Is Harry on the Boat?

By

Colin Butts

Is Harry on the Boat?

©1997 Colin Butts

ALL RIGHTS RESERVED

ISBN 0 9530457 0 6

Cover design by: Dominic James, Deep Design, London.
Cover photo by: Eddie Adoo.
Author's photo by: some git with an instamatic (probably Heather).

Published in the UK by:

Tuesday Morning Publishing
P O Box 12608
London
SE14 6ZR

Tel: 0181 244 0000   Fax: 0181 244 1000

Printed in Great Britain by Antony Rowe Ltd, Chippenham, Wiltshire

FOREWORD AND THANKS

As you read this book there will be occasions when you will wonder if some of the situations that the reps find themselves in are based on even a molecule of truth, as they seem to be so far fetched. Although the basic plot is fictional, many of the anecdotes which have been woven in are based upon my own personal experiences, or those of my peers. In fact, the rule of thumb should be that the more unbelievable the story, the more likely it is to have happened to me or someone I know at some point in the late eighties.

To give it a more contemporary feel and to allow for the development of the dance scene which is so important to the island, the action takes place in the present day (assuming of course that you are not a visiting alien now reading this in 2198 AD). Some of the bars mentioned (The Madhouse, The Charleston, Pub Ideas) no longer exist. Other places (The Star, Sgt. Peppers) have changed their names. A few are fictional(ish). In the same way that the reps are a composite of different holiday representatives I came into contact with, so some of the bars/clubs are an amalgam of different watering holes it was my pleasure to (over) frequent. So, if you think you can recognise yourself or one of the venues that I'm less than complimentary about, rest assured that you/it may have only partly been responsible for the inspiration (if you ever read this Lez, I promise you that Mario is in no way based on your good self). Whilst on the subject of my contemporaries, I would like to thank the following reps for inspiration and anecdotes (maiden names apply): Carl Verges, Tony Grant, Babs Pearson, Hursty, Gerry Boyle, Andrea Turner, Gresty, Des 'Fluffyflops' Ball, Debbie Bailey and Pete Fitzgerald. Also Reece Jensen for the Zakatek story.

To put a group of inherently outgoing 'characters' together to work in an environment such as Ibiza, especially when they are the same age as most of the clients, cannot help but lead to personality clashes, bizarre situations and all sorts of outrageous goings on. I had to edit nearly fifty thousand words from my original manuscript, partly because there was so much material to choose from and partly because even though they happened, some events would not be accepted even in a fictional context!

Club 18-30 type holidays remain enormously popular, but they still regularly attract bad press. This book might initially seem as if it is also knocking this type of tour operator; showing the seemingly callous way in which the clients appear to be manipulated; "lifting the lid" with stories of backhanders etc. Clearly though, these organisations fulfil a need, and however distasteful we might find it to see a procession of screaming, drunk, rampant holiday makers being led through a resort by an often equally drunk and rampant rep, at the end of the day they are having a good time, which surely is what going on a holiday is all about. As Greg says to Brad in Chapter 5:-

"Because they are on holiday, they don't wanna have to make decisions. They don't wanna have to decide where to go - it's a lot easier if we do it for them".

Their clients are also in the main fairly well controlled. My experience is that because they are acutely aware of their image, the likes of Club 18-30 and Twenty's let clients get away with considerably less than mainstream tour operators do. This is mostly achieved by the reps being with the clients twenty four hours a day.

What we must not lose sight of is that these tour operators are businesses, and as such are there to make a profit. When you look at some of the fine profit margins within which they operate on the actual package, they could almost be forgiven for trying to supplement this revenue in other ways - the only argument is whether or not they do so to the detriment of the client. But enough - Club 18-30 *et al* are big enough and ugly enough to defend themselves.

Special thanks to Mick Crowley, Harry Ritchie and Rodney

Cooper for honest comments when reading drafts, Lindsey Fisher for photocopying, Dorise Mensah and Dominic James for contacts.

Finally, thanks to Bartolo Escandell and Steve Woods, for being Bartolo Escandell and Steve Woods.

Young Free & Single Staff

Resort Reps IBIZA - Start of Season

Alison	Resort Manager
Brad	First Year Rep
Mikey	First Year Rep
Mario	First Year Rep
Lorraine	First Year Rep
Greg	Third Year Rep
Heather	Second Year Rep
Kirstie	Resort Manager (previous year)

Head Office Staff

Adam Hawthorne-Blythe	Chairman
Felipe Gomez	Contracts Director
Sebastian Hunter	Financial Director
Jane Ward	Overseas Manager
Tom Ortega	Overseas Controller

PRE-DEPARTURE

'Ow.'

'What's up?'

'You've got your elbow on my hair,' said Alison grimacing. She tried to pull her head away, tutting impatiently.

'Sorry.' Jonathan transferred his weight onto his hands, slipping out as he did so. 'Is that better?'

Alison grunted.

Jonathan guided himself in and continued. He rested his head back on the pillow, but looked away from her towards the window. Parked directly outside of his Hampstead flat was the red Alfa Romeo that he had collected from Follet's in St. John's Wood the previous week. The engine was gleaming and the car purred like a cat. A pussy. Red and inviting. Pistons going up and down, tightly boring into the wanton, moaning engine. In and out, up and down. Shit. Desperately, his eyes scanned the room for something else which would hold his attention. In the corner was a TV and a video. That was no good - it made him think of porno's. Then, in a flash of inspiration, his stream of consciousness leap frogged to computer games. In his head he started going through the different stages of Mortal Kombat. This did the trick and the tightening in his loins temporarily subsided.

Alison looked at her watch over Jonathan's shoulder. Nine fifteen a.m. It usually took her about half an hour to get home from his flat, which meant that she would need to leave within twenty minutes to be sure of getting back in time. A small droplet of sweat trickled off of the end of his nose, landing on Alison's left cheekbone where it mixed with her own slight perspiration. It was quickly followed by his tongue, licking off their combined saltiness. Jonathan gently kissed her eyelids and their tongues briefly met as he worked his way down the nape of her neck. His breathing quickened, while his thrusts became slower. He'd lost concentration and the mental image of two computer generated characters kicking the living daylights out of each other had been replaced with images of yielding female flesh and bodily fluids.

Alison knew what was coming next. Sure enough, Jonathan completely withdrew his bursting member and swiftly replaced it with the middle and third finger of his right hand. At the same time he shifted position and started working his tongue down to her stomach, stopping to give each of her nipples exactly the same amount of attention.

'No Jonathan, I want it now,' breathed Alison, checking that the Ikea clock on the wall was showing the same time as her watch.

Alison knew that the only reason Jonathan had pulled out was that he was having trouble controlling his own orgasm. Usually she would have insisted on him using his fingers to bring her as close to a climax as possible, before re-mounting her for a minute or so to finish the job. But because her meeting with Kirstie was so important, she literally grabbed the opportunity to end proceedings prematurely with both hands. With one hand cupped beneath his bulging ball bag, she used the other to vigorously rub the length of Jonathan's circumcised phallus. As planned, in less than thirty seconds she felt the first hot spurt land on her forehead. Jonathan groaned, and then watched the rest of his thick white sperm fall between the crevasse of her breasts. Alison squeezed the last of it out, and then rubbed his already softening manhood into the white lake that he had just created. She was relieved that none of it had gone into her frizzy brown hair. Without saying a word, Jonathan slumped next to her. After a few minutes, Alison looked at her watch.

'Good ,' she thought, 'Not even nine thirty......'

She got back to her parent's house just before ten in the morning. Kirstie was due to arrive at eleven thirty. Alison had a shower and got herself ready. Kirstie and Alison were fairly similar, and probably because of this, not particularly close.

There was an unspoken rivalry between them which meant that they always went through the motions of liking each other, and this included not giving any reason to criticise the other's appearance, which was why Alison wanted at least an hour and a half to get herself ready.

Kirstie had completed her final season as Resort Manager for Ibiza the previous summer. Largely funded by the money that she made during this season she was now planning to open up a travel agency in her native Brecon. She was visiting her boyfriend's relations in Kent, and had agreed to make a detour to see Alison, who was to be replacing her as Resort Manager. She knew that Alison was desperate for advice on how to gain maximum financial benefit. Alison wanted to clean up.

Alison's parents home was typical of a suburban semi. At the front was a large bay window with Laura Ashley curtains, and at the back of the main two rooms (now knocked into one to form a dining room) was a patio door which opened onto a path leading to the neatly bordered garden. The room was not the room that the family spent most of their time in, more reserved for entertaining or impressing the neighbours. It was dominated with a majestic nonchalance by a seldom used mahogany dining table. The cold, well ordered discipline was broken by a number of holiday brochures, an open brief case and a six year old passport, all scattered impudently over the table's surface.

The crunch of gravel in the drive heralded Kirstie's arrival causing Alsion to hastily scoop all of the brochures into her brief case. She waited until the doorbell chimed before making her way to greet Kirstie, which she did by theatrically flinging open the door, and then both arms,

'Daaahling!' she shrieked, kissing Kirstie on both cheeks.

'How are you, alright?' smiled Kirstie politely.

'You look a bit wet. Don't you just loathe the British weather? God, I can't wait to get away again.'

Kirstie grunted, and changed the subject. 'Living room, dining room, bedroom or study?'

'Well, the drinks cabinet is in the dining room, and seeing as you're such an old alkie I think that will be our best bet. I've poured you a drink. Unless you want coffee......?'

'No, that will do fine.'

They sat at the table and smiled at each other. Alison started speaking first.

'So, any regrets?'

'No.' Kirstie replied flatly.

'Oh come on dahling. You're not telling me that after four summers abroad you're not going to miss it. Not even a teeny, weeny bit?' Alison tossed back her frizzy mane and laughed, spluttering smoke into the air. 'Still, I suppose we've all got to settle down some time. You never know, after the money I should make this year I might do the same myself.'

Alison paused and looked across the table. Kirstie's inside knowledge of Ibiza and in depth knowledge of the fiddles and the local contacts could save Alison a lot of time and make her a lot of money, so although they both knew why Kirstie was there, Alison didn't want to risk blowing things by winding her up too much or by being too blunt in her questioning. She said nothing and let Kirstie flick through the YF&S brochure. Kirstie recognised most of the people smiling out from them, as the company nearly always used its reps as models. She stabbed her finger at a picture of a good looking blonde lad, contorting his face as two nubile holidaymakers clung to his legs. He had short, very blonde hair, dark eyebrows (which made his natural hair seem highlighted), and green eyes which were framed by eyelashes so thick and long, that had he been a woman he would probably not have had much use for eyeliner or mascara. Apart from the fact that he was just over five and a half feet tall, he was almost certainly the closest thing you could get to what most peoples pre-conceived idea of a 'typical' rep would be.

'He's with you this year, isn't he?'

'Who's that?' enquired Alison.

'Scouse Greg.'

'Oh him? Yeah. What's he like to work with?'

4

'He's fine. You just have to leave him to it. Shags himself silly, but to be fair he's pretty discreet.'

'Is he a good seller?' asked Alison, referring to excursion sales, in which the Resort Manager had a vested interest.

'One of the best,' replied Kirstie, remembering the money that Greg had made her the previous season. 'You'll have to watch him. If he can make a few quid on the side, he will.'

'Not this year he won't,' replied Alison sharply. 'The only person who's going to make any money this year is me.'

Kirstie said nothing. She knew that Alison meant it. She had seen it before; the enthusiasm for the job long since gone; the determination to have one last year with the sole objective of making as much money as possible, with little regard for anything or anyone else. To some degree Kirstie had been guilty of it herself in her final year. She had come home with nearly fourteen thousand pounds, and she knew Alison wanted more. But there was something about Alison. It was as if she had something to prove to herself. Kirstie had never seen anyone so ruthlessly determined to make her mark, almost as if she believed it was her calling. It actually made Kirstie feel slightly uneasy. Her instincts made her feel that it was going to be a strange season in Ibiza.

After Alison felt they had made enough small talk she started firing questions. She had a feeling that Kirstie wasn't telling her everything, and she was right. There were some things that Alison was just going to have to find out for herself. Once Alison was sure that she had leeched everything that she could from Kirstie, they started talking about reps, past and present. Eventually, they worked their way around to the new reps, all of whom Kirstie had been involved in interviewing. Alison should have also been involved, but she told everyone at the time (including Jonathan) that she was ill with 'women's problems'. If an abortion could be defined as 'women's problems', then she could not have been accused of lying. Only the father knew about it, and nobody was going to find out who he was.

'You'll like Mario,' said Kirstie. 'His parents are Italian.

Done a bit of modelling apparently. Very sure of himself. Shouldn't give you any trouble though - he wants to go all the way.'

'If he's anything like you say he is, I'll let him.' Alison laughed at her own deliberate mis-interpretation. 'What about the girls - what are they like?'

'There's a Brummie called Lorraine. I was surprised she got picked - seemed a bit timid. Wispy ginger hair, very fair complexion. Quite plain really. Jane liked her for some reason and you know what Jane's like when she makes her mind up,' said Kirstie referring to their Overseas Manager. Alison said nothing. 'I suppose you know that you've had another honour bestowed upon you, don't you?'

'What, you mean El Negro?'

Alison spoke surprisingly little Spanish for the amount of time she had been repping. But she knew what black was.

'That's right, Mikey Jarvis -Young Free & Single's first ever black rep,' replied Kirstie.

'He is actually, well, black. I mean we are talking 'as the ace of spades' here, and not just a half caste,' continued Alison, wallowing in political incorrectness.

'BLACK!' confirmed Kirstie, now enjoying watching Alison's suburban sensibilities being assaulted.

'I mean, don't get me wrong. I'm not a racist or anything. It's just - well, you know. Suppose we get racist clients and they start causing problems. It's me who'll have to sort it out, isn't it?'

Alison was looking for some re-assurance. Kirstie was giving her none.

'Well Alison. I'm sure Mikey knows he's black, and I'm sure he's quite capable of taking care of himself. He's got a brilliant sense of humour, as well as being built like a brick wotsit. And he's a Karate black belt.'

'Is he?'

If this was meant to re-assure Alison it was making her even more petrified. She remembered a film she'd seen where a huge black slave had turned on his masters, killing them all

6

(even the women) with his bare hands. Alison didn't consider herself to be a racist - she didn't go on any National Front marches or anything. She decided to move on.

'What about this blue eyed boy that Jane was going on about. Brad, is it?'

'Brad? Yeah, he should be really good.'

Kirstie thought back to Bridlehurst the country house-cum-hotel setting for the final interview for all YF&S rep's. This interview lasts for twenty four hours, and every aspect of each potential reps personality is tested to the full. Kirstie was one of the four interview panel, all of whom agreed that Brad would make a great rep. She continued with her assessment of him,

'Bit of a natural leader, really. S'pose it's 'cos he's older than the normal first year.'

'Why? How old is he?' enquired the twenty five year old Alison.

'Twenty six, I think,' replied Kirstie, beginning to home in on Alison's insecurity. 'Yeah, quite sharp too. Very quick witted. He finished that McQuaig test in six minutes.'

'The what?'

'McQuaig Institute test.' Alison shook her head. The company had only just introduced the test so Alison had never heard of it. 'It's like an IQ test. They have to answer fifty questions in fifteen minutes. When she first saw him Jane Ward assumed he'd give up when he realised there wasn't a pair of tits on page three of the question sheet. Mind you, she soon changed her tune when she marked it and found out he'd got them all right.'

'He what?'

'Every single one - and in only six minutes. Apparently he featured in a local paper when he was a kid for having an unusually high IQ.'

'I bet he looks like a right little swat,' said Alison hopefully.

'Hardly!' laughed Kirstie. 'Thats the funny thing about him. He actually looks more of a thug than a brainbox. He's a bit wider than Mikey - looks like he works out a bit, although he's

7

probably not quite as tall. Broken nose, light brown hair......'

Alison, had stopped listening, already beginning to worry that this new rep could be a threat to her position.

Kirstie could see that Alison was deep in thought. She tried a few more attempts at conversation, but Alison was preoccupied. Kirstie finished her drink then made her excuses and set off to her future in-laws in deepest Kent, half smiling to herself, with the words 'game, set and match' going around her head.

The sun was playing peek-a-boo through the row of uniform height poplar trees that lined the endlessly straight French country road. Brad had one of his favourite garage tapes playing that a DJ friend had mixed a week before. He would have liked to have had the roof off, but keeping the hard top on allowed him to get more merchandise on to the roof rack. He was taking in the scenery, and generally feeling very pleased with himself. During the first few hours of the journey he got the occasional pang of guilt when he remembered the way he had left his girlfriend Charlotte sobbing on the doorstep as he drove off. It wasn't so much the leaving her that made him fell guilty, more the 'Yeeehaaagh' and punch in the air he let out as soon as he turned the corner.

Brad didn't realise that there was a problem for quite a while. It might have been the music; it could have been the landscape; maybe he was just daydreaming. Whatever it was that had been monopolising Brad's attention, it certainly was not the Triumph Herald's temperature gauge. Cursing, he pulled into a lay by and thumped the dial with the outside of his fist, having a distant memory of how The Fonz had rectified a temperamental juke box in similar fashion in a much repeated episode of Happy Days. The Triumph failed to respond to Brad's pugilistic attempt at in-car maintenance so he got out to see what the problem was. The Sunday morning stillness of the Dordogne valley was only broken by the gentle hiss coming from underneath the Triumph Herald's bonnet. When he opened it he could see straight away that the fan belt was broken. His first thought was not on how to overcome the problem, but on what kind of retribution would cause Romford 'Word's me bond' Reg the most physical discomfort, and the most lasting pain. Brad had bought the car from Reg on the recommendation of a YF&S rep who had worked in Ibiza the previous season, where Reg had also been working. Because the car was being re-sprayed, it had not been presented to Brad until the day before he was due to leave. The car had an ill fitting Ford Sierra engine which gave it the turning circle of the QE2 and made it a nightmare to drive. However, he had gone through with the purchase partly because the tickets were booked and he had no other choice, and partly because Reg was going to Ibiza ten days after Brad to spend the season hiring out his speedboat during the day ('Honest geeze, it's me uncle's,'), and his Karaoke unit at night. Brad was about as good with cars as King Herod was with children, so having Reg promise to look after any problems that cropped up during the summer had been the final thing which had persuaded Brad to become the proud owner of a mutant Triumph Herald.

He was miles from anywhere. It was a Sunday afternoon and there was no sign of any life. The only option was to try and flag somebody down.

The first car that took pity on the Triumph Herald was a battered Citroen 2CV. It's occupant (a weathered five foot Frenchman of about sixty) couldn't help. He did seem very sympathetic, and Brad managed to pick up what French for fan belt was (courroire de ventilateur). With little else to stimulate Brad, the only thing that got him mildly excited was when one of the passing cars was a Ford Sierra (same engine therefore same fan belt) or a car with British plates (same language therefore no need to mispronounce 'courroire de ventilateur'). Just over two hours after first breaking down Brad's excitement level peaked when he saw that the car coming towards him was not only a Ford Sierra but also had

British plates. Unfortunately the occupants of the car also had a British mentality - healthily displayed by their shouts of "Wanker!" and accompanying hand signals.

Brad sat down on the grass verge and opened the last can of duty free Kronenburg. He definitely had a problem. There was no way that he could leave the car because all of the merchandise was on the roof rack, and the car was too full to put anything else inside. A night sleeping in the cramped drivers seat with no blankets was not particularly appealing, but he could see no other option. He sat back, crossed his fingers and scanned the horizon in the forlorn hope that somebody would come to his rescue.

Almost four hours after first breaking down his saviour arrived in the shape of one Samuel T Zakatek ('Please, call me Sammy'). Sammy had seemed fine to start with, especially when Brad discovered that he too was on his way to Ibiza where he had apparently spent the last ten years. Brad had initially assumed that any idiosyncratic personality traits were due to the fact that Sammy was American. But now some eight hours later the intensity of the man was proving too much and Brad dearly wanted to be out of his company.

During their search for a fan belt, they had stumbled across a hemp farm that had been given special dispensation by the French government to grow hemp to produce hempseed oil which was used as a machine lubricant. The laid back farm owner had contacted his brother who was going to bring up a selection of fan belts the next morning. With nothing else to do, Brad and Sammy had spent a few hours helping out on the farm and in return the farmer had arranged for them to stay in a friend's guest house a few kilometres away.

In the time they had spent together Sammy had told Brad increasingly bizarre stories. One of these was about how he had taken over a beach bar in Ibiza which had become so famous that the King of Spain 'dropped in' one day to congratulate him. In return for being so successful the King had offered Sammy anything he wanted. With potential fortune beckoning, the thing that Sammy had apparently wanted more than anything else in the world was the King's tie.

He also told Brad how he was going to kill his parents when he was twelve because they had sold his grandpa's tribal land which had been given to him by the Navahoe Indians, and didn't speak to them again until his brother's funeral (naturally, his brother had hung himself).

Brad had finally concluded that Sammy was a psychotic Vietnam veteran, and as they both laid on their beds in the guest house, Brad pretended to be asleep, thereby thwarting all attempts at conversation. He was praying for the morning and his fan belt to arrive.

Brad had almost fallen asleep when he felt Sammy shaking him.

'Brad. Wake up man, wake up.'

'Wassamadder!?'

'Sorry to wake y'man but I've just had a great fuckin' idea.'

'Oh for fuck's sake.'

'No, listen man. We ain't gonna get a chance to take anymore weed in the mornin' right? So I figure we drive up there now and help ourselves to some.'

'Leave it out. We've smoked ourselves silly all afternoon and I don't fancy smuggling any gear across the border. Besides, if you think I'm driving up there at what.' Brad looked at his watch, 'Three twenty in the morning you must be off your fucking trolley.'

'C'mon man! Where's your sense of adventure?'

'Somewhere just behind my sense of common. Look. Just go to sleep. We can probably grab a little personal in the morning.'

'Well fuck you man. I'm goin'. Y'can do what you want.'

This put Brad in something of a dilemma. Although going to the hemp field held little appeal to him, allowing psychotic Sammy to drive off into the night with the majority of the YF&S merchandise that Brad had temporarily stored in Sammy's jeep, held even less.

'Alright, give me a minute to get ready.'

Brad felt that Sammy was even more intense than before. Once in the jeep, Sammy started swigging a bottle of Jack Daniel's that had suddenly appeared. He was driving faster than normal and had a crazed look in his eyes. Brad was genuinely scared, and as often happens when struck by fear, was unable to say any of the thousand and one things racing through his mind.

The road leading up to the hemp farm was like one of those you see in James Bond car chases, or old movies when a moustachioed fiend has tampered with a cars brakes. In other words very windy, with steep drops and no railings. There was a car dawdling along in front of the jeep. Sammy started to thump the horn.

'C'mon. Get outta the road y'motherfuckin' French sonofabitch.' With that, Sammy rammed the rear bumper of the car.

'What are you playing at Sam?'

'Move it, fuck head.' He rammed the car again.

'Stop the car Sam.'

'Why? You scared Brad? MOVE you goddamn Frog!'

'Just stop the car and let me drive.'

'No way man.' Sam rammed the car, almost forcing it off of the road.

'Sammy. Please stop.'

'What's up Brad? No balls?'

Sammy started to overtake on a blind bend. This was enough for Brad.

'Stop the car you fucking psycho, or so help me I'll break your fucking neck you stupid CUNT!'

'That's the difference between us Brad,' said Sammy grinning maniacally. 'Two tours of duty. Hah - I've already died twice. But how about you? Are you scared to die Brad?'

This was all beginning to sound like a script from a bad 'B' movie. He hoped that Sammy would pull off a rubber face mask to reveal the grinning bearded face of Jeremy Beadle, thrusting a microphone under his nose. Brad looked at the hands on the steering wheel. Neither of them were deformed.

Bang went that theory.

'Sit tight. I'm the tour guide man,' drawled Sammy. 'I haven't been like this in a long time. It feels goooood! Y'know Brad. When I first saw you, d'you know why I stopped. When I saw you standing by the road I thought "Wow! That's my brother man". That's why I stopped.'

Brad was sure that there was now a tear in Sammy's eyes. The car seemed to be getting faster. They were approaching a sharp bend and Sammy was not slowing down. Brad had another look at him and he seemed to be in a trance. He made a decision. He pushed Sammy against the drivers door, grabbed the steering wheel, yanked on the handbrake and even though the car was still revving, managed to wrench the gearstick into neutral. The car skidded to a halt. Brad got out of the car and realised that the distance between the car and the drop was a matter of feet. He looked at Sammy who was staring straight ahead. Brad said nothing but turned around and started walking back to the guest house. Some things were more important, even than YF&S merchandise.

REPS ARRIVING

'On behalf of Captain Reynolds I would like to thank you all for flying with British Caledonian Airways and we hope that you enjoy your stay in Ibiza. Please remain seated until the aircraft comes to a complete standstill. You are reminded not to smoke until you are well into the airport terminal.'

There was a click and some classical music started playing. Mikey looked across the aisle and out of one of the windows at the terminal building, which was distorted by a heat haze rising from the tarmac. As he turned his head back he caught sight of The Idiot's face, grinning at him from two rows in front. He returned a half smile. Mikey's first impressions of people normally turned out to be correct. On this occasion he hoped that he was wrong - he sincerely hoped that he was wrong.

As they got off of the plane, The Idiot grabbed the stewardesses hand, kissed it and slipped her a sheet of paper mumbling something about 'next time'. Mikey shuddered at the thought of spending the next six months with him. When they had first met at the airport, Mikey was initially slightly put off by the psuedo-black attempt at bonding with the 'Hey Bro - how's it hanging' handshake and cocksure attitude. Then it was The Idiot endeavouring to chat up the check-in stewardess, followed by the duty free cashier, followed by a group of girls in the bar. All of these with his reps' badge unnecessarily emblazoned upon his chest. The final straw for Mikey was when The Idiot kept dropping his badge in front of the stewardess on the plane - just in case she was not entirely aware that he was a rep (as if this gave them some special bonding). No, Mikey had made up his mind. Mario was a complete and utter stain.

They walked into the cool terminal and made their way to the expectant baggage carousel. Mikey largely switched off to

Mario's self-centred ramblings, especially when Mario tried to tell him how he was sure that the stewardess was going to call, and that when she did he was going to 'Fuck her brains out man!'; Mikey wondered if too much wanking had caused Mario's cerebral organ to exit it's original habitat for similar reasons. He also offered a prayer of thanks to the inventor of both the Walkman and sunglasses, which were saving him from having to acknowledge or listen to Mario's egotistical waffle.

Mikey sat on the edge of the baggage carousel waiting for it to jerk into life. This was it - he was actually in Ibiza. Unfortunately, at that moment so was Mario who had just made his way over to Mikey, fresh from preening himself in front of the mirrors in the toilets.

'Spanish birds are fit man. That young one over there in the car hire bit keeps looking over. I bet she knows that we're rep's.'

'Yeah, I'm sure it's one of the condition's of employment.'

'What is?'

'Being telepathic.' Mikey read aloud the fictitious advert. 'Car hire receptionist wanted. Must get on with the public, speak at least one foreign language and be numerate. Telepathic skills and ability to spot Young Free & Single reps at a hundred yards an advantage.'

Mario looked at Mikey, totally baffled by his humour. He changed the subject.

'So who's meeting us then?'

'The Resort Manager,' replied Mikey.

'That's Alison isn't it?'

'Sure is.'

'She wasn't at the training course or the interviews, was she?'

'Sure wasn't.'

'I wonder what she's like,' said Mario sitting down next to Mikey, who moved away a little. 'Yeah. I wonder if she's fit. D'you reckon she shags?'

Mikey looked at Mario over the top of his sunglasses.

'Probably Mario, probably.'

When Mikey and Mario eventually came through customs the airport was fairly empty. Although they hadn't met her before, the YF&S bag draped over her shoulder ensured that they spotted Alison almost immediately. Mikey felt a sudden sense of anti-climax. It occurred to him that he had probably been expecting a herd of reporters and a brass band. Not only was it Mikey's first time abroad (apart from a visit to his grandparents in Jamaica when he was six), but he had gone through such mental turmoil deciding to become a rep and then such challenging interviews to actually become one, that Alison seemed somewhat, well - inadequate. Still, he was there and he was happy and he was pleased to see a familiar face other than Mario's.

'Ciao, Bella,' smarmed Mario, kissing Alison on both cheeks. 'Nice to meet you.'

'You too,' said Alison, thinking that Kirstie was right about how drop dead gorgeous Mario was. 'And you must be Mikey.'

'Don't tell me - my sunglasses gave me away.'

Alison laughed politely. 'There's not too many black rep's here.'

'Clumsy,' thought Mikey.

They kissed each other on the cheek. It was the first time that she had been kissed by a black man.

'How are you two getting on, alright?' enquired Alison.

'Yeah man, great,' replied Mario offering Mikey his hand for another handshake. Mikey had no choice but to take it and to go through the motions. He noticed that whenever Mario spoke to him, his semi-cockney accent changed into that of a Brooklyn Mafia type street punk. They put their luggage into the white estate car that Alison had hired. YF&S supplied her with a moped for the season, but on special occasions she was allowed a car. Mario sat next to Alison in the front, whilst Mikey clambered into the back with his Head sports bag. He took his portable hi-fi unit out of the bag, looking for a cassette to put in to his Walkman.

'Hey, great wog box man.' Mario realised his faux pas

almost before the words were out of his mouth. 'Shit. Sorry man, I didn't mean...well, when I said wog.....what I meant man was....'

Mikey put him out of his misery. 'It's alright Mario. That's what I call it.' A relieved Mario laughed. 'You can do me one favour though,' added Mikey.

'Yeah man, whaddya want?' replied Mario, eager to please.

'Stop calling me man. I'm from London and we're in Ibiza - not New York. My friends call me Mikey.' He paused before adding, 'You can call me Mr Jarvis.'

'Oh, uh right ma-, I mean right. What, so that's your full name then, is it - Mike Jarvis?'

'No.'

Michael Jarvis silently and expressionlessly chuckled to himself. His dry humour and totally flat delivery were lost on most people, who could never tell if he was joking or serious. Mikey realised at that moment that Mario and he were on totally different wavelengths - it was just a shame that they were not on totally different resorts.

Most reps never bothered to research much more than the prospective nightlife of their chosen destination, but Mikey had found out a little about the history of the island before leaving the UK. He guessed that Mario, and probably Alison would have absolutely no interest in the subject, so largely for his own amusement he thought it would be fun to share this knowledge with them on the journey into San Antonio. As they drove away from the airport, Mikey saw a sign pointing towards Las Salinas, the salt flats.

'See those salt flats Mario?'

'Yeah.'

'Well it's mainly because of those that this little island has been invaded through the years.'

'Yeah?'

'Yeah. Well, that and it's location of course.'

'And now it's being invaded by Young Free & Single,' chipped in Alison.

'And loads of Krauts,' added Mario.

17

'Funnily enough Mario, a Germanic tribe called the Vandals invaded Ibiza in the fifth century.' As Mikey expected, there was no reaction from either Mario or Alison. 'Then the Byzantines.' He looked directly ahead and soaked up the disinterested silence. 'Then of course there were the Saracens.' Mikey smiled to himself and stared out of the window, pausing for nearly a minute. 'I think it was the Moors next - or was it the Normans.' He took some chewing gum out of a wrapper and popped it into his mouth pushing himself down in the seat to become more comfortable. 'No, I'm sure it was the Normans.'

After nearly half an hour they arrived in San Antonio. Mikey remembered reading that San Antonio used to be a small fishing port until tourists started arriving in the sixties. It really took off however, during the tourist boom which followed Franco's death in nineteen seventy five. By the end of the late seventies and early eighties, package holidays had started to become more and more common place. With them came the advent of the specialist holiday, in particular those catering for young people. These saw the 'West End' of San Antonio grow to service the demand for bar crawls, with a whole variety of theme bars and night clubs springing up. It's peak was probably reached in the mid eighties, when the same island gave birth to the rave scene. Although there was still a strong demand for 'Ere we go' type bars, it was the stylish clubs and more laid back, drug dominated places that started to come back in vogue. Places like Cafe del Mar, which until the mid-eighties had been the domain of locals and a few backgammon playing 'in-the-know' workers, were suddenly overrun with Moschino clad ravers and wannabes.

It was quite close to Cafe del Mar that the majority of YF&S's accommodation was based including their principal unit, The Bon Tiempo Apartments (The Bon), which was where Mikey was initially to be staying. The area around The Bon was undeveloped and barren. The building stood there, a solitary white block like a lone tooth in a mouth of decay, caused by the apathetic dentistry of local planners unable to shake off the deep rooted mañana mentality. As the car pulled up outside Mikey counted that The Bon's white paintwork and brown shutters rose five storeys, although he also observed that all of the shutters were closed and the only towel draped over a balcony was on the top floor. They took their cases out of the car and walked down the side of the apartments, weaving their way between the steel framed chairs and wicker and glass tables that were there to offer the imminent guests an al fresco dining or drinking option. As Mikey walked into the reception there was a huge contrast both in brightness and temperature. Mikey shivered slightly and draped his sweatshirt over his shoulders. Their rooms were not quite ready, so they left their things in reception and went into the bar where Alison got them all a drink. The conversation was dominated by Mario trying to impress Alison, which contributed to Mikey refusing the offer of another drink - he was in far greater need of a spliff.

Having told Alison that he was going exploring, he walked out of the apartments, lightly tapping his balls with his fingertips to confirm that the small lump of solid he had smuggled over was still there.

The apartments overlooked the man made beach in San Antonio called Calo des Moro. It was evening, and there was a slight breeze but it was still warm enough to wear a T-shirt. Looking out from the beach, Mikey could see an island. He squinted at it in the evening light and it's shape reminded him of an oil tanker; rising almost vertically from the sea then gently undulating along it's deck until it rose again to the bridge, before dramatically plunging back into the sea at it's stern. Between him and the island, about four hundred metres out from the beach, was a boat. It seemed to be pumping out or sucking up something from the sea. Mikey sat down at a white plastic table outside the beach bar and ordered himself a coffee. He grew curious as to what the boat was doing. Mikey spoke reasonably good Spanish (quite unusual for a YF&S rep), and when the waiter came back he decided to ask him what was going on.

'*Que pasa, alli con el barco?*' (What's happening there, with the ship). The waiter informed him that the boat was pumping sand in to the sea so that it would be washed up on the beach. He also told him that over the next few days, lorries would come and dump tons of sand on the beach ready for the beginning of the season. He was intrigued to know why Mikey spoke Spanish, and why he was in Ibiza so early in the season. When Mikey told him that he was a rep at the local apartments, the waiter wouldn't let him pay for his coffee, and brought over a bottle of San Miguel and a schnapps. He then showed Mikey the menu saying that the food was second to none, and that if any of Mikey's clients ever wanted to eat there, they would be given a ten percent discount.

Mikey thanked him, shook his hand and walked further around the bay. When he got to the peninsula of a rocky outcrop, he sat down and pulled out of his pocket a packet of red Rizlas. He turned his back to the wind, put the necessary ingredients along the length of the Rizla and settled down to his first joint in Ibiza. Between the island and the opposite mainland, a red sun quickly sank into the gently rippling sea.

There were no sounds apart from the steady chug of the sand boat, and the call of three seagulls circling overhead. Mikey was in his element. As he laid on the rock, his foot unconsciously tapped along to the boat's hypnotic rhythm. He looked at the island and remembered reading that it was called Conejera and that the ancient warrior Hannibal was supposed to have been born there. He spent a few moments daydreaming, trying to imagine what the island would have been like in ancient times. After a while his thoughts turned to more recent events, in particular the months leading up to his decision to become a rep. The catalyst had been the split with his girlfriend of four years (her parents didn't approve of him although they had only met him twice). No amount of persuasion had been sufficient to win her back, and he couldn't stand the thought of seeing her with someone else. A friend had suggested repping for YF&S and almost before he knew what was happening he had found himself at Gatwick ready for a season in Ibiza.

When he got back to the apartments, Alison was waiting for him.

'Where have you been? I've just been going through some of the paperwork with Mario.'

'Sorry. I didn't realise that you wanted me. I've just been having a look round. The guy at the beach cafe said he'd give our clients a ten percent discount. Even said he'd give me free food,' offered Mikey helpfully. Alison suddenly looked stern. She puffed out her thirty four B chest and sat upright in the chair.

'There's something that is very important that you must understand. The only places that we take clients and the only places that we go for free food are where I tell you. Is that understood?'

'Sure. It's just that-'

'There are no just that's. You are a first year rep, and those kind of things are left for the Resort Manager to look after.'

Mikey could see that logical discussion was futile,

'OK. No problem.'

'Good. I hope I've made myself clear. Now, if I can attract that fat deigo's attention, I'll get us all a drink,' said Alison, seemingly oblivious to the blood line of her two new reps.

'Oi-yaay. See- nyor. Dos San Miguels and a gin tonic.' Mikey winced at her accent and command of Spanish even more than he had her previous comment.

'Gracias.'

Mikey looked at the Spanish waiter and half raised his eyebrows as if to say 'I know'.

Alison and Mario eventually left leaving Mikey alone in the bar. It seemed strange to think that in just under one weeks time it would be overrun with young British holidaymakers.

The next morning every rep apart from Brad had arrived on resort and were gathered in the bar area of The Bon. Alison was sitting at the bar drinking coffee and looking at the flight manifestos that had arrived that morning. Mikey was practising his Spanish on Frank, or rather they were teaching each other the best swear words in their respective language. Greg was telling Mario about a Danish girl that he had got a wank off of on the beach the night before. While he was telling him, Mario was looking across at Heather thinking that he wouldn't mind getting a wank off of her. Didn't even have to be on the beach. Heather was a petite and extremely pretty second year rep from Heald Green, not far from Manchester airport, who had only recently become aware of the effect that her looks had on men. Working in Spain, she had quickly learned how to use them to her advantage, and her confidence had grown tenfold during her first season as a rep.

She was whispering to the Brummie, Lorraine. Every minute or so they would explode into fits of giggles. Although Heather was 'blessed' with Barbie doll looks, she was cursed with a laugh that sounded like a cross between a hyena sitting on a stinging nettle and a kookaburra with whooping cough. In the background the TV in the bar was showing a very old dubbed episode of Knight Rider.

Alison looked up from her manifesto and just as she did so she caught sight of an over-burdened red English car turning the corner. It was a Triumph Herald. Mikey was the next one to see the car.

'Brad's here.'

Lorraine jumped up from her seat and ran out to meet him. Greg, Heather and Mario had never met him before - Greg and Heather because they were second year reps, and Mario because he was on a different training course. These three walked out and stood by the doorway, curious to see what their workmate for the next six months was like.

Mikey, Lorraine and Brad all embraced each other. They had shared the experience of the Bridlehurst twenty four hour interview, and then a one week training course in Warwick. Reps who went through these two stages together and then who ended up on the same resort nearly always had a special bond.

Brad put his things into a room on the second floor, where Alison told him he would be staying until the first clients arrived.

When Brad got back downstairs there was a row of chairs facing Alison. He went and sat next to Mikey and told him about his encounter with Samuel Zakatek and how he had eventually left him the following morning trying to stuff a bin liner full of weed into the boot of his jeep. Mario was in the middle of a story, which Brad only caught the tail end of.

'.........so I said to her "What's wrong?" and she said "You called me stupid" and I said "No I didn't, I said I was going to fuck you STUPID"!'

Mario burst out laughing but the story only elicited the politest of laughter from the rest of the group. Mikey looked at Brad trying to silently convey what he thought of Mario. Lorraine decided to be a little more verbal in her appreciation of the story.

'Well, she would've 'ad to be bloody stupid to shag you, wouldn't she?'. This got a better response. She turned her attentions to Mikey, putting on the thickest of Brummie accents. 'So coom on then Mikey. Is it true what them all say about black men?'.

'What, that we make great lawyers, accountants, politicians.......'

'No yer pillock, that you've all got cowin' big dadgers.' She was blunt as well.

'Even if he was hung like King Dong, Lorraine,' said Brad, 'He'd be able to put it in that trap of yours and you'd still be able to hold a conversation. Could probably get mine in there as well.'

'The only way yem'll be putting that thing of yours near me gob is if I need a tooth pick.' Lorraine's retort started Heather off on another hyena impression..

'Jesus, could you imagine shagging that,' said Mario pointing at Heather, doing a poor impression of her laugh. 'Is she always like this?'

'No' said Lorraine, 'Only when she sees Italian dicks.'

Heather now had tears rolling down her eyes, not because it was particularly funny but because she was prone to giggling fits.

'Aye, well you've seen enough of those, eh Heather?' Scouse Greg decided to join in.

'Oh you can talk,' said Heather rubbing her eyes and still laughing, 'You were down the clap clinic so many times last season that you were on first name terms with all the doctors. How many did you shag last year? Eighty? Ninety?'

'Fuck off. Be serious you daft ol' bag.'

'Well how many was it then?'

'Sixty four.'

'What! In a season!?' exclaimed Mario, looking at Greg convinced that if Greg could do that many then he should be able to do at least the same, if not more.

'Jesus,' said Mikey. 'Did you take any precautions?'

'Aye....... I didn't give 'em me fuckin' phone number.'

'FOR CHRIST'S SAKE!' screamed Alison. 'Can't you lot talk about anything other than SEX!'

There was a general mumbling of 'Sorry' and then silence.

'See, we can't think of anythin' else to talk about,' said Greg.

'Don't give me that,' said Alison. 'There must be something else you've all got in common.'

'Like what?'

'Oh I don't know. Anything! Talk about the weather for all I care.'

Greg looked at Alison, then looked out of the window at the sky, then looked back at Alison again. His face broke into a grin,

'Nice day for a fuck.'

After the meeting and some coach microphone training Alison took everyone to a bar called The Cockney Pride. The exterior had a large dirty white canopy with the bars name written on it in brown computer generated vinyl (although the 'P' was missing from 'Pride'). The small window panes at the front of the bar were surrounded by dark panelled wood in an attempt to make it look as Englishly rustic as possible. By the door was an 'A' board which informed potential customers that they sold draught Guinness and English sausages. Like many of the bars in San Antonio, The Cockney Pride was the shape of an oversized garage. Once inside, Alison sat on a stool at the end of the bar and introduced all of the reps to Trev, the professional cockney ex-pat turned bar owner, who's shock of white/grey hair was emphasised by his deeply tanned face.

Trev asked everyone what they wanted to drink. He had a gruff cockney voice and rolled his r's so that they sounded like 'w's. Although Mikey knew that it would taste disgusting, he ordered a bwandy and owange and some dwy woasted peanuts - just for his own amusement. They sat and chatted for a while. Reading between the lines, Mikey got the impression that Trev wasn't too keen on black people - he certainly wasn't too keen on Asians ('Bloody Pakis evewywhere back 'ome. Wunning the Off License, Newsagents - even the wuddy Gweengwocers'). After ten minutes Trev and Alison went and sat at the other end of the bar, which pleased Brad and Mikey in particular who were already bored by Trev's opinions on everything.

Brad went to the toilet. When he got back Greg was explaining something to Mario and Mikey.

'So, are you sure you've got it?'

'I think so,' replied Mario.

'What about you Mikey?'

'Nah dread. I don't want to get involved.'

'Well you're in the wrong job mate,' said Mario. 'Just run it by me one more time Greg to see if I've got it. It's one point for a wank....'

'That's it. One point for a wank; two points for a blow job and three points for a shag.' Greg took a satisfied swig of his San Miguel, confident that everyone understood the rules.

'And what sexist mother invented this game?' asked Mikey.

'You'll soon change your tune lad,' laughed Greg. 'Within two months, you'll be so bored with shaggin' that you'll be desperate for anything to liven it up. No object in your room'll be safe unless it's bolted down. It's just a bit of harmless fun between the reps and some of the other workers.'

'Yeah. Come on Mikey, it'll be a crack,' implored Mario.

'So who exactly is the competition between again?' asked Brad, trying to catch Trev's eye so he could order some more drinks.

'Well, primarily like, it's between all of us reps. But some of the other lads join in - y'know, DJ's, props, guys on the beach party.'

'What about bonus points then?' asked Brad, finally catching Trev's eye and mouthing 'same again'.

'Bonus points?'

'Yeah, y'know. Threesomes, missing the pink and potting the brown...'

'Fucking hell. We're not playing snooker,' said Mario. 'What's all this pink and brown nonsense?'

'I think young Bradley is referring to the rusty bullet hole,' said Mikey.

'The what?' Mario was still struggling.

'The chocolate starfish.'

'Backdooring.'

'Uphill gardening.'

'What the fuck are you all on about?'

'What we're on about Mario lad, is 'ow many points you score if you gerrit up the dirt box.'

'What, you mean shoving it up their arse!!?' exclaimed Mario.

'Delicately put,' said Mikey.

'What, are you all queer or something?'

'Um, we are talking about women Mario.' Greg could feel a wind up coming on and looked over at Brad and winked. 'Mind you, if we say four points for a bit of backdooring, but only three if you do it to a bloke. Whaddyer reckon Brad?'

'Sounds fair. But what about if a bloke does it to you?'

'Depends how big his dick is.' Mikey decided to join in, seeing as it was Mario they were taking the piss out of. 'I mean, it's only fair that you get more points if a baby's arm goes up there. If someone's got a dick like Mario's, then....'

'Well if it's as small as Mario's you should actually lose points.' Brad was having trouble keeping a straight face. Greg had already cracked.

'What are you all laughing at?' asked Heather as she walked passed the group on her way to the toilet.

'Old Mario was just telling us how much he loves anal sex and how he's always felt he had homosexual tendencies,' said Mikey totally straight faced.

'Ooohh, what a waste,' said Heather squeezing his cheek.

'I'M NOT A FUCKING QUEER!' screamed Mario. Alison looked over.

'It's alright Al,' said Brad, 'Just sorting out who the homophobic reps are.'

Alison smiled and nodded. Brad could tell that she didn't have a clue what he had just said. It crossed his mind that the way her head moved would have been better suited to the parcel shelf or back ledge of a car.

'Well that's a shame,' teased Heather. 'I like effeminate men.'

'No, what it was Heath darlin', was old Mario here was getting a bit queezy over the thought of anal sex,' explained Greg.

'Quite right too. It's bloody painful.'

'What, you mean you've tried it!!?' asked a horrified Mario.

'It's not so much that I've tried it. It's more that it seems that it's every blokes obsession to stick it up there. I mean what's the point?'

'Exactly!' Mario was hoping he had an ally.

'So come on then. Why do you all do it?'

'Yeah, why?' echoed Mario.

'For the same reason men swim rivers, explore jungles....' started Greg,

'What, to get covered in shit,' offered Brad.

'Yuk!' said Heather screwing her face up.

'The reason we do it,' continued Greg, 'Is the reason we do

most things - 'cos it's there and 'cos we're not s'posed to.' Greg finished off his drink and got the conversation back to the 'serious' topic of the competition. 'So. Let's make sure everybody knows the points system. One point for a wank; two for a blow job; three for a shag; four for a bit of backdooring and two bonus points for a threesome. That means eight points if it's two new people.'

'Is that two blokes or two girls' enquired Brad.

'Either,' replied Greg. 'Youse girls can join in too if y'like.'

'I'd love to,' said Heather. She nodded over to Alison who was cooing into Trev's ear, 'But I think there'd be only one winner!'

The male reps finished their drinks, left the girls in the bar and walked down the road into the West End to see if anything interesting was going on. En route, Greg left the group to see if a girl he had been shagging the previous season was still working in a bar called The OK Corral. The other three went into Sgt. Peppers where a very talented mixed race piano player/singer was belting out soul songs. After one drink Brad decided to leave them to it, the drive over finally catching up with him. Mikey and Mario moved towards the front of the stage to introduce themselves to the singer once he had finished playing, because they were to be using the bar during bar crawl nights and Alison had told them that they would be expected to get up on stage and sing ocassionally. Mario had noticed a really fit blonde standing on her own between the stage and one of the bars, so he left Mikey to swoop upon the poor unsuspecting girl with the enthusiasm of a malnourished golden eagle spotting a paraplegic field mouse. Mikey was sure that he recognised her from somewhere.

When the singer finished playing, he came over to where they were all standing. He nodded acknowledgement and then touched fists with Mikey, after which he tapped Mario on the shoulder. At first Mario swung round, but when he saw who it was his face broke into a smile and his voice, back into a Brooklyn accent.

'Wicked set man, wicked.'

'Cheers la'.'

'Yeah man, wicked.' Mario looked at the blonde and then at the piano player.

'Sorry, I don't know your name,' he said addressing the piano player.

'Ray.'

'Ray, this is Cheryl.'

'Alright,' said Ray nodding at Cheryl and winking, 'Are youse two an item then like?'

'Not yet,' said Mario talking to both Ray and Cheryl, 'I've got to wine and dine her first - then if she plays her cards right she'll see why Italian men are the worlds best lovers. What d'you think of that Cheryl?'

'Cheryl Pitt,' thought Mikey.

'Well,' said Cheryl thoughtfully, 'As tempting as your offer sounds, I've always found black scousers to be the best lovers and Italians to be all mouth and no - well, you know.'

'Hang on. What do you mean, black scousers? You mean like -'

'Like Ray,' offered Mikey helpfully.

'What you and Ray, you're.....' Mario's voice trailed off as he saw the first opportunity to gird his loins in Ibiza disappearing.

'Fucking 'ell la', you Italians may be gash in the sack, but yer fucking quick when it comes to catching on. Cheryl, is me girl. So, I'm afraid t'say that you've spent the last ten minutes trying to chat up me bird. But I tell yer what, gerrin a round o' Jaegermeisters an' I won't get me minder to come over and do yer.'

Mario went to the bar mumbling to himself, and for once actually ended up paying for a drink. Ray turned to Mikey,

'I 'aven't really gorra minder. Still, seems to 'ave done the trick.' Mario was scurrying back with four small glasses of a black liqueur.

'Anyway, what's yer name?'

'Mikey.'

'Well Mikey, as long as yer don't try and chat 'er up as well, meet me girl Cheryl........'

'......Cheryl Pitt,' interrupted Mikey. 'Haven't seen you on page three for a while'.

'Oh, you recognised her then,' laughed Ray. Mario had just got back with the drinks.

'I'd recognise those cheekbones anywhere,' said Mikey, trying to avoid referring to her obvious assets.

Mario, who had suddenly realised who Cheryl was, had no such tact.

'Fuck. I thought I recognised those tits.......'

''Ey, steady on.'

But Mario was just getting into his stride.

'Jesus. There's me trying to chat up a girl who I've probably knocked one out over on countless occasions. Cheryl, fucking, Pitt. Strewth! Wait 'til I tell my brother about this. He reckons you're the dirtiest looking of all of them.'

'Steady on lad.' Ray was trying to keep calm.

Mario carried on. The only way he could have surpassed his lack of sensitivity to the situation would have been if he had entered an animal rights meeting and started giving out tickets for a bullfight.

'Jeez, what he wouldn't like to do to you.' Mario fumbled in his jacket pocket for his camera. It was obvious he was slightly pissed. 'Here, Ray. Take a picture of me and Cheryl. No open leg shots, but you can get your tits out if you like, ha, ha, ha, ha!'

Ray hadn't grown up in Kirkby without being able to take care of himself. He also hadn't grown up in Kirkby without recognising a prize idiot when he saw one. He decided he was seeing one.

'Mikey. Do us a favour and take your dick of a mate out of this bar before I break this bottle over 'is thick 'ed.'

'C'mon Mario - let's go.'

'Nah, wait, wait. There's no need for this Ray. I didn't mean to offend you or your woman. Fuck, man. I respect you. Y'know, the way you sing and everything... Do you like good music....' Mario broke into song.

'Alright, alright. Just forget it.'

30

Ray decided that anything would be better than hearing Mario demolish one of his favourite songs. Unfortunately, Mario had a habit of always saying the wrong thing.

'Yeah man, no hard feelings. Listen, just because your girlfriend takes her clothes off and loads of blokes wank over her, it don't mean a thing. I mean, shit, even I'VE wanked over her. Fuck, it doesn't mean she's a filthy slut or anything.'

Ray picked up a bottle at the same time Mikey grabbed Mario's arm. If he wanted, Mikey could have easily taken the bottle off of Ray (and any non existent minder) but he figured that the chances were that he would probably end up being more friendly with Ray by the end of the season than he would Mario.

'It's alright Ray. I've got him. C'mon Mario, we're leaving.'

'No, no. I've got to make it up with Ray first.'

'You can make it up with Ray tomorrow. We're outta here.'

Mikey mouthed 'sorry' to Ray and Cheryl, and almost carried Mario out of the bar. When they got outside Mikey let him go and said,

'Mario, how much have you had to drink?'

'Whaddya mean? I've had the same as you.'

'What about in the bar at The Bon Tiempo while I was getting ready.'

'Oh, just a few aniseedy type drinks with Frank.'

'It wasn't called hierbas by any chance, was it?'

'Yeah, something like that. Meant to be a local drink or something.'

Mikey realised that Mario was obviously a lot more pissed than he had at first thought. There was little point in engaging him in conversation, so he walked him down to the taxi rank at the harbour and stuck him in a taxi, telling the driver to take Mario to the Apartmentos Bon Tiempo.

Mikey needed to unwind. He couldn't have a late one because of the meeting with Alison the next morning. He walked passed the outdoor restaurants and fountains that line the bay in San Antonio, and ended up at a small bar near the Es Paradis and The Star night clubs. Next to the serving hatch there were four chickens sizzling on a spit. He ordered himself a coffee, and sat watching people pour in and out of the two clubs. He noticed that most of the stylish clubbers were going into Es Paradis, whereas the 'Here We Go' brigade seemed to favour The Star (or maybe it was just that Es Paradis didn't favour them).

It was almost two o'clock, so Mikey got up and started the ten minute walk back to the apartments. As he got to the top of the road, he heard a commotion behind him. He looked back but couldn't see what was going on, and decided not to get involved. He walked along the sea front, and up through the still busy West End. A very pink looking girl in a long T-shirt and shorts was throwing up outside Joe Spoons Irish Bar. Various sun-tanned boys and girls tried to get him to go into different watering holes as he walked up the bustling hill, and it was not until he had got passed a bar called The Highlander that he felt he could relax. He turned left and eventually started walking down a hill which took him to a road which had wasteland on either side of it. He recognised this as being the road which led to the apartments. He had only just turned into the it when a police car drove past him with it's lights flashing. Police cars always made Mikey feel uneasy. But he was in Spain now, and he was sure that the Spanish police didn't assume that every black face belonged to a drug dealer, a mugger or a car thief. The police car got about fifty yards down the road before it swung round and screeched up in front of Mikey. 'This doesn't look too promising' he thought. He was right. Three policeman got out of the car and started yelling at Mikey in Spanish, whilst prodding him with their batons. They very roughly bundled him in the car. Mikey's first thought was to tell them that he was a rep, but he remembered that earlier Alison had said that there might be a problem with some of the work permits. He decided to use this as a last resort if things got rough. The car sped through San Antonio. When they got to the roundabout next to Extasis night club, Mikey assumed that they would carry on along the road which connects San Antonio with Ibiza Town, because this was where the police station was situated. Instead, they turned right and then took the second left down the busy road where Mikey had enjoyed a coffee but ten minutes earlier. When the queuing crowds saw the police car, they instantly got out of the way.

'What the fuck is going on?' Mikey mumbled to himself. When they got to the bar, they dragged Mikey out of the car and paraded him in front of the bar owner.

'*Mira. Es este el chico?*' (Look. Is this the boy?) said the burliest of the policeman.

'No,' replied the bar owner.

'*Pero me hablas dicho que era Negro.*' (But you said he was black.)

'*Verdad. Pero no era este. Este habla Espanol. Creo que es un guia.* (I know. But that's not him. He speaks Spanish. I think he's a rep.)

'So that's what it's all about' said Mikey thinking aloud. The burliest of the policeman turned to Mikey, took off his policeman's cap and scratched the back of his head.

'We are very sorry. The owner, he say that a boy eat chicken and drink wine but no pay. The boy is negro like you. But now the man say that you are no he. He also say that he think you might be guia - how you say - a rep. Tu habla espanol?'

'*Si, un pocito.* But I think your English is better than my Spanish,' said Mikey trying to win him over. The burly policeman turned to the other two and said something which Mikey couldn't hear. They all laughed. A quick bar of the laughing policeman went through Mikey's head, but he decided not to share it in case the joke got lost in the translation.

'Come. Where you stay? We take you home.'

On the short journey back Mikey got on surprisingly well with the policemen. Once again, he was sure that his Spanish endeared them to him. He discovered that the smallest of the three shared his interest in Karate. When they arrived back at the apartments, all three of the police got out and shook his hand. As they were leaving, the little one, having a bit of fun, aimed a karate kick at Mikeys ribs, pulling back just before he connected. They all laughed, in a male bonding type of way.

From the bar of the apartments, all that the inebriated Alison could see was Mikey having a 'fight' with some Spanish police. Alison had arranged to meet Trev when The Cockney Pride closed, so she had popped back to The Bon to grab a few bits and pieces. When she saw Mikey and the police she went running outside.

'What's happening - *que pasa?*' demanded Alison.

Mikey quickly explained that this was his boss. The burly policeman asked her if she spoke Spanish.

'*Si,*' lied Alison who had the most basic grasp of the language. The policeman told her what had happened speaking very quickly in his native tongue. Mikey noticed that Alison was shaking her head at all the wrong places. When the policeman had finished, she invited them in for a drink, which they accepted. Alison made sure that they were all comfortable and then walked over to where Mikey was left standing. As she walked towards him, the policeman all raised their glasses and mouthed 'Salut' to Mikey. Mikey smiled back at them. Alison only saw the smile.

'This is no laughing matter.'

'What do you mean?' asked Mikey innocently.

'What I mean is, that tomorrow I am going to get you on the first flight back to London. Still laughing? No. I thought not. You're fired!'

'WHAT?'

'You heard. Thank God I was able to calm them down or I dread to think what could have happened. Because of you, our whole future on this island could be in jeopardy. No, that's it. You're off home tomorrow.'

Mikey thought he was hearing things. 'Why, what have I done?'

'You know what you've done, and by tomorrow so will Jane Ward.'

'What exactly did they tell you Alison?'

This was probably a silly question on Mikey's part because he had heard virtually the whole conversation, but he thought he would ask anyway.

'Everything. Don't you care what that poor girl must have thought?'

'WHAT POOR GIRL?' Mikey was beginning to feel himself get exasperated.

'The white girl. The one you got your..your... oh do you really want me to make me say it?'

'YES!'

'Alright then. The white girl that you made look at your cock outside The Star Club.'

'WHAT!?' Mikey was almost laughing.

'There's no point in denying it. The police told me everything.'

'So your Spanish is good enough to understand all they said is it?'

'I understood most of it.'

'Alright then. What's Spanish for cock?'

'Pollo,' replied Alison matter of factly.

'I think you'll find that's chicken. Poll-A is cock,' said Mikey putting the emphasis on the last syllable.

'Well that's as maybe. But I know that white is blanco.'

'Yeah, but they were referring to white wine - vino blanco - not a white girl!'

Alison was beginning to realise that she had probably filled in a few too many of the blanks in her Spanish vocabulary for herself.

'So you didn't expose yourself in an alleyway then?' The policeman were leaving and waved at Mikey.

'Hasta luego Mikey,'

'Adios amigos,' replied Mikey, returning their wave before continuing the conversation with Alison. 'No I did not expose myself in an alley nor anywhere else for that matter. Believe it or not Alison, I have progressed from clubbing girls over the head and dragging them back to my cave. I've actually got my own flat at home with running water and electricity. I've even learned how to use a knife and fork.'

'Alright, there's no need to be sarcastic. They must have been speaking a local dialect,' said Alison tartly.

Mikey felt like saying that it wouldn't have mattered if they had been speaking in 'Klingon'.

'Anyway, I've still a good mind to sack you. Stealing isn't exactly what we expect from our reps either. Or I suppose that because you were wearing your reps badge you thought you'd found somewhere else that you could get free food? And you have the audacity to have a go at Mario for wearing his badge all the time. Hah!'

Mikey felt like he did not want to waste his breath on Alison. But if he wanted to have anything like the summer he had planned, then this kind of situation had to be dealt with, even though it was her problem and not his. It was time to tactfully, slowly and deliberately extricate himself from the situation without making a total enemy of his Resort Manager; the woman who could send him home the next day without any reason other than 'he wasn't suitable'.

'Alison. Like you said, the police were speaking Ibizenco so it was quite hard to follow what they were saying.'

'I know. But I got the gist of it.'

'Well you did and you didn't. Basically, what happened was another black guy ran off without paying for his food, and because at this time of year there aren't too many of the broth- there aren't too many other black guys over here, they picked me up. It was a case of mistaken identity, so believe me there isn't a problem. I'm not a thief; I'm not a flasher and I wasn't poncing food.'

'Alright then.' Alison lit a cigarette. 'I'll go down to the police station tomorrow and smooth things over.' She took a long, self important drag on her Marlboro. 'I just hope that tonight has taught you a lesson.'

It had. Mikey had learned that his Resort Manager couldn't speak Spanish, couldn't hold her drink and couldn't give a toss about anyone other than herself. He had also learned that the 'Italian Stallion' was not going to be on his Christmas card list, although he could think of quite a few other lists that he would like to have put him on.

Although she was pissed, Alison drove back to The Cockney Pride and picked up Trev. They had a bite to eat at San Antonio Grill then went back to his neat and spacious one bedroomed apartment around the bay at Port des Torrent.

Alison's original plan had been to go round some of the bars that they would be visiting on the Sunday night bar crawl to finalise the payments and the length of time that she would keep the clients in each bar. During her first few days on resort she had introduced herself to all of the owners of the bars that YF&S were to be using. She felt that of them all, Trevor would be the most receptive to a little womanly persuasion, so for this reason she decided to invest the whole evening into making sure that Trevor agreed to what she wanted. Although having the exact payments sorted out wasn't so crucial at the beginning of the season, by the end of June there would be several hundred clients on resort, so she had to be sure that the whole thing would then go like clockwork. YF&S nearly always chose bars that were not particularly busy. The reason that these bars were normally as popular as a beach at Sellafield was because they were on the whole, crap. Most of the bars in the West End didn't need the business. Many of them didn't want the business. The reason for this was that when YF&S went into a bar they would normally take it over. This would scare off their customers, so that when YF&S left (which they normally did after a maximum of forty minutes) the bar would be totally empty, and this could ruin a bars normal nightly momentum.

A lot of bars would like 'small' groups of up to about twenty people, but the only way they could get these would be through individual reps. It was made absolutely clear to all reps from day one that if any of them were caught taking money from bars then they would be instantly dismissed (as indeed they would if they were found to be doing any kind of fiddling). The only backhanders that were allowed were those which were officially sanctioned by the company. This 'black' money was organised on every resort through the Resort Manager, presenting him or her with an ideal opportunity to do some creative accounting to their own benefit. It was with this in mind that Alison had visited The Cockney Pride. Kirstie had told her that the previous year Trev had paid her seventy five pesetas a head for all of the clients that they brought in on the bar crawl. Alison knew that Trev was a lecherous old sod, and had decided to pay him a visit with as much flesh on show as possible to try and get the payment up to one hundred and fifty pesetas. It would certainly be worth her while. She would tell head office that she was being paid only fifty pesetas a head. Every week she would say that there was a third less clients on the crawl than there actually was. This one bar alone could be worth between three and five thousand pounds to her personally during the season. And there were four bars on the crawl. Plus two night clubs. Then there were the excursions, restaurants, car and bike hire...... the list was gloriously endless!

When they got back to Trev's, Alison was fairly sure that she had him where she wanted him. She kissed him on the cheek, kicked off her shoes and flopped giggling on to the cream leather settee.

'Awight then luv, what's it ter be? Whisky ter make yer fwisky, or bwandy ter make yer wandy? Ha! ha! ha! ha!'

'What about some wine, to make me pine,' teased Alison in a Lumleyesque sexy drawl.

'And what's me little tweasure pining for exactly?'

Alison licked her lips and 'innocently' looked at Trev's groin then up at his face.

'Well it depends what you're offering Trevor.'

Trev put down his bottle of Jack Daniel's and walked over to the settee. He stood behind her, and leant over to kiss her. As they were kissing, Alison knelt up, feeling Trev start to grow hard against her ribcage. He grabbed her hair and roughly pulled it back, gently biting her neck and shoulder. Alison stretched up so her right breast softly brushed against his bursting zip. Trev slipped his hand down her shirt, flicked her left nipple and then undid the remaining three buttons. Alison hesitantly started rubbing the front of Trev's trousers, taking her hand away and then putting it back again. Now she was in control and could start playing games. Trev was obviously getting worked up. Alison kept touching him, and then taking her hand away as if she was doing something that she shouldn't.

'Oh Trev, I really want to, but -'

'But what? Come on darlin'. We're both gwown ups.'

'I know we are Trev.'

'So what's the pwoblem?'

'Look Trev, you're a very horny man. The thing is I've only ever slept with three men and I've never done it on the first night,' lied Alison. 'Come and sit down. Anyway, where's that wine?'

Trev reluctantly walked over to the breakfast bar and poured Alison a wine. She thanked him by kissing him on the lips and then running her fingernails down his chest as he sat down next to her.

'Wine, wine, it makes me pine.' Alison giggled and snuggled up against Trev's chest, squeezing her arms into her side and crossing her legs so that the only way he could have successfully groped her would have been if his arms grew by a metre and had at least another two joints. It took Trev two minutes of clumsy fumbling to realise this for himself, after which he resignedly kissed the top of Alison's head and gave up.

'I'm sorry Trev. You don't mind do you?'

'No luv. There'll be uvver times,' replied Trev optimistically.

Alison purred. 'That's why I like older men - they understand women so much better. I'm sure we will soon. Mind you, all of this worry about hitting black money targets doesn't help me to relax.'

'What's that then Al baby?'

'Well, we have to draw a certain amount of money from the bars, and we're not expecting as many clients on resort as last season. That's why I'm trying to get more from the bars this year.'

'You're kidding! I fought that was just you being a gweedy cah.'

'Trevor! How could you think such a thing? Greedy cow indeed.'

'I know, I know. I'm sowy. I fought that most of the money went to you.'

'No, that's all changed. All of the money goes to the company.' Alison truly was an excellent liar. 'So,' Alison paused, took a deep breath and sat up in the chair looking directly into Trev's eyes. 'Are we going to be alright at one fifty a head?'

'We'll see.' Trev still wanted to play games.

Alison had decided to go in for the kill. 'There's no time for "we'll sees" Trevor dearest. I need to let head office know what bars we're using by tomorrow.' The lies were coming thick and fast now. 'So, are we going to be using you this year or not?'

Trevor stood up and walked over to the kitchen. He positioned himself behind the breakfast bar and poured himself a drink. His face looked stern. Alison began to wonder if she had blown it. He took a sip from his glass, swishing the whisky around his mouth before swallowing. Then, as Alison held her breath, his face broke into it's familiar grin.

'Go on then. Do us a favour though.'

'Of course darling. Anything.'

'Show us yer tits before you go!'

'Oh Trevor!' Alison got up and gave him a kiss on the cheek, assuming he was joking although guessing that he probably was not.

Five minutes after leaving, Alison lit a cigarette and breathed out a huge sigh of relief at a job well done.

Five minutes after Alison left, discarding a sticky, crumpled piece of tissue paper into the bin, Trev did the same.

CHAPTER ONE

CLIENTS ON RESORT

Alison eventually walked into the bar at ten o'clock - half an hour later than she had arranged the meeting for. Mikey turned to Brad and said that she looked liked she'd had a late one and then made a sarcastic comment about her being a stickler for time keeping. Alison didn't apologise for being late and proceeded to open the meeting.

'Right then you lot. Good morning.'

'Good morning Alison,' they replied in unison like a group of six year olds.

'Well it's good to see looking round that none of you appear to be too rough. I'm sure none of you will need any reminding that today is the day that our first clients arrive. I've got all of the flight manifesto's here.' Alison gave them out. 'You will see that we have thirty seven arrivals. This is made up of two couples, fifteen males and eighteen females.'

'REEEEEESULT!' yelled Greg, punching the air at the news of this female heavy ratio.

'Thought you would be pleased Greg,' smiled Alison. 'The majority of the clients will be staying here at The Bon Tiempo, although three will be at The Delfin. You'll be bringing the flight in Greg, and Brad - I want you to be at The Delfin to welcome the three arrivals. When Greg has checked his lot into The Bon Tiempo he'll walk down to check everything is alright. Clear?' Brad nodded and looked over at Greg who gave him a reassuring wink.

'Tomorrow night we'll be taking them out on a bar crawl. Thursdays won't normally be bar crawl nights, but things are always a bit up in the air at the beginning of the season so we

41

need to improvise. On the subject of improvising, the official beach party doesn't start until next week, so on Friday we'll be doing our own down on the man made beach over there.' Alison waved her arm towards Calo des Moro which was just a hundred yards from the apartments. 'Included in the three thousand peseta price of the beach party will be a Bar-B-Q back here at the apartments, where we will also be doing a pop quiz. Right, everyone got that?' There was a general mumbling of agreement. 'Good. That takes us through to Saturday. Everyone needs to be in the office in Ibiza Town no later than midday. Heather and Greg know where it is and there's a map in your information pack. There are another two flights in from Gatwick on Saturday night. Heather and Mikey will be doing the bigger one and Brad will bring in the smaller one - I think there are eighteen arrivals Brad - in a minibus. Also Brad, if you could be up to meet two arrivals who are being stuck in a taxi from the Bristol flight. Should be here at about eight o'clock Sunday morning. Lorraine and Mario, you'll be bringing in the Manchester arrivals.'

Alison noticed that the colour had visibly drained from Lorraine's face when she heard the news. Lorraine had not been too good on the microphone either and hitherto Alison had been wholly unimpressed with her performance. The quality that Jane Ward saw in Lorraine that Alison was unable to, was that although she was not really an entertainer, Lorraine was very good with small groups. Other girls in particular warmed to her very quickly. The secret to having a good team was balance. Jane Ward understood this (which was one of the reasons why she was Overseas Manager) and Alison did not. She gave Lorraine a look of contempt and continued,

'That flight is due to land at eight thirty five Sunday morning. Unfortunately the flights are all over the place this weekend. There are another three clients staying at Las Huertas turning up Sunday evening, so I'm sorry to have to do this to you Brad but you'll have to go and pick them up. You'll be sharing a coach with a rep from a company called

Summerplan, so she'll probably do the microphone.'

Most of this went over Brad's head. He had no experience of airport nights and the whole thing seemed quite exciting. He was trying to work out when he would get a chance to sleep but he was sure everything would be alright. If Greg had been given such a heavy workload Alison knew she would not have had such an easy ride.

'Ok then,' said Alison bringing the meeting to a close. 'The rest of today should really be spent getting your information books and posters ready. You'll be moving to your respective hotels on Saturday, but I'll speak to you all individually about that on Friday. If any of you need help I'll be up in my room, but only come up if it's absolutely necessary because I've got a mound of paperwork to get through. Any questions?'

There was no reply, so Alison got into the lift up to her apartment on the fifth floor, where she took off her shoes and fell on the bed to catch up on some much needed sleep.

Downstairs, Greg started examining the flight manifestos. He explained to the new recruits that the beginning of the season was a great time to score points. This was because a lot of places were not yet open, which meant that most of the girls who came away would stay within the group. Also, because it was the cheapest time of year a lot of nurses came away - a category with which Greg claimed to have had particular success.

Looking down the manifesto Greg explained the difference between 'single shares' and 'single rooms'. 'Single shares' were clients who came away to share a room with a stranger. Although they could be quite normal, in Greg's experience they were normally weirdo's, slappers or both. 'Single rooms' often fell into the same category, although they were more likely to be clients who had booked at the last minute and were prepared to go anywhere to get a tan. They would normally be horrified when they discovered what YF&S was all about.

Apart from pulling women, Greg's other main talent was selling. He had never had a proper sales job in the UK or any official sales training, but he truly did possess the gift of the gab and a razor sharp mind when it came to a scam. His selling skills were what made YF&S largely turn a blind eye to his 'indiscretions' when it came to clients of the opposite sex.

Excursion sales were very important to YF&S. Apart from allowing them to keep control of clients on resort they produced a valuable source of revenue. Reps were targeted to get at least sixty percent of their clients to buy the excursion block, i.e. all of the excursions. To encourage this they were paid a small basic salary (just over fifty pounds a week) but a commission structure which was very much geared towards achieving and exceeding their sales targets. Part of the reason that YF&S holiday's were so cheap was because they counted on excursion sales to maintain profitability.

Because the excursion sales targets were so high, any large groups who decided not to join in could decimate sales figures. The strategy in this situation was to try and identify the natural leader and home in on him or her. As a team, Heather and Greg were brilliant. They were both very attractive and knew how to flirt and charm; gently persuading at first using pleasant logic ('If you book the block you get two excursions free', 'It's much more fun with everyone sticking together'); then maybe a bit of flattery ('With you lot on the excursions they'll be great.', 'We really enjoy the excursions when we get groups like you on them.'); finally resorting to a virtual snub as a last resort ('Well if you don't book them don't come crying to us when you get ripped off by someone selling crap excursions around town, or when you run out of money.'). It took a very strong individual to resist their combined pressure, and once the leader had been won over there would be three strong personalities cajoling any reluctant member of the party into parting with their money for a block of excursions.

Because he had to be at The Delino hotel by six in the morning, Brad didn't go into town with all of the others. Mikey decided to stay at the apartments where the pair of them had a bite to eat after which they took a few bottles of San Miguel up to Brad's room. They sat on the balcony listening to music and putting the world to right. Although they couldn't see it in the dark, they could hear the sea as the small waves washed against the man made beach a couple of hundred yard away. In the distance they could hear a singer guitarist ruining Eric Clapton's 'Wonderful Tonight' and the occasional shriek of a middle aged woman who had obviously drank too much sangria. After an hour or so Mikey could tell that Brad was tired, so he left and popped into town to try and score some puff. After Mikey had left, Brad got his uniform ready for the next morning, set his alarm for five thirty, cleaned his teeth and hit the sack.

Five thirty came a lot quicker than Brad would have liked. Had he been on holiday he would probably still have been in a club. Instead he showered himself into life, put on his uniform and went down to reception to wait for Greg's coach. Although he was still tired, once he put on his uniform he began to feel quite excited. It was a strange feeling, the thought of actually meeting 'clients'. All of the training was geared towards looking after clients; entertaining clients; selling to clients; disciplining clients - Brad was almost expecting supernatural beings rather than ordinary people.

A little after six thirty Brad heard the rumble of a diesel engine. He looked up to see the newly risen sun reflecting off the dewy blue and red paintwork which was the livery of the San Jose coach that had just pulled up outside. Through the closed door he could just about make out Greg's voice on the microphone giving the new arrivals instructions before leading them off the coach. As they all walked past Brad he tried to look as relaxed and experienced as he could, although inside he felt totally hopeless. A group of three girls looked at him and started giggling.

'Alright girls.' Brad smiled at them. They just giggled some more which made Brad feel like a grinning vacuous banana standing there in his bright yellow uniform. He sought refuge in Greg. 'Alright Greg.' Greg was busy checking people in and didn't even notice Brad for almost a minute. When he did see

45

him he was quite impatient.

'You should be on the coach taking the other three to the Delfin. Get a move on. I'll be there in five minutes.'

Brad shuffled off feeling useless. He got on the coach and smiled at the driver. 'Alright?' The coach driver didn't reply but pressed a button which hissed the door closed. Brad glanced at the three clients, raised his eyebrows and mouthed 'Alright,' whereupon he sat himself down in the front chair with his back to them. Two minutes later they were at the Delfin. Brad got off of the coach and walked through to the reception. Two of the three clients were girls who had come away together. He checked them in, and stood at the reception with the night porter waiting for the single share male client to walk through the door. A couple of minutes passed without sign. Brad went out of the hotel to find the coach driver ushering the final client around to pick up his case. Brad looked at the flight manifesto to get the lone travellers name.

'Stewart Collins is it?'

Stewart Collins nodded. He was wearing a pair of brown crimplene trousers, white trainers and a brown V- neck jumper with a red inlay of Chinese writing down the sleeve. His hair was black and worn in an unfashioned side parting. Brad went round to the side of the coach to help him with his case, which was larger than normal and of a brown leather design. It looked heavy, so Brad grabbed it with both hands to yank it off of the coach. As he did so, the case flew out and swung into the groin of the driver who was standing next to him, which left the unfortunate Spaniard in a crumpled heap mumbling something that Brad did not exactly understand, but could guess was not particularly complimentary. Unless the gravitational pull of the earth in Spain was considerably less than in the UK, Brad surmised that the case was probably empty. Without saying a word, Stewart took the case and walked towards the hotel door. Brad followed him and after checking him in, showed him his room. All attempts at conversation elicited only grunts and stares at the floor. Brad went down to reception where Greg had turned up. Greg started laughing.

'Told you single shares were normally weirdo's, didn't I?'

'Thank fuck for that,' sighed Brad. 'For one horrible moment I thought it was me.'

'No mate. Our man in brown is a one 'undred percent nut-nut. I don't s'pose you picked up his case?'

'YEAH! It seemed as if it was empty!'

Greg grinned and nodded. 'I tell you wha'. We're gonna 'ave some fun and games with that one this week.'

No sooner had Greg finished speaking than they heard a crash which sounded like a charging elephant, followed by a gradual wail which turned into a blood curdling scream. They ran up to Stewart's room, and as they approached they could hear very heavy breathing. Brad got there first and opened the door.

They were greeted with the sight of the man in brown crouching on the step leading to the shower. He was staring into space and had already picked off three of the tiles which were scattered around his feet.

'What's the matter?' asked Brad. 'Are you OK?'. Crimplene man just rocked back and forth on his haunches and said nothing. Brad crouched down next to him. 'Stewart. What's wrong. Do you need any help?'

Stewart stood up and walked out of the bathroom and flopped onto his bed.

'I'm just tired.'

'Oh, that's alright then,' said Greg sarcastically. 'Do us a favour though lad. If you suddenly get 'un-tired', leave them fucking tiles alone, eh? Come 'ed Brad, let's go.'

As they walked out of the room the two girls who had just arrived were standing in the corridor.

'Is everything alright?' asked the blonde one.

Brad was just about to reply that there was no problem and that they should go to bed when Greg piped up,

'No. We're going to move you into a different room and it will probably be safest if we stay at this hotel for a few hours until the welcome meeting just in case there are any more problems. The guy isn't really dangerous but he is a little disturbed at the moment. Come downstairs and we'll get you a drink while I organise another room.'

Brad was confused. He could not understand how Greg had made such a thorough analysis of the situation with such little information. He guessed that it was just experience. He certainly had a lot to learn.

Brad sat drinking coffee while the two girls knocked back vodkas and orange. They seemed as if they were already a bit tipsy. Both were only about five foot two. The blonde one introduced herself as Emma. She started asking questions about Greg.

'He's a northerner, isn't he? I don't normally like northerners but he seems really sweet. He's ever so good looking isn't he? I was talking to him on the coach. He's a right laugh. Has he got a girlfriend?'

'No I 'aven't, and I don't want one,' said Greg, walking in and catching the tail end of the conversation.

Emma blushed. Brad noticed that the dark haired girl was staring directly at him. He smiled at her a little uncomfortably.

'What's your name?'

'Linda. And you're......Brad,' she replied looking at his badge. 'What about you Brad, have you got a girlfriend?'

'Course he 'asn't,' butted in Greg. 'He's too fucking ugly.' Greg started laughing.

'Well I don't think he's ugly,' said Linda. 'I bet you get loads of girls don't you?'

Brad started to relax. It dawned on him that just because these were clients he didn't have to watch everything he said. He could just be himself and have a laugh. Greg was already whispering into the giggling Emma's ear. He caught his eye. Greg winked and nodded his head towards Linda mouthing 'go on'. The penny dropped.

'Actually, I've not been with a girl for over a year now,' lied Brad. 'That's why I became a rep. I was seeing this girl who dumped me for a rugby player. I tried to win her back but him and two of his mates from the team beat me up.' Emma and

48

Greg started listening. 'I was in hospital for ten weeks. They kicked me in the - well, you know,' Brad put his hand around his groin. 'The specialist was worried that I'd never be able to make love again. I couldn't get a decent hard on so they put this thing in my wotsit - it's a bit like one of those bendy things that you put in your hair. It just means that it's hard all of the time and when I want to use it I just have to bend it from the side to the front. I'm really embarrassed about it. I've not let anyone see it up until now - God knows how anyone will ever fancy me.' Brad looked at the floor, convinced that the girls knew he was bullshitting. He caught Greg's eye and winked.

'You'd show it to us though Brad, wouldn't you?' asked Greg. 'I mean, you girls wouldn't be embarrassed would you?'

Before they could reply Brad said, 'Well if I do show it to you it will have to be one at a time and you've got to promise not to laugh.'

'Alright then' answered Greg assumptively on everyone's behalf. 'Let's go upstairs.'

Brad led the way with a huge grin on his face. The two girls followed giggling. Greg kept telling them to sshh, so as not to embarrass Brad. When they got to the room Brad said, 'OK, Greg first.' Greg walked into the room and the two of them burst out laughing.

'Fuckin' brilliant. Right. You get Linda in 'ere and I'll ger' Emma next door. They're definitely up for it. That's why I came out with all that bullshit about staying 'ere for a few hours. Emma was making a serious play for me on the coach. Remember we've got the welcome meeting at eleven so don't be too long.'

'There's no danger of that with the way my bollocks feel at the moment. I just hope she comes across otherwise they'll probably explode - very messy.'

'Yeah, well don't fall asleep either. I'll see you back at The Bon later. Good luck.'

Greg walked out and ushered Linda in. Brad and Linda stood facing each other.

'Look Brad. If you're embarrassed I underst-'

'No. It's fine Linda,' said Brad solemnly. 'It's something I've got to do. Give me your hand.' He took Linda's hand and rested it against his 'injury'. It was already rock hard and pointing to the left. 'Right. All I have to do is to undo my zip and bend it forward.' He undid his trousers and lifted his member over the top of his pants. 'There you go.' He put her hand onto it. Does it feel any different?'

'I'm not sure. Maybe. It's hard to tell.'

'Linda. Can I ask you to do me a huge favour. You see, I've not come since the operation and -' Brad could take no more and burst out laughing, falling onto the bed with Linda on top of him.

'You bastard. I knew you were lying.' With that she bent down and bit his dick before taken the majority of it in her mouth. After a minute or two Brad put his hands on either side of her head and gently pulled her up so that they were face to face. As he kissed her she slipped off her panties, and then pulled off her all in one blue and white striped dress. She straddled his thigh and started to rub herself up and down it. Brad raised his knee, and pushed two fingers inside her. She let out a low moan and rammed herself against his hand. Brad turned her over without taking his fingers out, so that she was lying on her back. He worked his tongue down her body until his tongue was flicking her clitoris, while his fingers probed her.

'Have you got a condom?' he asked.

'No. Haven't you?'

'Yeah. A hundred and eighty quid's worth, but not here. SHIT!'

'Never mind. Here.' With that Linda slid down the bed so that she was underneath the kneeling Brad. She licked and then sucked his balls whilst deftly rubbing his member. Just as Brad was about to come she raised her head and put her mouth around his helmet where she received Brad's first ejaculation on Spanish soil. Brad looked down at her grinning from ear to ear.

'What a fine woman! God, I definitely owe you one.'

50

'Actually you don't,' replied Linda. 'I've never been much of a screamer, but believe me, we're quits.'

Brad stayed with her for about fifteen minutes before making his way back to The Bon. When he got there the only person in the bar was Greg, who was getting the flipchart ready for the welcome meeting. As he walked in, Greg wrote '3 POINTS' in big red letters on the flipchart. He looked at Brad for some feedback, whereupon Brad lifted up two fingers.

'WHAT! You didn't shag 'er.' Brad shook his head. 'Why not?'

'No dunkies mate.'

'I thought you brought two hundred quids worth with you to sell.'

'I did - only some bastards apparently supplied all the bars with condom machines. I'll have to try and sell them to our clients.'

'Knowing our lot you'll probably 'ave more chance of using 'em. Anyway - I'd've still shagged 'er. She seemed clean enough to me.'

'Well Dr. Greg. I'm taking no chances this season.'

'Fair enough. Still, good early points eh? I've gorra 'and it to you Brad, that was a great story. What a fuckin' team. Almost fuckin' telepathic.'

Greg and Brad had a self congratulatory breakfast and waited as the other reps gradually filtered down for the welcome meeting. The only other people in the bar were one of the couples. As it was the first 'real clients', each of the reps made a point of talking to them and telling them how wonderful all of the excursions were. Feeling totally intimidated, the couple fled for the nearest beach clutching their towels and Piz Buin as they left. All of the other new arrivals apart from Emma and Linda turned up - including Stewart. He was wearing the same brown clothes and spent the welcome meeting rocking backwards and forwards in a chair making motor bike noises.

Because there were so many reps in relation to clients, all of those who attended the welcome meeting booked an excursion block. This was also largely due to a thoroughly entertaining welcome meeting by Greg, where he even convinced the rest of the reps that there was little else to do at the beginning of the season other than the excursions.

The bar crawl started at seven thirty. Linda and Emma both turned up, and Brad was pleasantly surprised at how nice they looked compared to when they arrived that morning. There was also a red head that Brad hadn't noticed at the welcome meeting. Mario noticed her too.

'Cor! What would I do with that?' whistled Mario.

'Come too quickly?' replied Mikey.

'I can go for ever mate. Everything you've ever heard about Italians - it's all true.'

Mikey considered the comment and had to agree.

Mario continued, 'You watch - by the end of tonight she'll be putty in my hands.'

'The only thing that'll be in your hands at the end of tonight will be your dick, soft lad,' said Greg, catching the conversation as he walked past.

'Oh I don't know Greg,' added the ever sarcastic Mikey. 'Let's face it - Mario is a very good looking lad. Alright, so he dresses a bit strange...' Mikey looked Mario up and down. Because they were going on a bar crawl all of the reps had to wear YF&S T-shirts. All of them apart from Mario were wearing either jeans or tracksuit bottoms. Mario had a pair of very baggy black trousers held up with wide black braces, tucked into ankle high buckled boots. 'Actually Mario, you're not going anywhere for a few minutes are you?'

'No. Why?'

'I thought I'd pop upstairs and get you a little red nose to complete the outfit.'

'Whaddya mean?'

'I think what he means is that you bear an uncanny resemblance to a clown,' offered Brad helpfully.

'Fuck off! Do you know how much these trousers cost? A hundred and twenty quid!' Mario stood there looking pleased with himself.

'They might have cost that much when the original owner bought them, but how much did they cost you?' Mikey knew that he shouldn't be winding Mario up, but he couldn't help himself.

'What do you mean, how much did they cost me?'

'Mario, it's obvious that some ex-New Romantic has donated them to a charity shop where they've no doubt caught your sartorially inelegant eye. So what were they? A fiver? A tenner?'

'What the fuck do you know about fashion,' said the now agitated Mario, before proudly adding, 'My cousin runs one of the best clothes shops in the King's Road.'

'So why don't you shop there then?' Mikey was finding this too easy.

'I suppose you could always go and get changed.' Brad could sense that it was getting nasty so he thought he would try to deflect some of Mario's rage away from Mikey. It was too late. Mario's face contorted into an ugly scowl as he prepared himself for his final retort.

'Well at least I can change my clothes - what are you going to do about your skin?' With that Mario turned on his heel and went to the bar. Brad looked at Mikey worried that the next stage of the confrontation was going to become physical. Mikey sensed his concern.

'It's alright Brad. I've learnt how to deal with idiots like him. I'm just glad he's shown his true colours so early in the season.'

'Well I admire your control. If he can't stand having the piss taken out of him what's he doing in this job?'

'I guess the odd bad one slips through the net. Apparently he was outstanding at Bridlehurst - one of the best candidates.'

'I don't believe that for one minute.'

'Well, from what I hear it's true. Obviously all of the girls loved him and he comes across as being pretty confident. Mind you, a little birdy told me that he knew one of the rep's from last year who gave him the lowdown on what to expect during the twenty four hour interview.'

53

'What, so he knew all about being woken up in the middle of the night and dumped in the wilds of Hereford?'

'Guess so. He also knew what kind of five minute sketch would go down well - and all about that two minute after dinner speech.'

'Oh fuck - I forgot about that. I reckon that must've been the scariest part of the whole interview.'

'I think it was for everyone. I mean, one minute you're relaxing eating, the next they're telling you that you've got two minutes to prepare a two minute after dinner speech on a subject they give you. I had to talk about Dolphins. What about you?'

'Eating a Cadbury's Cream Egg underwater.'

'You what!?'

'Seriously. I had to talk about eating a Cadbury's Cream Egg underwater. They spring it on you to see how good you are at waffling and how you react under stress. I s'pose if Mario knew all about it, it made it a bit easier.'

'For sure. The other thing that I heard is that he's brother's a bit of a 'face' back home, sorts out someone in head office with coke or something. By all accounts he pulled a few strings for him.'

'That figures.'

They both looked over at Mario who had knocked back two quick glasses of hierbas. He stared at Mikey and Brad and then made a point of making a bee line for the red head. Just at that moment Alison came in. She walked over to Greg who was standing a few feet away from Brad and Mikey. As she passed them she said,

'Come on you two. What are you doing standing there? You should be mingling with the clients like Mario is.' She turned round to Greg. 'Right. Shall we get this show on the road?'

The first bar they visited was The Cockney Pride. Brad was conscious of Alison sitting at the top of the bar watching their every move. She seemed to be on Lorraine's case, going up to her and telling her to do things every few minutes. After about half an hour Brad was standing near Lorraine so he bent over to her.

'You alright?'

'Yeah fine.'

'I noticed that Alison keeps pulling you over. Anything up?'

'Oh she keeps telling me not to spend too long speaking to one group of people. It seems really superficial to keep saying 'having a good time?', 'have you booked the excursions?' - some of them are really interesting to talk to. If I keep walking away it makes me seem ignorant.'

'Mmmm. Still, she's the boss.'

'I know. It's just that - oh what the hell!' Lorraine changed the subject. 'Old Mario seems to be getting pissed. He's making a right twat of himself with that Patricia.'

'Who's Patricia?' asked Brad.

'The pretty redhead,' replied Lorraine. 'That's the other thing that pisses me off. Mario's spent the whole night trying to chat her up yet Alison hasn't said anything to him.'

'Where's Patricia from?' enquired Brad.

'Nottingham, I think.'

'What does she do for a living?'

'She's a student.'

'What's she studying?'

'Economics. Don't tell me you're after her too?'

'Alright, I won't. What does she drink?

'Malibu and pineapple I think.'

Brad smiled at Lorraine, ordered a Malibu and pineapple from Trevor and walked over to Patricia. Mario had left her alone to get himself another drink.

'Patricia, isn't it?'

'That's right. And which one are you?' She looked at his badge. 'Brad. Well hello Brad.'

'Well hello Patricia.' Brad smiled. 'Enjoying yourself?' Patricia looked over at Mario.

'Hardly.'

'Oh don't worry about him. He's just a bit pissed.'

'A bit!'

'Alright - very pissed.'

55

There were a few seconds awkward silence which Patricia broke. 'So Brad. Have you come over here to tell me how wonderful you are and how three thousand people applied for thirty jobs, and how you've got to be a special person to be a rep, and how thrilled any girl should be if a rep tries to chat her up, and -'

'WHOA! Steady on. Strewth! It would seem my fellow rep has been giving you a bit of an ear bashing.'

'Oh come off it - it's not just him. All of you reps obviously love yourselves. You think that all you have to do is snap your fingers and we'll all just fall into bed. Old wotsisname over there has spent the last three quarters of an hour telling me how great he is and how lucky I am that he's chosen me,' said Patricia pointing at Mario. 'I suppose it's some kind of competition between you all.'

'Hang on, hang on. Although I'm sure that there are numerous benefits to wearing this badge, it does also mean that I have a job to do and part of that job is to go around talking to our clients to make sure that they are enjoying themselves. Now if you're saying to me that you'd enjoy yourself more by me making myself scarce then that's fine, but please do me a favour and don't tarnish me with the same brush as that cretin. He's got the brains-'

'BRAINS!' interrupted Patricia. 'You're not going to tell me you need brains to do this job. I thought all you needed was the ability to ponce drinks and a mirror to look at yourself in. You'll be telling me next that you need two 'A' levels to be a rep.'

'No, it's not a pre-requisite but it does help.'

Patricia started laughing in a semi-mocking way. 'So what are your 'A' levels in Brad? Sunbathing and chatting up girls?'

'No, I only got 'O' levels in those.' Brad thought that now would be an opportune time to use the information that Lorraine had just given him. 'So judging by the way you put such an emphasis on intellect I assume you're in the middle of taking a degree yourself.'

'I am actually.'

'Mmm.' Brad looked thoughtful. 'I suppose you're doing a cop out degree like Sociology or Economics.'

'Economics isn't a cop out degree. Anyway, how did you know that I'm studying Economics?' Patricia looked at Brad quizzically.

Brad could feel himself in danger of becoming a little too smug so he brought the conversation to a close. 'Anyway Patricia, just to show that we're not all vainglorious drink ponces obsessed with acquiring notches for our bedpost I'm going to carry on doing my job by talking to other clients, and whilst I'm sure they won't be as interesting as you...' Brad put on a voice of mock sincerity, '...I've just gotta do, what I've gotta do.' Brad gave her the glass he had in his hand. 'There you go. You look like you drink Malibu and pineapple.'

As Brad walked away Mario arrived, dropping a pint of beer on the floor right next to Patricia's feet and soaking them in the process. Brad didn't wait around to see what happened next and went over to Greg who was talking to Emma and Linda. They had a brief conversation before Greg looked at his watch and turned to Brad.

'Right. We've been in here forty minutes now. Time to move on.'

With that Greg looked over at Alison and pointed at his watch. Alison nodded, so Greg went over to the tape deck, turned the music down and switched on the microphone.

'OK. Have we got anyone here from Young Free & Single?' A smallish cheer went up. 'That was PATHETIC! I said DO WE HAVE ANYONE HERE FROM YOUNG FREE & SINGLE?' With that the whole of the Cockney Pride erupted into a unified drunken yell. 'That's more like it! Right then Young Free & Single. It's time to knock back yer drinks 'cos we're moving on to our second port of call. If you want to follow Heather and Brad they'll show you round to The Angler's where your reps will be DJ'ing and gerrin' you into the party mood.' Greg switched off the microphone and came over to Brad. 'Right. Lead them round to The Angler's. Me, Lorraine and Mario will make sure there aren't any stragglers.

57

When you get there start playing some records and gerr'em all going. I'll take over as soon as we've cleared this place.'

'Any idea how long you'll be?' asked Brad.

'I don't know. Ten, fifteen minutes. Why?'

'It's just that I've never DJ'd before.'

'Well, now's your chance to learn. Come on, gerra move on.'

Brad and Heather led the majority of the 'ere we go' singing holidaymakers to The Angler's. The place was totally empty. As they turned up they were greeted by the owner, who seemed quite flustered.

'What time do you call this? You're ten minutes late. You'd better stay an extra ten minutes or you won't get -' the bar owner checked himself just before he revealed his 'arrangement' with Alison. 'Well now you're here get some music on.'

'Would you mind showing me how to work the decks. I've never DJ'd before,' asked Brad.

'Fucking great! You're ten minutes late and they send me round a rep who's never DJ'd before.' The bar owner shook his head. 'Alright. Follow me. I'm Russell. Who are you?'

'Brad'

'Alright Brad.' They shook hands. Russell's tone mellowed. 'I'm not having a go at you personally, it's just that I get a bit stressed at the beginning of the season. Ironic really. That's why I came out here in the first place, to avoid stress. Tried everything back home. Even took up fishing. Never go fishing if you want to relax Brad. It's one of the most stressful bloody pastimes there are. Trying to get those horrible little maggots on the hook without ripping them in half or not getting them on at all. Then getting the bloody line all tangled up. Then some idiot fishing next to you letting his float drift up to yours. And then you can sit there all sodding day in the wet and cold and catch nothing, drinking stale coffee and eating crispy sandwiches. What a fucking waste of time.'

Brad nodded his agreement.

'Is that why you called your bar Angler's?' asked Brad,

stuck for anything else to say.

'Couldn't think of anything suitable to call it. I had a shoe repair shop back home. Hasn't got the same ring to it, has it?' Russell laughed. Brad raised his eyebrows. 'I mean, Trev's got The Cockney Pride 'cos he's from London. I think it's always good to call a small bar after something that relates to the owner, so I thought why not call it The Angler's seeing as I was doing so much fishing. Quite appropriate don't you think?'

Brad actually thought that 'The Manic-Depressive-Paranoid-Schizophrenic' would have been a more appropriate name, but he kept that suggestion to himself.

'Right Brad. There's the speed select, thirty three or forty five. These are your fade controls, this one controls the left deck and this one the right deck and this is your cross fade. These control treble and bass and these are your headphones. If you want to listen just in the headphones you flick this switch. Got that? Good. What do you want to drink? San Miguel ok?'

Brad nodded still trying to take everything in. He looked through the record collection which wasn't particularly awe inspiring. He successfully managed to put on three records before Greg arrived. When Greg took over Brad was amazed at how easy he made it seem. He was on the microphone getting everybody going and although 'Happy Hour' and 'Shout' were not the sort of records Brad would have chosen to listen to, they were certainly suitable for the occasion. Every time Emma and Linda walked past the DJ booth Greg would catch Brad's eye, hold up three fingers and mouth 'three points'. A couple of times that Brad brushed past them they would both pinch his bum. Just before they were all due to leave, a very drunk Emma cornered Brad as he came out of the Gents.

'This is great isn't it?'

'I'm glad you're enjoying yourself,' said Brad. Emma put her arm through his, which made Brad look around to check that Alison wasn't looking over. He also found himself checking that Patricia wasn't watching either.

59

'Brad, I've got some good news and some bad news,' slurred Emma.

'And what's that then.'

'Well, the bad news is that Linda wants to sleep with Greg.'

'Oh. Oh well, that sounds more like the good news to me,' replied Brad, his ego defence mechanism kicking in.

'No, no. The good news is that I want to sleep with you.' Emma giggled.

'Emma, I don't want you thinking I'm easy or that I sleep with just anyone.'

'I don't think you're easy,' grinned Emma running her fingernails up the inside of his thigh.

'Well that's alright then. You do know that we don't finish this bar crawl until gone midnight don't you? Do you think you can last that long?'

Emma stood on her tiptoes and whispered into his ear, 'I can last forever.'

Brad smiled and rushed over to Greg, who had just started playing an Edwin Starr record.

'Greg. Greg guess what?'

'What?'

'You'll never guess what's just happened.'

'Go on.'

'Emma just came up to me and says that they want to swap - y'know, me with her and you with Linda.'

'Oh that.' Greg put another record onto the turntable and cued it up ready to play. 'Yeah I know all about that. It was my idea.'

'Your idea?' Brad looked bewildered.

'Yeah, I sorted it out in The Cockney Pride. Hang on a minute.' Greg started Gary Glitter's 'Leader of the Gang'. 'It's obvious that they'll shag anything with a badge.'

'How can you tell,' interrupted Brad.

'I just can,' replied Greg. 'Anyway, I've already got maximum points out of Emma 'cos she won't take it up the shit box so there's no point in shagging her again.'

Ten minutes later the bar crawl proceeded to Sgt. Peppers.

Somewhere on the way Patricia got lost, denying Brad the opportunity to speak to her again. Once finished in Peppers, Mikey and all of the other reps were going down to The Star Club to round things off and Greg was going back to the apartments to increase his points tally. As Brad was feeling pissed, tired and randy he opted to join Greg, Linda and Emma. The two girls went on ahead and were waiting for them in the bar of the apartments when Brad and Greg got back. Brad sat down with the girls and got himself a toasted sandwich and a coffee while Greg went to see the receptionist to check that there were no problems.

When he got back Brad yawned.

'Well I don't know about anyone else, but I'm knackered.'

'That's a shame,' said Greg slipping his arms around the shoulders of both girls, 'Guess I'll just 'ave to take these lovely young ladies upstairs an' look after 'em on me own.'

'You must be joking. It's bad enough that the love of my life has dumped me for you,' he said looking at Linda half joking, 'I'm just lucky that this fine specimen of womanhood has got some sense of justice....' Brad tousled Emma's hair '...and taste.'

'Aye, well I've got something for you to taste,' said Greg, grabbing Linda's hand to lead her upstairs. 'See you on the beach party tomorrow.'

'He's a real charmer, isn't he?' said Brad to Emma. 'Such a way with words.' Emma just smiled. She was obviously very drunk. 'Come on then. Time for bed.'

Emma hiccoughed and stumbled to her feet picking up her handbag as she did so. Her high heels made an embarrassingly loud clip clop on the marble floor, so much so that when they got out of the lift on Brad's floor, he managed to persuade her to take them off.

Brad didn't particularly enjoy the sex. They were both pissed and the whole thing lacked any passion. There was a short period of fumbling, followed by less than ten minutes of missionary position sex, after which Brad all but dribbled into the first of his hundred and eighty pounds worth of condoms.

It did nothing to make him feel any better when Emma kept asking questions about Mario and revealed that at least half of the girls on holiday that week fancied him - herself included. Emma was dead to the world within minutes, so after he got back from cleaning himself up he made a point of switching the light on to set his alarm in an unsuccessful attempt at waking her up. It was just gone two o'clock. He set the alarm for eight thirty and climbed into bed next to the now snoring Emma, thinking that if the season carried on like this he would probably end up using all of the condoms himself.

When Brad woke up Emma had already left, which was fortunate because Alison knocked on his door before he went down for desk duty to give him a list of things to buy for the beach party. It consisted of consumable's and accessories which seemed to be aimed at getting the clients as drunk and as messy as possible (Sangria, champagne, eggs and other sticky/runny foodstuffs). During desk duty Brad noticed that two of the reasonably attractive holidaymakers were in fact a pair of twins. He surmised that he was either a lot more drunk than he thought during the bar crawl, or that the twins had not been in the same place at the same time. Towards the end of Brad's desk duty the bar gradually filled up with all of the rest of the clients who were going on the beach party. Brad had to go over to a group of four young lad's who called themselves the Plymouth Possee who had their ghetto blaster on full volume playing thrash metal. This did not go down too well with the clients who had more refined musical tastes, or who simply had a hangover.

'Alright lads?' No reaction. 'Do you think you could turn that down a bit?'

'Sorry mate, can't hear you - the music's too loud.'

Brad wasn't sure what to do. These were clients and he didn't want to be confrontational. On the other hand, he couldn't allow himself to lose respect, and the music was annoying the majority of the rest of the gathering. It was his first minor dilemma. He decided to be firm but tactful. It was however, a decision that he had no need to execute. At that moment Greg walked past, snatched the music system from the offenders lap, slammed it on the table, and pressed the Stop/Eject button.

'That's enough of that fuckin' shite,' he said, throwing the cassette out of the window. The Plymouth Possee's protestations were abridged by the cheering of everybody else. 'Right then you lot. Get your skates on 'cos it's beach party time.' He turned to the Plymouth Possee. 'And you four....' Greg bent down so he could talk to them without everyone else hearing, his face totally stern. Brad felt the hairs on the back of his neck stand on end, convinced that there was going to be an 'off'. Greg's face broke into a half smile, half scowl. '....are going to get so fucking pissed on this beach party, 'cos I'm going to throw so much fucking ale down your necks, that you won't be able to tell the difference between Megadeath and Lisa fucking Stansfield.'

'Yeee-haaah!' whooped the Possee in unison.

Greg looked over at Brad and gave him another 'that's the way to do it' wink. Brad could only stand there in inexperienced acknowledgement of a master at work.

As they made their way to the beach, Brad noticed that there was definitely an imbalance in the sexes. A few of the males who had booked the excursion block had obviously overdone things on the bar crawl, and had chosen to look on the beach party as being one of the 'free' ones that buying the whole block gave them.

A dozen steps led down to the semi-circular beach, which at the sea was about a hundred metres across. The beach continued on both sides, but rocks rather than sand provided access to the sea. Above these rocks, sand had been sprinkled over an area of concrete to provide additional 'beach'. There were only fifty or so holidaymakers there apart from the YF&S beach party. Greg chose the most deserted spot he could and proceeded to draw out a makeshift volleyball court in the sand, tying a piece of string between two poles to provide a net. Some cheap bottles of champagne were opened, music switched on and the beach party slowly got under way. For the

63

first hour or so the drink flowed freely. Brad went round making sure that everybody was getting into the right mood (i.e. pissed). It proved to be an ideal opportunity to acquaint himself with the rest of the group. There were four nurses from the highlands of Scotland, who were all on holiday abroad for the first time. There was another nurse from Cambridge called Vanessa who was with her best friend, a student called Abigail. Vanessa and Abigail, on first impressions, seemed quite dowdy, with very bland faces. But the more he spoke to them the more their personalities came through. Both had very lively eyes, and exuded a genuine warmth. It was this, and not the fact that they had the biggest, roundest tits that Brad had yet set eyes upon that made him spend at least half an hour engaging them in conversation. It also gave him the opportunity to avoid Linda and Emma, who seemed to be competing with the Plymouth Possee to see who could get pissed the quickest.

Brad noticed that Patricia the redhead kept looking over, but in light of the previous nights conversation his game plan now was to treat her no differently to any of the others - at least for the time being. He did find it difficult not to occasionally look over, but this was mainly due to the fact that Mario was losing any remaining credibility by doing handstands in front of her, and displaying feats of 'strength' (trying to pick Patricia up and throw her into the sea). Stewart (the man in brown) was still wearing exactly the same clothes as he had been since he arrived. He had no beach towel, and despite the fact that it was already in the nineties the only sartorial concession that he had made was to roll up his sleeves and trouser legs. The brown shoes and socks remained firmly in place, which was probably just as well in view of the amount of time they had been on his person. Stewart did dab some suntan cream on the few areas exposed to the sun, and he seemed quite happy to sit on a rock ten yards or so from the rest of the group, with his hands in his pockets. Every so often he would look up to see what was going on. Each of the reps in turn went to see if he was alright

64

and to see if he wanted any more drink, even though he had not touched his glass of champagne. When Brad went up to see him, Stewart was absolutely drenched in sweat and was showing the first signs of burning. Despite Brad's attempts at getting him to sit in the shade, or to take a drink, Stewart just lay there making a random motor bike noise whenever he felt so inclined.

After about an hour, Greg got the games under way. It started with an egg throwing competition, where six couples had to face each other and in turn, throw an egg to their 'partner' without breaking it. After each round the remaining couples had to both take two steps back making the distance greater. During the second round an egg broke over Vanessa's collar bone, and the resulting gooey mess gently dripped down her perfectly formed right breast where it teasingly dripped off of her nipple. Every male on the beach stood there in salivating silence; instantly and momentarily bonded by the shared thought, and shared desire to return in the next life not as a mammal, but as an unfertilised bird.

Over the course of the next hour the games and the participants got messier and messier. For anyone with indifferent culinary requirements, the eggs, flour and other ingredients cooking in the afternoon sun on various torso's and craniums, would probably have provided a hearty meal. The drink quickly went so Lorraine had to go to the supermarket to get some more. By the time they got to the final game everybody (including the reps) was completely sloshed. It is of course, sod's law that a crisis always happens when those supposed to deal with it are in their least able state. Today was no exception. Just as Brad was in the middle of a cruel laughing fit brought about by seeing that Stewart Collins had bright red shins, bright red forearms and a bubbly forehead, one of the Scottish nurses came running over.

'Brad! Brad help! I can't find Glenda. She went swimming twenty minutes ago and she hasn't come back.'

'Has she been drinking?'

'Of course she's been drinking. We all have.'

65

'Where did she swim out?' asked Brad, quickly beginning to sober up. The Scottish girl pointed out towards the boat that was still pumping out sand.

'You don't think she's been sucked up by that boat do you?' asked the ever helpful Mario, who had come running across the beach.

The Scottish girl started howling. Brad gave Mario a filthy look eliciting a shrug of Mario's shoulders, after which he walked back across the beach to Patricia to do more handstands. The other reps and a few of the clients spread along the half mile stretch of coast to begin the search. Brad went to the left with the other three Scottish girls, Vanessa and Abigail. Greg, Linda, Emma and the reps went to the right. Brad was becoming genuinely concerned because he could see absolutely nobody out at sea. One of the other Scottish girls with Brad turned out to be her sister, called Margo, who was quickly becoming hysterical. As they started walking back to the area of the beach party, Brad saw Mikey waving his arms in the air and pointing at a short girl in a white swimsuit walking next to him.

'Is that her?' Brad asked Margo pointing at the girl next to Mikey.

'Aye, oh thank God,' she replied as she started running towards her sister.

Brad relaxed, and stopped off at the beach bar to get himself a lolly. When he got back, something wasn't right. There was a group gathered around the Scottish girls.

'What's up?' asked Brad. 'I thought she was alright?'

'SHE is!' replied Mikey. 'It's Margo. All the worry about her sister has brought on an asthma attack.'

'Oh fuck,' said Brad.

'She needs a ventalin. She's having a bad one.' Vanessa the nurse had sort of taken charge of the situation.

'I've got one back at my apartment,' replied Brad.

'You have?' said a surprised Greg.

'Yeah, I'm allergic to cats.'

'Obviously not all pussies,' mumbled a very drunk Linda

lamely.

'Well don't just stand there,' yelled Greg, 'GO AND GET IT!'

Brad went sprinting back to his apartment. It was very hot, he had drank a hell of a lot, but he suddenly felt stone cold sober. When he got back to the apartments Alison was sitting in reception.

'Brad. What are you doing here? You should be at the beach party.' Brad was so out of breath that he could hardly speak.

'Sorry - emergency - explain - can't stop - move - get passed - fuck -' panted Brad. Alison was standing in Brad's way and her chair was stopping him from getting passed.

'Right. Calm down and tell me what you're doing back at the apartments.'

Brad just panted, unable to utter another word.

'Brad, get your breath because I'm not moving until you tell me exactly what's going on.'

Brad looked at her. He shook his head, mouthed the word 'Can't' and barged past her. He could hear her shouting after him, but Brad felt like a man possessed. Once in his room he found the ventalin. He grabbed it, and ran for the door. As he opened it a flustered Alison was walking in. He crashed into her sending her sprawling across the corridor.

'STREETER!' she screamed, 'If you don't come back here now I'll...'

Brad heard no more. He ran out of the apartments and headed for the beach. He felt as though his lungs were about to explode. All he wanted to do was to stop, but he seriously believed that Margo's life could depend on him. He'd had one bad asthma attack himself and he remembered how petrified he was. As he approached the beach though, everybody seemed to be behaving normally. There was even a volleyball game going. Brad had been expecting to see a group huddled around Margo, but as he got closer he saw her sitting with her friends smiling. He stopped next to Vanessa and Abigail.

'What - why - Margo -'

'It's alright Brad,' said Vanessa. 'Just after you left I found a paper bag and got her to breathe into that, and she was fine two minutes later. You were bloody quick though. I'd better look into your trunks to make sure that you're not really Linford Christie.'

Brad flopped onto the sand unable to respond. All of a sudden he felt dizzy, and couldn't breathe. At first Vanessa and Abigail thought he was messing about, but as soon as they realised he wasn't Vanessa yelled over to Greg to get some water. She gave Brad his own ventalin and poured some cold water over him. After about five minutes the panic was over and Brad got his breath back.

'Fuck me. What happened there?'

'I don't know,' replied Mikey, ' But if you can run like that again I can probably get you a game with the London Monarchs.'

'No thanks,' replied Brad. 'Jesus I'm shagged.'

'Well after that performance I think you might just be,' said Lorraine who had joined the group of reps around Brad. 'I think the lovely Patricia was impressed. Oh Brad, you're such a hero,' she added sarcastically.

Brad looked over at Patricia and smiled. She actually smiled back. Brad picked himself up and walked over to her. Her friends were playing volleyball.

'Hello Patricia.'

'Are you alright?'

'Yeah, I am now. Pretty pathetic, eh? Nothing like nearly passing out on a beach full of people - guaranteed to impress.'

'Oh - and who were you trying to impress exactly?'

Brad cursed his subconscious for letting that one slip. He laughed. 'It's a shame you hate reps so much. Just think, if I'd died then you'd have never known how horrible I really am.'

'Oh, I think I've a good idea.' She was smiling. 'Anyway, you would have probably come back to haunt me.'

'I wouldn't have haunted you Patricia. I would have been your guardian angel, making sure that no horrible reps made a pass at you.'

'And what about nice reps? Would you have stopped them too?'

'There are no nice reps. We're all egomaniacs who think we can sleep with anyone we want. Remember?'

'Mmmm,' replied Patricia thoughtfully. 'And do you think that you can sleep with anyone you want Brad?'

'Let's just say that sometimes you meet someone where sleeping with them isn't the main priority.' Brad looked directly into Patricia's eyes and smiled. Should he make some smart comment? Should he just tell her he fancied the hell out of her? Should he wait until another time....? The decision was made for him. Greg yelled Brad over to give him a hand to start clearing things up. 'Saved by the yell. I'll speak to you later.' Patricia nodded, rolled onto her back and sat up, facing away from Brad so that she could do up her bikini top.

Brad never did catch up with Patricia later that evening. After the beach party was a Bar-B-Q and pop quiz, and following such a hot day on the beach with so much alcohol, the numbers started dwindling. Patricia did not attend either event, and later in the evening Brad found himself propping up the bar in Sgt. Peppers. He had ignored all messages that Alison wanted to speak to him urgently. He guessed what it was about, but he felt that he would prefer to face her after a good night's sleep. Sgt. Peppers was the fourth bar that Brad had visited with mainly the male members of the group in tow. Having spent most of the day with all of them, Brad felt qualified to have an opinion as to whether or not they were all dick heads. Sadly, they were, and after the days events Brad no longer wanted to be in their company. He went and stood by the door to talk to Danny, one of the props. After about five minutes he saw the rather tipsy twins walk past arm in arm giggling. He bade farewell to Danny and chased after them. The first five minutes walk back was fine, and Brad felt rather pleased with himself having a twin on either arm. However, Brad was so tired that he actually kept on momentarily falling asleep while he was walking.

When they all got back to the apartments Brad made a half

hearted attempt at inviting the twins up to his room for coffee. This was not a particularly well thought out invitation as Brad did not in fact have any coffee, nor anything to boil hot water with. Moreover, the twins couldn't understand his incoherent mumblings, and even if they had, there would have been little chance of them going back to a room with a man who had spent the last two hundred yards of the walk home treading on both their feet and gurgling incomprehensible bullshit. Therefore, alone, Brad finally flopped onto his bed, snoring and dribbling himself into an exhausted sleep.

CHAPTER TWO

The first thing that struck Brad was the noise; coaches revving, tannoys blaring, kids screaming, adults laughing or yelling - and so many PEOPLE. Ibiza airport on a Saturday night was no place for an agoraphobic. Brad felt that everybody was looking at him in his bright yellow uniform. In truth, the majority probably were. Brad remembered the mystique that had surrounded the holiday reps when he had been abroad; seeming so calm and in control; so familiar with their surroundings; confident and unflappable - at that precise moment in time a humming bird from the planet Krypton would have flapped less. Externally though, he was holding things together well. Heather was trying to be re-assuring, and Mikey was too busy trying to control his own nerves to be able to offer any words of comfort. The three of them were sitting outside the doors to the airport so that they could still see the flight arrivals board. Brad was having trouble keeping still, partly through nerves and partly because he had seen a vision of beauty in a Thomson's uniform by the agency desk in arrivals. He went to wander into the airport.

'I'd stay here if I were you Brad,' said Heather. 'You know what Alison told us.'

'Yeah. What was all that about?' enquired Brad.

'Oh, I don't know,' replied Heather. 'All she told me is that there was a delay in getting our work permits sorted out and that it would be best if we kept a low profile at the airport until they're ready. In theory I suppose they could arrest us and deport us if they find we're working without them.'

'Well that's bloody sensible,' joined in the until then, quiet Mikey. 'Spend all that time training us, let us all leave our jobs, girlfriends or whatever back home, and then after a few days on resort we end up back in Blighty because some dumb bitch hasn't filled in the right forms. Brilliant.'

'We don't know that it's Alison's fault Mikey,' defended Heather half heartedly.

'I didn't say it was. All I said was 'some dumb bitch'. If you think I was referring to Alison, well.......' Heather only grunted a response. Mikey changed the subject. 'So I see that Greg scored another three points last night.'

This was the first Brad had heard of it. 'Who with? It can't have been either of the twins 'cos I walked them home.' Brad cringed slightly as he remembered the embarrassing end to the previous night.

'No, it was Vanessa, you know, the nurse.'

'Oh you're fucking joking! Jammy bastard. You mean he's had his hand round those lovely-'

'More than just his hands from what he was telling me.' All Brad could do was to shake his head and repeat 'Jammy bastard'.

Heather started telling Mikey and Brad some stories about Greg from the previous season. She was half way through a story about Greg and the hotel owners fifteen year old daughter when Brad interrupted her.

'Oh no!'

'What's up?' asked Heather.

'My flight's just arrived.'

Sure enough, there on the board was flight MON746 from Gatwick.

'It's alright Brad,' said Heather 'You'll do fine.'

Brad was unconvinced. He picked up his brief case and clipboard and drifted into the airport like a condemned man. There were reps everywhere, wearing a whole spectrum of different coloured uniforms, and all confidently laughing and joking with each other as if they belonged to an exclusive club to which Brad had yet to gain membership. He tried to appear confident, but he didn't know where to look, what to do or how to act. He stood by the door leading out from the arrival lounge with his clipboard, staring intently at the luggage of every person who came through in case it had a YF&S label on it. He was so engrossed in this that he didn't notice her walk up behind him. There was a tap on his shoulder.

'Hello.'

'Uh, hello,' he replied.

It was The Vision. She had curly black hair that cascaded down her shoulders, framing a perfectly symmetrical face dominated by a pair of gorgeous green eyes. She also had full red lips which were the same bright red as her uniform. She continued the conversation,

'First time at the airport then?'

'No, no - well actually yes.'

'I thought so,' she laughed.

'That obvious is it?'

'Afraid so. I'm Kelly.'

'Hi, I'm Brad.'

They shook hands. Her smile was captivating, so captivating that he forgot to let go of her hand. There was a couple of seconds awkward silence before Kelly slipped her hand from his.

'Well, I'll leave you to it then. Good luck.' Brad mumbled thanks and she was gone. He could have kicked himself. When he had first seen her from outside the airport he had planned at least half a dozen witty/charming things to say, but he had forgotten all of them.

'Lovely, isn't she?' said a deepish voice with an Irish lilt. Brad turned around to see that the voice belonged to another Thomson's rep, who's badge showed his name to be Leo. 'You know what gave the game away, don't you?'

'What game?' replied a confused Brad.

'That it's your first time at the airport.'

'Oh that. No I don't. How can you tell?'

'Easy. The flights that landed before the Gatwick one were both from Germany. You can normally wait at least fifteen minutes before the first passengers come through - you've been standing here since it's arrival was first announced.'

Brad felt a little silly, but he did not have to feel silly for long. At that moment, Leo caught sight of some very English looking tourists coming through the door.

'Here they come now. See you later.'

Brad's stomach knotted again. He marvelled at how easily all of the reps around him just seemed to 'switch on'. It took ages for the first person to come through with a YF&S sticker. There was a flurry of activity and then before he had time to blink, it was all over. He checked his manifesto, and thankfully all eighteen had arrived - not one more, not one less. Brad went and found Heather and Mikey.

'Everything alright?' asked Heather.

'Yep. No problems.'

'Good. Off you go then. We'll see you at tomorrow's welcome meeting.'

Brad approached the mini bus as slowly as he could, knowing that the clients were waiting for their experienced, know-everything rep. He felt like he should have a green 'L' plate around his neck, so that they would all be more inclined to show a degree of benevolence to someone who had only just started the job. As he stepped onto the coach, he was greeted with eighteen faces looking at him with tired expectancy. Brad smiled at them then turned his back and sat down to try and compose himself. The coach driver said something to Brad in Spanish, which sounded like a question. Brad was feeling self-conscious enough as it was. He had no intention of letting the new arrivals know that he couldn't speak the native lingo, so he mumbled 'Si'. It was a lucky guess on Brad's part because the driver had asked if everybody was on board. Following Brad's response he closed the doors and they were off. Brad was painfully aware of the absolute silence behind him, so to appear that he was doing something, Brad kept putting exaggerated ticks on the clipboard, hoping that this would make the new arrivals think that he was important and professional. Eventually, he composed himself and switched the microphone on.

To his horror, there was a mind numbing squeal of feedback. Mercifully, the driver rectified the problem, but the little confidence that had remained in Brad was fast draining

74

away. When the microphone was at a satisfactory volume, Brad read through the 'do's and don'ts' at least five times faster than he had originally planned and with a very shaky voice. He got only a minimal reaction, so he looked for salvage in one of his tapes. 'AAAAAARRRRGGHH!!!' Brad had left his brief case which contained all of his tapes at the airport. He could feel the sweat pores on his scalp working overtime. He looked at the cassette player and noticed that there was already a tape in it, so he pushed that in. Unfortunately, what followed was an aural assault of the magnitude that only a Spanish coach driver's musical tastes could inflict. Gingerly, Brad switched the microphone back on. After the obligatory squeal of feedback he asked if anyone had any decent tapes. A girl sitting about halfway back gave him a tape of Madonna, and although under normal circumstances Brad would have asked her to define the word 'decent', under these circumstances Madonna was just fine. Feeling slightly more confident, Brad had a go at pointing out some of the local landmarks and telling some jokes. The response was not too dissimilar to that normally only reserved for Jim Bowen, so Brad sheepishly pushed the tape back in, and sat down to add another couple of hundred ticks to his clipboard.

Brad only managed to get an hour's sleep before his alarm woke him in time to greet the two new arrivals from the Bristol flight, who eventually turned up at just gone nine thirty in the morning. Brad spent a little while talking to them, and advised them to try and stay up for another hour or so in order to attend the welcome meeting. They took their bags up to their rooms just as Mikey came down.

'What are those two like?'

'Both single shares. He's been on holiday with Young Free & Single for the last five years and thinks he knows more about repping than we do....'

'He probably does. What about the girl?'

75

'Well you saw her. She's not about to be the next pageant queen of San An is she? Never mind, at least there were probably some decent fillies on your flight.'

'Well if there were they must have missed the plane. Mind you, I was shitting myself so much that a gaggle of nude page three girls could have walked through and I wouldn't have noticed.'

'I know what you mean,' agreed Brad. 'Oh well, at least there's the Manchester flight.'

At that moment, Lorraine's coach pulled up outside with the Manchester arrivals. As they noisily filtered off of the coach, Brad and Mikey looked out for any obvious specimens of glorious womanhood. As the final girl picked her case from the underbelly of the coach Brad and Mikey looked at each other. Mikey said it;

'Never mind. At least there's the Birmingham flight.'

By ten thirty, The Bon Tiempo bar had over a hundred boisterous holidaymakers in it, all waiting for the welcome meeting. The reps were going around pouring out complimentary bucks fizz (a four hundred peseta bottle of sparkling wine with orange juice). Brad was actually quite excited. He was to be running through the information part of the welcome meeting, and although he was nervous, the performer in him was actually looking forward to being up in front of all of these people. As it was Brad who was to be starting proceedings, it was his responsibility to get everyone to settle down and listen to what was to be said. Greg came and stood next to Brad.

'Nervous?'

'A little,' replied Brad honestly.

'You'll do fine and you know it. Your one of the best new rep's I've seen.' Brad didn't know if Greg was just trying to make him feel better or if he actually meant it. Over the course of the first few days on resort he had grown to admire Greg, even be a little in awe of him. There was no doubting that Greg was an absolute hound where women were concerned, but there was also no denying that he nearly always had clients eating out of the palm of his hand. Greg was undoubtedly very itinerant, and for him to say what he had was just the confidence remedy that Brad needed. 'Alright then - off you go.'

Brad had brought a whistle which he blew as loudly as he could to attract everyone's attention.

'Right you lot. If you could all shut up for ten minutes.'

The other reps went round making ssshhhhing noises and telling the clients to be quiet. After thirty seconds or so the noise and chattering diminished to just the odd whisper.

'Thank you,' said Brad.

Everybody was now looking at him, including the other reps. Brad was walking around with a soda siphon in his hand.

'What's that for?' Heather whispered into Greg's ear. Greg just shrugged his shoulders.

'Ok everyone. Good morning.'

There was a general cry of 'Good morning' in return, followed by a few embarrassed giggles.

'Right I'd like to thank you all for turning up to this welcome meeting. If you've all got a full glass I'll teach you your first bit of Spanish, the Spanish for cheers.' Brad raised his glass. 'Salut.' The whole room took a drink and responded. That was the first of the free drinks you'll be getting on this holiday. Believe me, there'll be plenty more, but we'll tell you about that later. Before we start, what I'm going to do is to introduce you to everyone. My name is Brad, your ever smiling, ever friendly rep, and I'm going to be looking after you lucky people in The Las Huertas.' This drew a small cheer from those staying at The Las Huertas. 'Over there,' continued Brad, 'Is my partner in crime at The Las Huertas, the lovely Lorraine.' Lorraine gave a nervous wave and blushed slightly. 'You'll also be seeing quite a lot of Greg. He's the little fella over there, but as he'll be the first to tell you, size isn't important.' Greg smiled at everyone, and grabbed hold of his balls, and mouthed indication that they were massive, which made one group of girls in particular go into giggling fits. 'Those of you who are staying here are going to be looked

77

after by the beauty and the beast. If you like your men tall dark and handsome girls.....' Mario puffed his chest out. '.....we've got Mikey,' Mikey sank to the floor in an impromptu display of the splits and sprang back up again, gaining a few whoops of appreciation for his athletic display from the assembled throng. 'And the beast - no only kidding - the beauty is the best thing to come out of Manchester since the M6 was built, the beautiful Heather.'

There followed a sixty second chorus of 'Get your tits out for the boys' before the meeting was brought back to order. 'Standing next to Heather we have the best dressed man in Ibiza, Mario.' Mario tried to give all of the girls the most smouldering look that he could. Brad had noticed Alison standing at the back of the room. He wasn't sure whether or not to introduce her. Although they had spoken to each other since the beach party, Alison had not mentioned the incident with the ventalin. Brad guessed that she had found out what had happened and decided to leave it. He knew she wouldn't apologise so silence was probably the next best thing. Brad didn't think that Alison would appreciate being pointed out, so he moved on. 'Last but not least is Sid.' All of the reps looked at Brad quizzically. Brad raised the soda siphon. 'This is Sid the soda siphon, and he's here to help me make sure that you pay attention and that nobody heckles. If Sid doesn't like you he has a tendency to spit at people, so you have been warned.' Greg smiled at Brad and nodded re-assuringly.

'Ok. I'm going to spend about five to ten minutes telling you a bit about where you're staying, a few do's and don'ts and the best way to keep out of trouble. Then Heather is going to spend about the same amount of time telling you all about some of the brilliant things we've got lined up for you. If I could just ask you all to pay attention, because apart from the risk of upsetting Sid, this is for your benefit, and giving us twenty minutes of your time now will make the next week or two a lot more enjoyable. Most of what we're going to cover today can be found in the information book at reception. There is also a notice board, which will keep you informed as to all of the special things that we've got in store for you. We do actually stay in the same hotels and apartments as all of you, and although we're always around please remember that we do occasionally sleep, so if you need us we do have allocated times when we'll be in the bar to answer questions or have a chat. These times will normally be between nine thirty and ten thirty in the morning, and six and seven in the evening.

Right. We'll start off with the hotels. Try and get to know the people who work there, because contrary to what you might think they are not all called Manuel and none of them respond particularly well to being whacked around the head. They all speak English, even a few swear words.' Brad turned around to Frank who was standing a couple of feet away, as Brad had previously arranged. 'Isn't that right Frank?'

'Yes, you bloody wanker,' he replied in his best English.

This brought the house down. Brad looked over at Greg who mouthed 'Nice one'. Brad began to feel more confident.

'You can buy most things at reception. They sell postcards, stamps, sweets..'

'What about condoms?' shouted one of the lads who Brad had brought in the previous night. A few people chuckled.

'I'm glad you asked me that.' Brad might have been glad, but he was certainly not surprised. He had spent five minutes before the welcome meeting talking to the question asker, promising him a free drink if he asked about condoms. 'You might find machines in some bars, but as this is a Roman Catholic country our little rubber friends aren't as easy to get hold of as back home. But luckily I've come prepared - arf! arf! - so if any of you need some I've six different varieties which I'll be happy to let you have for a modest fee. Obviously used ones will be slightly cheaper.

If any of you have valuables or money that you want to keep safe then all of the hotels have safety deposit boxes that you can hire for the week. You can change money at reception. The best way of working out what something costs is by understanding that one of those green notes is worth roughly a fiver. The green notes are a thousand pesetas and are referred to as a Mill. If you don't want your money to run through your hands like water, or you don't have shares in Spanish Telecom, then I suggest that you use the phone boxes rather than the ridiculously expensive phone in The Las Huertas. Isn't that right Lorraine?' Lorraine nodded. The previous night she had rang home to speak to her mother because just prior to leaving England her eleven year old dog had not been well, and she was naturally concerned. She had rang from The Las Huertas, and the owner had charged her a fortune for doing so. Greg and Heather had both agreed that it was bang out of order, but Alison had simply said it was her own stupid fault and that she would know better next time. Brad continued, 'Everything you need to know about phoning home can be found in the information book.

One last thing about the hotels. As I said before, we do stay in them as well, and we do occasionally get a chance to sleep. Whilst we're not asking you to tip toe around, do just spare a thought for your reps and also for people who have come away to relax, as opposed to chucking alcohol or whatever else down their necks. On the subject of drugs...and this is very important.' Brad looked at everybody sternly. 'If any of you are found with any kind of narcotics...' Brad paused and looked round, before his face broke into a grin, 'Then you will of course, be made to share them out with all of us.' The rest of the reps seemed to be enjoying Brad's welcome meeting as much as the clients. 'Seriously though, do not do anything at all to risk getting in trouble with the police over here. There are three types. You have the locals - they're the ones in the blue uniforms - who are in actual fact meant to be the nicest. Having said that, I certainly wouldn't be inviting them round for tea. Then you have the Guardia Civil, or Civil Guard. They are the ones in green with the silly hats. Now then, I know that they're silly hats, you know that they're silly hats but please, don't tell them that they're silly hats. The guns they have are real, the batons they carry are real, and the bruises they cause are real. So, make sure you stay out of trouble. Later in the season we will be joined by the Nationals who wear brown uniforms, but luckily you won't be meeting them.'

Before the welcome meeting, Greg had advised Brad to go over the top about the police. The reason was that providing you made the clients scared enough of them then you could always use the threat of calling them as a last resort if you had trouble makers you couldn't deal with.

Brad went through all of the other informative parts of the welcome meeting before handing over to Heather. He felt it had gone reasonably well, although he had rushed it a little, and not cracked all of the 'funnies' he had planned. When he finished Greg made everyone give him a big cheer, which put Brad on top of the world.

Sales at the welcome meeting were good. By the time they had got around everybody it was nearly three p.m. As the adrenaline wore off, Brad began to feel very tired. He sat in the corner of the bar and ordered himself a coffee, and was joined by Heather and Greg.

'How do you feel?' asked Heather.

'Bloody knackered,' replied Brad.

'You've got to go back to the airport at six o'clock, haven't you?'

'Yeah. I must admit, I didn't realise I wouldn't get any sleep.'

'You'll get used to it,' said Greg. 'Mind you, it is a bit harsh for yer first time.'

Heather nodded her agreement. A few seconds silence fell, during which they simultaneously each took a sip from their respective cup or glass.

'So, did you enjoy the welcome meeting?' Heather said to Brad, changing the subject.

'Yeah. I thought you were really funny. Sales were good as well so you obviously got the point across.'

'Oh I didn't mean did you like what I did,' replied Heather, 'But thanks anyway. No, I meant did you enjoy doing your bit.'

'Well I was a bit nervous to start with, but once I got a bit of feedback I suppose I settled down a bit. Seeing this scouse git giving me the thumbs up really helped.'

'Aye, well y'deserved it,' said Greg enthusiastically. 'That bit where you got Frank to call you a wanker was brilliant, wasn't it Heath.'

'Yeah, really good. I thought that thing with the soda siphon was a great way of setting the tone - firm but still having a laugh. Loved the way you stitched up Mario as well. Mind you, I don't think he noticed.'

Brad was a little embarrassed by the praise, but also relieved. To be respected by his peers was very important to him, especially as they were going to be so close to each other all season. After about ten minutes Alison came into the bar.

'How were sales?' she asked.

'I've not worked it out exactly,' said Greg, 'But I think it's over eighty percent, and I'm sure we'll get a few more when we do the bar crawl tonight.'

'Excellent,' said Alison. 'You did really well explaining the excursions Heather - I knew sales would be good.'

'Thanks. Brad did well didn't he?'

'Not bad for a first time,' replied Alison. 'Actually, if you could leave Brad and me alone for a while I've got a few things to go through with him.'

'Aye, well I'm gonna hit the sack,' said Greg. 'Come on Heath, I'm sure your good for five points.'

'You must be joking,' laughed Heather. 'Frank's got more chance than you. Anyway, you'd probably need a splint to keep it up.'

'There's not a splint big enough darlin'.'

'God, hark at him,' said Heather. 'Don't you turn out like him Brad.'

'There's no danger of that,' replied Brad. 'I'd have to chop my legs off to be the same height as him for starters.' Greg's height was the only physical imperfection Brad could home in on.

'Yeah, and after you've chopped your legs off you'd have to grow your dick to double it's size,' retorted Greg, as quick as a flash. 'Anyway, we can't have two of me around - it wouldn't be right to bring such joy to the female population.'

'Oh 'scuse me while I'm sick,' said Heather. 'I'll see you

later Brad. See you tonight Alison.'

Everyone said their good-byes. Brad sat there for a moment feeling very content. He felt as if he was beginning to belong; almost like an apprentice finally being accepted as a 'grown up' member of a team. Greg and Heather had given him a real feeling of warmth, and even though he wasn't looking forward to going back to the airport, he felt that it was all part of his initiation and that it could only help him to be accepted by the experienced reps and to be respected by the new reps, even quicker.

'How did you think your part of the welcome meeting went Brad?' asked Alison.

Brad's self-doubts had been quelled somewhat by the previous conversation with Greg and Heather. He didn't want to come across to Alison as being negative or deliberately self-effacing, so he gave Alison an honest self-appraisal.

'I was a bit nervous to start with, but once some of the jokes got a bit of feedback I felt quite confident and began to enjoy it. I'm sure I can do better though.'

'By 'jokes', did you mean that thing with the soda siphon?'

For once, partly due to fatigue and partly due to Greg's previous approval, Brad failed to pick up on the inflection in Alison's voice. He naively replied,

'Oh that. I only thought of it on the way back from the airport. It worked quite well, didn't it?'

'So what would have happened if someone had started heckling?'

Brad began to pick up on Alison's tone. However, he could see nothing wrong in what he had done, so he continued to be honest and light hearted.

'Well, someone would have got wet I suppose.'

Alison was not amused.

'Someone would have got wet,' repeated Alison slowly. 'And after you'd had your fun, do you not think that all hell would have broken loose - drinks being thrown over everyone maybe?'

Brad thought carefully before replying.

'No, I don't actually. If someone had started heckling I would have warned them a couple of times and gauged whether or not they were annoying everyone else. If they were, then I would have put it to a 'shall I shan't I' vote with the rest of the group. That way if I had to squirt someone then all of the group would have been on my side.'

Alison was not expecting such a carefully thought out answer. He was of course right, but she could not concede - not to Brad.

'Well I'm sure with your vast experience you know best, but let me tell you - with my limited experience - that you are wrong, and I don't want to see it again.' Alison moved on before Brad had a chance to argue the point further. 'Another thing I don't want to see again is that nonsense with the condoms. Most of these kids come away on a tight budget, and we want them to spend as much as possible on excursions, T-shirts and products associated with Young Free & Single. We don't want their money going into your pocket. You should know that head office take a very dim view on any illegal earnings.'

'Hang on a minute. I'm not trying to make a profit. For all I care Young Free & Single can keep any profit, as long as I get back what they cost me. Like you said, most of them are kids and being here will probably be the first or best chance that many of them will have had to be promiscuous. They're in a foreign country that doesn't make condoms as easy to get hold of as back home. What do you want them to do - have unprotected sex?'

'What I want is a hundred percent excursion sales.'

'Oh come on Alison. Buying a packet of condoms for a couple of quid is hardly going to effect excursion sales.'

'Well I disagree. You should not have done that without first asking my permission -'

'Ok,' interrupted Brad, trying to be conciliatory, 'I should have asked you first and I apologise for not doing so. But surely you can see the logic in why I did it. Apart from anything else it was entertaining.'

'Well that's a matter of opinion and I don't want to see it again. Understood?'

'Yes, but-'

'I said, UNDERSTOOD?'

Brad shut up. Alison began to assert herself even more.

'And what the hell do you think you were doing telling them not to use the hotel phone.'

'Because it's a bloody rip off,' replied Brad. 'Lorraine got charged four mill and she was on the phone for less than five minutes. That would have cost less than a mill from a call box.'

'Well the clients can find that out for themselves. Our relationship with the hotels is of the utmost importance and we cannot do anything to jeopardise it.'

'What, even if they're ripping off our clients?'

'Like I said, let them find out for themselves.'

'But a minute ago you were saying that Young Free & Single wanted to get all of their money and now you're saying that you don't care if they spend almost as much as a flight home on a couple of poxy phone calls.' Brad knew that he should shut up, but he was sure that Alison would be able to see the flaws in her argument, thereby allowing them to agree on what was best for the clients. What Brad had yet to fully discover was that in Alison, logic and emotion mixed like oil and water. Seeing the flaws in her argument and admitting them to Brad was as likely as Ayatollah Khomeni admitting that he liked nothing better than a mug of cocoa and a nice read of the Satanic Verses before going to bed.

'Look. Just do as you're fucking told for once. Jesus,' said Alison slamming her clipboard on the table, 'Who's the manager here, eh? You?'

'No, of course not, but-'

'Oh good. I'm glad we've got that sorted out. Is that why you didn't introduce me during the welcome meeting? Didn't you want the clients all to know that I'm your manager? What is it? Because I'm a woman? Because I'm younger than you?'

'No of course not. I just thought-'

'Well don't think. You're paid to do as your told, not to

think. You've got a lot to learn Brad - a LOT to learn.' Alison picked her things up, and calmed down. 'You should remember that you've got two ears and one mouth - learn to use them in that ratio. I don't say the things I do to be awkward or to win arguments. I say them because I've got six years experience. Why do you think I was chosen to be Resort Manager for Ibiza?' Brad bit his lip. 'I know you're keen and ambitious. Listen to what I can teach you and one day you might be in this position. Alright?'

Brad just grunted. He was utterly drained.

'Right then. Don't forget you've got to be at the airport in a couple of hours, so if I were you I'd go up to your room and freshen up. Providing the plane's not delayed I'll see you on the bar crawl. Ok?'

Brad nodded and gathered up his things. When he got to his room he slumped on his bed. Any enthusiasm for going to the airport had gone, along with his little remaining energy. He put his shorts on and walked round to the Tanit apartments where Danny, the prop from Sgt. Peppers lived. Danny shared with a Kiwi called Robbo who taught windsurfing. They both supplemented their incomes by selling speed, dope and most other narcotic substances. Robbo answered the door wearing a sarong, his blonde hair matted and his eyes as red as the Moroccan sun.

'Yoah man. What's happening. Hey Danny, it's Rod.'

'Actually my name's Brad.'

'Sorry man. D'ya wanna skin up?'

'No thanks, I've got to go to the airport and I'm fucked enough as it is.' He walked into the main living area. 'Alright Danny.'

Danny was laying on a settee surrounded by empty coke bottles, cigarette butts and an overflowing ashtray. The apartment looked like the Enola Gay had recently deposited her payload onto it. Despite the fact that the balcony door was open, there was a smell of rancid feet mixed with the sweet aroma of some recently smoked hash. Brad bought a gram of whizz (he couldn't afford coke), exchanged pleasantries then made his way back to his own apartment. When he got there Alison had left a note instructing him to move his things over to The Las Huertas. By now, there was only time to have a shower and get ready for the airport, so Brad packed his things up as best he could so that he would be ready to move first thing in the morning.

The airport was a lot quieter than his previous visit. The flight was delayed by forty five minutes so he got himself a coffee, dabbed some speed and sat on a wall outside the airport next to where the coaches lined up. It was a lovely warm evening, and Brad felt like he could easily lay on the grass and fall asleep. After another coffee and a slightly stale cheese roll, Brad heard his flight announced over the tannoy. He made a point of waiting ten minutes before going through. The only other English rep in arrivals had short black hair and an horrendous uniform. Brad walked up to her, looked at her badge and introduced himself.

'Hi, I'm Brad. I believe we're sharing a coach back to San Antonio.'

'Yes. Oh am I glad you're here. It's my first time at the airport and my manager hasn't turned up.' She paused, before remembering to introduce herself. 'Sorry, my name's Stella.' They shook hands. 'So you work for Young Free & Single then do you? I applied for a job with your lot - got through to Bridlehurst, you know, the final interview, but....' her voice trailed off. 'Still, never mind. At least I'm here. How long have you been with Young Free & Single?'

'Actually this is my first season too.'

'You're joking!' replied Stella. 'Oh shit, I was hoping you'd do the transfer for me. I know it's a bit of a cheek seeing as they're mostly going to be my clients, but I guess I assumed that you'd be an experienced rep.'

'Well it depends what you mean by experienced,' offered Brad suggestively. He looked at her for a reaction. She blushed and almost smiled. 'Oh well - I don't suppose I could possibly cock it up any more than I did the last one. Are you sure you want me to do it?'

'Positive!'

Brad's clients were one of the first lot to come through. He showed them on to the coach, then went back into the airport to ring Mikey at the apartments. It struck Brad that the speed had started to work. After a minute or so, Mikey came to the phone.

'Mikey?'

'Brad. Where are you?'

'I'm at the airport. You know we said there's always the second Gatwick flight...'

'Oh don't tell me it's three blokes.'

'No, they're all female - but only just.' Brad could hear a lot of noise in the background. 'You all set for the bar crawl.'

'Yeah. I tell you what, some of the girls who arrived last night are looking quite fit made up.'

'Well don't you go spoiling them for everyone else.' The pips started going. 'Listen, I'll catch you later.'

Brad went back out to the arrivals to find Stella surrounded by about a dozen black cockney teenage males, giving her a good-natured hard time. Brad thought about helping, but Stella was handling them more than adequately.

The coach transfer went infinitely better than Brad's first attempt. He spoke on the microphone for at least half the journey and established an excellent rapport.

The black cockneys were a British Rail football team who came away every year together. Brad arranged to meet them at the football stadium in San Antonio, so that YF&S could give them a game. Brad thought it would be a good idea to get them all on the bar crawl, so he arranged to meet everyone at a small bar in town called The Charleston. The reason for this choice of venue was that he had briefly met the London owners during the winter, and it was central enough for everyone to find easily. He could have chosen Sgt. Peppers, but he felt that he needed to score some Brownie points with

Alison, and what better way to do so than to walk in with a group of holidaymakers from another tour company?

Brad therefore found himself at ten o'clock with thirty newly arrived, non-YF&S clients and one increasingly pissed rep (Stella), on full throttle in The Charleston. The Charleston was quite small, long and narrow. The bar itself ran almost the whole length of the premises and faced on to a mirror which ran along the opposite side, giving the illusion that the place was bigger than it actually was. It's colour scheme was pink and grey, and the ultra-violet type lights picked out white clothes, teeth and dandruff. The bar was popular with the workers who used to do a lot of coke in there, so the ultra-violet lights also gave a good indication as to who had indulged by the white smear that was often to be found around their nostrils. The owners were only in their early twenties themselves, and the music was so good that nobody wanted to leave. Brad had to wait until just gone ten thirty before he was able to persuade them all to follow him to Sgt. Peppers. He couldn't believe he was still going strong. As he left, the blonde co-owner who everybody called Duffy, came over to Brad and shook his hand.

'Cheers Brad, if you can keep them here a bit longer next time it'll be more.'

As Brad took his hand away and opened it he found a crumpled two mill note. Before he had a chance to even think, he was being swept along with the rest of the crowd towards Sgt. Peppers. Brad knew that taking backhanders was a dismissable offence. His first thought was to give the money to Alison and explain what had happened, but the way she had been lately he did not really want to put himself at her idiosyncratic mercy. Alternatively he could have asked Greg what to do. Brad guessed that Greg would have told him to keep it, but it was a long season and there was no way of really knowing what Greg's relationship with Alison was, or how his own relationship with Greg would change. If he just kept it and said nothing then apart from his own conscience, The Charleston boys would have one over on him. In the end the solution was obvious.

'Stella, you got a minute?'

By now Stella was fairly drunk. She was wearing a lacy white halter neck which pushed her ample breasts together to produce a glorious cleavage, that her rep's uniform had previously done nothing to enhance. With her black hair spiked up Brad thought that she looked quite dirty. He could not help himself ogling her obvious orbs of womanhood, especially as she bounced her way next to him.

'Enjoying yourself,' she said as she put her arm through his.

'Yeah.' Brad snatched another sneaky look. 'Stella, I've got a bit of a problem.'

'Don't worry Brad,' she giggled. 'It happens to men of your age.'

'Very funny. It's nothing like that - well, I'll admit to the odd spot of premature ejaculation - no, what it is...' he said pulling out the two mill note, '...is this.'

Stella took the money and looked at it.

'Oh, I see,' she said slowly. 'So you can only manage to have sex with women if you pay them first.'

'If that was the case Stella dearest, then I would be expecting at least one thousand nine hundred and ninety five pesetas change.' They both laughed. 'Duffy gave it to me for taking all of this lot into his bar and seeing as they are mainly your clients, it's only fair that you should have it.'

'Don't be silly,' said Stella. 'You persuaded them to come along so you should have it.'

'No honestly Stella - you take it. It'll make me feel better.'

'Oh you are a cutie.'

She lent up and kissed him on his cheek. He felt her right breast yield against his elbow. Stella was definitely becoming more attractive as the night wore on.

When they all walked into Sgt. Peppers it was in full swing. Greg and Lorraine were on stage singing with Ray; Mario was talking to Alison, and Mikey was talking to a group of three girls that Brad didn't recognise. Mikey was the first to see

Brad and the BR football team. Mikey stopped talking to the girls and went over to Brad, offering him one of his elongated handshakes.

'So where did you pick up all the brothers then.'

Mikey acknowledged them with a nod and a grin as they all came in. The BR boys were there to party, and as soon as they were in the bar, whistles and horns were going and the place immediately took off. Alison looked over to see what all of the commotion was about. She saw Brad in the centre of the melee. She immediately recognised that the BR football ream were not YF&S clients. She turned to Mario.

'Who are that bunch of troublemakers with Brad?'

Mario shrugged his shoulders. Alison stood up, craning her neck as she walked down the four steps leading to the dance floor to get a better look at what was going on. It had got to the stage where her gut reaction was to give Brad a dressing down, based upon the paranoid assumption that everything he did was aimed at undermining her authority. She was preparing herself to ask Brad to step outside when Noel, the Irish owner of Sgt. Peppers, gestured for her to come behind the bar, where he was standing next to the till. When Alison was next to him he slipped her a brown A5 envelope.

'There y'go me darling. I already had it all counted up for yeh when that big rep o' yours brought in all them dark fellas. I've stuck in another six mill which should cover it. I know he brought more than t'irty in with him but they didn't get here until a good half hour after all o' the others. What was the problem? Could yis not persuade them t'leave The Angler's?'

'Uh, no, I mean yeah, uh something like that.'

It dawned on Alison that Noel had assumed that Brad's crowd were with YF&S, and as a result had paid her on the previously agreed 'per head' arrangement. She smiled to herself and slipped the envelope into her handbag. All she had to do now was to make sure that they all went down to The Star Club and another bulging brown envelope would be hers. She went over to Brad.

'Brad.' Brad could barely hear her over the music and

shouting. She gestured for him to come up to the bar where it was slightly less noisy. 'That's better. How did the transfer go?'

'Yeah, good. I ended up doing the microphone - that's where I got this lot from. You don't mind do you? I just thought that if I showed them what a good time we all have then they might book with Young Free & Single next year.'

Alison was glad that she hadn't reprimanded Brad because apart from the money he had just made her, he did have a very good point. However, she still had to let him benefit from the wisdom of her experience.

'No, it's not a problem Brad. Just be careful with large gangs of lads that they don't disrupt things and ruin it for the rest of the group. This lot seem alright though.'

She looked over at one of the loudest of the BR group. Rayon had his shirt off. He was sliding his lean muscular torso up and down the twins as he danced on one side of them, while Mikey did the same on the other. A small crowd had gathered around them and were whistling and clapping. Alison reached into her bag and pulled out a handful of tickets. She handed them to Brad.

'Here. Give these to them.'

'What is it?' asked Brad

'Free entry into The Star. I shouldn't really do it but you've done well tonight and as you say, they might come on holiday with us next time.'

'Nice one,' enthused Brad.

Alison watched him go over to the group and give them the tickets, pointing to Alison as he did so. In a flash, Rayon leapt over the railing and was at Alison's side. He took her hand and kissed it, then looked up at her and smiled, his gold tooth glistening as he did so.

'Until The Star.'

With that he leapt back on to the dance floor and continued grinding away at the twins. Alison smiled uncomfortably before shuffling off to the Ladies to make sure the brown envelope was still in her bag.

An hour after the BR football team's arrival, Greg got on

the microphone to tell everyone that YF&S were off to The Star Club. Normally only about half of the group would have had sufficient energy to make it to The Star. However, the atmosphere was so good that not only did the whole of the YF&S crowd leave, but also virtually everyone else in the bar. When Alison saw this she ran outside and jumped on her moped. She got to The Star five minutes before everybody else.

The owner of The Star was a suave Spaniard called Jimmy. He always looked immaculate, and he always made a point of being on the door when a tour company was expected. He had a near perfect English accent, apart from a tendency to be very guttural when he had to say a word that started with the letter 'H'. When he saw Alison he held out his arms to welcome her. He had not yet made up his mind whether or not he liked her. He preferred to deal with men, but Kirstie had been tolerable the previous year so for the time being he put his prejudices to one side.

'Alison, guappa. How are you tonight. You look adorable.'

Alison blushed slightly. She fancied Jimmy like mad. He was an attractive man in his late thirties and exuded a debonair charm. He effortlessly commanded respect and had obvious power brought about by his wealth and status.

'I'm fine thanks Jimmy. We've got quite a few coming down tonight.'

'Yes. This is good - how many you have?'

'Well that's why I've come down, Jimmy. We've got a lot more than we normally have for this time of year so I wanted to help you to count them in.'

'Oh don't worry. Javier will do that. Come, you have a drink with me. A nice chupito perhaps.'

Jimmy put his arm around Alison's shoulder and escorted her through to the first bar. He clicked his fingers and two slammer glasses were immediately placed on the bar in front of them.

Outside the first clients had arrived. Although the bar crawl had officially finished and the reps could have gone home, most would normally stay for a few drinks, certainly at the beginning of the season. Apart from anything else it was expected of them - another of the unwritten rules which made it a twenty four hour a day job.

Brad and Stella were at the front of the group that had made the five minute walk from Sgt. Peppers to The Star. The short corridor opened up onto the smaller of the two rooms. Ahead of them was the dance floor; to the right a bar and to the left two other bars. They walked passed the DJ booth which was in the middle of the two rooms so that the DJ could monitor all of the crowd. Brad didn't know the DJ's name, but they nodded 'Hi' as they caught each others eye. Most of the club was painted white, with bright primary colours splashed randomly around in the form of soft furnishings, tiles or abstract murals. Large plants and small trees helped to give the club a lively fresh atmosphere. Brad and Stella walked through to the larger, brighter room which was totally rammed. There was a small bar in every corner of this room, and a large rectangular bar towards the back of the club from which customers could order drinks from all sides. They walked passed this bar to the bar furthest from the entrance which was known as bar five. This was where all of the reps would normally congregate because at this bar they only had to sign a docket to be given free drinks.

Brad got the feeling that Stella had already made her mind up that she was going to sleep with him. Her character was actually quite strong, so he did not feel comfortable with being totally assumptive by just saying something like 'shall we go then'. He felt that Stella wanted to tease him a little.

'So which hotel are you staying at in San An then?' asked Brad.

'I'm not.'

'What, have you got an apartment?'

'No, I'm in a hotel.'

She smiled and took a sip of her drink. Brad was a little confused. He thought, optimistically, that maybe she meant that she wasn't staying in her hotel because she was intending to stay at his. They stood there not talking for a couple of minutes. Brad was sure that Stella was smirking.

'So go on then. Where are you staying?' asked Brad, unable to work out what Stella was up to.

'I told you - in a hotel.'

'Alright, alright. What's it called - how many syllables?' said Brad, losing patience slightly.

'You won't have heard of it.'

'Oh, and why's that?'

'Because it's in Playa d'en Bossa.'

'WHAT! That's the other side of the island.'

'Very good Brad. Ten out of ten for your geographical knowledge of Ibiza.'

Brad was not sure whether to be pleased or disappointed by this news. There was no way he could go to her place because he had to move his things to The Las Huertas first thing in the morning. It was time to test the water. He forced a cough.

'You can stay at my place if you don't want to do the journey home tonight.'

'Can I?' she replied, still looking directly ahead whilst sucking her drink through her straw.

Brad still wasn't sure if she was being sarcastic in tone, so he slightly watered down his offer.

'Well, you know, it's late and there are no more buses. Anyway, I've got a spare bed if you're worried about my intentions...'

'Ooooh, you've got a spare bed have you?' Now she was being sarcastic. 'Well if you've got a spare bed then there's not much point in me coming back.' Stella put down her drink and picked up her bag. 'Best I go and get a taxi. Bye!' Stella started walking towards the door, looking over her shoulder and grinning as she did so.

Right, thought Brad. Two can play at this game.

'Yeah, ok - I'll walk you to the taxi rank.'

Rather than taking the main road to the taxi rank they went around the dark alleyway at the back of the Star. Halfway down, Brad spoke.

'Stella.'

'Mmmm?'

Brad span Stella round. He stretched out her arms and pinned her against the cold white wall by her wrists. He looked into her eyes. She smiled, then lifted up her right knee, flicking it from side to side against his crotch. Brad let go of her left wrist, and with his right hand undid the top two buttons of her halter neck whilst their mouths passionately engulfed each other. Once there was enough room, Brad cupped his hand under her fleshy right breast, lifting it so he could move his head down slightly to roll her huge brown nipple between his tongue and top lip. Stella's breathing became heavier, and she started squeezing and digging her nails into Brad's cock through his shorts. Just at that moment, the emergency exit at the back of The Star Club opened. It was less than twenty feet away so Brad and Stella froze. First of all he heard a man's voice with a slightly Spanish accent.

'I don't know. It's more than we paid per head last year.' Brad noticed that the 'h' in 'head' was pronounced very gutturally. 'And I think you should not say to your head office that you only have a quarter of the real figure. Last year Kirstie told them sixty or seventy percent.' There was a pause before the Spanish voice sighed, 'Oh well. As long as you keep bringing the people in like you did tonight then I don't care where the money goes.' The man laughed. 'Anyway, you be careful on that moped. I would have thought you would have had a car.'

'So would I Jimmy. So would I.'

It was Alison! Brad dragged Stella two yards to the end of the wall where they couldn't be seen.

'What's up?' asked a slightly spooked Stella.

'Ssshhh!' hissed Brad. 'That's my boss'.

'What was she doing?'

'I'm not sure.' Brad went silent for a few seconds. 'So that's why she gave me those free tickets.'

Brad waited until Alison had driven passed. His erection had subsided and although he still wanted to do very rude things to Stella, he was deep in thought as they walked to the taxi rank. After a couple of minutes Stella spoke.

'Are you alright Brad?'

'Yeah, fine. Do you know anything about backhanders?'

'What do you mean, payments to reps and tour companies?'

'That sort of thing, yeah.'

'Well only that it goes on and that the higher up you are the more money you normally get.'

'So do you think my boss would have been paid by the owner of The Star Club for taking all of our lot in?'

'Yes of course.' They had arrived at the taxi rank. 'Do you still want me to come back?' asked Stella, not sure whether Brad could manage being thoughtful and passionate at the same time.

Brad smiled and opened the taxi door. 'Get in.'

When they got back to the Bon, there were a few clients in the bar. Brad went in first and told Stella to leave it a couple of minutes before coming up, so the clients wouldn't know what was going on. When he got into his room he got a pot of yoghurt out of the fridge and put it next to the bed. Two minutes later Stella knocked on the door. As soon as he closed it they were pulling each others clothes off. Within a very short period of time Brad had his shorts around his ankles, and Stella had just her halter neck (minus it's buttons) hanging off of one shoulder. She had her back to the wall with her legs around his waist and his cock inside her. Still in this position, Brad carried her through to the bedroom, although the size of his steps were limited by the shorts that he was unable to kick from his ankles. Brad's intention had been to cover her in yoghurt, but events overtook him, and the only thing that Stella ended up covered in was Brad's spunk. It wasn't until Brad had got his breath back and saw the thick white stream trickling down her chin that he cursed himself - he hadn't worn a condom. It was only the first week and already he had broken the promise he had made to himself not to have unprotected sex. He did not have long to chastise himself though. Stella went to the bathroom, and within the four minutes it took to clean herself up, Brad had sunk into a long overdue sleep.

Although she was prepared to stay the night she was none too keen on walking into her hotel in the morning adorned in the previous nights apparel. She had enjoyed the night with Brad and wanted to see him again, so she made a half hearted attempt at waking him before realising that he was out for the count. Her clothes were scattered around the apartment. She picked up a black felt pen which was on the bedside cabinet, and then her panties from the bedroom floor. On them she wrote her name, hotel and phone number and three x's. She smiled to herself then slid the panties up his left leg, so they were just below his knee. Brad didn't hear her close the door, or the taxi pull up outside. He didn't hear the giggling twins come back with Mikey and Rayon or Greg come back with Linda and Emma. He didn't hear Mario being sick outside the apartments or a drunk Vanessa yelling and giggling that she wanted Greg's baby. Brad was at last, catching up on some much needed sleep.

CHAPTER THREE

Felipe Gomez walked up to his wife who was at the kitchen sink cutting the stems off of some flowers.

'Another week beckons,' he said, kissing her on the cheek.

'Are you off then?' she said, putting the flowers down and drying her hands. 'Will you be overseas at all this week?'

'I don't think so. Nothing planned anyway. I was expecting a call from Luis in Ibiza. If he calls get him to ring me at the office.'

'When's Luis coming over again? He hasn't been over since before Christmas.'

'It's a busy time of year my darling, but I'll ask him when we speak.' Felipe looked at his watch and kissed her on the cheek. 'Anyway, must go if I'm going to miss the traffic. I'll call you later.'

He walked over to his new Range Rover and opened the door so that he could get to the brief case on the back seat. For now, all that he wanted from it was his packet of Ducados cigarettes. When he had first smoked them he remembered that he had not liked them, but countless trips to Spain as Contracts Director for YF&S meant that he had grown used to their harsh taste. They were always readily available and cheap. Not that cost was a primary concern to Felipe. Over the years his position had allowed him to accrue a good deal of wealth, many times more than any other Contracts Director had ever earned. He now had a beautiful house in Dulwich Village; a house that none of his workmates had ever visited, apart from one - and she had only spent one night there when his wife was away.

He had enjoyed spending the weekend at his luxurious home and driving his new car. During the week he would normally stay in the company flat near their offices in

Teddington and drive the company Audi. Still, that was the way he liked it. Nobody at YF&S knew his private business. A few colleagues knew where he lived, but as far as they were concerned the house was left to him by a relative. They would have been shocked if they knew that the small loan he had taken to buy the property would be fully paid within eighteen months.

Felipe Gomez was in his late forties, swarthy and obviously Mediterranean. He had grown to like the good things in life, and the one hint at his wealth that he did not try to hide was his clothes. He was always immaculately turned out - suits from Saville Row, shirts and ties from Jermyn Street, shoes by Church or occasionally Lobb. His hair was longer than it should have been; only slightly greying at the temples but receding significantly on top. It was always greased back, and the length of his hair at the back meant that the collars of his shirts became grubby very quickly. Although not as jowly, Felipe did not look too dissimilar to Asil Nadir, the exiled Polly Peck chairman whom he admired greatly.

He was a little annoyed at himself for leaving the invoice in his brief case. If his wife had seen it she could have put two and two together and the game would have been up. He could not pay it out of their joint account because his wife took great pride in managing the home with stoic efficiency. Her stoicism however, would have soon changed to zealous rage at any hint of infidelity. He could have easily paid it out of their Spanish account, but Felipe wanted YF&S to pay it. Although he was a director, the size of his shares with the company were not large enough to educe any company loyalty from Felipe. It had not always been so, but three and a half years had passed since Felipe had confidently applied to be Financial Director with the attendant share options. He was so sure that the position was to be his that most of his family and friends also assumed it to be a foregone conclusion. There was nobody else working for the company at the time who was better qualified than Felipe. He remembered all too vividly the day he was called into the Chairman's office.

'Good morning Felipe. Please take a seat.'

Adam Hawthorne-Blythe had a luxurious Oxbridge educated voice and a grey handlebar moustache, the legacy of his ten years in the RAF. He had the sort of presence that would have had the populous of a bygone era tugging their forelocks and saying 'Gawd bless yer guv'nor.'

'I'll come straight to the point.' Felipe recalled the excitement that this statement had caused him at the time - the prelude to a whole new lifestyle. 'As you know, we have been looking for a new F.D. and your name was put forward as a suitable candidate. Whilst there is no doubting your integrity and commitment the board felt that you possessed insufficient relevant experience for this post. We shall soon be undergoing an extensive expansion programme, which is why it was felt that we needed someone who had experience of actually being in that role. The man we have coming in is Sebastian Hunter, who you may know is the Financial Director of our rivals......'

Felipe heard little else. The board limited the disappointment by promoting him from Contracts Manager to Contracts Director. The job was just the same however. The only difference was a small amount of shares, a slightly bigger office, a slightly larger salary and a title.

It was inevitable that Felipe would not like Sebastian Hunter who was a good fifteen years his junior. Moreover Sebastian brought about numerous sweeping changes within a very short time of joining so Felipe and Sebastian had locked horns on a number of occasions. This was why Felipe wanted YF&S to pay the invoice - not that he could not afford it but more that he liked the idea of tricking Sebastian into paying an invoice that was for something totally unconnected to YF&S.

If Sebastian asked why Felipe had been to a private hospital Felipe was going to tell him that it was for laser corrective surgery to his eyes, and although he knew that he really would not have a leg to stand on he was looking forward to a fierce argument to justify why it should be paid. He half suspected that Sebastian would pay it without saying anything. Because he was passed over for promotion Felipe was allowed the occasional privilege, and for such a small amount he was curious to discover whether or not Sebastian would wish to have a big showdown.

The black company Audi swept onto the road, and within ten minutes he was stuck in traffic in Brixton. If he left early enough he normally drove over Vauxhall Bridge, down the Embankment to Chelsea, through Earl's Court, along the A4 to Chiswick then down the A316. Sometimes he preferred to go around the South Circular, through Wandsworth and Kingston. As he had left later than planned he changed his original route and went left down Acre Lane to get out of the traffic and headed for Wandsworth.

It was eight thirty in the morning but already nearly twenty degrees - a 'mid May mini heat wave' the forecaster had called it. Felipe just called it bloody hot. It was a different kind of heat to the Med, more industrial and dirty. How he wished he was driving his air conditioned Range Rover. He stopped his car outside a newsagent in Clapham High St. just past the Spanish tapas bar called La Rueda to get a bottle of water. He also bought the Daily Mail and the Financial Times to see how his shares were doing and what his stars were saying. Both were looking good.

As he came off the A3, London threw off it's grey overcoat of uniformity, gradually turning into the manicured hedgerows and detached individuality of suburbia. The traffic queues seemed to get smaller as the cars got bigger and all around the colours appeared richer. Felipe relaxed and made a slight detour to look at the houses next to the river. If he did not eventually move to Spain then this is where he would probably put down his roots. The younger of his two sons would be leaving Dulwich College the following year, so it was not premature for him to start considering a move.

Felipe Gomez had a position in YF&S senior enough to warrant his own parking space. As he locked the door to the

Audi he heard a chirpy Scottish female voice behind him.

'Morning Felipe.'

Felipe looked up. The voice belonged to Jane Ward, the Overseas Manager for YF&S.

'Good morning Miss Ward. And how are we on this beautiful morning?'

'Very well Felipe, very well. Not too sure if I like this heat though.'

It never failed to amaze Felipe how the British always complained about the weather. It was either too hot; too cold; too windy; too humid; too wet or too dry - an endless source of useless conversation.

'Well, I'm sure it's hotter in Spain.'

'Aye, you're probably right there Felipe. When are you off again?' Felipe held the door to the reception area open for Jane. 'Thanks.'

'I'm not sure Jane. I'll probably be off to Ibiza shortly. I was in Tenerife last week.'

'What was that like?'

'Oh, give me Ibiza any day.' Felipe looked at the receptionist. 'Any messages for me Amanda?'

'Only to call Luis at Viajes Diamante in Ibiza,' replied the bespectacled blonde temp.

'Dear oh dear Felipe,' said Jane. 'Looks like there's no way of you getting away from Ibiza. I'll see you later.'

'Yes. Good-bye Jane.'

Felipe turned and walked in the opposite direction to his office. What did Jane mean by that comment? It was probably innocent, but was his association with Ibiza becoming a little bit too high profile? He never knew how to take Jane Ward. She was one of these people who always gave the impression that she knew something that you did not. There were rumours going round that she had been secretly seeing Sebastian Hunter. All this did was to add to the enigmatic mystique which surrounded her. Certainly all of the reps were in awe of her, but Felipe did not feel comfortable that she had the same effect on him, a Company Director. He was certainly higher up the company ladder than her, but Sebastian Hunter was considerably more powerful than him, and if Sebastian and Jane were lovers then Jane could be more influential than her official position within the company suggested.

Felipe walked into his office. He liked dark wood and traditional English furnishings. Leather dominated his office. An executive leather chair behind a leather inlaid desk, on which were placed a neat pile of various leather bound diaries and information books, and next to the window a leather two seater Chesterfield. The window had wooden Venetian blinds, the desk a gold and green lamp and the floor boasted an expensive Lahore rug. There was even a drinks cabinet with crystal glasses and a whole range of spirits purchased duty free on the way back from his constant trips abroad. There were a few executive toys on various surfaces and in the corner was a grandfather clock. Although the room was not particularly big it had a well ordered opulence which was obviously dictated by a very neat man. Felipe was in fact the only director who had gone to the trouble and expense of furnishing his own office. It's splendour surpassed even the Chairman's (although it was less than a third of the size) and he had justified this extravagance by using the same excuse as he had for acquiring the house in Dulwich, namely that the furnishings had all been left to him by a rich relative. He had explained to his colleagues that there was no room in his house for them and that putting them in his office was preferable to going to the expense of putting them in to storage.

Felipe closed the office door before ringing Luis at Viajes Diamante. Viajes Diamante were the local agents in Ibiza for YF&S, and amongst other things they were the link through which Felipe contracted all of the accommodation for every holidaymaker who went to Ibiza with YF&S. He conducted his conversation with Luis in Spanish. Nobody else was aware that he had known Luis for more than thirty years. Luis was a native Ibizenco, unlike Felipe who was from just outside Seville, but they had met at college in Madrid and had remained in touch, visiting each other frequently. During the last few years the opportunity had arisen for them to have a business relationship, so their personal relationship had flourished even more, particularly since Luis had divorced his wife.

Felipe had been in the UK for more than twenty years, eighteen of which had been spent married to his English wife Rosemary. His English was near perfect and he had adopted what he considered to be the best of English manners. Adjectives such as 'polite' and 'charming' were ones often applied to describe Felipe. However, his English associates would have been surprised to have realised that when Felipe spoke Spanish it was with a regional dialect which most Spaniards would recognise as suggesting that he was from the lower end of the social scale. It had only been in his twenties that Felipe had started to try and better himself when he was living in England. As such, he had not refined his Spanish accent or vocabulary anywhere near as much as he had his English.

When he finished his call he looked at his Gucci watch. He had a game of golf arranged near Liphook at two thirty. He made a couple of more calls and then took the invoice out of his jacket pocket ready to take in to Sebastian Hunter. It was from The Chamberlain Clinic. It did not specify what the treatment was. Felipe stubbed out a half smoked Ducados on the marble ashtray on his desk, gathered his things and headed for Sebastian Hunter's office. When he got there the door was slightly open. He opened it a little further and realised Sebastian wasn't in. Just at that moment, Jane Ward walked by.

'Ah, Jane. Have you seen Sebastian this morning?'

'No, I haven't seen him in the office,' she replied truthfully.

'Have you any idea where he is or what time he'll be in?'

'I think he had a meeting with the bank or something. Amanda said he's expected in about lunchtime.'

'Ok. Thanks.'

Felipe went into the office and put the invoice on a pile of papers on Sebastian's desk. He attached a yellow Post-it note to the invoice with 'Sebastian, please speak to me about this' written on it. As Felipe left the office he accidentally slammed the door. What he did not see was the invoice float under the desk as it got caught in the draught, causing the Post-it note tp separate and tumble onto the floor next to the waste paper basket.

'Come on darling, you'll be late.'

'Well that doesn't matter - you are my boss.'

'Technically that may be so Jane, but I'm not the one you report to, am I?'

'No Sebastian,' sang back Jane in a child-like manner. 'Right, I'm ready. What have you got on today?'

'Oh, just a meeting with the bank. I should be back about lunchtime.'

They got into Sebastian's company Mercedes and headed for the office. The journey from Weybridge normally took less than half an hour.

'I'm surprised that people haven't sussed us out yet,' said Sebastian. 'What with you nearly always arriving a couple of minutes after me. I'm sure someone must have seen me dropping you off around the corner.'

'Aye, well they better not,' snapped Jane.

'Alright, alright. I really don't know what your problem is though. I mean we've been seeing each other now for what, nearly a year?'

'Forty seven weeks and three days,' replied Jane.

'Exactly! That's a long time to keep something like this secret. I want everyone to know how I feel about you.'

'I know you do honey but I've never hidden what my thoughts are about it. I want to progress through merit. I don't want people thinking that I've achieved something just because of my relationship with you.'

'They wouldn't -'

'You don't know that for sure. Please let's not go over this again. I had a career before we met and I want to continue with it - at least for a few more years. You do understand don't you?'

Sebastian stopped at the red lights at the Sunbury Cross roundabout. He turned to see Jane's doleful eyes looking at him.

'You know I do.' He leant across and kissed her. 'I do love you, you caber tossing savage.'

Jane moved to the edge of her seat and kissed Sebastian on the lips and playfully squeezed his balls.

'Was that a request, or are you just talking dirty again?'

The lights changed, and they smiled at each other as Sebastian joined the cars coming into London from the M3.

Once in Teddington Sebastian dropped Jane off at the usual place.

'See you about lunchtime. Hope it goes well with the bank. Love you.'

'You too. See you later.' They kissed and Sebastian drove off towards Richmond.

As Jane walked into the office car park, the black Audi of Felipe Gomez was manoeuvring into his parking space.

'Good Morning Felipe.'

Sebastian arrived a little after one o'clock. He put his head around the door to say hello to Jane, but her assistant Tom Ortega was at his desk in their shared office and Jane seemed to be engrossed in a deep telephone conversation, so he simply mouthed 'talk to you later'. Jane was on the phone for almost another ten minutes and when she finally hung up she slumped in her chair and let out a huge sigh. Tom had caught some of the call.

'What was all that about?' he asked.

'That was a very distressed young Zena ringing from Crete.'

'What's up with her? She's only been out there a week.'

'Mmm, I know. Poor wee girl, her first week in her first season and she has that to deal with.' Jane shook her head. Tom looked at her quizzically, allowing her a moment or so to continue. Jane sat forward in her chair and explained what had happened. 'Zena was guiding a coach back from the beach party - it was the first time she'd done a coach on her own as well. Anyway, a couple of girl clients had met up with a couple of local Greek guys and decided to get a lift back in their jeeps rather than getting the coach. One of the Greek guys was obviously giving it the big macho bit and tried to overtake the coach but there was a car coming in the other direction, so he had to pull in sharply and you know how unstable those jeeps are.'

'So what happened?'

'Well, the jeep flipped over and landed in a ditch.'

'Were they alright?' asked Tom.

'Hardly. Zena stopped the coach and went over to the jeep. The Greek guy just had some cuts and grazes, but when Zena looked at the girl - oh God, it's so horrible - her nose and lips were gone -'

'What do you mean, gone?'

'Apparently the metal rim of the jeep had sliced away half of her face. Apart from that her legs were all twisted, an eye was missing and the top of her skull had flipped open.'

'WHAT! So was she still alive.'

'That's the worst part. She was wriggling and moving around.'

'Oh my God. So what did Zena do, call an ambulance?'

'They were miles from anywhere so there was no point. She got the other Greek guy to put the girl in the back of the other jeep. When the clients saw the state she was in a few of them were sick - God knows how Zena wasn't. She got the coach driver to take the clients back to the hotel -'

'Hang on a minute,' said Tom. 'Where were the other reps?'

'Well there's only Chas and Debbie. Debbie was back at the hotel and Chas was guiding the other coach which was about two minutes in front of Zena's.' Jane had temporarily lost her train of thought. She reflected blankly and looked at Tom for a prompt. 'Where was I?' Before Tom could answer she continued. 'Oh yeah. So Zena sat in the back of the jeep and had to keep pulling the girls tongue out. She said that she was gurgling and mumbling incoherently all the way to the hospital.'

'What was Zena gurgling and mumbling about?'

'TOM!?'

'Sorry.'

'When they wheeled her into the hospital even the nurses were covering their eyes. The other Greek guy, bastard, just drove off with his mate and left poor Zena to it. Can you imagine the state she must have been in? She doesn't speak Greek and she's running around trying to find a doctor. She reckons it took nearly fifteen minutes before some fat bellied, fag smoking mess of a doctor sauntered in. He told Zena to leave her there. When Zena rang back later to find out what happened no-one knew anything about it. Eventually Chas got the British embassy to call and they've just found out that the girl is dead.'

'Jesus. Mind you it's probably a good thing, if you know what I mean,' said Tom.

'Aye, well you're probably right there.'

'So who tells the parents, assuming that the local police don't know any friends of the family who can do it? It's got to be your turn Jane.'

'I'll wait until I've got all the info together first. Christ! What a start to the season.' Jane stood up. 'I'm just going to pop up to Sebastian's office. If anyone from Crete calls get it transferred to his extension will you?'

'Sure,' replied Tom.

When Jane left Tom smiled to himself. It was so obvious to him that Jane and Sebastian were having an affair that he wished that Jane would confide in him.

When Jane got to Sebastian's office he was on the phone. She closed the door behind her and sat down opposite him. His window was open, allowing the murmur of traffic to sweep

109

in with the gentle early summer breeze. Every so often this inoffensive noise was punctuated with the roar of a bus or lorry revving it's engine. This caused Sebastian to screw up his face and put his finger in his left ear so he could hear what the person on the other end of the phone was saying. Eventually he put the phone down and smiled at Jane.

'Are you alright darling, you look a bit stressed?'

'Aye, well I've just been speaking to a poor wee lassie in Crete who's had to deal with the first death of the season - a particularly gruesome one as well.'

'What happened?' asked Sebastian.

'Oh I'll tell you tonight,' said Jane waving her hand not wanting to go through the whole thing again. 'Anyway, what's the problem with Majorca that you wanted to talk to me about?'

'I was talking to our agent out there, and as of yet no excursion money has been liquidated. Majorca's been live two weeks longer than all of the other resorts and I'm more than a little concerned. What's this Resort Manager...' Sebastian looked at his notes, '.....Jason Barnes, like?'

'Barnesy,' replied Jane. 'Loads of experience, very shrewd. Popular with all of the other reps as well. In fact I think that Kirstie Davies has just gone out to pay him and some of the other second year rep's a visit.'

'Isn't that the Welsh girl who ran Ibiza last year?'

'Aye - and she worked in Majorca the year before so I guess she knows a lot of the bar owners and that. She's got her own travel agency in Brecon now.'

'So this Jason Barnes character - is he loyal?'

'Was. Not sure about now though.'

'What do you mean?'

'Nothing to worry about in isolation, but one of his first year rep's was on the phone last week in tears, moaning about the way he was treating her and the fact that she'd not received any commission. Also, there were a few rumours going around before the season started that it was going to be Barnesy's last season, and that he was going to try and make

110

as much as he could.'

'So why didn't you do anything about it?' snapped Sebastian probably a little too harshly.

Jane was proud of the way she did her job and would not tolerate any invalid criticism, even from Sebastian. However, in a slow and deliberate voice she explained,

'Because every year I get phone calls from first year rep's who suddenly realise that they're not on holiday and who didn't fully appreciate what was expected of them. Also, every year there are rumours going around about Resort Manager's who are intending to rip us off and scarper. If I listened to every rumour and whimper then we'd have no Resort Manager's and no reps.' Jane paused and looked at Sebastian, who realised from Jane's tone that he was close to upsetting her. He therefore wisely said nothing and allowed her to continue. 'Of course there is an element of fiddling going on, but we have managed to eliminate most of it. We know through historical analysis what a resort should be producing, and if there are any major discrepancies from our expectations then we start fishing. When we go out to resort we talk to the reps, and it's very easy for them to unwittingly give the game away. Sometimes they can be so fed up with a manager that they'll do the investigating for us.'

'Well, you obviously know what you're doing,' said Sebastian tactfully. 'So what do you propose doing about this Barnes character?'

'I'll get Tom on a flight out there tomorrow, and if there's any hint of foul play - dear Jason Barnes' feet won't touch the ground.'

'You'll make sure you get the excursion money first won't you?' said the more fiscally motivated Sebastian. Jane glared at him. 'Yes, of course you will.' Sebastian hurried, changing the subject. 'What about the other resorts, have we got any other managers that there are, er, 'rumours' about.'

'Not really. Only Alison.'

'Alison.' Sebastian looked down his list. 'Alison Shand in Ibiza?'

'That's her,' replied Jane.

'Isn't she the one that Felipe Gomez recommended?' asked Sebastian.

'More than just recommended - he virtually insisted on her going out there. We had her earmarked for Benidorm. She's very good at entertaining and her paperwork's superb, but we didn't think her 'people' skills were strong enough to manage one of the big two,' said Jane, referring to Majorca and Ibiza. 'Anyway, Felipe spoke to our beloved Chairman and that was that. So I suppose it's your fault really Sebastian.'

'What do you mean, my fault?' he asked, puzzled.

'Well you know how Hawthorne-Blythe still feels a bit guilty about giving the F.D. job to you rather than Felipe. I suppose it was his way of giving Felipe some kind of recompense.'

'So why was Felipe so keen for Alison to get the job?'

'Beats me,' said Jane shaking her head. 'Felipe does seem to take a special interest in Ibiza though.'

'All the more reason why Alison wouldn't dare to be on the fiddle,' said Sebastian, satisfying himself with this explanation and standing up as he did so. 'Come on, let's nip over the road and have a quick pint - my treat.'

Jane picked her things up from Sebastian's desk. She was not as convinced as he was of either Alison or Felipe's loyalty. There was no reason for her to suspect foul play other than a gut feeling that something was not quite right.

CHAPTER FOUR

The room was pitifully dingy. Moreover, because The Las Huertas was a hotel rather than apartments there were no cooking facilities. Just a bed, a bedside cabinet and a wardrobe. The bathroom consisted of a toilet without a seat, a shower and a cracked mirror. Brad was not impressed. This was to be his 'home' for the next six months. The most depressing thing though was the lack of natural light; just a window that opened on to the adjoining building with only a three foot wide gap between them. Brad started to unpack his case. At the top were Stella's panties which he threw into the bottom of the wardrobe. As he did so, he recalled the event's of the previous night, although he was unable to recall Stella leaving.

He thought back to Alison outside The Star Club. What a bitch! She had made out that she was being so magnanimous by giving the BR football team free tickets to The Star when all of the time she was lining her own pocket. Brad was desperate to talk to somebody, but it had to be someone with experience which meant that it could only be Heather or Greg. Although he got on well with Greg he was unsure whether or not Greg gave a toss about anything other than scoring points. Heather had stuck up for Alison - albeit half-heartedly - during the conversation with Mikey at the airport, and Brad had not really built up any kind of rapport with her to know where her loyalties lay. Brad decided to have a quiet word with Greg later in the day to try to find out exactly what were the implication's of Alison's conversation outside The Star.

Greg did not turn up at The Las Huertas pool until early afternoon. Every other Monday was a free day (in other words no arranged official excursions), so the reps were supposed to keep the clients amused as best they could. The Pon did not have a pool, so the majority of the YF&S holidaymakers who

113

were not in a bar or on the beach gravitated to the one at The Las Huertas. Even though Greg looked a little the worse for wear, Brad noticed that the majority of the girls looked up when he arrived. He slumped on a sunbed next to Brad.

'Fuck me, was I caning last night.'

'What do you mean, caning?' asked Brad, unfamiliar with this northern expression.

'Shagging.'

'Three more points?'

'Two bonus points.'

'What, a threesome?!'

'Fuckin' right.'

'Who with?' demanded an envious Brad, already guessing the answer.

'Linda and Emma.'

'You're kidding.'

'I wish I was. My dick is so fucking sore......still, puts me on to eleven points, wa-hay. Whar' about you - any luck last night?'

'Yeah, that spiky haired rep I brought back from the airport.'

'Nice one. Was she as dirty as she looked?'

'Can't really remember. Plenty of 'Harry on the boat' though.'

'Plenty of WHAT?'

'You know, Harry-' Greg shook his head, not having a clue what Brad was on about. 'Harry Monk, spunk. On the boat.'

'On the what?' Greg was confused.

'It's cockney rhyming slang. Harry Monk, spunk, on the boat race, face.'

Greg started laughing. 'What, so Harry on the boat means you gism'd all over her face?'

'Basically yeah.'

'Fucking brilliant. I'll have to start using that one.' At that moment one of the Scottish girls came past. 'Hey, darling,' called Greg. 'Do you want some Harry on your boat?'

Brad hid his face in his sunbed with embarrassment. Fortunately the Scottish girl had no idea what Greg was on

114

about, which amused Greg even more.

Mario had been sitting on the other side of the pool and came over to join them.

'What's so funny?' he asked.

'Have you ever 'eard the expression 'Harry on the boat'?' asked Greg.

'Yeah. Spunk on the face.'

For some reason Greg found this expression so amusing that Mario repeating it sent him into apoplexy again.

When Greg finished laughing he turned to Brad. 'Sold many condoms yet?'

'Have I fuck,' said Brad. 'No one seems bothered. The only time any of the stupid bastards want one is when they want to blow it up over their head, or to use as a water bomb. Apart from that, Alison's none to keen on me knocking them out. I've given a few boxes to the lads at The Charleston and Vince at The Madhouse on sale or return. Guess I'll just have to try and use the rest myself.'

The peace and quiet that had descended upon the pool was interrupted by the four members of the Plymouth Possee, who came and sat by the pool near the reps with their ghetto blaster once again blaring out thrash metal. Mario stood up.

'It's alright, I'll deal with this. I saw how you dealt with them last time Greg.'

'I know but there's more to -'

'Don't worry, I know what I'm doing,' insisted Mario, walking over to them.

'Oh dear,' said Greg. 'I was about to tell 'im that there are ways and there are ways. This should be interesting.'

The Plymouth Possee had just sat themselves down when a grinning Mario approached them.

'Turn that fucking shit off.'

With that, Mario pressed the eject button and threw the tape into the pool. He looked round to Greg and Brad for approval. This meant that he did not see the biggest of the Plymouth Possee come up behind and half punch, half push him into the pool.

'And don't come out till you've got our cassette.'

A humiliated Mario looked out from the pool to be greeted with universal mocking laughter.

'Told you,' said Greg.

'Shouldn't we do something,' said Brad.

'No. He'll learn from 'is mistakes - 'opefully,' replied Greg.

Mario was about to get out of the pool when a crescendo of yelling came from the bar. Everyone looked up, just as Mikey and half a dozen or so of the BR football team came running into the pool and bombed Mario, also soaking most of the other sunbathers in the process. Mikey sprang out of the shallow end, beat his chest letting out a Tarzan type call, then pushed Mario back in the pool just as he had struggled out. Mario was looking totally drained and defeated.

'Me Masambula, King of the reps,' roared Mikey sending himself up. 'Me no let this white oppressor out of pool to torture me more with bad clothes and bad chat up lines. Me have tribe who make sure he no escape.' As Mikey said this, Rayon stuck his foot out sending the hapless Mario once again into his new, chlorine filled temporary home. All of the clients loved this, joining in to make sure that Mario stayed in the pool for at least another quarter of an hour, by which time even the Plymouth Possee had tired of this new game.

Mikey eventually came over and sat with Brad and Greg.

'You seem full of beans,' said Brad. 'What did you get up to last night?'

'More like 'who' did 'e get up to,' corrected Greg.

Mikey smiled. 'Well if you must know it was one of the twins. Rayon did the other one.'

'Any good?' asked Greg.

'Oh, it gets better,' said Mikey. 'Tell me Greg - not that I'm joining in this points thing you understand - but if I was, how many points for a pair of twins?'

'Oh you didn't,' said Brad. 'Please tell me you didn't.'

Mikey looked at Brad grinning from ear to ear and started nodding.

'What, at the same time?' asked Greg, worried that his

points lead would be threatened.

'Not exactly,' said Mikey. 'They changed half way through without telling us.'

'So 'ow d'ya know for sure that they changed?' asked Greg.

'Believe me man, I know. Rayon reckons that their biffs are shaved differently, though to be honest I didn't notice.'

'You lucky bastard,' said Brad. 'I walked them home the other night as well.'

'Yeah I know,' laughed Mikey. 'They said that you kept falling asleep as you were walking and talking crap.'

Brad hid his head in his hands and groaned.

'So, six points to you last night, five points to me and three points to Brad,' said Greg. 'That puts me in the lead on twelve, Mikey on six, Mario on zilch and Brad on nine. No hang on a minute, you didn't shag Linda 'cos you didn't have a condom so that means you've only got eight points.'

'So I don't get any points for sleepwalking and talking crap then,' said Brad.

'You're lucky we don't deduct any.'

Brad was sitting next to Lorraine at the front of the coach, while Heather was explaining the evenings proceedings to all of the holidaymakers over the microphone.

'.....And after the bucking bronco you'll have a chance to show what you think of your reps by giving us the thumbs up or thumbs down in the amphitheatre. If you give us the thumbs down, then we get chucked into a slimy pool. Now I should warn everyone that I can't swim, so.....'

The inevitable chorus of 'Get your tits out' followed. Lorraine leaned across Brad to speak to Greg who was sitting on the other side of the aisle.

'So what exactly happens tonight then Greg?'

'First of all we give them their own raw meat to cook over the Bar-B-Q. While they're eating their meal they can drink as much wine and draught beer as they want. Then we take 'em onto the bucking bronco's..'

'What are they again?' asked Lorraine

'Mechanical bulls,' replied Greg. 'After that we all go up to the amphitheatre. Basically the venue used to be a zoo an' the amphitheatre used t'be where the seals performed. All it is, is a small stage with a titchy moat like pool between it an' the audience. They've got some nutter compering and singing called Woodsy and 'e warms everyone up first with a ten minute singalong. Then we go on one by one and start singing. 'Alfway through the song Woodsy stops playing, takes the piss out of you and gets this lot to give you the thumbs up or the thumbs down. If you get the thumbs up you walk away, if you get the thumbs down, in you go. Simple really.'

'So did you ever stay dry last year?' asked Brad.

'Well I got the thumbs up once, but the bastard still pushed me in.'

'This Woodsy sounds mad,' said Lorraine.

'Yeah, that's a fair assessment. He's the funniest bloke I've ever met though - really quick, and does not give a fuck,' said Greg, highlighting the point by pausing between each of the last five words of the sentence.

'Can't wait to meet him,' said Lorraine foolishly.

Once they had completed the five minute journey to the excursion which was just outside San Antonio, the reps led the hundred or so clients to the front gate. There to greet them were two men dressed as cowboys, one obviously Spanish and one obviously English. The one who was obviously English had what looked suspiciously like a spliff in one hand and a bottle of beer in the other. He caught sight of Greg from thirty yards,

'Ah, Greg, you short arsed little twat. How's the dose - cleared up yet?' The Wigan accent turned it's attentions to Lorraine who was walking next to Greg. 'And who's this, your mother? Well, she's certainly ugly enough for me,' He put his arm around her, 'Don't worry darling, you're not fat enough.'

Mikey made the mistake of trying to talk. 'Oh hang on a minute, I'll just go and get me drums so you can understand.

Hold on,' Woodsy turned around to shout up to where they were preparing to give out the meat for the Bar-B-Q. 'Juanito, grab a couple of missionaries for the Bar-B.' Mikey looked at Woodsy, not smiling. 'Oh fuck me,' said Woodsy, 'I hope he hasn't got one of those effigy things or I've had it. Oi you,' he said, running and grabbing Brad, then hiding behind him. 'You look big enough and stupid enough to look after me. Fuck me, you've even got a broken nose.' Woodsy pushed his own nose flat against his face and started speaking like a retard. 'Der, my name's Brad, and my specialist subject is...'

'Flattening northern comedians,' interrupted Brad.

'Oh it fucking is, is it.' With that Woodsy tweaked Brad's nipple causing him to yelp. 'Well if that's the case you'd better come up to the bar so I can get you all a drink before you do any serious damage to me.'

As they were walking up the hill to the bar, Woodsy was about ten yards ahead of them all with his arm around Lorraine's shoulder. Every few seconds they'd both break out into bursts of laughter. Brad was walking next to Greg.

'Christ,' said Brad, 'He's like a human tornado.'

'I did warn you,' smiled Greg.

'How does he get away with it?'

'Timing,' said Greg. 'I've seen people about t'lay 'im out an' the next minute 'e's got 'is arm round their shoulder at the bar, and by the end of the night that same person'll be treating 'im as if 'e's their best friend. Thing is, 'e'll still be taking the piss out of 'em.'

'I still don't know how he gets away with it,' repeated Brad, shaking his head.

'Well he doesn't always, does he Heath.' Heather had caught up with Greg, Brad and Mikey.

'No he doesn't,' replied Heather. 'Do you remember that time last year?'

'DO I!' laughed Greg.

'What happened?' said Mikey.

By now they had reached the bar, and Woodsy sent them all some drinks before walking off to sit down to have a more

119

serious conversation with Alison.

'Well,' said Greg swigging his beer, 'We 'ad a group of squaddies over. They were real div 'eads an' they'd been giving us a few problems, 'adn't they Heath?' Heather nodded her agreement. 'Anyway, we weren't actually 'ere, we were at Hoe Down - we'll be going there next week. Woodsy was compering and taking the piss as 'e does, but 'e was really layin' into these squaddies. One of 'em in particular reckoned 'imself to be a bit of a comedian an' kept trying to come back at Woodsy - fatal mistake. Woodsy spent literally five minutes just coating 'im until everyone in the place was cryin' with laughter. Obviously he 'ad the microphone, so even if the bloke 'ad been funny - which he wasn't - 'e would've still been slaughtered. When it all finished the squaddies surrounded 'im an' at first it seemed pretty good natured. I was standing nearby an' the only bit I heard Woodsy say was something like, "Listen, you've all obviously joined the army 'cos you're too fucking thick to get a proper job. Then you come over here hoping to get a shag but you're all too fucking ugly so what do you do? The same as when you're in your barracks - all wank over a biscuit or shag each other." After that I think 'e turned to the one who thought 'e was funny and told 'im that he 'ad as much chance of gerrin' a laugh as Simon Weston (that bloke who got burnt in the Falklands) 'ad of starring in a Gillette advert. Well that was it, they all laid into him. Mind you, 'e certainly 'ad a go. He can 'ave a scrap can our Woodsy.'

'I should think he'd have to,' said Mikey

During the evening Brad couldn't take his eyes off of Patricia, who he had not seen since the beach party. Tonight was her penultimate night before returning back to Nottingham and nearly a week's exposure to the sun had made her look even more gorgeous. When Brad went on stage for his turn in the amphitheatre he was conscious of her sitting in the audience far and away above anybody and everybody else.

Brad had chosen to sing Stevie Wonder's 'I Just Called'. To assist him in his task he had a black stocking over his head with some sunglasses, a red yellow and green hat with dreadlocks hanging out of the back and a telephone. Before he got to the first chorus Woodsy had stopped playing the guitar and following an extremely loud thumbs down, Brad found himself jettisoned into the eight foot deep seal pool. As Brad went under, the stocking over his head immediately filled up with water, totally disorientating him. He came up for air, but all that he got was another mouthful of water and an earful of uproarious laughter.

He couldn't find the side of the pool and was genuinely beginning to panic, as it was clear that everyone believed him to be play acting. When Brad came up coughing and spluttering the third time, a strong pair of arms dragged him out of the water and ripped off the stocking. Brad gulped in the welcome fresh air in between coughing up the contents of the seal pool from his lungs. Mikey had been his saviour and was crouching over him as Woodsy had already started playing 'Hey Big Spender' for Lorraine.

'You alright mate?' asked Mikey.

'Yeah, thanks to you.'

Brad walked to the back of the stage and quickly dried off before walking down to the client free DJ tower to catch up with Mikey.

'Jesus, I thought I'd had it then.'

Mikey laughed, reached into his bag and pulled out a spliff.

'Do you think this will help your recovery?'

'Probably.' Brad lit it, inhaled deeply then let out a satisfied groan. 'I know what would really help my recovery though.'

'What's that,' said Mikey taking the joint.

'Patricia.'

'Yeah man, she's looking badly fit. I thought you were getting on alright with her.'

'Mmm, I was,' said Brad reflectively. 'The problem is Mikey, if I really like someone I've got this real bad habit of putting them onto a bit of a pedestal, and then I can't talk to them.'

'What a load of bollocks. She's the same person that she was when you were talking to her on the beach the other day.

121

The only difference is that she's got more of a tan and you've romanticised the whole thing. The one thing that's certain is that she's going home the day after tomorrow, and if you don't do something about it you'll never know. If you approach her what's the worst thing that's going to happen? She's not going to poke your eye out or put a curse on you. The worst that's going to happen is that you'll get rejected, and if you can't handle one little bit of rejection getting all of the ego boosts that this job gives you then you're not the bloke that I thought you was.' Mikey paused and half smiling added, 'Any chance of some of that spliff?'

'Yeah, sure.' Brad was a little taken aback. 'Jesus. I'm the one who normally plays the agony uncle.'

'I'm sure there'll be times for you to return the compliment.......I'm sure there'll be times.'

Brad could hear Woodsy telling everyone to make their way down to the bar area for the final hour of 'The finest beer and the finest tunes.' The former never existed and Greg quickly put paid to the latter when he took over the DJ'ing.

Brad was standing near the pool, deep in thought wondering what to say to Patricia and pondering Mikey's advice when he felt a tap on his shoulder.

'Not talking to me then?' It was Patricia.

'Oh, hi.'

'I thought I'd done something to upset you. You haven't said a word to me all night.'

'No, don't be silly,' said Brad.

He stood there, cursing himself at not being able to think of anything to say. In truth, he was trying too hard. Patricia stood next to him. He could tell by her body language, the way she was breathing, the look on her face that she was interested, but still he could say nothing. After a thirty second eternity of silence Patricia spoke,

'Oh well, I'd better go and see my friends. I might see you later.'

'Yeah, maybe. See you later.' Patricia started walking away. Brad suddenly had a rush of blood. 'Patricia.' He skipped a couple of paces to catch her up. 'Look, I know I'm in danger of making a berk of myself here, but I guess that's what I'm paid to do, so here goes. I can't think of anything to say to you that doesn't sound corny, because I know you've got a pre-conceived idea of us all and that you think we believe that we can have who we want at the click of a finger. Maybe we can but as I've only been doing the job a week I've yet to find that out. You've only got a couple of days left, and the thing is I'd like to get to know you better.' Patricia's face lit up as she smiled. Brad continued, 'That's doesn't mean that getting you into bed is the top of my agenda - although I'd be lying if I said it wasn't on the agenda at all - it's just that...'

'Sssshhhh!' Patricia put her index finger to Brad's lips. 'I'm not stupid Brad. I've known that you've liked me ever since the beach party, probably before that actually. I just don't want to be another three points or whatever it is Mario said you all do.'

'Oh that,' said Brad, cursing Mario under his breath. 'Yeah, it's pathetic. Mikey and me don't get involved in it. Even if we did Patricia, there really is something about you that - oh God, this is going to sound corny - that's special.' Brad could see Alison walking towards him. 'Shit, here comes my boss. Look, we're all going down Bugala's after this. Will you come along?' Patricia nodded. Brad blew her a kiss and ran off to join one of the larger groups before Alison had a chance to have a go at him.

After leaving Bugala's they went to a little Spanish bar that no English used, and ordered two carajillos, expresso coffee with brandy. The more he spoke to her, the more Brad liked her. The conversation flowed freely, as they both gradually showed a little bit more of themselves to each other. Patricia admitted that she had a boyfriend back in Nottingham, but told Brad that things were not going too well.

They finished their drinks and made their way back. As Brad was staying at the Las Huertas and Patricia at the apartments, Brad realised that at some point during the walk home the topic of sleeping together would have to come up. He was hoping it would come up naturally, but they became embroiled in discussing Mario, so that by the time they got to the end of the wasteland, just fifty yards from the apartments, the subject had still not been broached. They arrived at the corner of the road which led down to the apartments. Brad took hold of Patricia's other hand so that they were facing each other. He softly kissed her lips. Patricia slipped her hands from his and encircled him with her arms. Brad began to kiss her more passionately, pushing his right thigh between her legs as he did so. Patricia rubbed herself against him, but Brad noticed that she kept stopping herself from getting too carried away.

Brad wanted her badly, but he was acutely aware that Patricia did not want to become another three points. He suspected that he could have probably persuaded her to consummate their friendship. However, his instincts told him that she still did not trust him entirely which would mean that not only would it have been a battle, but also that she would have felt a little uncomfortable the next day. If Brad was going to have her he wanted her totally.

'Patricia.'

Patricia was kissing Brad's neck and moaning slightly. This was going to be hard.

'Patricia, stop.' Patricia stopped kissing Brad and looked at him quizzically. 'Come on Patricia. Let's get you home. I'll walk you to the reception. I've had a wonderful, special evening, and I don't want to ruin it by making a clumsy lunge. If this is going to happen let's make sure that it happens properly, yeah?'

Patricia smiled, and snuggled up to Brad. He kissed the top of her head and they walked over to the door of the apartments, where he kissed her softly on the lips and looked her in the eyes.

'I'll see you tomorrow. You are going to come to the match, aren't you?'

'I wouldn't miss it for the world.'

Brad watched her float up the stairs. As she disappeared from view Brad started the walk back. When he was out of earshot of the apartment balconies he muttered, 'Well Bradley Streeter, I hope you know what you're doing.'

Alison woke up not feeling none too happy with the events of the previous night. Manny, the Spanish owner of the excursion had made her feel extremely awkward by not picking up on any of the hints she had dropped about wanting a payment for taking customers to his excursions. Kirstie had told her before leaving England that Manny never gave backhanders. He was so well liked by the bosses of YF&S that any blatant attempt at getting money out of him would have meant treading on very thin ice. Alison felt that maybe she had overstepped the mark and was feeling worried that Manny might speak to someone in head office informing them that she was trying to make money on the side. She decided that a call to the UK would be prudent to pre-empt that possibility, by pretending that she was trying to get extra money for the company.

She had also tried to get some money out of Woodsy, but all that she got out of him other than the piss taken at the size of her nose, was a small cut from raffling the video of the evenings proceedings. Another thing that Alison was none too pleased with was the way that Brad and Mikey had already seemed to have formed some kind of bond. Even as individuals they played on her insecurities, so the thought of them forming any type of alliance made her even more paranoid.

With all of this playing on her mind Alison went down to reception. Mikey was there doing his desk duty. Despite his cheery 'Morning', Alison virtually ignored him, grabbed a coffee and went to the reception desk to call head office. She picked up the receiver of the grey phone and put her finger into the old fashioned dial. When she got through to Jane

Ward's office it was a male voice that answered the phone. Tom Ortega.

'Good morning. Overseas.'

'Hello, who's that - Tom?'

'Speaking.' Tom recognised the voice. 'Is that the dulcet tones of Alison Shand?'

'Is Jane there?' Alison did not particularly like Tom and did not want to indulge in polite conversation.'

"Fraid not Ali.' Alison hated having her name abbreviated. 'Can I help?'

'When's she due back?'

'Don't know. She's in a meeting with Sebastian. Anything wrong?'

Although Alison did not want to deal with Tom, she was aware that she needed to make some kind of contact with head office in case Manny called and mentioned the fact that she had asked for money.

'No nothing wrong. If you see Jane tell her that I tried to get some money out of one of the excursion owners but he wouldn't play ball. I did my best.' What Alison failed to mention was that it was her own pocket that she was trying to line and not the company's.

'Alright, I'll pass the message on. Anything else? How are the new reps getting on?'

'Oh not bad. Mario's getting on really well. Lorraine is a bit timid but I should be able to knock her into shape.'

'What about Brad? How's he doing?'

'Well to be honest -,' Alison cleared her throat, 'I'm not so sure about him. He's a bit arrogant, thinks he knows it all. He spends a lot of time chasing girl clients and loadsa time sleeping so he's always late. I can probably sort him out, I just hope that he doesn't lead Mikey astray.'

Tom was somewhat surprised. What Alison was unaware of was that Tom had been on Brad's panel at the twenty four hour interview called Bridlehurst and the one week training course at Warwick. Just prior to Brad leaving for resort Tom had even been out with him socially a couple of times. Brad had excelled at both the interview and the training course and Tom was ninety percent sure that Brad was going to turn out to be a first class rep. He did however know that Brad was a bit of a womaniser, and his dry sense of humour and quick wit could have been mistaken for arrogance. So, although Tom's gut feeling was that Alison had got it wrong, he half accepted that Alison's comments could have had some substance.

When Alison put the phone down she smiled to herself, happy that she had not only avoided any problems that could have arisen from her attempt to get money out of Manny, but also happy in the belief that she had weakened the position of one she saw as being a potential threat.

After Brad finished his desk duty at The Las Huertas he walked over to The Bon to join Mikey and all of the others who were to be participating in the football match with the British Rail mob. As he walked in, Mikey was standing on a chair changing the channels on the TV. Mikey flicked passed the local news channel which was running a story about an American who had rammed his jeep into a police car near Las Salinas, preferring to watch the ever present cycling which he concluded the Spanish were totally obsessed with.

'Alright Harvis.' Brad deliberately mis-pronounced the 'J' in Jarvis as an 'H', like the Spanish.

'How did you get on last night?' asked Mikey.

'What, with Patricia? Yeah we had a good night.'

'And......?'

'And what? If you mean did I score any points, the answer's no. I want to do things properly. I think it might have been on the cards but it didn't seem right.'

'Jesus. You sound almost human. Go on, she wouldn't let you, would she?'

'To be honest mate I don't know. I didn't really try. Maybe I just didn't want to shatter my illusion of her.'

'What, you mean if you shagged her she'd fall off of that

pedestal of yours?'

Brad winced a bit as Mikey scored a home truth.

'Just remember Jarvis, nobody likes a smart arse.' They both laughed. Brad continued, 'Yeah you're probably right. Thing is, for the sake of twenty four hours I'd rather wait until tonight and do it properly. What about you? Much happen?'

'No. I had a fairly early night. Alison was in a foul mood this morning though.'

Alison! Brad had been so wrapped up in Patricia that he had almost forgotten the events of the night before last. He still had not spoken to anyone about it. He had considered telling Mikey but he did not want to demotivate him so he had chosen to say nothing until he had spoken to one of the senior reps. Brad changed the subject.

'Actually, I had a few problems myself last night. You know the tallest one of the Plymouth Possee, that group of four lads we shifted from the apartments to the hotel at the weekend?'

'Yeah, is that the ginger one? Peter, isn't it,' replied Mikey.

'Yeah, that's the one. Well he came down this morning with a black eye. Reckons that the hotel owner's son stormed in last night and whacked him for virtually no reason.'

'Do you believe him?' asked Mikey.

'As it happens, I do.' Frank the waiter put a pot of tea on the table in front of Brad. 'Gracias Frank.' Brad poured the tea out of the stainless steel teapot, managing to get half of it over the table. 'Bollocks! I hate these bloody tea pots.' He took a couple of serviettes out of a glass and dabbed at the table before resuming the conversation. 'It's funny, I know that the four of them come across as dick heads but they're alright. Pretty harmless really. I wouldn't say that they were troublemakers, would you?'

'Do you know what they do for a living?' asked Mikey. Brad shook his head. 'Peter and Timmy are both paramedics - ambulancemen.'

'Really? No I didn't know that.' Brad took a sip of his tea. 'I suppose I'd better speak to Alison.'

'Well, now's your chance.'

At that moment Alison walked in. She could scarcely disguise her displeasure at seeing Brad and Mikey together again.

'What are you doing here Brad?'

Brad looked at Mikey and raised his eyebrows as a way of confirming that he also thought that Alison was in a bad mood.

'Two reasons actually Alison. First of all you probably remember that we arranged a football match with that British Rail mob.' Alison nodded vaguely. 'Also, I wanted to talk to you about something that happened in the hotel last night.'

'What was that then?' asked a fairly dis-interested Alison.

'One of my clients got battered by the hotel owners son.'

'Who was it?'

'Peter Turner, the tall ginger lad with the Plymouth Possee.'

'Who?' Alison had not had much contact with the clients.

'The group of four lads from Plymouth.'

'Oh them. They're that bunch of wankers aren't they? No doubt he probably deserved it,' dismissed Alison.

'Actually they're not bad lads when you get to know them,' contradicted Mikey.

'That's right,' agreed Brad. 'Besides, you should see the state of his face. All he did was have the stereo on a bit loud, and I wouldn't say that warranted what was dished out.'

'How do you know? Were you there?'

'No Alison I wasn't but-'

'Well if you weren't there how do you know what happened?'

'Because he told me and I believe him. Well that's my judgement anyway,' replied Brad.

'Yes. Well we all saw how good your 'judgement' was when you came out with all that nonsense at the welcome meeting,' said Alison tartly. 'Look, if you're that concerned do a report. Now if you'll both excuse me I've got important things to be getting on with.' Alison swung on her heels and headed for the lift.

'Slut!' muttered Mikey under his breath.

'Mmmm,' nodded Brad. He badly needed to talk to somebody.

The turn out for the football match was not particularly good, largely a result of it being such a hot day. Apart from Brad, Greg, Mikey and Mario, the only clients willing to play were two of the Plymouth Possee, and Simon, the single share from Bristol. A few 'ringers' were roped in, but the British Rail team still thrashed YF&S six - two. Four of British Rails' goals were scored in the first half when Mario was in goal. By the end of the half the rest of the team were screaming at him for his reluctance to dive on the floor. Brad took over in goal for the second half, and although he had assumed that Mario had not wanted to dive for fear of getting dirty, Brad's own first dive resulted in badly grazing his knee on the hard surface. This made Brad think that maybe Mario wasn't so stupid after all.

The girl reps and a handful of female clients watched the match. Brad was disappointed that Patricia wasn't there. However, she turned up near the beginning of the second half, which unfortunately coincided with Brad letting in his first goal.

After the match, Brad sidled up to Patricia as discreetly as he could and squeezed her hand.

'You're all sweaty,' she said. She looked down at his left leg where a line of blood had trickled down his shin from the graze on his knee. 'And you're bleeding.'

'It's alright Patricia, I'm hard.'

'Not yet you're not.' Patricia lowered her voice. 'But you will be.'

Brad felt a tingling in his loins. He felt randy as hell, having falling asleep with his dick in his hand thinking about Patricia, and awoken in similar fashion.

'You look as though you need a shower,' said Patricia. She looked at Brad with a gaze that made him melt, and started running her fingernails along the inside of his wrist as they

130

were walking along. 'Have you tried the showers in The Bon? They're really good. I'd let you use ours but I'd have to ask the girls. Oh, hang on a minute...' Patricia put her hand to her mouth in mock surprise. 'I've just remembered. They're out for the whole afternoon and probably aren't going to be back until gone six.' She looked at her watch. 'Well that's another four hours. Now what can I do until they get back?'

Brad took off his shirt and tucked it into the front of his shorts in an attempt to conceal his fast growing excitement. Patricia looked over her shoulder to make sure that nobody was watching and slowly pulled the shirt out of Brad's shorts, allowing the back of her knuckles to slowly brush against his cock as she did so. Brad was now rock hard, and it was obvious. He snatched the shirt and put it back in his shorts. Patricia was totally aware of the effect she was having and was enjoying being in control. 'Any ideas Brad? What would you like to do for the next four hours?'

'The way I feel right now,' he said slipping his right hand underneath her mane of red hair and squeezing the back of her neck, 'You'll be lucky to get four minutes out of me.'

They walked off together ahead of the others. Mario saw what was going on. Mikey walked up behind him,

'Still think she fancies you Mario?'

'Who?'

'Who! You know who.'

'What, Patricia? That slag? I could have had her easy. She thinks she's really smart. No man, I'm not interested.'

'Why don't I believe you Mario?'

'You can believe whatever you fucking like man,' snapped Mario, causing Mikey to grin ever more. 'Anyway, I don't know what she see's in him. I mean, I'm better looking than him, I dress smarter, I've got more money and I've probably got a bigger dick. What's he got?'

Mikey patted Mario on the back and shaking his head, sighed, 'A personality Mario, a personality.'

When Brad and Patricia got back to the apartments there was hardly anybody around. They got into the lift and as soon

131

as it started it's ascent they were all over each other. As they got out of the lift and opened Patricia's door which was directly opposite, their mouths barely disengaged. Once inside, Brad started to try and pull Patricia's vest over her shoulders.

'Whoa there,' she said panting. Brad ignored her, his fingers pulling aside her bikini bottoms. He put one finger inside her, slowly, rhythmically exploring her warm flesh. As she became moist, he gently circled her clitoris with his middle finger before plunging first one, then two fingers back inside her. As she started writhing, Brad curled back his two fingers and began pulling them towards him more and more vigorously, at the same time letting his palm brush against the top of her lips and her magic button. After a few minutes Brad felt her contract around his hand, after which she let out a scream as she released a torrent which ran down Brad's arm.

'Jesus, what was that?' she said as she slumped against the wall. Brad put his hands on her hips and kissed her.

'God. What did you just do to me?' Patricia looked down at her leg. 'Oh shit, I'm bleeding.' Brad started laughing. 'What's so funny?'

'You're not bleeding. That's blood from my knee.'

Patricia looked at herself a little more closely.

'So it is. Phew!' She started laughing. Brad joined in and they hugged each other, rocking back and forth as they laughed. 'Come on, let me show you our bathroom.'

They both stepped into the bath. Brad had his back to the shower, and because he was bigger he stopped most of the water going directly into Patricia's face. Patricia looked up at Brad, and without losing his gaze, ran her tongue down his body. When she reached his groin she licked around his thighs and then slid her tongue up the inside of his leg. Every so often her mouth would fill with water from the shower. When this happened Patricia would let it pour out of her mouth and dribble down her chin. Eventually she lightly ran her tongue along the length of Brad's cock, barely touching it as she did so. Then she squeezed his balls and pulled them towards her mouth, flicking them every so often with her tongue. Brad was desperate,

'Please, Patricia - put it in your mouth.'

Patricia engulfed Brad's cock with her mouth, managing to barely touch it as she did so. When it was two thirds of the way in, she closed her lips around it and sucked hard as she pulled away from him. This time it was Brad's turn to let out a loud moan. As she released Brad from her mouth she laid back in the bath supporting herself with one hand. With the other she started probing her own womanhood, all the time staring directly at Brad whilst the shower water dripped off of Brad's cock onto the hand that she was using to indulge herself. Brad looked at his throbbing, plum coloured helmet.

'Don't just look at it Bradley.' Patricia stood up, turned her back to him and bent over, putting one hand between her legs and opened herself up. She looked back at him over her shoulder. 'This is where I want it.'

Brad could hardly believe that a girl he had thought so innocent was talking and being so dirty. He took hold of his cock in his left hand and looked skyward,

'There is a God.' With that he brushed his bell end up and down her lips before ramming himself inside her. They moaned in harmony. After a while Patricia reached back and started squeezing Brad's aching balls. It was too much.

'Oh shit,' said Brad as he pulled out. He stood there for a second or two hoping that he had managed to stop himself. But he felt his balls tighten and sure enough, a string of cum shot up Patricia's back. Although he had come, Brad did not feel as if he had come properly. It was as if somebody had been shaking a bottle and opened it, but only the froth had come out - the rest of the contents were still in the bottle.

'Quick, get out of the bath.'

Patricia got out of the bath and they went into the bedroom. Brad got on top of her, surprised and relieved to find that his erection had not subsided. Not only that, but he also felt more in control and was able to be less frenetic in his lovemaking. The whole thing felt very special to Brad. At one point, Patricia was on top of him, slowly circling and grinding her hips to take

133

him as deeply into her as she could. Her hair tumbled over her shoulders and she gurgled with delight, her tongue slowly sliding between her lips. Behind her, the balcony door was open, and the setting sun made the sky seem as though it were veiled in blood. The diminishing heat touched their ardoured skin, and as she twisted, impaled on top of him, the silhouette of perfect womanhood that she formed made Brad want to go and buy the biggest pedestal he could find. He felt pure emotion, and as he rolled her over, the synchronised rhythm and shuddering, simultaneous climax that followed made Brad realise he had badly under estimated the power of foreign climes.

Brad had not expected to fall in love so early in the season.

CHAPTER FIVE

'Fuck, fuck, shit, shit, shit, shit FUCK! Bitch, whore, Judas slag bag!'

Brad was not a happy man. He picked the phone off the receiver and slammed it back again twice, yelling 'Bollocks' as he did so. It had only been ten days since Patricia had kissed him at the airport and with tears rolling down her eyes, promised that she would come out to see him again within the next two months. There had been one letter, written as soon as she had got back. That was fine. Then there had been a phone call every other day. But for the last four days Brad had sensed that there was something wrong, and sure enough there was. Brad recalled parts of the just finished conversation in his head as best he could.

'The time we had together was special Brad..........You did things to me that no-one has ever done before.........I don't know how I feel......You're so far away .....Things seem so different now.......It's just that he's here and you're there....I know I said I couldn't stand him........He's changed........He really loves me........We can still be friends.'

'We can still be BOLLOCKS!' said Brad out loud, picking up and slamming down the phone one more time for good measure.

He walked back to the hotel from the phone box with his hands thrust into the pockets of his track suit bottoms and his head hung. The brown and white hotel mongrel that Brad normally made a fuss of came running up to him yapping.

'Fuck off.'

The dog ignored him and ran around Brad barking even louder. In the end Brad sat on a wall and tickled the dog behind the ear.

'I don't know. Women, eh?' The dog sat down, tilted his

135

head and wagged his tail. 'You don't know how lucky you are. It's easy for you. All you've got to do is find someone you like, sniff her bits and jump on her back. You don't have to worry about whether or not she's got a boyfriend, do you eh?' The dog barked. 'That's it. You just toddle off until you see someone else you like and do the same again. Who says it's a dog's life?' The dog began to tire of Brad's conversation and started sniffing a nearby tree. 'What a load of bollocks. One minute I'm the best thing since sliced bread and her boyfriend's a stain, next minute I'm last year's model and she's getting him his pipe, slippers and cardboard cut out of Match of the Day. Slag!' Brad clicked his fingers to attract the dog's attention and beckon him over. 'Nah. She's not a slag really. Jesus. I've only been here two weeks or so and it's already bloody obvious that this ain't the real world. What was the phrase I read in that book the other day? "Well peopled solitude?" That's this place for you. I've seen them everywhere already. Sad fucks surrounding themselves with people when all the time they're really just lonely sad old gits. Do you think that's what I'll become? A lonely sad old git.' The dog cocked his leg up the tree. 'Well there's obviously no point in talking to you. I doubt if you've even read Camus.'

Brad got back to The Bon half an hour before the pre-airport meeting. Greg was in reception.

'Alright mate?'

'Is that a pleasantry or are you genuinely interested?' asked Brad.

'Oh fuck me. What's up with you? No, don't tell me, let me guess.' Greg leaned back in his chair and examined Brad. 'Women problems. Only thing it can be.'

'Spot on Einstein.'

'Don't tell me. That redhead you've been going on about for the last week and a 'alf 'as dumped you and gone back with her boyfriend.'

'Hmmm. Go on then. How did you work that one out?'

'Didn't 'ave to. It 'appens all the time.'

'What do you mean?' demanded Brad.

'We'd better get some drinks in.' Greg gestured to Frank. 'Two beers and two carajillo's por favor.' Frank nodded. 'It's obvious if you think about it. Because we work 'ere we get blasé about the place. But to the majority of Brits this place could be the fuckin' moon - it's a million miles away from their real world. That means that you're a million miles away from their real world. Sure, while they're 'ere it seems as if 'love will find a way', but the end of the day they go 'ome, go back to their normal lives and go back to their normal routines. When some of 'em think of what they've done or the people they've turned into on 'oliday it scares the fuckin' shite out of 'em. All they want to do is scurry back to their comfort zones, and if that comfort zone includes an old boyfriend then tough titty.'

'Yeah, but surely it must work out sometimes,' insisted Brad.

'The only time it ever works out-' Frank put the drinks on the table. 'Cheers.'

'Cheers.'

'The only time it ever works out is if you gerra girl over at the end of the season who doesn't live too far away from you back 'ome an' who isn't particularly settled. Either tha', or start seeing someone who works 'ere. I guess there are exceptions but I don't know of many.'

'That's really sad,' said Brad sipping his drink.

'Is it fuck,' said Greg. 'Try telling that to Mikey. Why do you think 'e's on nearly as many points as me?' Greg knocked back his carajillo in one. 'It's like I just said. Girls come away and become somebody else for a week or two, without their family or friends 'ere to judge 'em. There are loads of girls who'd like to sleep with a black guy. Most of 'em wouldn't dare do it back 'ome. But they come 'ere and it's their ideal chance, especially 'cos Mikey's a rep an' 'e's gorra be even more discreet about it than they 'ave. Look at that policewoman from Torquay last week. I guarantee she was a bit racist. Didn't stop 'er though

137

did it? We should've given 'im a bonus point for that one.' Brad smiled. Greg continued, 'On the subject of points, I'm afraid that due to your misplaced loyalty with Patricia or whatever 'er name was, you've slipped down the old league table.'

'Don't worry, I'll catch up.'

'I'm sure you will. Another drink?' asked Greg.

'Yeah, why not,' replied Brad. They were both silent for a moment. Brad started to pick the scab off of his knee which had still not healed properly although almost two weeks had passed since the football match. The top part was all yellow and pussy and only the bottom half had anything worth picking. He seemed absorbed in his task, but as he flicked one of the last remaining pieces on the floor he resumed the conversation with Greg without looking up. 'I've got to say Greg, you've surprised me a bit. I didn't realise you thought about things so deeply.'

'Only certain things. The way I look arr'it is that these years are probably gonna be the most enjoyable of my life and I'm gonna to make the most of 'em. My advice to you is to do the same. Cheers,' he said raising his newly acquired glass.

'Yeah cheers.' Brad took a long swig of his beer. 'Seeing as we're on this male bonding trip there's something I want to ask you.'

'No y'can't sniff me fingers.'

'Don't worry mate, I wouldn't want to the amount of time you spend scratching your balls. No, it's about Alison.'

'Oh y'can't wanna shag 'er surely. That'd be minus ten points straight away.'

'No. It's something quite serious Greg.' Brad looked around to make sure that nobody else was listening. 'Do you think she's taking backhanders?' Greg went very quiet. He stared at his glass. 'It's just that I saw her outside The Star Club,' continued Brad, 'And-'

'STOP.' Greg interrupted him. 'Listen to me. I just told you thar' all I'm concerned with is 'aving a good time. Wha' she gets up to is 'er business as long as it doesn't effect me. Yes, she probably is at it but to be honest I don't give a flying fuck.

I've got ways of supplementing me income and maybe when I get t'know yer better I might tell yer what they are. As far as Alison is concerned I'd keep out of 'er face.'

'The thing is Greg, her whole attitude is effecting the way I do my job.'

'Well you'll just 'ave to ride the punches and go with it. She's the manager and that's tha'.'

At that moment Lorraine walked into the bar.

'Hello darling. You alright?' asked Brad.

'No I'm not.'

'What's up?'

'Nothing and everything.' Lorraine pulled out a chair, ordered a cider and sat at the table. 'It's that cow Alison.'

Brad looked at Greg with a 'now will you listen' type of look. The only response it drew was for Greg to get up from the table.

'I'm going for a dump.'

'What's up with him?' asked Lorraine. Brad shrugged his shoulders and said nothing, allowing Lorraine to continue. 'I don't know Brad. I'm doing the best I can but it never seems good enough for her. She's always on my case. Lorraine do this....get up and dance......stop talking to this person...stop talking to that person....tidy yourself up....learn to put your make up on properly....learn to sing...don't drink so much....talk more clearly on the microphone....your sales are crap...sell more merchandise.....every time I see her she's got something to say, and it's doing my head in. I'm not that useless am I Brad?' Brad looked at her and saw her eyes welling up. He put his arm around her shoulder and she started snivelling. 'I don't know. I just feel like giving up.'

'Come on,' said Brad. 'Don't let it get to you.'

Working so close together and being a bit older, Brad had already began to feel like a big brother to Lorraine. He had noticed that Alison had been giving Lorraine a hard time, and as far as he could see the only reason for doing it was that Lorraine allowed her to. Although Lorraine could be foul mouthed and come across as being sure of herself, Brad knew that she was actually quite timid and sensitive. This was what made her so popular with the other girl clients. She was not and did not try to be glamorous. She was down to earth, always taking the time to talk to clients and to be genuinely interested in what they had to say, unlike ninety per cent of all other reps. She was certainly the total antithesis of Alison, which was probably part of the reason why Alison was none too keen on her.

'I'm sorry Brad,' said Lorraine wiping her eyes. 'Maybe I'm just homesick.'

'Well if it's any consolation Lorraine, I don't think she particularly likes me either.'

'What is her problem? I sometimes wonder how she got the job in the first place.' Lorraine got up to get her cider. As she did so Alison walked in with Mario behind her.

'Where is everyone?' snapped Alison.

'Greg's answering the call of nature. Lorraine's at the bar and unless my eyes deceive me, Heather and Mikey are just coming out of the supermarket.'

Alison lit a cigarette and sat down in the chair that Lorraine had just vacated, whilst Mario pulled up a stool and sat next to her. Greg came back from the toilet at the same time Heather and Mikey walked into the bar. They all swooped for the last remaining chair. Mikey was first there, but he gave it up to Heather and grabbed a couple more from outside. Lorraine joined the group carrying her glass of cider.

'Not drinking again are we Lorraine?' said Alison half serious. She looked her up and down and focused on her sunburnt nose. 'No wonder you've got a red nose, you'll be on the meths next.' Lorraine forced out a smile. 'On the subject of looking like a down and out, I saw you when you left for your airport transfer on Wednesday. When you go to the airport tonight make sure that you iron your shirt.'

'I did iron my shirt on Wednesday,' protested Lorraine.

'Well if you did,' said Alison, 'You either didn't have the iron switched on, or your skin's creased.' Alison looked round the table for an appreciative response to her 'joke'. Mario

140

guffawed. 'Anyway,' she continued, 'Back to the business in hand and tonight's transfers. I can't believe that it's the third Saturday of the season, can you?' All of the reps apart from Mario mumbled 'no'. Mario said 'UNBELIEVABLE' in a loud voice shaking his head. 'Right, before we start, any problems?'

Lorraine whispered to Brad, 'Yeah you, you bitch.'

'What was that Lorraine?' pounced Alison.

'Lorraine just reminded me,' said Brad thinking as quickly as he could, 'That the hotel owners nutty son Rafael decked another one of our client's the night before last.'

'Why did he do that?'

'Same as before. No reason.'

'Don't give me that Brad,' said Alison, 'He wouldn't hit someone without reason unless he was a total psycho.'

'Well there you go. That's your reason. He IS a total psycho.'

'I very much doubt it. The end of the day Brad it's the responsibility of you and Lorraine to keep your clients in order. If you can't do it we'll have to think about moving either one, or both of you.' Alison got a file from out of her briefcase. Lorraine went to say something but Brad shook his head to stop her. Alison flapped open the file on the table. 'Now then. Tonight's transfers.'

The Triumph Herald had proved to be both a blessing and a curse. It had given Brad a status of sorts - the rep with the old convertible - but it had already cost him nearly a hundred pounds in repair bills. Romford Reg was supposed to have come over a week after Brad to sort out any teething problems, but Brad had not yet seen hide nor hair of him. He was therefore more than a little annoyed when, shortly after the meeting with Alison he had bumped into Duffy from The Charleston, who had told him that Reg had been on the island for nearly a week. As soon as he found this out Brad drove around to where Reg was staying at Port des Torrent to remind him of their agreement.

The car started making funny noises just after the roundabout, and by the time it had reached the road which led to the tennis club it was spluttering badly. Brad stopped on the main road outside Hotel Es Puchet, where it stalled and refused to start again. Brad got out and had a cursory look under the bonnet but could see nothing particularly untoward, so he disconnected the battery (he had to do this as it was the only way he had of making the ignition light go off) and started to push it towards a side road. As he was doing so he heard a girl's voice,

'Do you need a hand?'

He looked round. It was Kelly 'The Vision' coming out of the Hotel Es Puchet.

'Oh, hi. Yeah, if you wouldn't mind.' He saw that she was wearing her red uniform. 'Actually, you'd better get in and steer while I push.' Kelly jumped into the car exposing a tanned thigh that Brad could not help leering at. 'Do you like the way I had the car sprayed especially to match your uniform,' he added, noticing the similarity in colour between the two. She smiled at him. Brad tried to push the car in the most dignified way he could and Kelly turned the car down a small dusty side road. She got out of the car, once more exposing her perfectly formed thigh.

'Thanks,' said Brad. 'Are you at the airport tonight?'

'Yeah, you?'

'Providing I get this bloody thing sorted out and back in time. I'm bringing in a Gatwick flight at about one.'

'Good, I'll see you there then.'

'Which way are you going?'

'Well I only live about a hundred yards up there,' said Kelly pointing in the direction of Port des Torrent.

'That's the way I'm going. I'll walk with you if you want.'

They walked up the road together. Kelly did not say very much but she smiled a lot. Brad was a little confused because the way she looked at him and her body language suggested she might be interested in him, but the few attempts he made at making conversation were greeted with more or less a monosyllabic response. They parted company at her apartments and Brad continued his journey to see Romford Reg.

It was late evening, but the heat still meant that the walk made Brad feel uncomfortably sticky. Romford Reg lived in a bungalow at the end of a dirt track which was up a steepish incline, flanked on either side by a long white wall and the ocassional bungalow. By the time Brad got to Reg's he was knackered, and his knee was killing him. He had also formed the opinion that every bungalow he passed must have had a shrieking Spanish woman and yapping dog installed at the same time as its bidet and shutters.

When he knocked on Reg's door there was no answer. He tried again but this time banged a lot harder. Still there was no answer.

'Fucking wanker,' he spat in frustration.

He wanted to leave a note but he did not have a pen or paper. A couple of bungalows away a Spanish looking middle aged man was doing some gardening. Brad walked up to him.

'Excuse me,' he said. The man looked up. Brad started to speak very slowly to make himself understood. 'Do-you-have-a-pen-and-paper-por-favor.'

Brad made an action as if drawing on imaginary paper with an imaginary pen. The man didn't say a word, put down his tools and walked into his bungalow. Brad guessed that he hadn't understood him or didn't like the English, so he started to write a message as best he could in the dirt with a stick. He had just finished the 'g' in Reg, when the man re-emerged from his bungalow.

'There you go lad,' said the man in a Yorkshire accent, handing Brad a pen and paper. 'You looking for Reg?'

'Um, yes.' Brad was surprised that the man was not Spanish.

'You've just missed him. He'll be out for the night now. Any message?'

'Yeah, if you wouldn't mind. Could you tell him that Brad called round and give him this.' Brad quickly scribbled a note telling Reg where the car was and where to find him, and handed it to the man along with the car keys.

'Aye, right. So are you a friend of his then?'

'Well I wouldn't so much say a friend,' said Brad truthfully. 'I bought a car off of him back in the UK.'

'What, not that old Triumph?'

'Yeah, it was actually.'

The man started laughing. 'He tried to sell that to me at the end of last season. Wanted five hundred quid for it. I told him he had to be joking. Ha, ha. Five hundred quid,' he repeated shaking his head. 'Good job he sold it to somebody back in the UK. So how long are you on holiday for?'

'I'm not. I'm working out here as a rep.'

'Oh right,' said the man sounding surprised. 'So how's the car doing? Did it manage to make it to the airport?' He chuckled.

'Um, no. I er, drove it out here. Had a few problems bringing it over though.' Brad briefly wondered what eventually happened to Samuel Zakatek.

'Go on! It's never made it back to the island. Well I'll be.'

'Yeah, well it's here now and it's broken down, and I want that fu-,' Brad hesitated, 'Is Reg a friend of yours?' The man shook his head. 'Good. Well I want that fucking wanker to sort it out for me like he promised he would.'

'So that's what these keys are for then.' The man put them in his pocket. 'Alright. I'll give them to him as soon as I see him.'

Brad thanked the man and started the long walk back. When he got to the main road he changed his mind and caught a taxi so that he would be able to grab a little more sleep before going to the airport.

Brad woke up to find Greg in his bedroom.

'How did you get in here?'

'Your door was open,' said Greg. 'Talking of which, the scores on the doors. Interested?'

144

'Yeah, give me a chance to wake up though eh? What time is it?'

'Five thirty,' said Greg looking at his watch. 'Bloody 'ell. Your knee looks bad.'

'What?' said Brad still half asleep. 'Oh that? Yeah, not too clever is it? What did you say the time was again?'

'Five thirty, p.m.'

'Jeez. That's pretty good. We finished the welcome meeting at what, one this afternoon? Four hours sleep. Not bad, huh?'

'Why? Not been getting much sleep lately?'

'No. Alison keeps giving me dodgy flights. Not only that, but the day before last I was meant to be having a lie in and she came in and woke me up at eight thirty after some T-shirts or something. Still never mind. How did the airport go?'

'Yeah, alright,' replied Greg. 'Some fit fanny.'

'Bet they're not as fit as that Thomson's rep Kelly. I've got to make a play for her before the end of the season,' said Brad lustfully.

'Never mind 'er lad, it's tonight's bar crawl that you wanna be scoring some points on.'

'Oh joy,' said Brad, flopping back in his bed. 'Another bleeding Sunday bar crawl.'

'Don't knock it mate. It's the best place to blag.' Greg pulled out a sheet of A4 paper. 'Right then - the scores to date. In last place we 'ave Mario. Reckons 'e's shagged seven, but 'e's such a bullshitter we'll just disqualify 'im. The props and other workers aren't really in the running, so it's between you me an' Mikey. Mikey 'ad a good week last week. Three shags an' a blow job. He was on eight, so that puts 'im on...' Greg did some quick mental arithmetic, '...Nineteen points. You did diddly squat 'cos you're a soft twat..'

'Fuck off.'

'...So that means you're still on eleven. Or should we give you a bonus point for being DUMPED!' added Greg, yelling the last word at Brad. Brad swung a lazy kick at him, half swearing and half laughing. 'And finally we've got yours truly. I shagged three last week but I slipped it up that Irish girls 'oop,

145

so I'm on a grand total of twenty three.'

'The only thing you're on, you short arsed little git, is a fucking big ego trip. All this points lark is a smokescreen isn't it? It just gives you a reason not to shag a girl more than once 'cos you're probably gash in the sack and none of 'em want second helpings. That's it, eh?'

'Bradley lad,' said Greg grinning, 'If thinking that makes your eleven points easier to bear then you believe that. Even better, why don't you shag that Irish girl I rumped the other night so you can fall in love with 'er? She said she wanted to get back with 'er boyfriend back 'ome.' As Greg finished the sentence he burst out laughing and ran out of the way just as Brad aimed a pillow at him. 'So, what's your new arrivals like?'

'There's a group of half a dozen or so lads from Hammersmith who seem like a good laugh. A bit OTT but definitely away for the crack. Oh, and there was another group of eight seriously pissed blokes from Orpington all wearing Molson Dry T-shirts. Seemed harmless enough.'

'Fanny?'

'Yeah a few bits and pieces. Some girl turned up who reckons she's just had a pacemaker fitted.'

'WHAT!!!'

'Seriously. She reckons that this could be her last holiday,' said Brad shaking his head.

'What's she like?'

'What do you mean - "like",' said Brad knowing exactly what Greg meant.

'You know, points potential.' Brad started laughing. 'What you laughing at? I'm serious. Suppose I manage to get her palpitating. That's gorra be worth a couple of bonus points.'

'You're sick,' said Brad, still laughing. 'Go on, piss off back to your own hotel.'

'Why's that? Do you need to knock one out 'cos you've not 'ad a shag for so long?' said Greg as he opened the door to leave. 'I'll see you in an hour or so.'

'Yeah, see you later,' said Brad.

After Greg left, it crossed Brad's mind that he could indeed do with 'knocking one out'. He started to recall a particularly rude session he had been involved in with his ex-girlfriend, Charlotte. Just over a month before he left for resort she had turned up on his doorstep wearing only a raincoat, stockings and suspenders and knee length boots. Before going out, they had agreed to spend the whole night winding each other up sexually. During the course of the evening they brought each other quite close to climaxing on several occasions and in various locations. When they eventually got back to Brad's house they had virtually raped each other. As Brad recalled the evenings events, he started to think how nice it would be to get Charlotte out to Ibiza to indulge in a Mediterranean repeat performance. The memory had brought Brad quite close to ejaculating, but on the spur of the moment he pulled his shorts up, sorted out some hundred peseta coins and headed for the phone box. As he made his way down the stairs he knew that he shouldn't be ringing Charlotte, but as often happens when the male member fills with blood, the brain empties of logic and reason.

Charlotte's mother answered the phone. Brad heard Charlotte come running down the stairs.

'Hi. Brad?'

'Yeah. How y'doing?'

'Oh not bad. I'm missing you.' Brad winced. 'I knew you'd call.' Brad winced some more and contemplated abandoning the idea of inviting her over. But the memory of a suspender clad Charlotte spread eagled on his dining table was too much for him.

'I was just wondering,' said Brad hesitantly. 'I was just wondering how you'd feel about coming over for a long weekend.'

'Really!!!' replied Charlotte, just a little too excitedly.

'Yeah, well I can probably sort you out a flight through the company.'

'Oh that'd be brilliant. Mum.....'

'Oi, hang on a minute, don't tell your mum yet. I've a bit of organising to do.'

'Sorry. It's just that I'm so excited.'

Brad began to realise that he might have underestimated the strength of Charlotte's feelings.

'Look, my money's running out. I tell you what Charlotte, let me see what I can arrange out here and I'll give you a call as soon as I've got something sorted. Alright?'

'Yeah, brill,' replied a still obviously excited Charlotte. 'Miss you.'

'Yeah, er, miss you too,' mumbled Brad.

Brad went up to his room, took off his shorts and finished off his wank. As soon as the first shot hit his hairy stomach he started to curse himself for making the phone call. He grabbed a dirty T-shirt to wipe away the majority of his sperm, then had a shower before getting his clothes ready for the bar crawl. After a few minutes deliberation he pulled on a pair of track suit bottoms, made sure that he had some more hundred peseta coins and headed for the phone box again. This time Charlotte answered the phone, which was hardly surprising as she had been virtually sitting on it for the last hour.

'Hi Charlotte.'

'Hiya. I managed to get in touch with my boss-'

'Charlotte....' Charlotte was not or would not listen.

'I got in touch with her at home-'

'Charlotte.....'

'And she said that I can have a few days off so I can come for longer if you want.'

'Oh.' Brad sighed. 'Look Charlotte. I don't know how to say this but..'

He paused to try and find the right way of putting it. The truth? Sorry Charlotte, I only wanted to get you out here because I've not had sex for over a week, but now I've finished my wank I've changed my mind. Probably not a good idea. Sugar coated truth? How could he sugar coat that? Oh well, there was only one answer. An outright porkie.....

'I was really looking forward to you coming over but my boss has said that we can't have girlfriends out here. She reckons it would distract us from our job. Do you believe that?

148

I'm really pissed off. Obviously I did my best but - Charlotte? Charlotte, are you still there?'

Brad opened the door of the phone box and stepped out, where the hotel mongrel was waiting for him. 'Well, I know a stiff dick's got no conscience, but I feel like a real bastard now. I guess that's fucked up my Karma again.'

The hotel mongrel displayed his usual disinterest in Brad's ramblings, and ran across the road to introduce himself to an underfed canine which looked like a cross between an Irish Setter and a Dingo. Brad guessed that he was going to have to get himself a more receptive confidante.

When Brad got to The Angler's, Greg was DJ'ing and the bar crawl was already in full swing. After a while it became clear to Brad that The Molson Boys sole mission in life had become to get him as drunk as possible. Although other reps would often let clients buy them drinks Brad always refused. He couldn't see the point - he got all of his drinks for nothing. But The Molson Boys did not give him a chance to refuse, and in truth, Brad only offered token resistance.

The six lads from Hammersmith had tried it on with every girl in the bar within the first half hour, and Brad noticed that they had also had quite a lot of luck with the fruit machine. The constant stream of snakebite's that The Molson Boys had been pouring down his neck and the packed atmosphere had made Brad feel a little light headed, so he went outside for some fresh air, where he was soon joined by a surprisingly pissed Greg, who had just finished his DJ stint.

'Alrigh' lad?'

'Yeah. Bit pissed though,' replied Brad.

'Fuck me, you're not the only one. I'm caned.'

'What have you been drinking?'

'Those bloody La Mumba's,' said Greg, raising his glass to exemplify the point. 'What about you?'

'Snakebites - cider and lager. The Molson Boys have been getting them for me.' They both took a swig from their respective glasses. 'Who's DJ'ing?'

'Mario. Can't believe 'ow good 'e is for someone who's never done it before. Where's that girl with the pacemaker?'

'I'm not sure,' said Brad looking around. 'There she is,' he added spotting her by the DJ stand. 'I feel a bit responsible for her to be honest. She's a single share so she hasn't come away with anybody. I'll leave her to her own devices for a while and try to catch up with her and have a chat later.' He noticed Greg eyeing her up. 'Keep your grubby little hands off you perv. She doesn't want corrupting by you, she's a nice girl.'

'There's no such thing,' said Greg emptying the chocolate contents of his glass.

Brad was about to turn around and go back into the bar when he noticed Robbo, the Kiwi windsurfer and dealer sauntering down the road, virtually oblivious to his surroundings. He was wearing a ripped pair of jeans, flip flops, a brightly coloured waistcoat and about a dozen sets of beads around his neck. Brad interrupted his daydream.

'Robbo, just the man.'

'Uh,' Robbo looked up slightly startled. 'Yo, Rod. What's happening?'

'Brad, not Rod you knob.' He ushered Robbo out of earshot from everyone else. 'I might need to pay you a visit a bit later.'

'Yeah man, no problem. Whaddya need? I've got some wicked doves at the moment.'

'To be honest Robbo, I've not had any of the old fifth letters since I've been here. Not sure how I'd cope being pilled up and having to do this job. I wouldn't mind some Charles but I'm a bit skint at the moment. What about the fast stuff?' asked Brad.

'Speed?' replied Robbo. Brad nodded. 'I've got some more powder turning up tomorrow, but all I've got for now are speed pills called Red Devils.'

'How much are they?'

'Five hundred pesetas to you.' Robbo saw one of Brad's clients walking over. 'Look out.' It was one of The Molson Boys carrying yet another snakebite.

'Hang on a minute Robbo.' Brad turned round.

'Alright Brad,' said The Molson Boy handing him the drink, 'There you go.'

'Cheers,' said Brad, taking the glass.

'Can I have a quick word?' said The Molson Boy.

'Yeah sure. What's up?'

'Oh no, nothing's wrong. I just wondered if you knew where we could score some pills.' Brad started laughing. 'What's so funny?' added The Molson Boy, slightly paranoid.

'It just so happens that the man you need to speak to is standing right here.' He turned back round to face Robbo. 'Meet Robbo. Robbo this is...'

'Kieran,' said The Molson Boy.

'Kieran,' repeated Brad. Robbo and Kieran shook hands. 'Kieran was wondering if you could sort him out.'

'Yeah sure man. What do you need?'

'Depends. What pills have you got?'

'Doves.'

'What are they like?'

'Oh wicked man. Seriously,' added Robbo sincerely, 'They're fucking wicked. Best on the island.'

'How much?' asked Kieran.

'Three mill each.'

'How much is that?' asked Kieran turning to Brad.

'About fifteen quid,' replied Brad.

'Oh come on mate,' said Kieran, 'You must be able to do better than that.'

'How many do you want?' asked Robbo.

Kieran started counting under his breath. After about ten seconds he finished his calculations.

'Twenty, for now.'

'Twenty,' repeated Robbo, his eyes lighting up. 'I'll tell you what. Make it twenty five and you can have them for two mill each.'

'Alright, done,' said Kieran shaking Robbo's hand. 'Give me a minute and I'll go and get the money.' Kieran disappeared back into the bar.

'Nice one Ro- I mean Brad,' said Robbo.

'No problem,' said Brad.

Robbo reached into his trousers and pulled out a bag of pills. He counted out twenty five and put them into a smaller bag. He then took out another one, after which he reached into his pocket and pulled out two red capsules.

'There you go,' he said, giving the three pills to Brad.

'What's this?' asked Brad.

'A dove and two Red Devils,' said Robbo.

'But I don't know if I want them yet,' said Brad. 'I was going to come down The Star Club later and see you then.'

'No worries mate,' said Robbo. 'I don't want anything for them. Put the odd bit of business my way when your clients ask you, and I'll always sort you out.'

'Oh right. Nice one,' said Brad, thrusting the pills deep into his pocket.

Kieran came back with the money.

'There you go mate.' He handed Robbo the money in exchange for the bag of pills.

'Cheers man,' said Robbo. 'Listen. I'll catch you guys later.'

They both waved him off. As he disappeared down the road Kieran turned to Brad and handed him a pill.

'There you go Brad. Cheers.'

'What's this for?'

'For sorting us out.'

'Don't be silly,' said Brad handing the pill back to Kieran. Kieran wouldn't take it.

'No it's yours. From the boys.'

'Well, thanks Kieran.'

'That's alright,' said Kieran smiling. 'Oh, by the way I almost forgot. Lorraine wanted you in the bar. Apparently a group of lads have upset the owner or something.'

At that moment Brad heard the sound of breaking glass. He ran into the bar where he saw the owner Russell, squaring up to one of the Hammersmith crew that the others called Pit Bull. Pit Bull was actually being very calm whereas Russell was prodding him and yelling. Brad had to question the

152

wisdom of this as Russell was middle aged, fat and about five foot seven, whereas Pit Bull was five foot ten with a Tysonesque neck, and in training to be a competing body builder. Pit Bull actually seemed to be finding the whole thing quite amusing, which was having the effect of irritating Russell even more. Brad stepped between them.

'What's up?'

'I dunno,' said Pit Bull dismissively, 'Ask this silly old sod.'

'I'll give you silly old sod you bloody troublemaker. First you clear out my fruit machine...'

'We won fair and square,' said Pit Bull calmly.

'Then you come in here breaking up my bar...'

'What are you on about? Breaking up your bar...?'

'You and your bloody mates,' sprayed Russell.

'Oh get a life,' said Pit Bull, turning away.

'Get a life? Get a life!? It's 'cos of scum like you I left England in the first place.'

'Steady on Russell,' intervened Brad, surprised at the self control that Pit Bull had thus far displayed.

'Steady on? I'll give this lot steady on. I've a good mind to...'

'You've a good mind to what?' Pit Bull was beginning to lose his temper.

'If I was a few years younger...'

'If you was a few years younger you'd still be a fucking idiot.'

'If you think you can come in here and wreck my bar....'

'Wreck your bar?' Pit Bull picked up a bar stool by one leg, 'I'll show you wreck your bar you fucking mug.'

'Hang on a minute mate,' said Brad grabbing the stool. He turned to Russell. 'What's he done exactly?'

'They came in here and didn't let anybody else use the fruit machine,' said Russell.

'Bollocks,' said Pit Bull. 'Nobody else wanted to use it. You're just pissed off 'cos we kept winning.'

This was true. Russell was annoyed that they kept winning. Not only was he annoyed but he was also surprised, because he had rigged the machine so that it never paid out a jackpot.

153

'And then they start to wreck my bar.'

'What have they done exactly?' said Brad, finding it increasingly difficult to mediate.

'Look,' said Russell pointing at the floor. On the floor was a broken mirror and picture frame.

'Is that it?' asked Brad, a little surprised that this was the cause of such a fuss. He moved the stool out of Pit Bull's way. 'So how did it happen?'

'We were just mucking about and I fell against the wall and accidentally knocked them off,' said Pit Bull.

'Accident my arse,' said Russell.

'Alright, alright. Did anybody else see what happened?' enquired Brad looking around the group.

'I did.' A girl in a tight white top with large conical breasts stepped forward.

'The bloke with the crew cut fell against the wall and the mirror and picture fell off. Simple as that.' There was a general mumbling of agreement.

'Oh that's right,' said Russell. 'This slag's probably his girlfriend.'

Brad stepped forward before Pit Bull got to Russell.

'Alright mate, calm down. I'll deal with this.'

Brad looked at Russell shaking his head, but before he had a chance to admonish him, Russell was off again.

'Bloody yobs. That mirror and picture cost a fortune.'

'Fucking liar!!!' yelled one of Pit Bulls mates, a blonde lad called Kempy. 'The mirror was one of those shitty old Jim Bean one's - you probably got it from the brewery for nothing.'

'And what about the picture?' demanded Russell.

'That thing. Look...!' said Kempy picking it up. 'It's just a cheap old Ferrari print.'

'Who asked you to poke your nose in anyway, you cockney bastard,' said Russell. It crossed Brad's mind that maybe Russell had a death wish. 'Someone's going to be made to pay for this.'

'You want paying do you eh? You want fucking paying, you fat CUNT!' Kempy was getting very riled. He put his hand in his pocket, and for one horrible moment Brad thought that he was going to pull out a knife. Instead he pulled out a huge handful of change from his pocket, freshly won from Russell's fruit machine. 'There you go,' he said throwing it at him. 'There should be more than enough there to cover the shit that's just fallen off of your wall. There should even be enough left over for you to buy some breath freshener you smelly bastard.'

Things had gone far enough and Brad realised that any further escalation in the situation would have probably meant a physical confrontation, from which Russell would have undoubtedly not benefited. He therefore decided that although they were not due to leave for another five minutes, a slightly shorter visit would be to everyone's advantage, not least of all Russell's. Apart from anything else, Brad felt that Russell had brought a lot of it on himself. He turned to the DJ stand to get the microphone, but Greg was obviously of the same opinion and had already taken the microphone from Mario.

'Right then, Young Free & Single. If you want to drink up we're going to make our way round to our next port of call, The Cockney Pride.'

As they got outside Heather came up to Brad.

'Well done Brad. That could've got quite nasty - you handled it well.'

'Thanks Heath,' replied Brad. 'Is it just me or is that Russell off his trolley?'

'No, he's definitely not the full shilling. I'm surprised those lads didn't do him.'

'Not as surprised as I was,' sighed Brad. 'They're not bad lads really are they?' Brad caught up with Greg.

'Nice one mate,' said Greg. 'Thought it was going to go off then. Good job those boys are 'alf sensible.'

'Yeah, I'll have a word with them later.'

They were not in The Cockney Pride long before the party mood was resumed. Brad slowed down on the drinking, but for the first time since he had been away he was genuinely enjoying the company of the clients. He was getting loads of female attention; the girl with the conical breasts, the girl with the pacemaker, a girl from Hounslow, a blonde from Stafford, a freckly Scot - all were giving the right signals.

The Molson Boys were proving to be a great crack, and Pit Bull and Co. were like a group of whirling dervishes and spent all of their time surrounded by women, when they were not getting money to pour out of the fruit machine. After Brad spoke to Pit Bull and Kempy, he realised that they were probably not too dissimilar to the kind of friends that he knocked about with in the UK. One of the main reasons that he got on with them was that they were more or less the same age as him, whereas most of the YF&S holidaymakers were normally only about twenty years old. They also shared Brad's enthusiasm for a wind up and for taking the piss. In the Cockney Pride they started tapping people on the shoulder as they walked passed, then totally changing their body position so that the person they had tapped thought it was someone else. Brad started to have a go at it, and although at first he kept getting caught out, after half an hour he was pretty much getting the hang of it and, childish as it was, finding it highly amusing.

Heather and Greg were no longer treating him as a novice; Lorraine and Mikey were beginning to look up to him and ask his advice. Greg had even said that later in the evening he would tell Brad how to make money out of the cruise. Brad looked at his badge and at that moment realised it was more valuable than any gold card. It was getting him instant respect and popularity, women, free entry into everywhere, free drinks - now even free drugs. It all seemed a little too good to be true.

It was.

Alison just missed YF&S leaving The Angler's. She was greeted by Russell's wife, Jean. Jean's leathery skin had not responded particularly well to the Spanish sun. She also insisted on applying the type of make up that teenage models in the sixties favoured. Unfortunately, on a fifty year old face it served to caricature her appearance rather than enhance it. Her strongly coloured red hair often had people guessing as to whether or not it was a wig. She smoked constantly, and if she had no-one to gossip about or nothing to worry about, then she would worry as to why not. She loved to poke her nose into other people's affairs; she would have looked more at home behind a pair of net curtains than a bar.

Alison did not particularly like either Jean or Russell - not many people did. She spent as little time as possible in The Angler's. It was a horrible bar which was normally empty. The only reason she used it was because they paid fifty pesetas a head more than anywhere else. Alison had told head office that it was a great little bar with it's own DJ booth and that although they didn't pay as much as some of the other bars it was perfect for YF&S. This meant that The Angler's provided Alison with a healthy personal weekly income. She therefore did her weekly PR bit and shared a glass of wine with Russell and Jean whenever she went in to pick up her money directly after the bar crawl. As Jean caught sight of Alison walking towards her, she poured her usual and mouthed hello.

'Thanks Jean.' Alison took the drink. 'How are you tonight?'

'Ooh, can't complain. Fitz was late again delivering our ice. I shouldn't really tell you this...' Jean leaned forward and lowered her voice, '....but I've heard that he's having an affair with that Callum's wife. You know, the couple who run the Irish bar around the bay.'

Alison did not know who she meant, but she did not want the conversation to progress any further, so she smiled and changed the subject.

'So where's Russell? Many in tonight?' Alison wanted to get her money and get out.

'I think he's out the back. Hang on.'

Jean walked through a door at the back and yelled for her husband. Alison looked across the bar and forced a smile at the two remaining customers. A minute later, a very flustered Russell came walking into the bar.

'Hello Alison. Do you want a drink?'

'No, I've already got one thanks,' she replied pointing at her half full glass. 'Good night tonight?'

'You must be joking,' said Russell pouring himself a large Jack Daniel's.

'What do you mean?' asked Alison. 'There were nearly a couple of hundred wasn't there?'

'Oh yeah. There were two hundred alright. They wrecked my bloody bar.'

Alison looked around for some obvious signs of damage, but could see none.

'What do you mean, wrecked your bar?'

'I've cleared it all up now haven't I Jean?' Jean nodded her agreement. 'Bloody hooligans. If I hadn't stood up to them I don't know what they would have done, eh Jean?'

'No knowing what they would've done,' repeated Jean lighting another cigarette from her existing one.

'Fat lot of good your bloody reps were.'

'Fat lot of good,' said Jean nodding and folding her arms.

'There was about ten of them, wasn't there Jean?'

'Oh definitely. At least ten.'

'Are you sure they were our clients?' asked Alison. If she had given the question a bit more thought she would not have asked it because other than YF&S The Angler's had probably barely had more than ten clients all season.

'Course I'm sure,' said Russell. 'They were with that big rep.'

'Yeah, that's it. The big one,' added Jean nodding furiously.

'What, Brad?' asked Alison.

'Yeah, that's the one, Brad,' said Russell.

'Brad,' said Jean.

'All him and the others did was to wait until it was all over and then leave early.'

'Left early they did,' added Jean.

'Who made them leave early?' asked Alison, trying to make some sense out of what they were saying.

'I think it was that Brad,' Russell scratched his head.

'Brad!' snapped Alison.

'And I tell you something else Alison. I'm not giving you any money tonight 'cos I've got to pay for the breakages.'

As soon as Alison heard the name Brad she stormed out. Brad had just cost her, her usual brown envelope. As she walked round to The Cockney Pride and began to calm down a little she knew that the chances were, Russell was making a mountain out of a molehill. However, she had been looking for an excuse to pull Brad up and this presented her with the perfect opportunity.

By the time Alison got round to The Cockney Pride, YF&S had just finished taking their weekly group photograph which was to be subsequently sold to the clients. Brad was standing outside the bar when he caught sight of Alison. He went to say hello, but he didn't get a chance.

'STREETER!' yelled Alison in front of all the clients. 'Get over here. NOW!'

Brad walked over to her, a little annoyed at the way she had just embarrassed him.

'What's up?'

'I've just come from The Angler's,' said Alison. 'It's bad enough that your clients wrecked the bar, but how dare you leave before the agreed time. How dare you!'

'Would you rather Russell got his head kicked in?'

'Of course not. Which lads did it, because I'm telling you now, they're on the next flight home?'

'No they're not,' snapped Brad.

'I beg your pardon,' said Alison, unable to believe her ears.

'I said, no they're not,' repeated Brad slowly.

'If you're not careful you'll be on the flight with them.'

At that moment Greg walked up to join them, closely followed by the other reps.

'What's up?' asked Greg.

'Nothing,' said Alison sharply. 'Go back to the bar. That goes for the rest of you too. This is between me and Brad.'

'Is this all about wha' just 'appened in The Angler's?' persisted Greg.

'Yeah,' interjected Brad before Alison had a chance to reply.

'Look, I've already said I'm dealing with it,' said Alison.

'Do you know what 'appened?' asked Greg.

'No she doesn't,' jumped in Brad again. Alison was getting very wound up. 'She wants to send the Hammersmith lot back home.'

'You must be joking,' said Heather, who had spent the last hour growing to like them.

'It wasn't their fault,' added Greg. 'It was that fuckin' idiot Russell - 'e was lucky 'e didn't get a clump. In fact, if it weren't for Brad 'e probably would 'ave.'

'Yeah,' said Heather, 'Brad was brilliant.'

'Well that's as maybe. But you still left early and things were still broken,' insisted Alison.

'Yeah, but the reason we left early was to stop Russell getting killed,' said Greg. 'Anyway it was only five minutes, an' it was only a poxy mirror an' picture frame that got broken.'

'And the boys paid for it,' said Brad.

'Mmmm,' grunted Alison, 'Well I can't claim to be happy about this, but for the time being I'll leave it until after I've spoken to Russell again.' She placed her bag on the floor, then added, 'Right you lot, get back to work, I want to have a quick word alone with Brad.' They all stood there for a moment not moving. 'Go on, off you go,' said an increasingly impatient Alison.

After they had gone she turned to Brad, He was half expecting an apology. He should have known better.

'Right,' said Alison. 'I'm going to go back and sort this all out with Russell. God help you if I find out that there's more to this.' Brad tutted raising his eyes skyward.

'Is that it?'

'No, that's not 'it',' said Alison. 'I was going to speak to you anyway, even before all this happened. I've been watching you closely over the last few weeks and frankly I don't think you are pulling your weight.'

'WHAT!!!' exclaimed Brad, unable to believe his ears.

'This isn't a holiday Brad. Every time I see you you're chatting up some girl or doing your own thing. You were late for desk the other day-'

'Hang on a minute. I'm not taking this. Do you know how much sleep I've had in the last week? Twenty hours. Twenty fucking hours in a week. And do you know why? Because you keep giving me all the poxy flights.'

'Everyone gets the same airport duties,' contradicted Alison.

'That's bullshit and you know it,' said Brad. 'I've only been doing the job a few weeks and already even I know that there are good flights and bad flights. And as for the desk duty, I missed one, and that was only because you changed the rota without telling anyone.' Brad shook his head laughing. 'And what happens the only day I get a chance to lie in? You come knocking on my door at eight thirty. Oh no. Don't you dare say that I'm not pulling my weight.'

'Well, that's my opinion. If I compare you to Mario-'

'Hold on Alison,' interrupted an increasingly impatient Brad. 'You've obviously got some kind of problem with me-'

'I haven't, it's just that-'

'Yes you have. I don't know why, and to be honest I'm getting to the stage where I don't care. I enjoy this job, and I think I'm pretty good at it. I'll listen to constructive criticism, but I'm not going to be your whipping boy.'

Alison was not sure what to say. She could not admit it but she did not want a major confrontation. If she was going to get rid of Brad she was going to have to do it more deviously. She would have to compromise - for now.

'Well I'm sorry if that's how you feel Brad, but I can assure you that I haven't got a problem with you. I think you're very able, but as I've said before, you've got a lot to learn, and it's up to you whether or not you do so. I'm here to help, but I've got a resort to run and believe me, it's not an easy job.' Alison felt that she had said enough, and knew that she was arguing on thin ice. 'Right then, I'm going to see Russell. I'll see you tomorrow.'

Brad walked back to The Cockney Pride, not totally convinced by Alison's 'pep talk'. When he got there Greg was waiting. Greg could tell that Brad was not very happy. He leant over and had a quiet word in Heather's ear. Heather nodded, and Greg came over to Brad.

'Come on mate, we're going for a drink,' said Greg.

'What do you mean? We're in the middle of a bar crawl,' said Brad.

'Fuck the bar crawl lad. It can wait. I've spoken to Heather and there's more than enough reps to look after the clients.'

'What about Alison?'

'Don't worry about 'er. She'll get down 'ere just after we've gone an' she'll be propping up the bar with dear old Trevor until gone midnight. She won't get down The Star until at least one, if at all.'

'What about Peppers?' asked Brad.

'She 'ates it in there. Old wotsisface - the owner?' Brad shook his head unable to remember his name either, 'Anyway, 'e's not there tonight so there's nothing for 'er to pick up an-'

'So you ADMIT she's taking backhanders,' said Brad, swooping on what Greg had said.

'We'll talk about that later, eh lad? Finish your drink an' let's leave all these giddies an' go an' 'ave a proper night out.

'Giddies?'

'Yeah. Tourists. Come on, drink up.'

The first hour was spent having a laugh together and going into bars that they would not normally visit. They ended up in The Charleston. As they walked in, Brad put his finger to his lips to indicate to Duffy that he should say nothing about the money he had given Brad a couple of weeks before. Although Brad had given the money to Stella and although he was getting on well with Greg, he wanted to take no chances. Duffy's partner Jake gave them both a drink and would not accept Brad's offer to pay. After Brad had introduced Greg to them both, Duffy poured out four schnapps.

'Salut,' they said simultaneously before downing the drink in one. Brad and Greg had just started a conversation when Duffy came over.

'Just a quickie Brad,' said Duffy. 'You know the bloke you

bought that car of yours from.'

'What, Reg?'

'Yeah, that's him. Well I thought you might be interested to know that he was in here earlier on, and I heard him mouthing off.'

'About what?'

'About the car. He was talking to some bloke saying how he'd stitched you up, and how if you thought he was going to spend all of the season with his head under the bonnet then you had another think coming.'

'He did, did he?'

'Yeah, just thought that you might be interested.'

'Thanks.' Brad turned to Greg. 'That's all I need.'

'What's up?' asked Greg.

'Oh, just the dick head I bought the Triumph from trying to have me over. My problem,' sighed Brad. They sat and said nothing for a while. Eventually Greg broke the silence.

'Come 'ed then, let's 'ave it.'

'What?'

'You've obviously gorra lot you wanna ger'off your chest.'

'Not really. I'm just having trouble understanding how she got the job. She never stops to think before she opens her mouth. I don't care what she says but she's definitely got a problem with me, and she certainly gives poor old Lorraine a hard time. Mikey hasn't said as much but I know he hates her. She treats him like a performing seal; "Oh go on Mikey do your impressions; show so-and-so how you dance; do that Jamaican talking". The only rep she's got any time for is Mario and he's probably the worst rep on the island.'

'Aye lad, you're right abou' that one,' agreed Greg.

'She knows as much about motivation as Tracy Lords does chastity.'

'Who's Tracy Lords?' asked a baffled Greg.

'Oh, er, some porn star.' Brad returned to the subject before Greg had a chance to question him further. 'I mean look at me. I was on top of the world tonight - really enjoying the job. If you're enthusiastic about repping clients pick up on

163

it and it rubs off. Now look what she's done. That Russell is a total wanker. He's a fucking fruit cake. But does she bother listening to what really happened? No. She engages her mouth before her brain as usual and has a go at me. I feel like telling her to poke the fucking job.' Greg sat there saying nothing. Brad continued. 'I appreciate that you don't want to get involved Greg, but I know that she's on the fiddle. I'm not sure how exactly, but I'm going to find out.'

'What's the point,' said Greg.

'What's the point?' repeated Brad. 'The point is that I don't feel safe, and if she's going to try and get shot of me then I'm going to make sure I've got something on her. I know she's taking money from bars-'

'Of course she's takin' money from bars.'

'What?'

'Of course she's takin' money from bars,' repeated Greg.

'So why doesn't somebody tell head office?' asked a bewildered Brad.

'Because 'ead office already knows.' Brad looked at him aghast. 'Oh come on Brad. You're not telling me you didn't know that the company gets paid by the bars for us taking our clients into 'em.' Brad shook his head. 'Why do you think we go into shit 'oles like The Angler's?'

'I did wonder,' said Brad, still shaking his head.

'It's not just the money. Look around you.' Greg gestured to Capone's and Tropic's, two of the most popular bars in the heart of the West End of San Antonio. 'Why do you think we don't bring our mob to these places?'

'Probably because they wouldn't pay us,' said Brad.

'That's one reason,' conceded Greg.

'But the whole thing sucks. I mean, apart from a few exceptions we take them to the crap bars and march them past all the good ones that they really want to go into. And what about bar nights!? Who on earth wants to come away and spend three or four nights getting pissed in a hotel bar?'

'You're missing the point,' said Greg. 'The reason a lot of them come away with Young Free & Single is to be part o' summit. It's to be part of a group, all doing summit together.' Greg took a swig of his drink before continuing. 'Of course these bigger bars won't pay us for bringin' our clients in - they don't need the business. But by the same token our lot would get lost in here - there'd be no, no..........' Greg struggled to find the word.

'What, corporate identity?' offered Brad.

'No, nearly but not quite. There'd be no......oh what's the fuckin' word I'm lookin' for?'

'Camaraderie? Team spirit?'

'No, but it'll do. Ok, so bars like The Angler's are shit, but when we go in there it becomes a Young Free & Single bar. They feel that they belong; they feel part o' summit. We do the DJ'ing an' wherever we want an' the clients love it.'

'Alright, fair enough,' said Brad, 'But we herd them around like sheep. We make them knock their drinks back as soon as we leave and hassle them if they straggle. It's worse than being at fucking school.'

'Some of 'em still are at school. What you've gorra remember lad is that a lor' of 'em are coming away for the first time-'

'I know that, but-'

'An' because they're on 'oliday,' continued Greg, not allowing Brad to interrupt, 'They don't wanna 'ave to make decisions. They don't wanna 'ave to decide where to go - it's a lot easier if we do it for 'em.'

Brad sipped his drink, thinking through what Greg had said. Brad was not in the least bit pig-headed, and if an argument was put to him that was well presented, logical and made sense, then he would take that opinion on board as his own rather than playing devil's advocate for the sake of proving a point.

'Don't get me wrong Brad. I'm not saying that we always choose the right bars or that we don't spend too many nights in the hotel, just that in principle the philosophy is right.'

Brad sat quiet for a few moments before he spoke.

'Bit of a smart arsed little scouser on the quiet aren't we.'

165

Greg smiled. Just at that moment Duffy brought two bottles of San Miguel over.

'There you go lads.' They both thanked him, and clinked the bottles together.

'Well I tell you what Greg,' said Brad, 'It all makes sense. What I can't understand is why Alison didn't tell me all of this.'

'Yeah,' said Greg, running his fingers through his spiky blonde hair, 'I was wondering that too. It's not as if it's a big secret or anythin'.'

'Maybe she has got something to hide after all,' said Brad.

'Mmmm.' Greg looked as though he was deep in thought. After a minute or so he asked, 'What exactly did you hear 'er say outside The Star that night when you were with that rep, Stella weren't it?'

'Yeah,' said Brad, suddenly preoccupied. 'Hang on a minute.' Brad sat up in his chair clicking his fingers. 'It's just beginning to make sense.'

'What is?'

'That night round the back of The Star,' said Brad getting more and more animated. 'Jimmy the owner said something about it not being a good idea to tell head office that only a quarter of the actual figure had been in-'

'A QUARTER!!!' said Greg incredulously, 'Greedy bitch.'

'So what's she doing? Only declaring part of the amount she should be to head office,' asked Brad.

'Exactly that. But a quarter? Phew,' whistled Greg. 'That's stronging it a bit. I wouldn't mind betting she's lying about 'ow much the bars are paying too. All Resort Managers do it a bit, but it sounds like she's takin' the piss.'

'So how do we get shot of her?' said Brad, in a matter of fact manner.

'WE!!?' yelled Greg. 'Oh no mate, your on your own with this one. I've already told yer that I don't give a toss what she's up to,'

'Even if she's shit at her job-?'

'She could be the Group 4 of Resort Manager's for all I care,' said Greg. 'Like I've already said, I do my own thing and that's it. I'd advise you to do the same.'

'I would do my own thing,' protested Brad, 'And I wouldn't care how much she makes if it wasn't for the fact that her money grabbing is effecting the way she does her job, and even if it doesn't effect you it's effecting me Mikey and Lorraine.' Brad purposefully put his near empty bottle down on the table. 'First thing tomorrow I'm going to ring head office and tell them what's going on.'

'Ha,' said Greg mockingly, 'An' I 'eard you were meant to be intelligent.'

'What's wrong with doing that?' said Brad.

'You've just said she's shit at the job - 'ow d'yer think she gorrit in the first place?'

'I don't follow.'

'Use your loaf, lad.' Brad still looked at him baffled. 'Well put it this way,' continued Greg, 'If you do ring 'ead office, make sure you've got loads of firm evidence and be careful who you talk to.'

'What, you mean......'

'What I mean Brad, is that she's got friends in 'igh places - 'igh enough for 'er to be given the job when she probably didn't deserve it.'

'Who?'

'I don't know for sure and if I did I wouldn't say. Just be careful.'

'Oh come on,' insisted Brad, 'You must have some idea.'

'Look, just fucking leave it. I'm saying zilch.'

An awkward and uncomfortable silence followed. Brad was still trying to take it all in, and Greg was trying to find a way of not causing a rift between himself and Brad, so he eventually broke the gap in conversation.

'I tell you what though, providing you drink up and come down The Star right now I will let you in on summit else.'

'What's that?'

'How to make money on the cruise.'

The dog end was precariously perched upon a broken Izal block. Greg tried to blast it off first, but his aim was not particularly true, which was hardly surprising considering the amount of alcohol he had consumed. Brad was closer to the block and once his bladder allowed, his subsequent torrent dislodged the dog end, after which he chased it down towards the plug hole. Unfortunately, Brad had also consumed far too much alcohol, and as he swung his hips to try and attain sufficient velocity to complete his task he managed to catch the bottom of Greg's white jeans and shoes.

'Oi, watch where you're pissing you clumsy bastard.'

'Sorry mate,' laughed Brad, rocking backwards and forwards as he spoke. He noticed that when Greg did his flies up, he mumbled 'Bollocks' and then pulled his jeans up as high as he could. 'What you doing?' he asked, puzzled by Greg's actions.

'I didn't shake it properly and I've dribbled so there's a stain on me jeans.' Greg stumbled slightly as he made his way over to look at himself in the mirror above the wash basin. 'Fuck me, I'm pissed.'

'But why are you pulling your trousers up around your chest?'

'So that the stain's lower down me leg when I pull 'em back down again. Make's me dick seem bigger.'

Brad shook his head. 'Greg, you really are a sad fuck.'

They rolled back into The Star Club where the rest of YF&S had just arrived. Heather was at the front of the group. She took one look at Brad and Greg with their arms wrapped around each other and started laughing.

'Had one too many have we boys?'

They both stopped and looked up at her trying to focus.

'The lovely Heather,' said Brad, burping as he spoke.

'Alright 'eath?' said Greg.

'Is that cow Alison with you?' asked Brad forgetting himself for the moment.

'No, she's having an early night,' replied Heather ignoring

168

Brad's alcohol induced comment. Brad punched the air. 'Looking at the state of you two you'd better make yourselves scarce. Bar five wouldn't be a bad idea.'

As they made their way through the club Brad bumped into the girl with the conical breasts.

'Sorry,' slurred Brad, before realising who it was. 'Oh, it's you. How the devil are you?'

'Not as pissed as you,' she replied.

'Ah,' said Brad pulling himself upright. 'I may be pissed, but in the morning I will be sober. Whereas you madam,' he looked at her chest, 'Will still have absolutely massive tits. If I thought that there was the-' Greg pulled him away. As he went Brad added, 'What's your name?'

'Veronica.'

'Well Veronica I owe you one for helping out in The Angler's.' By now Brad was at least six feet away. 'And if I catch up with you later I'll give you one. Weh-hey!'

Veronica gave Brad an embarrassed smile then carried on dancing with her friend.

Brad and Greg positioned themselves on two bar stools in the corner of bar five. On the walk down to the club, Greg had started to tell Brad how to fiddle money on the cruise. Brad was keen to resume the conversation.

'So before you get too pissed, go over the cruise thing again. I still don't get the accounting bit.'

'It's easy. If anyone turns up in the morning who 'asn't already booked the cruise, then you take their money an' just keep it.'

'But surely those people will show up on the figures as extras,' said Brad, finding it difficult to unravel things in his current state.

'Yeah, but only if everyone turns up.'

'Huh?' Brad was still confused.

'Just say for example that in the morning you've got three people who turn up wanting to come on the cruise who didn't book it earlier.' Greg looked at Brad for acknowledgement. Brad nodded. 'Ok. So now let's say that three people don't turn up who 'ad booked it. Bingo. The figures balance an' you pocket the money.'

'Yeah, but why would someone pay for an excursion and then not bother turning up?'

'Think about the welcome meetings. What do we say during the sales pitch? We tell 'em that by booking a two week block they're basically gerrin' three trips for nothing. They'll always miss one or two, so that's when you do it.'

'What, so it doesn't have to be the cruise then - it could be any excursion?' asked Brad, slowly grasping the concept.

'Course it can. But the cruise is the best.'

'Why's that?'

'Mainly because it starts so early in the morning. Plus you can help things along a little,' added Greg with a twinkle in his eye.

'What do you mean?'

'If we weren't so pissed tonight, then this bar crawl is the perfect opportunity. All you do is go round some of the clients who've booked the block an' try and get 'em as pissed as possible. As you're doing that you tell 'em that the cruise is a crock of shit an' not worth getting up for. Chances are in the morning they'll have such a hangover they won't wanna get up anyway.'

'Looks like we'll know how they feel tomorrow then.'

'Oh don't remind me,' said Greg burping loudly. 'Where was I? Oh yeah. So the other thing you do is go round all of those who ain't booked the cruise an' tell 'em 'ow good it is, an' if they're only gonna book one excursion it should be that one. Then in the morning you make a point of knocking on the doors of those who you think will come along, an' leave the one's you put off of the idea the night before. Another little thing I do is bung Frank a bit of wonga to put the clock forward in reception so that we can leave early. That's it really.'

'Brilliant,' said Brad. 'I can't wait to get stuck into doing that.'

'You've changed your tune lad,' said Greg. 'A couple of hours ago you were all for grassing up Alison for fiddling, now you're thinking of doing the same.'

'There's no comparison and you know it,' protested Brad. 'What she's doing effects the way the resort is run, her attitude to us, and the client's enjoyment. All we're doing is going a small way to supplementing our meagre income.'

Greg mumbled his agreement and ordered another two drinks, signing for them once they were brought over. Greg looked around the club. As he did so he caught sight of Romford Reg, who until then he had temporarily forgotten about and had not actually seen since leaving the UK. Brad walked up behind him and tapped him on the shoulder. Reg looked shocked when he saw Brad.

'The illusive Romford Reg,' said Brad sarcastically.

'What do you mean, illusive?' said Reg defensively.

'You were due over here two weeks ago. The car's fucked and we had an arrangement. You know I paid over the odds for that car, and I swallowed it because I didn't have a choice. But you were supposed to look after it for me during the season.'

'I didn't say the whole season,' said Reg.

'Look, I'm not gonna stand here arguing with you...'

'Neither am I,' interrupted Reg, wanting to make himself look a little more credible in front of the two friends that he was standing with. 'I sold that car fair and square. I'll sort it out this time but that's it.' Brad glared at him. 'Just get the fucking thing fixed,' said Brad aggressively. Before walking away he added, 'And do yourself a big favour and don't take me for a mug.'

When Brad got back to bar five, Greg was still sitting on the bar stool but with his eyes closed.

'Greg, wake up.' Brad shook him. Greg stirred slightly. 'I'm leaving. Are you coming?'

'No, I'll stay another 'alf 'our.' Greg was only just able to get the words out.

When Brad got to the hotel he ordered himself a coffee and also bought a litre bottle of water in an attempt to fend off the inevitable hangover. He had been sitting there for five minutes when Veronica and her friend came in. Brad called Veronica over. Her unimpressed friend marched upstairs making a point of saying 'see you in a couple of minutes' in a very loud voice.

'Do you want a coffee?' asked Brad.

'No thanks.'

'Look, I'm sorry about that comment earlier on.'

'That's alright,' she replied. 'I get comments about them all the time. At least yours was nearly funny.'

'What's up with your friend? I get the impression she doesn't like me very much,' said Brad.

Although he was pissed, he was instinctively already beginning to steer the conversation. He knew that if he was going to get Veronica upstairs he would have to keep things brief, mainly due to the fact that he could feel he was having trouble talking.

'Oh she's alright. She just gets a bit moody sometimes.'

'Yeah, that often happens,' said Brad slyly. 'You get one friend who gets all the male attention, and the other one doesn't like it.'

'What me! Male attention! You must be joking.'

'Oh come off it. Blokes have been coming up to you all night. I've been watching,' lied Brad.

'They were just silly little boys,' said Veronica blushing slightly.

'You make it seem as though you're ancient. How old are you?'

'Twenty one,' she replied.

'Twenty one,' repeated Brad sarcastically. 'My, my. That's really old.'

'I just can't be bothered with kids,' she said.

'Kids? So what you're saying is you prefer older men,' said Brad grinning.

'Yeah definitely.'

'How old is old?'

'I dunno really.'

'Is twenty six too young?' asked Brad looking her in the eye.

'No that's about right. Why how old are you?'

'Funnily enough twenty six,' said Brad leaning back in his chair.

'You're not. I thought you were younger than that.'

'Well I tell you what. I've got my passport upstairs. You can come up and have a look at it if you like. Then you'll know I'm not lying.'

'Uh, I don't know,' said Veronica hesitantly. 'I don't want you getting the wrong idea.'

'Look. I'm enjoying talking to you and I'd like to carry on the conversation, but if we stay down here and someone tells my boss that I've been spending loads of time with one client then I could get into serious trouble. I've got some Southern Comfort upstairs so we'll just have a night-cap and take it from there.'

Veronica followed Brad upstairs. Once they got to his room he poured her a drink and they made polite conversation for a few minutes before they started kissing. Brad undid her bra, releasing the two mounds of flesh which had been struggling to escape all night. He rolled on top of her and as she spread her legs wide open, Brad started rubbing himself against her while he buried his head in her chest. Things were going well, so he put his hand down her panties, and got himself ready to enter her. At that moment Veronica jumped up and pushed Brad off.

'No, stop it. I knew you'd get the wrong idea.'

'Well I must admit, having your tit in my mouth while you had your legs wide open maybe did give me slightly the wrong impression, yes.'

'I'm not like that. I never sleep with anyone on the first night.'

'Well can't we just pretend that we've already been out?' asked Brad lamely.

'No. I'm not saying that I don't want to - just not tonight.'

'Are you going on the cruise tomorrow?' he asked.

'Yes. That's another reason why I want to go back. I'll never get up in time otherwise.' Veronica straightened her clothes and did up her bra.

'I'll see you tomorrow,' she said.

'Yeah, see you tomorrow,' replied a defeated Brad.

Brad was feeling as randy as hell so he lurched back downstairs to see if there were anymore stragglers. He ordered himself another coffee and sat down. He was almost asleep when the girl from Hounslow came in on her own.

'Hello,' said Brad, 'Where are your friends?'

'Fu'in bitches lef' me.' She was very drunk.

'Come upstairs. I'll look after you,' he said in desperation.

To his surprise she followed him upstairs. Without saying barely a word they both get undressed. The next thing Brad remembered was hearing a door slam. He awoke with a start, and stumbled towards the door where he saw the Hounslow girl disappearing down the corridor.

'Oi. Where are you going.'

'Y'fell 'sleep with y'tongue out,' she slurred.

'Sorry, come back.'

Wobbling, she made her way back to his room and got undressed again. Within a couple of minutes he was on top of her, and a couple of minutes after that he came in her mouth without warning. She ran out to the bathroom and spat it out. When she came back in she glared at him.

'You bastard.'

'What? You only had to say.'

'You di'n give me a chance.'

'Sorry.'

'You don' even know m'name.'

'Yes I do,' protested Brad.

'Wha'issit then?

'I'll tell you in the morning.'

With that Brad fell asleep, smiling in the knowledge that another three points were in the bag.

'Oh God,' moaned Brad. 'I knew it would be a rough crossing.'

Greg said nothing. He just leant over the back of the boat

staring at the sea.

'Do you want some sangria?' asked Mario walking round with a pouron full of red liquid.

With that, Greg turned his head and threw up over the side, the sight of which caused Brad to follow suit seconds later. When they had finished the two of them looked at each other, faces crimson and eyes streaming, and started to laugh.

'Fuckin' hell lad. We sank some ale last night.'

'You're not wrong Greg. I forgot what a hangover was like. Give me class A drugs anytime.'

They went back to the front of the boat where the small flat island of Espalmador was growing larger.

'So you got three points last night, did yer?' Greg asked Brad.

'Yeah. I tried with that girl over there,' he said pointing towards Veronica. 'But she wouldn't have it - mind you I've got a bit of a plan for later. Anyway, I went back down to reception, and that girl from Hounslow came in totally pissed.'

'What was 'er name?'

'Dunno,' said Brad. 'I never asked her.' They both chuckled. 'I chanced my arm and blatantly propositioned her and she didn't say no, so...'

'Is she 'ere today?'

'No,' replied Brad. 'That's what makes it even better. She booked a block and didn't turn up, so I got someone else to take her place. Brilliant eh? Not only did I get three points out of her but I also made best part of twenty quid.'

'That's it Bradley lad - you're learning.'

Espalmador is small enough to completely walk around within an hour, and is predominantly made up of sand dunes with sporadic clumps of coarse grass. It is almost totally flat and offers little protection from the sun, although the shallow bay is perfect for sprinting in to cool off. There are nearly always a number of yachts moored within swimming distance of the beach, gently bobbing and loosely pulling against their anchors. The island also contains a mud bath, which is basically a pool of sewage that a previous Resort Manager for

YF&S thought would be fun for clients to cover themselves in and then to take pictures ('Oh look mum, this is me covered in a load of shit.'). Brad and Mikey did not share the opinion that this was a 'fun' way to spend an afternoon, so they stayed with half of the clients while Mario, Heather, Greg and Lorraine shepherded the other half to the mud bath.

The early light cloud gave way to a sultry sun, which seemed even hotter to the bathers as it reflected off of the white-ish sand which blanketed the flat, shelterless island. The only respite from the heat was to run down the gentle slope into the sea, scattering the shoals of small fish that were waiting for the scraps which would soon be thrown from the moored boats as the visitors had their lunch.

Apart from YF&S, there were another two largish boats that had moored on Espalmador, one carrying Italian families, the other German families. Mikey had brought his American football with him, and after a while he got a few clients together and started to throw the ball around. Because it was such a hot day, this was the only real activity taking place on the beach, so most eyes were on them. There is a certain knack to throwing an American football correctly, and apart from Mikey, only an Asian lad called Rashid, who was one of The Molson Boys, came anywhere close to achieving this. As those in the group tired of unsuccessfully trying to make the ball spin through the air, it whittled down to just Mikey and Rashid. Mikey wanted a little more variety, and as he had shown Brad how to throw the ball during the first few weeks of the season he decided to get him involved.

'Brad. Get up off your backside and catch this,' yelled Mikey throwing the ball at him.

Brad jumped up and caught the ball on the half volley. He positioned his fingers towards the back of the ball, with the first joints over the laces as Mikey had shown him.

'Ready?' he shouted to Mikey.

'When you are.'

'Well go on then, move back a bit.' Brad was preparing a monster pass.

'Far enough?' said Mikey at the top of his voice.

Brad skipped a couple of paces forward, pulled his arm back and launched the ball. As soon as it left his hand he knew that it was a bad throw. He started to hop on one foot willing the ball to change direction in the same way that a cricketer does when he knows he is about to be caught out, or a tennis player when they are trying to make the ball stay in. His hopping became more frantic as he saw where the ball was heading. An adorable looking child of about three, naked apart from a white sun hat that barely covered cascading golden curls, was innocently and happily running towards it's parents, oblivious to the projectile that was descending from the clear blue Mediterranean sky.

'Look out,' yelled Brad in a strangled voice, turning away in the hope that contact would be avoided.

His sense of hearing was all that was required to know the outcome. There was a loud THUD! followed by the whole beach collectively going OOOHHHH, closely succeeded by the howling of a small child who's first experience of American football had not been altogether painless. Brad looked up and saw a crowd of people running towards the prostrate infant. His first thought was to run in the opposite direction, but his conscience got the better of him so he ran over to see if there was anything he could do and to face the music. The father was a very overweight six foot plus blonde man in his mid-thirties. He came running at Brad swearing in German. Mikey intercepted him and managed to calm him down, showing him that the child was perfectly alright, much to everyone's surprise. Brad mumbled his apologies and slid off to the other end of the beach, convinced that he was at that moment, probably the most unpopular man on Espalmador.

His self imposed solitary confinement was broken by Veronica walking over to him. Brad had seen her coming but had continued to pretend he was asleep, so that he could perve at her topless form as her magnificent breasts appeared to defy all the principles of modern physics. She spread her towel out and sat down next to him, and Brad groaned as if he

177

had just been awoken from a deep sleep.

'What time is it?' he asked rubbing his eyes.

'I don't know.' She rolled on to her front, much to Brad's disappointment. 'I heard about your bit of baby bashing.'

'Don't. I feel really bad about it. I'm scared to go back down there.'

'I wouldn't worry. Most of our lot thought it was hilarious.'

'Even so, I don't think I'll bother for a while.' Brad suddenly realised that events had given him the perfect opportunity to put his plan for getting off with Veronica into action. 'I'm going to get a pedaloe out. Fancy coming along for the ride?'

They made their way down to the pedaloes which were just out of sight of most of the YF&S sunbathers. Once they were about a hundred metres out to sea Brad pulled out a bottle of suntan oil.

'We'll have to be careful out here Veronica. The sun reflects off the sea so we'll burn easily. Here, I've got some factor eight oil. I'll rub it in for you.' Veronica turned her back and Brad started massaging in the oil. 'Now the front.' She turned round and Brad poured the oil over her reddening breasts. As he began rubbing it in he could feel himself getting hard. He moved down to the inside of her thighs and then tried to slip one finger inside her. Veronica groaned slightly, but the angle he was sitting was such that he could not move his hand in the way that he wanted. He stopped and handed the bottle to Veronica. 'Your turn.' Veronica took the bottle and poured liberal amounts all over Brad's chest and legs. She spent barely a minute rubbing it into his chest before working her way down to his tummy and legs. Brad was straining to be released from his swimming trunks, and Veronica quickly obliged. The suntan oil enhanced the sensation as she ran her hand up and down his length. Brad asked her to stop, partly because he thought he was going to come and partly because a yacht was approaching with a deck full of people. 'Come on, let's head for that deserted bit of beach over there.'

At the back of the beach was a crudely constructed stone wall. What little clothing they both had on was soon discarded.

Veronica was sitting on the wall with her arms around Brad's neck as he stood in between her legs. The outside of his hips slid against her oily inner thighs. She reached down and grabbed him, deftly slipping on a condom.

'Where did that come from?' asked a slightly surprised Brad.

'You men think we're so stupid. Don't think this was all your idea Brad. Like I said, not on the first night. But it's not the first night now, is it?' Brad shook his head. Veronica grabbed hold of his manhood so hard that he almost winced. Her face almost turned into a scowl as she said, 'So come on then - fuck me.'

After the initial shock Brad grabbed her hair and pulled her head back sharply, sensing that she wanted some aggressive role play. He started biting her neck and then quite roughly put a hand on her right breast. Brad completely withdrew and started teasing her, each time ramming himself in as hard as he could, waiting until she was almost crying with frustration. On the fifth thrust she let out a blood curdling scream. Brad pulled out again, holding her tightly and kissing her as she writhed frantically. She carried on screaming and Brad rammed himself into her again. The screaming got louder and Brad thought to himself that this was some performance, although he couldn't exactly put his finger on what he was doing right. He began quickening his thrusts and Veronica scratched and wriggled almost as though she were trying to get free. Brad had been kissing her all of this time, so he stopped and rather optimistically said, 'What's up, am I too big for you?' This was the first opportunity that Veronica had of speaking.

'No, get off, get off you pillock! There's a lizard running up my leg.'

With that she pushed herself away from Brad, and in so doing fell backwards over the wall with her legs splayed in the air. A startled gekko disembarked and scurried into a hole under the wall. Brad started laughing but he was extremely close to coming, so while she was on the floor Brad leapt onto

179

the wall, threw off the condom and finished himself off showering her with his hot semen, laughing maniacally as he did so. When she regained her composure she ran her fingers over her sperm covered breasts and realised what Brad had done. He looked at her slightly sheepishly expecting an earful. Part of the reason for doing it had been out of devilment - a good story for later raconteuring. He was therefore slightly surprised when, instead of calling him a bastard as he had expected, she just laid there and looked at him.

'Come on then. You've had yours. Where's mine?'

'What do you mean?'

'If you think you're going to walk away without making me come then you've got another think coming.'

'Sorry darling. I'm a one shot wonder. You're not going to get any life out of this for a while,' he said flicking his shrinking dick from side to side.

'Well, you'd better use something else then.'

Brad picked up his T-shirt from the other side of the wall, placed it underneath her and started to drip suntan oil up her legs. He moved his middle finger around the outside of her clit, and then ran his other fingers up and down her lips before plunging the middle finger inside her. As he slowly moved his fingers in and out of her, he flicked her clit with his tongue. The first time she came surprisingly quickly, but she grabbed hold of his hair and wouldn't let him stop until her body had shuddered another two times.

'Bloody hell,' said Brad, 'We're going to have some filthy sex this week.' Veronica smiled at him nodding, still breathless and unable to speak. 'Come on. Let's get ourselves cleaned up.'

Brad helped her to her feet and kissed her. They both put on their bathing costumes and ran into the sea, then gathered their things and got on the pedaloe. On the way back they passed close to the beach where YF&S were gathered. Veronica was sitting on the side of the pedaloe which was closest to the beach, so she did not see Brad raise three fingers behind her head as he caught sight of Greg and Mikey. Seventeen points. He was catching up.

180

CHAPTER SIX

Mario was wound up. He was getting on well with Alison; Greg didn't seem too bad; Lorraine and Heather probably fancied him. It was Brad and that black bastard Mikey who were annoying him. He had shagged seven girls, and he was sure it was because of Brad and Mikey's shit stirring that he had been banned from The Competition. They were always trying to take the piss out of him. They thought that they were so funny but Mario never understood their humour. He wasn't too bothered about them because he had made his own friends, well, more like his brothers friends from back home. There were two bouncers and a couple of scallies, all Anglo-Italian, who he had started to hang around with when he was not working. It was one of the bouncers that he had bought the stolen video camera from.

He had already filmed the last three of his conquests, none of whom had any idea that there was a hidden camera in the room. Over the course of the first couple of weeks of the season his restaurant owning father had wired him enough money to buy not only a knocked off video camera, but also a similarly sourced portable TV and video recorder. It was his intention to get Greg, Brad and Mikey round to his apartment to watch a video of him in action so that they would no longer be able to ban him from the competition. He knew, of course, that the real reason they had banned him was because he was better looking than all of them and they knew that they didn't stand a chance.

Mario made the five minute walk to The Las Huertas, but the bar night had finished and Brad was nowhere to be seen. When he got to The Bon Mikey had gone into town and Greg was at the bar talking to a girl with short dark hair that he had spent most of the cruise with and most of the bar night trying to persuade to come up to his room. Mario nodded at Greg mouthing 'got a minute'. Greg held up five fingers to indicate that he wanted another five minutes, so Mario went and sat with a group of three lads, where the conversation quickly got round to sex, and in particular the girl reps. They all agreed that they would 'give one' to Alison and Heather, but then they started discussing Lorraine.

'Wouldn't shag her with yours,' said one of the lads, called Lester.

'Nah man, she's a pig,' agreed another, called Ryan.

'I'd have to be really pissed,' said the third, called Paul. 'You'd have to give me at least fifty quid.'

'Me too,' agreed Ryan again.

'I'd do her for fifty,' said Lester

'You should get Mario to knob her,' said Paul, 'I've seen him in action. He could pull anything.'

'Is that right Mario? Are you a bit of a stud with the ladies?' asked Lester.

'Yeah man. I reckon I can pull just about anything,' said Mario without any hint of modesty.

'Go on then,' taunted Ryan.

'Go on then, what?' asked Mario.

'Go on then - pull Lorraine.'

'No I couldn't-' Mario was interrupted by Paul.

'Yeah come on superstud. We'll make it a hundred quid. A hundred quid to shag Lorraine.'

'What,' said Mario, 'You mean to say you'll give me a hundred quid just to shag her?'

'Yep.' said Lester.

'What about if I don't?' asked Mario. 'What's the bet?'

'If you don't you'll have to keep us in drinks all night at one of the excursions next week,' said Paul. 'We'll need some proof though.'

Mario grinned. 'Will a video do?'

When Greg walked into Mario's room he was surprised how tidy it was and how many home comforts he had. He was still wondering why Mario had insisted on dragging him away from the bar - something really important he had said.

'Right. Sit down.'

Greg sat on the bed and watched as Mario switched on the television and put on a video.

'If you've dragged me down 'ere just to watch a porno when I 'ad the real thing waiting for me, I'll not be an 'appy man.'

'Just wait,' said Mario. 'You won't be disappointed.'

'I bet you say that to all the girls you bring back 'ere - assuming you ever 'ave that is.'

Mario looked at Greg and smiled confidently.

'Just watch the video. You can save your apologies until later.'

Mario pressed the play button. There was no remote control; the retired couple had come back earlier than expected so the Italian bouncers had to leg it out of the back door of the villa without getting a chance to grab it.

As the screen flickered into life, Greg let out a sigh of disappointment as a not particularly good looking porn star who he half recognised laid on a bed with her legs slightly apart. He was on the point of getting up to go back to the girl with the short dark hair back at the Bon, when to his astonishment, a naked Mario walked onto the screen.

'That's you!' was all he could say. Mario just grinned. 'And that. That's not a porn star. That's old, er, thingybob, that girl...the one that was 'ere last week.....'

'Theresa,' said Mario smugly.

'Yeah, Theresa,' said a still slightly shocked Greg. Mario bent down and fast forwarded the video to his next conquest.

'And that's Ruth,' said Mario stopping the video briefly when the night time action in his hotel room changed to daylight on the screen. 'You'll probably recognise the next one.' On to the screen came the girl with short dark hair that Greg had spent best part of the day trying to pull. 'Letitia, I think her name is,' said Mario, rubbing it in as Greg groaned.

He allowed the video to continue playing. 'I only got the camera last week so I didn't record the first four.' Greg wasn't really listening, he was engrossed in what was happening on screen, his opinion of Mario reluctantly going up every time Mario did.

'Good show Mario lad. Good show.'

'Thanks,' said Mario beaming. 'So. Are you going to stop listening to those two wankers and put me back in The Competition?'

'Mario me old mate, if it means that much to you, you're back in.' Mario punched the air. 'I'll even give you a bonus point for filming it. How many d'you say you've bonked?'

'Seven,' said Mario.

'Seven times three, that's twenty one, plus one for the filming puts you onto a grand total of twenty two.'

'Am I in the lead then?' asked a freshly enthused Mario.

'No. I'm on twenty three - probably twenty six after tonight. Mikey's on nineteen-'

'WHAT!!!' excaimed Mario. 'He can't be. He must be lying.'

'Don't think so,' said Greg. 'Anyway. He's on nineteen and Brad's on seventeen.'

'So I'm in second place?' Greg nodded. 'Yes!' said Mario punching the air again.

'Right. Well unless you've gorra wench 'iding in the wardrobe for me, I'm off.'

'Alright mate,' said Mario feeling like one of 'the lads'.

After Greg left, Mario laid on his bed feeling very pleased with himself. He had achieved his first goal of getting back into the competition. Now he was going to concentrate on his next goal - to earn that hundred quid.

Greg walked into the Las Huertas where Brad was talking to a sunburnt blonde girl. Greg beckoned him over, whereupon Brad excused himself and crossed the bar to where Greg was standing.

184

'Alright mate,' said Brad, 'Fuck me, am I on a roll.'

'I thought you were going to see that Veronica again tonight. Brilliant sex and all that.'

'I am,' replied Brad, 'But she's had to go out with her miserable mate so she's going to come up to my room when she gets back.'

'What time's that then?'

'She reckons about three. The thing is,' said Brad nodding over towards the blonde girl, 'I started making improper suggestions to that one over there during the bar night and she seems well game.'

'Well, you need the points if you're gonna catch up with Mario.'

'What do you mean?'

'He's back in The Competition.'

'How come?' asked Brad. 'I thought you said he was bullshitting.'

'Yeah, I thought 'e was. But our Mario's gor'imself a video camera and it seems 'e fancies himself as a bit of a porn star.'

'What, have you seen it?'

'That's where I've just come from. And I've got some more bad news.'

'What's that?'

'He's 'ung like a fucking donkey.'

'Oh please tell me you're joking,' groaned Brad.

'Nope. Wish I was. I reckon it's gorra be 'eading for a niner.'

'What, nine inches?'

'Maybe a bit more. And 'e's got a massive bell end.'

'Is there no justice? As if he isn't conceited enough,' sighed Brad shaking his head. 'Oh well. I suppose he was at the back of the line when brains and personality were dished out so he had to make up for it somewhere. It's just a shame he's been over compensated in the tadger department. God could have just made him good at badminton or something instead.' Brad sat on the edge of a table, smiled re-assuringly at the blonde girl and folded his arms. 'So how many points is he on?'

'Twenty two. Seven shags and a bonus point for filming.

You're in last place so you'd better get your finger out, or should that be in?'

'Yeah I intend to. What's the time?'

'Quarter to one,' said Greg looking at his YF&S watch.

'Shit, that only gives me a couple of hours before Veronica gets back. I'd better get a move on. You out anywhere later?'

'Well I've been blagging that girl with short dark 'air all day. She's meant to be waiting for me back at The Bon, but after whar' I've just seen I'm not sure if I'll bother.' Brad looked at him quizzically. Greg explained, 'I've just seen her in action. Letitia's her name - cellulite on celluloid, co-starring Mario. I'm not sure I wanna stir 'is porridge 'cos if she can manage that thing of his without yelping then mine'll be like a dick in a bucket.' Brad laughed. 'Mind you,' continued Greg, 'Mario didn't stick it up the rusty bullet 'ole, so I should be alright there - extra points as well.'

The hand dryer in the men's toilets didn't swivel upwards which meant that Mario was unable to blow dry his hair. He punched it then looked at himself in the mirror, smoothing his damp hair back with the palms of his hands, turning a few degrees to the right as he did so. Mario always felt that this particular angle offered the best profile. He straightened the badge on his blue denim shirt and drew his gun on his own reflection, trying a few 'Billy the Kid' type fancy spins. Mario felt he would make a good wild west hero. He gave himself a smouldering look and tried spinning the gun from one hand to the other. Unfortunately it span straight out of his hand, onto the floor and into the urinal. As he picked it out Mikey walked in.

'Ah, Mario dear boy. Searching for dog ends or are you hoping to find a personality down there?'

'Is that meant to be funny?'

'Mmmmm,' said Mikey, 'I daresay that in some quarters that would be considered humorous, yes.'

'You really think you're so smart. Why don't you just fuck off.'

Mikey walked over to the urinal and unzipped his fly. He looked at Mario and smiled, which aggrevated Mario even more.

'Why do you keep having a go at me? What is your problem?'

Mikey finished his task, zipped his flies back up and walked over to the sink to wash his hands without saying a word.

'Come on man. What's your problem?' Still Mikey said nothing. 'Ok, I'll tell you what you're problem is shall I? Is that what you want? Eh? Alright. You're problem is that you've got one almighty big fucking chip on your shoulder. You can throw an American football around better than me, you can probably dance better than me, but other than that you're as jealous as fuck of me. You'd give anything to be able to change this,' said Mario pointing at his skin.

'Is that right?' said Mikey wearily.

'Fucking right it is man. I'm not racist - I've got lots of black friends, but I tell you what, most of them are the same as you. A fucking big chip on their shoulder.'

'Well, Mario,' said Mikey calmly, 'Why don't you just put a white hood on, wipe the piss off of that toy gun of yours and do the world a favour and shoot me if that's how you feel.'

'What the fuck are you on about?'

'What I'm on about,' said Mikey raising his voice, 'What I'm on about shit for brains is that you have not got a clue. You go on about me wanting to change the colour of my skin. Have you listened to yourself? Have you listened to the way you talk, looked at the way you dress - seen the way you try and shake hands? If anyone wants to change the colour of their skin it's you. You're so desperate to be a brother it's sickening.'

'Bollocks, I-'

'And as for not being racist, bullshit,' continued Mikey, almost singing the last word. 'You've got a pre-conceived image of what being black is about, and all the time there are people like you around we'll carry on having doors slammed in our faces, unless we're wearing boxing gloves, running shoes or carrying a microphone. As soon as we don't conform to type, then people feel threatened - you Mario, you feel threatened by me.'

'I ain't scared of you,' said a very riled Mario, defiantly pulling himself up to his full height, 'I could fucking do you any day.'

'Q.E.D. Mario. You're too stupid to even understand what I'm saying, aren't you? You're threatened by me because you know I'm smarter than you. The thing you still haven't sussed is that I didn't start off disliking you. In fact, I probably don't give you any more stick than I do anybody else. Your problem is that you take everything, especially yourself, far too seriously.' Mikey turned towards the door, shaking his head and laughing, continued, 'It's a shame really, because apart from being racist, having a shit personality and no sense of humour, you're not a bad bloke.' Mikey walked out of the door leaving Mario still trying to make sense of what he had just said. He had been gone a matter of seconds when he put his head back round the door. 'Oh, and for the record, if you are going to 'do me', make sure you've got a few friends with you.'

The noise from the hall as Mikey walked back into the Hoe Down was deafening, with Woodsy pounding out 'Country Roads' and three hundred drunk holidaymakers swaying and singing along, many of them with bottles or glasses in the air indicating that they wanted a refill. He quickly calmed down following his confrontation with Mario and focused his attention on a girl from Kent. Brad was having problems juggling between several different women, as he was going through his most promiscuous period since arriving in Ibiza (or in his life, for that matter). He had slept with Veronica a couple of more times, and she alone was just about enough to wear him out. Two days had passed since he had been supposed to shag her and Melanie, the blond girl, in the same night. He recalled how he had almost been caught by Veronica. After Greg left him he had managed to persuade Melanie to go up to his room. He had lost track of time, on top of which Veronica had also cut short her night out. When she knocked on the door Brad had not heard her knocking at first because he had a pair of thighs for earmuffs. When he heard her trying the door he told Melanie that it was his boss and bundled her into the bathroom, and then fell against the unlocked door just as Veronica was opening it, mumbling to her that he was puking up and would come up to her room when he was finished. He rounded off proceedings with Melanie, using his first Black Shadow durex. Then he went up to Veronica and brought her down to his room. He had not felt ready to perform again right away, but this had helped to validate his story about being sick, because Veronica knew that he had been feeling rampant. He did however, have a mammoth session with her the following morning, and later in the day he had sex with the girl from Hounslow.

This time she was sober, and at least he discovered that her name was Francesca. The following night he had got off with the Scottish redhead, but had not got anywhere mainly because as they had walked into her apartment her friend had been sitting in a chair facing the door pulling out a tampon, and for a reason that Brad never did discover, examining her genitals with the same enthusiasm that a babboon examines another's backside. As her friend was five foot two and thirteen stone not only had Brad's ardour been somewhat dampened, but the embarrassment factor was such that there was no way that Brad could have stayed in the apartment.

Veronica, Francesca, Melanie and the Scottish redhead were all at the Hoe Down, and Brad really was not sure which way to turn. Greg had given him a lesson in how to have more than one girl on the go when they had been out the previous night. The standard line was to say:-

"I really like you, but if we get caught getting off with clients then it's instant dismissal (at this point, page fifty six of the Courier's Manual could be shown as validation). Obviously, we'll still be seeing each other, but you mustn't get upset if you see me flirting with somebody else 'cos it's just part of the job. It doesn't mean anything. And the reason that sometimes we have to see each other during the day instead of night is because our boss has a skeleton key and believe it or not has a habit of checking up on us."

According to Greg, it didn't work with everyone, but the afternoon bit was a good way of persuading girls to have what Greg called 'afternoon delight.'

When Mario finally emerged from the Hoe Down toilets he made his way over to Lester and his two friends with whom he had the hundred pound bet to shag Lorraine. They wound him up sufficiently to goad him into action.

Later in the evening, just after the square dancing, Mario approached Lorraine.

'Hi gorgeous. How's tricks?'

'Not bad. I hate this bloody excursion already though,' replied Lorraine.

'Yeah me too,' agreed Mario. 'So, are you enjoying the job?'

'Yeah, I'm loving it. You?'

'Brilliant.' Mario paused for a while. 'Met anyone you like yet?'

'No.' Lorraine looked at Mario suspiciously. 'Mario, what are you up to?'

'Nothing,' replied Mario defensively, 'What do you mean?'

'Well, since we've been in Ibiza we've probably only ever had two conversations, and I initiated both of those. Even then all you did was speak about yourself. So why this sudden interest in my well being?'

'It's not a sudden interest,' protested Mario. 'The only reason we haven't spoken much is that we don't work in the same hotel and we've both been really busy. You know how it is.'

'Hmmm,' replied an unconvinced Lorraine.

'I see you've caught the sun,' said Mario trying to keep the conversation going. 'It suits you. Makes you look.........sexy.'

Lorraine burst out laughing. 'Fuck off Mario. Since when did a red nose look sexy to anything other than a reindeer?' She did have a point. Lorraine had a very fair complexion, and her only dermatological response to the sun was a bright red forehead and nose. 'Sexy? Don't make me laugh.'

'I'm serious,' said Mario as genuinely as he could. 'You shouldn't put yourself down you know. You're a nice looking girl, you ooze sex appeal.'

'Yeah, well it must be oozing somewhere else 'cos I've not had a shag since I've been here.'

'Really. You must be getting desperate.'

'No Mario, I'm not desperate. If I don't meet anyone I like then I'll stay celibate until the end of the season.' Lorraine took a sip of her wine. 'Anyway, how's your love life going - how many points are you on now?'

'What?' said Mario, a little taken aback that Lorraine knew about The Competition. 'Oh that. I don't get involved in it to be honest, it doesn't interest me. I think it degrades women.'

'Right,' said Lorraine, 'So videoing yourself shagging them and showing it to the other reps doesn't, is that it?'

'Huh? Who told you about that?'

'Oh sorry Mario, I didn't realise that it was a secret.'

'You don't understand Lorraine-'

'Look, I don't know what you're playing at Mario, but whatever it is don't get me involved.' Lorraine put her drink on the bar. 'Now if you'll excuse me I've got to go and dress up as a can-can girl.'

Mario stood at the bar and looked over at Lester and his friends. Lester put his thumbs up as a way of asking Mario how he had got on. Mario replied with a thumbs up and a smile. There was no alternative - he was going to have to lie.

Brad eventually walked into The Las Huertas at three in the morning. After the Hoe Down he had gone back to The Bon with the Scottish redhead. They had sex in the shower, a blue Fiesta durex this time. It had taken him nearly an hour to persuade her to indulge in carnal activity once they had got back to her apartment, and consequently Brad felt totally exhausted. He was therefore less than happy to see Melanie waiting in reception for him. He was even less happy when the night porter came running up to him saying that there was a problem with some clients on the third floor. When Brad got there he heard doors banging and people laughing. The first person he saw was Pit Bull running around in a pair of boxer shorts, closely followed by a giggling Kempy. Pit Bull saw Brad first.

'Oi Brad me old mucker. Over 'ere. I've got something to show you.'

'Keep the noise down, eh lads.' Brad knew that he wouldn't have a problem with them. He got on well with the whole group and had even been down the gym a few times with Pit Bull.

'Sorry Brad,' said Kempy lowering his voice, 'But you've got to come and see this.'

Brad walked into the room. On the bed on all fours was the girl with the pacemaker. In her mouth she had the tallest of the group, Matt, and just preparing to enter her from behind was William, who's severe acne even reached down to his buttocks. The girl let Matt's cock spring out of her mouth and turned her head round to see what William was doing. When she saw Brad her face lit up.

'Brad, come over here,' she said lunging for his belt.

Brad brushed her aside, briskly ushering Kempy and Pit Bull outside. 'What the fuck is going on?'

'We're all shagging her - what does it look like?' said Kempy laughing.

'I can see that. What's she taken?'

'Oh we gave her some GBH,' said Kempy.

'Oh Jesus.' Brad knew about GHB, or GBH as it was more commonly known. It was like a liquid ecstasy and Brad had in the past, witnessed fairly normal girls turn into total sex fiends once under it's influence. He had also witnessed people pass out in spectacular fashion when they had over indulged, especially if they had mixed it with alcohol.

'How much has she had?' asked Brad.

'Dunno. Not a lot,' said Pit Bull.

'Only a couple of cap fulls,' added Kempy.

'And did she happen to mention any reason why she shouldn't take drugs?' asked Brad, his voice heavy with irony.

'No.'

'Did she mention anything that made her different to other girlsl?' said Brad.

'Like what?' asked Pit Bull. 'Don't tell me she's a sex change.'

'The only thing I've noticed different about her that she can talk with her mouth full,' said Kempy laughing.

'So she didn't mention anything about having a pacemaker.'

'What?!!' said Pit Bull.

'Fuck off your winding us up,' said Kempy. He could tell by Brad's face that he wasn't. 'Oh shit,' said Pit Bull and Kempy in unison.

'What's 'appening?' said a voice from the top of the stairs. It was Greg, who had popped in to The Las Huertas to see Brad and had heard from the night porter that something was going on.

'This motley crew have given the girl with the pacemaker some GBH and they're in the process of gang banging her.'

'Steady on Brad,' said Pit Bull, 'That makes it sound as though we're raping her.' Brad said nothing and just looked at the pair of them. Pit Bull got the message and went into the room.

'Will, Matt. Get off of her.'

'Bollocks, I haven't finished yet,' said William. Pit Bull grabbed William's mousey pony tail. 'Aaaagghhh.'

'Yes you fucking have.'

'What's your problem,' said Matt, sub-consciously stroking his manhood, still wet with saliva.

'It's not my problem, it's hers,' said Pit Bull. 'She's got a fucking pacemaker and we've given her GBH.'

'Oh bollocks,' said Matt, moving away from the girl as if she had a highly contagious disease.

'Come on, put some clothes on,' Brad said to the girl, picking her dress up off of the floor.

'Spoilsport,' said the girl, throwing her arms around his neck. He slowly extricated himself from her grasp. 'Oh God, I'm so drunk,' said the girl.

'I don't think you are drunk,' said Brad.

'Yes I bloody am. I must have had ten Tequila slammers. Oh hell, I'm going to be sick.'

With that she retched, just missing Brad but managing to score a direct hit on Kempy's bed.

'You dirty fucking bitch,' cried Kempy.

'That didn't seem to bother you five minutes ago,' said Brad flatly. He turned to the girl. 'What's your name?'

'Peggy.'

'Pacemaker Peggy,' Pit Bull whispered to Matt, who burst out laughing.

'Are you sure you're only pissed?' asked Brad.

'Of course I'm sure,' said Peggy.

'It's alright,' said Greg, 'I'll take care of it if y'want. I think you're wanted downstairs,' he said, referring to Melanie.

Brad had forgotten all about her. Groaning, he made his way back to the bar. Peggy got dressed and left the room with Greg. As they left Greg turned to the group,

'Be'ave yersleves lads.'

He walked her to the top of the stairs. 'Right. Wha' room are yer in?' She waved her key at him. Greg looked at it. 'Two one one. Come 'ed then, follow me.'

They walked down the stairs and went into her room, where she flopped onto her bed.

'Why did you have to ruin my fun?' said Peggy without opening her eyes. Greg took his shoes off. 'I've always wanted to do that,' she said, her eyes still closed. Greg threw his shirt onto the floor. 'All those lovely blokes and you two have to bloody stop it.' Greg stepped out of his trousers and pants. 'SPOILSPORTS!!' She opened her eyes and was surprised to see a naked Greg walking towards her. 'What are you do-' Her sentence was cut short by Greg sticking his dick in her mouth. Peggy quickly warmed to her task, and Greg smiled at the reflection he saw in the mirror on the wall next to the bed.

194

'This has gorra be worth a bonus point,' he thought.

'Brad, you'll be late for desk.' It was Lorraine knocking on the door.

Brad looked down at Melanie who was in the middle of giving him a blow job. He had not been enjoying it and was having trouble maintaining an erection. He had woken up with a chronically sore throat, and the thought of anybody sticking their tongue down it - especially Melanie - was enough to make him feel sick. His knee had still not properly healed from the fooball match when Patricia had been on holiday, and his helmet was beginning to get the hot itch which he knew normally preceeded an onset of thrush. He was not in the best of health. Lorraine knocking on the door had been a blessing, and he was starting to realise that morning desk times were a great excuse for not performing. He figured that if he was with a girl he did not particularly like, then he could time things so that he got a hard on just a couple of minutes before Lorraine knocked, which would give him the opportunity to either halt proceedings or, if feeling selfish, to come himself and not have to worry about indulging in any sexual olympics. Sex had always been very important to Brad, and although he knew that this new attitude had to be caused by fatigue and simply getting too much sex, he pushed it to the back of his mind. Contrary to what he originally thought, he was getting caught up in the momentum of 'The Competition'.

'Sorry Melanie, I've got to go down to desk. It's a shame 'cos I was looking forward to a really good session as well,' he lied. 'Do you want me to come?' Melanie looked up at him and nodded, leaving her mouth positioned over his semi-erect cock. Brad quickly brought himself to a very poor climax, regretting doing so almost as soon as the first drop of semen hit the back of Melanie's throat. Brad could feel himself becoming a complete bastard, but was unable or unwilling to stop it. For no obvious reason, Melanie had been really annoying him. Maybe it was the way she followed him around like a lap dog, or always seemed to be looking at him; maybe it was the fact she rarely said anything of any consequence or seemed to have little respect for herself; he was not sure. What he was sure of was that he wanted her out of his room.

'Come on Mel.'

'What?' she replied sleepily.

'Come on, get up. I've got to go to desk duty.'

'That's alright. I'll wait here for you - we can carry on where we left off when you get back.'

'We can, can we?' Nothing could have been further from Brad's mind. 'Sorry darling, but I've got to go and see the boss later. If she find's you here then I'll get the sack and we don't want that, do we?' Melanie shook her head and reluctantly started getting out of bed. 'Good girl.' Brad went into the bathroom. When he came back Melanie put her arms around his neck and tried to kiss him. Brad started to become irritated. 'Melanie - STOP IT! Come on, let's go.'

She sulkily walked down the corridor to her room and Brad walked down the stairs, promising himself that no matter how randy he felt he would not sleep with her again. He would tell her that someone had told his boss about them and that for the sake of his job he had to stop things.

Brad decided to call in to Peggy to see how she was. He knocked on the door but there was no answer. The door was unlocked so he walked in. He saw that someone was next to her and straight away thought it was Pit Bull or one of his mates.

'For fuck's sake. After everything I said.....' He pulled the sheets back and was startled when he saw who it was. 'Greg! What the fuck?!'

'Alright lad. Told yer I'd shag 'er. Gorra be worth a bonus point - whaddya reckon?'

'You can fuck right off. I don't believe you - you're bang out of order.'

'So you wouldn't 'ave shagged 'er then?'

'Of course I wouldn't. I could've done. Mind you, the state

she was in anyone could have.'

'So why didn't you?'

'Because she was drugged up and she's got a pacemaker. Fuck me Greg, what other reasons do you want?'

'Well you didn't miss anything - she was a gash shag.'

'Shut up you bastard - she'll hear you.'

'No she won't - she passed out when I was in the middle of shaggin' 'er. I carried on for about five minutes but she didn't move so I gis'd all over 'er 'air. What's rhyming slang for 'air.'

'Barnet,' replied Brad without thinking.

'There you go then. 'Arry on the Barnet. Ha! Ha!'

'What, so you shagged her while she was unconscious?'

'Course I did. I tried to gerrit up the rusty bullet 'ole but it wouldn't fit.'

Brad could only shake his head in disbelief. 'We'd better wake her up to see if she's alright.'

They both shook her and called her name but she didn't move. They shook her more vigorously and said Peggy louder, but still there was no response. Greg gently slapped her around the face and began to look a little worried.

'Is she alright?' he asked, his voice sounding slightly shaky.

'I don't know,' said a now concerned Brad.

'I can't see her chest moving,' said Greg. 'What about scratching the soles of her feet?'

Brad tried Greg's suggestion but there was no response. Greg took her wrist, trying to find a pulse.

'Oh shit,' he said, 'I can't feel anything.'

'I think we're in trouble,' said Brad.

'Oh Christ no,' said Greg, running around the room in a blind panic. 'Oh fuck no. She's snuffed it in't she? Oh fuck, fuck, fuck. What should I do?' Greg sat down and stood up again half a dozen times in as many seconds. 'I've gorrit,' he said, clicking his fingers. 'Come on - let's just fuck off an' leave 'er, then you can come up 'n discover 'er in an hour or so.'

'Don't be stupid,' said Brad looking at him incredulously

'Why not?' asked Greg, looking wounded.

'Apart from the fact it's totally out of order she's got all your

Harry in her hair.'

'Let's chop 'er 'air off then.'

'Greg, think properly. Pit Bull and all the boys saw you leave with her.'

'Exactly. They all shagged 'er. One of 'em might 'ave the same kind of 'Arry as me. Anyway, it was them who gave 'er the GBH - not me.'

They both stared at the lifeless body. 'Come on,' said Brad finally. 'Let's call an ambulance.'

Greg knew Brad was right and followed him down the stairs, thinking aloud all of the way. Brad got through to the medical centre, who said that they would send an ambulance as soon as they could. Brad and Greg went back up to Peggy's room but when they opened the door and looked at the bed she wasn't there.

'Is this the right room? asked a confused Greg.

As he said it, Peggy came out of the bathroom.

'Hello. What are you two doing here?'

'Are you alright?' asked Brad.

'Never better. I know I was a bit of a naughty girl last night but I can't remember exactly what I did. That GBH is lethal. I can still feel it now. God, it makes you feel as randy as hell.'

'Yeah, you were a bit naughty,' said Greg.

'Well if you can't be naughty on holiday when can you be? I suppose I should be embarrassed but.......who cares? I can remember being with Pit Bull and his mates. What about you two, did you both, you know....?'

'No/Yes,' said Brad and Greg, simultaneously and respectively.

'What we mean is,' said the scheming Greg, 'Is that we both started but you passed out before we both 'ad a chance to come.' Brad groaned, guessing what was coming next. 'The thing is, we're both meant to be doing desk duty so we can't stop.'

'That's a shame,' said Peggy.

'Tell y'what though girl. Do y'fancy wankin' us both off before we go like? Y'know, to make up for not makin' us come

198

last night.'

Brad shook his head and sank his face into his hands, unable to believe that she was so rude and Greg so forward.

'Alright then.'

Brad felt as though he had just witnessed two people bartering over the price of a bunch of banana's. However, he still took part in the transcation. Greg already had his cock out and was vigorously wanking himself to an erection. Peggy pulled down Brad's tacksuit bottoms and greedily put his cock into her mouth. Once she had achieved the desired effect, she sat on the bed squeezing their balls as they both remained standing. Even while he was wanking, Brad was still shaking his head in disbelief with his face buried in his free hand laughing.

'Ready to put some Harry on the Boat, Bradley lad?' asked Greg after a couple of minutes.

'When you are.'

'On five. One, two, three, four..........FIVE.'

The two reps spurted over Peggy's face at exactly the same time. Greg made a point of aiming for her eye. Brad exploded into a fit of giggles. Peggy shrieked and gurgled with delight.

'Not bad for a corpse,' said Greg.

'Not bad at all,' agreed Brad.

As he said it, he heard the sound of an approaching siren. Brad and Greg looked at each other in horrified recollection.

'THE AMBULANCE!'

After telling the ambulance driver that it was a false alarm and completing his desk duty, Brad spent the rest of the day trying to track down Romford Reg. Although he had got the car back, within one day it had started spluttering and was running very badly again.

During his travels, he was sure that he saw the jeep which belonged to Samuel Zakatek driving down the main Ibiza Town to San Antonio road. He probably wouldn't have noticed it had it not been for two police motor bikes tearing up behind it, although whether the former army vehicle was there intended victim, Brad didn't see.

He had no luck finding Reg, and by the early evening his throat and knee were killing him. On inspection he discovered that he did indeed appear to have thrush. That was it. He was going to have to go to the medical centre.

The medical centre that YF&S used overlooked the bay of San Antonio. When he went in and showed his rep's badge the casually dressed doctor was friendly, and asked him which hotel he was in and which other reps were working for YF&S this year. When Brad mentioned Greg's name the doctor started chuckling and repeatedly said 'Penicillin'.

After he had finished examining Brad he went over to a cabinet and picked out an assortment of medication.

'Ok, this ees for your throat.' He handed him some tablets and something to gargle with.

'This ees for your knee.' He handed him a bottle and some dressing.

'And this ees for your peenis.' He handed him a red and white tube of cream.

As Brad walked out of the door the doctor called out to him, laughing,

'And Welcome to Ibiza.'

CHAPTER SEVEN

The wind which gusted through the open balcony door blew the money off of the solid, dark wooden table, and all over the brown patterned tiled floor of her apartment. Alison quickly gathered up all of the notes and put them back into their respective piles, using a glass ash tray, calculator and lighter as makeshift paper weights. When she finished counting, the pile of five thousand peseta notes was the largest. She calculated that she had already made for herself the equivalent of nearly four thousand pounds. She gave a satisfied smile and lit a cigarette, staring at the money, working out that at this rate she should go home with over twenty thousand pounds.

A knock at the door interrupted her thoughts, causing her to quickly sweep all of the Spanish currency into her YF&S shoulder bag.

'Hang on a minute,' she yelled, 'Who is it?'

'It's me, Mario.'

'Hang on Mario.'

She put the shoulder bag under the settee, puffed her hair up and quickly put on some lipstick. When she opened the door she noticed how handsome Mario looked with a suntan.

'Alright, Alison. Just got in?'

'No, no. I've had loads of paperwork to do.'

'It must be really hard being a Resort Manager. I don't know if I'd be able to cope.'

'Well it's not easy.' Alison sat down and beckoned for Mario to do the same. 'So, what can I do for you? Is anything wrong?'

'No not really.' Mario looked down at the table. If he was going to make this sound credible he was going to have to make Alison drag it out of him. 'No, nothing's wrong. I just popped up to um, see you.' Mario deliberately twiddled his fingers trying to look sorry for himself.

'Are you sure there's nothing wrong?' asked Alison. She briefly wondered if he was about to tell her that he had a crush on her. 'You seem like something's on your mind.'

'Nothing really,' replied Mario with rehearsed hesitancy, 'It's just that it's a bit, well, a bit.......delicate.'

'What is?'

'I mean I'm probably imagining it.'

'Imagining what?' She wondered if she had made it too obvious that she fancied him.

'It's just that I don't want to get anyone into trouble.'

'Who exactly?'

'Oh well, you'll probably notice it yourself anyway,' said Mario sighing. 'It's Lorraine.' Mario's voice suggested that the Iraqi secret police had just extracted his teeth one by one to obtain the name.

'Lorraine!?' Alison did not particularly like Lorraine. Moreover, she was also slightly deflated that Mario was not about to declare his undying lust. 'What's she done now?'

'Oh nothing,' exclaimed Mario quickly pretending to jump to her defence. 'Well nothing yet.'

'What do you mean, yet?'

'It's just that she's been........oh it's nothing, honest.'

'She's been what, Mario?'

'She's been sort of coming on to me,' blurted Mario. 'She's a nice enough girl but I don't fancy her, and even if I did I obviously wouldn't do anything, you know, working with her and all that. It's making me feel a little bit uncomfortable, that's all, and I'm not sure what to do.'

'Hmmm,' said Alison digesting what Mario had just said. 'I'll have a word with her if you want.'

'Oh no, don't do that,' said Mario pretending to leap to her defence again. 'I only wanted to make you aware of the situation in case it gets out of hand. I'm sure I can deal with it.' Mario stood up. 'I'm a big boy now,' he gave Alison the most suggestive look he could.

Alison blushed slightly and couldn't help herself from quickly glancing down at his groin.

'Well if you're sure that you can handle it - I mean deal with it then, alright.' Alison regained her composure. 'But if it carries on come up and see me. Ok?'

'Fine,' said Mario. He gently touched her on the shoulder. 'Thanks Alison. You've really put my mind at rest.'

'That's what I'm here for. Right, you better get your skates on or you'll be late for bar night. You've got quite a good crowd this week haven't you?'

'Yeah not bad. I can't believe how quickly the weeks are going. What's this, the fourth Tuesday with clients on resort?' asked Mario rhetorically. 'It's just whizzing by.' Mario made for the door. 'Anyway, thanks again Alison. I'll see you tomorrow. Are you coming to the hippy market?'

'Probably,' replied Alison.

Mario waited until he got into the lift before he started smiling. Five days had passed since the Hoe Down. He had lied to Lester and his friends (who were now into the second week of their holiday) by telling them that he had already shagged Lorraine but had not been able to video it. They wanted to see some evidence of it before they gave Mario the hundred pounds for 'winning' the bet, and Ryan (one of Lester's friends) had suggested a public display of affection towards Lorraine in front of them. The meeting with Alison had been purely to pre-empt any problems that might arise by Lorraine getting upset or by Alison witnessing any contact between them. Mario walked out to the lift smiling. When the door closed he looked at himself in the lift mirror.

'Good looking and clever.'

During the course of one's existence on this planet, it is possible that one will come into contact with someone (normally male), who derives his main source of entertainment from getting other members of the species horrendously drunk; who's sole purpose in life is to persuade other homo sapiens to consume vast quantities of alcohol, even if it is at his own expense. To own one's own bar would greatly assist such a mission. Monty had his own bar.

Monty's bar was near the hippy market at Es Cana. After the hippy market, YF&S would take all of their clients in there and spend the rest of the afternoon playing drinking games. Along with the hotel bar nights, this was the time when the reps encouraged their clients to drink more than any other. The main difference between Monty's and the hotel bar nights was that Monty was on hand to make sure that the reps got even more drunk than the clients. Because Es Cana was a quieter part of the island, Monty's had only been open a week, so this was the first time that YF&S had been there this season.

Greg had warned Brad and all of the other reps about Monty and his 'initiation ceremony'. The previous year one of the first year rep's had ended up in hospital with alcoholic poisoning directly after the first time he had visited the bar.

The bar itself was at the end of a dusty cul-de-sac which was only about twenty metres long. At the top of the cul-de-sac were scruffy four storey apartments, and the only other two buildings were an as yet un-opened pub called the White Lion, and at the end, Monty's. Opposite Monty's was wasteland upon which was a burnt out Seat, a mountain of bursting bin bags and an old washing machine.

As they walked into the near deserted pub Monty let off a klaxon and put on a record which turned out to be a rather strange version of 'Swing Low Sweet Chariot'. Mikey looked at Brad with genuine fear as if to say 'What have we let ourselves in for?'

All of the new reps were presented with a pint or a half pint of Piña Colada (depending on their gender), pints for males and half pints for females. This had to be consumed in one go, and anyone failing to do so had to empty the remaining contents of the glass over his or her own head.

Brad ended up helping Monty to serve behind the bar. Monty smoked constantly, which probably in part accounted for his gravelly Mancunian accent. It was difficult to tell his age. He had a full head of shoulder length mousey hair, yet his features were ravaged by years of over indulgence. He would have not looked out of place as a member of the Rolling Stones road crew.

Monty kept Brad supplied with a constant stream of snakebites, preparing another and ordering him to drink up as soon as he noticed that Brad's glass was less than half full. As Brad was serving he made a point of keeping tabs on which girls were getting the most drunk. Veronica had gone home the previous Saturday, and although she had been a great shag, he was glad to see the back of her. After the previous Hoe Down, he had discovered that Francesca (the girl from Hounslow), had slept with Kempy. Brad figured that this made it fair game for him to rump one of her mates, which he had done only half an hour before they left for their coach transfer on Saturday night.

Melanie (the blonde) had really started to aggravate him. She had turned up at his room the previous night, and although Brad ignored her knocking on the door she would not go away, so after five minutes he let her in. She had started to try and kiss him but Brad turned his back on her and went to sleep, farting loudly as he did so. That morning he had timed it so that he started shagging her five minutes before Lorraine was due to knock on his door to get him to come down for desk duty. Lorraine was early, which meant that he only had to shag Melanie for just over a minute before he was able to call a halt to proceedings. Melanie had not booked the excursion block and had all but ran out of money. She had dropped numerous hints to try and get Brad to allow her to tag along to the hippy market, but Brad ignored all of them and said that he would try and see her before she left to go back home that night. Fat chance.

The Molson Boys and Pit Bull & Co. were still there. They had been the life and soul of the first few days of the second week and had helped to persuade virtually all of the new arrivals to book the excursion block. Because of this, Brad slipped them the occasional free drink. Once again, Pit Bull and his friends were gathered around Monty's fruit machine and were, once again, doing remarkably well out of it. Brad took a break from serving behind the bar and made his way to the door to get some fresh air. The fruit machine was by the entrance and as he walked towards it Kempy nudged Will, who was playing the machine. They stopped putting money in and Pit Bull intercepted Brad, guiding him away from his little group and towards the door.

'Alright Brad. Come over 'ere so I can get you a drink.'

Brad looked at Pit Bull suspiciously. 'No thanks. You should know by now that I get them for nothing.' He looked back over to the fruit machine. 'So what's going on?'

'What do you mean?' replied Pit Bull indignantly.

'Pit Bull, you've been here for ten days now. Every time you go anywhere near a fruit machine it spews out money quicker than you spew out bullshit.'

'I don't know what you're talking about,' said Pit Bull fidgeting.

'CRAP!' said Brad almost laughing. 'I'll find out what you're up to anyway mate, so you might as well tell me.'

'If I tell you,' said Pit Bull looking around nervously, 'You've got to keep it a secret. Promise?'

'As long as it doesn't involve animals or children, yes I promise. Dib, dib, dib,' said Brad making a boy scout salute and raising his eyebrows.

Pit Bull proceeded to tell Brad that they were going home with nearly two thousand pounds more than they had arrived with. They had some kind of device which seemed to revolve around a false coin and a piece of cotton. In the ten days they had been there they had 'done' almost twenty machines. As well as this, they had paid for Matt's holiday in return for him being a 'donkey' and carrying seventy E's over (when they had arrived at the airport they were consequently all gutted when there were no customs officials). They had also brought over a couple of stolen credit cards, which had financed shopping expeditions and slap up meals.

Brad walked out of the bar laughing at the audacity of Pit

Bull & Co. Sitting on one of the walls which bordered the wasteland was a very pale looking Mario.

'What's up Mario? You don't look too clever.'

'I'm not. That Monty's a fucking nutter. He keeps forcing whisky down my neck.'

'I know how you feel mate. Even Alison's pissed.'

As if on cue Alison came stumbling out of the bar, gin and tonic in one hand and cigarette in the other. She spotted Mario and headed towards him spluttering smoke into the air. She plonked herself on his lap and put her arms round his neck.

'Isn't he lovely.' Alison squeezed his cheek between her forefinger and thumb. 'How long were you a model for?'

'Oh just a couple of years.'

'I bet you had girls falling at your feet,' she said, inadvertently blowing smoke into his face.

'If you have much more to drink he'll have another one,' said Brad.

'Don't be silly Brad,' replied Alison. 'I'm not in the least bit pissed (hic). Isn't he just the most gorgeous man you've ever seen?'

'Excuse me a minute. I think I'd rather Monty made me sick with snakebites than you making me sick by gushing all over him.' Brad made his way back to the bar. 'Give me a shout if your guide dog wants a bowl of water.'

'You're just jealous,' she called after him.

Brad walked behind the bar where Mikey and Heather were serving a constant flow of drinks. Three different football songs were being sung, all competing with Greg's DJ'ing. The furore was occasionally punctuated with a glass breaking or a girl shrieking. Anarchy was looming. Brad looked at Mikey and they both shook their heads.

'I am fucking wrecked,' said Mikey. Brad just nodded his agreement. 'Where's Mario?'

'Outside with a very pissed Resort Manager sitting on his knee.'

'NO WAY!' exclaimed Mikey. 'What, Alison's off her face?' Brad nodded again. 'This I must see. Take over for a few minutes.' With that, Mikey headed for the door.

During the course of the day Greg had introduced Brad to a new 'game', which further exemplified the almost total control that reps had over their clients. It involved going up to a girl, relieving her of her drink or whatever she happened to have in her hands and then getting her to raise both her arms in the air. She would then be instructed to lean forward, at which point her tits would be given a hearty slap. The male reps would then give her marks out of ten for 'wobblability'. At Monty's it had got to the stage where girls were actually taking their bras off and coming up to reps demanding to be slapped, and getting very upset if they subsequently received a bad score.

As incredulous as Brad first was when Greg demonstrated it to him, Brad had now wholeheartedly embraced the game as if it were his own invention. There were two girls that Brad had first tried the wobblability test on. Although they were mammalarily challenged (both only scoring four out of ten), they both had a wicked sense of humour and were highly flirtatious. As they approached the bar Brad noticed that they were both now also highly pissed. The first of the two who was called Clare, walked behind the bar, lifted her top up and said,

'I'm worth more than four out of ten. I want another go.'

Brad looked at Monty who's eyes were popping out of his head.

'Sorry,' said Brad, 'The judges decision is final. Anyway, you just want me to touch your tits again.' Clare put her top back down and started giggling. 'Unfortunately, as your rep I can't be responsible for ruining friendships and I know if I touch your tits your friend will only get jealous.'

'You won't get jealous, will you Trudi,' said Clare.

'Yes I will,' said Trudi laughing.

'See what I mean,' said Brad. 'If I'm going to have any kind of physical or sexual contact with you then it's going to have to be to both of you in even amounts.'

The girls looked at each other and started giggling again.

'You're all mouth,' said Trudi.

Brad walked into the kitchen which was at the back of the bar and beckoned them over. Without saying a word, he started kissing Trudi and put his left hand up her T-shirt. Next he pulled Clare towards him. Before he kissed her he looked at Trudi and said,

'Just so I do things evenly, it was the right one I just squeezed wasn't it?' With that he put his hand inside Clare's vest and started kissing her. When he finished he looked at them both and said, 'We'll see who's all mouth.'

Monty had witnessed what Brad had been up to and sidled up to him. 'You're a fucking smooth bastard, and no mistake.'

Brad smiled. 'More like a pissed bastard.'

'And getting more pissed by the minute,' said Monty pouring him a Ferna Blanca. There was something about the way that Monty offered a drink that made saying 'no' an option that could not be considered. Brad downed it in one and screwed his face up,

'Yuk, that tastes like shit.'

Monty gave Brad another snakebite as if to make things better, then went over to the microphone to announce a yard of ale challenge.

Rashid from The Molson Boys volunteered to go first. He took twenty three seconds to finish the yard of San Miguel, with everyone in the bar watching and cheering or jeering. Brad turned to Greg,

'Fuck doing that. Just looking at it makes me feel sick.'

'That's a shame,' said Greg, "Cos one of us'll 'ave to do it in a minute.'

'No way,' said Brad, shaking his head and holding his hands up with his palms facing outwards. 'I'm close enough to puking as it is.'

'How do you think I feel? One of us has to do it.' Greg put his arm around Brad's shoulder and turned him towards the door. 'Come on, let's go an' see Mikey an' Mario outside - maybe one of 'em fancy giving it a go.'

As they walked out of the bar, Pit Bull was downing the yard of ale, providing Kempy with the perfect distraction to

209

empty out what little money was left in the fruit machine. Once outside, Brad put his hand on the top of Mario's arm.

'Mario, me old mate. How would you like to get five bonus points.'

Mario looked at Brad suspiciously, and Mikey looked at him as if he had lost his marbles.

'What you on about?' asked Mario.

'One of us 'as to drink the yard of ale,' interjected Greg, before adding firmly, 'And there's no bonus points on offer.'

'After all we've already drunk - you must be joking,' said Mikey.

'I'm afraid he's not,' said Brad.

'I'd be sick,' said Mario.

'That's what I said,' agreed Brad.

'So I take it that there are no volunteers then?' Greg was greeted with total silence. 'That's what I thought. Right then. A game of spoof to settle it, loser does the yard. Agreed?' They all reluctantly nodded their heads.

'If we're all feeling so sick, can I make a suggestion?' asked Brad, 'Something for the, um, unofficial brochure.' He went to his bag and took out his camera, handing it to Clare, who was standing by the door. 'Here, take a picture of us when I give the signal.' He walked back to the rest of the reps. 'Right badges off for a team puke.'

'WHAT!' said Mario.

'Have you got a better idea?' exclaimed Brad. 'Look, we've got another sodding bar crawl tonight and I'm sure Monty hasn't finished with us yet. I can't see that we've got any other choice if we're not gonna pass out.'

The other three looked at each other before Greg finally said,

'He's right y'know. Come 'ed, let's gerron with it then.'

The four of them stood in a semi-circle facing a bemused Clare. They all took off their badges and held them aloft in one hand, whilst sticking their fingers down their throats with the other. Virtually simultaneously the four reps started retching, and Clare took the picture. When they finished they all began pissing themselves laughing in between gasping for breaths of fresh air and leaning against each other. Brad went over to Clare to get his camera.

'Cheers darling.' He got the camera and put one of his arms around her waist, opened his mouth and stuck his tongue out, 'Give us a kiss.' She wriggled out of his grasp screaming, which sent all four of them into a giggling fit.

A couple of minutes and a bottle of water later, they got down to the serious business of the game of spoof.

'How do you play it again?' asked Mario.

'We've all got three coins to start with,' said Greg, 'We put 'em be'ind our backs or in our pockets an' when we put 'em back in the middle we each 'ave either none, one, two or three. Then we each 'ave to guess 'ow many coins we're all 'olding in total. Got it?' Brad and Mikey nodded. Not wanting to appear stupid, Mario nodded as well. 'Right then.' They all put their hands behind their backs and then put their clenched fists back into the middle so that they were almost touching.

'So what do we do again?' asked Mario.

'You have to guess how many coins we've got in total,' said Brad. 'So if I've got two coins in my hand, Mikey's got one, Greg's got none and you've got three then the right answer would be six.'

'But I haven't got any,' said a confused Mario. The other three all groaned.

'You soft twat,' said Greg. 'Right, let's do it again. Just have none, one two or three coins in yer 'and an' say a number between nought and twelve. Got it?' Mario shrugged his shoulders. Once again they all put their fists back into the middle.

'Six,' said Greg.

'Five,' said Mikey,

'Eight,' said Brad. They all looked at Mario.

'What?'

'How many fucking coins!' screamed Greg, half laughing.

'Six,' said Mario.

'AAAAAAAGGGGHHHHHH!!!' yelled Greg, as Mikey and

Brad both doubled up. 'I said six. Just pick a number between nought and twelve apart from five six or eight, before one of us dies.'

'Seven,' said the hapless Mario.

'Right. Show,' said Greg.

Mario opened his fist to reveal three coins. Greg opened his and showed that he had two coins, and Mikey had the same amount in his. They all looked at Brad.

'Oh no,' moaned Brad opening his empty hand. Mikey started laughing, and Greg screamed.

'Oh you jammy, Italian, smarmy, fucking smeg-head.'

'What?' said a wounded looking Mario.

'You don't even realise, do you?' Greg glared at Mario. 'Go on, piss off back into the bar. You've won, soft lad.'

'Have I?' said Mario, his face lighting up. 'YES!' he punched the air and turned on his heels, heading for the bar.

'Do you fuckin' believe that?' asked a still incredulous Greg. 'Right, let's go again.'

It took another three goes before one of them guessed correctly, this time Mikey. Brad and Greg agreed that the last game should be the best of three. After a couple of minutes it was one-all, and they were facing each other for the decider. By now, a dozen or so clients had gathered around to see what was going on. Greg called first,

'None.'

'Brave call,' said Pit Bull who had downed his yard of ale in eighteen seconds and had come outside to get some air and to see what was going on.

'Why's it brave?' asked Clare, who had also returned, fairly confident that Brad was not now going to try and stick his puke coated tongue down her throat.

"Cos Brad already knows that Greg hasn't got any coins in his hand, so unless Brad hasn't got any either, then Greg's lost.'

Brad looked at Greg, keeping his hand closed and saying nothing. Greg looked at him nervously,

'Come on then you big lump - gerrit over with.'

Everybody watching was totally silent. Slowly, Brad opened his hand. It was empty. He put his head in his hands as Greg leapt into the air, before gleefully grabbing Brad by the arm to escort him through to the bar. The fifth client was in the middle of downing the yard of ale, but was doing hopelessly, which meant that Pit Bull was still in the lead. Brad went behind the bar and took the empty yard of ale from the previous competitor as soon as he had finished. He had to think quickly.

'I'll just give it a quick rinse,' said Brad, taking it through to the kitchen. Once out of sight, Brad got a litre of bottled water and poured it into the yard glass. As he returned to the bar, he kept his body between the glass and everyone in the bar, then as quickly as he could, put it under the San Miguel tap so that it changed colour, which made it look as though it was all beer. By the time it was full, everyone in the bar knew that Brad was about to undertake the challenge, and were rhythmically clapping and cheering. Brad made his way to the table and stood on it, saluting everyone like a latter day gladiator, holding the yard aloft in one hand. Monty leapt on the table next to him and beckoned for everyone to be quiet.

'Right then,' said Monty. 'Eighteen seconds to beat. Who thinks he can do it?'

The response was a drunken cheer with a few obscenities thrown in. 'Right then Brad. Are you ready?'

Brad nodded. Although he had a litre of water in the yard, and although he could drink a pint fairly quickly, this was a completely different ball game.

'Ok,' said Monty. 'Everybody. Three...two.....ONE!'

Brad put the glass to his lips and started pouring, opening his throat as best he could. He had no concept of time and was mainly concerned with completing the task without totally humiliating himself. As the yard got to the bowl at the bottom, Brad remembered someone once telling him to twist it so that the air bubble didn't send the beer shooting out all over him. It seemed to do the trick. The yard emptied, with only a mouthful spilling over his shirt. He put the glass down and looked at Monty, who clicked his stopwatch. He grabbed Brad around the shoulder. There was silent anticipation, before Monty announced in a slow voice, not too dissimilar to a dart's commentator,

'ELEVEN SECONDS!'

The place erupted. The Molson Boys and Pit Bull & Co. made there way over to the table and hoisted Brad on to Pit Bull's shoulders, whereupon they paraded him around the bar and outside, singing 'We're Proud Of You' to the tune of Auld Lang Syne.

Before Brad had a chance to bask in his oesophagusally inspired glory, he found himself in the middle a La Mumba boat race. Two teams of eight lined up, each member having a glass of La Mumba in his or her hand. It was a relay race where you could not start drinking your drink until the person in your team in front of you had finished theirs, which they demonstrated by tipping the glass upside down on their own head. This meant that if anybody didn't want to drink it then they had to pour the whole drink over themselves. La Mumba is a deceptively strong drink consisting of brandy and chocolate milk. The reason Monty chose this drink was that apart from it's alcoholic content and it's price (four hundred and fifty pesetas a glass), it was sticky and very messy, thereby dissuading contestants from taking the option of emptying it over their own heads. Monty made them do three consecutive boat race's.

At the end of the afternoon, not one sober person got back onto the coach. The coach drivers hated doing this particular excursion, and they only agreed to do it on the proviso that YF&S supplied a cleaner as soon as all of the client's had disembarked to mop up the inevitable mess.

Mikey and Brad sat in the seats by the entrance to the coach and agreed to do the microphone between them. Mikey had everyone in stitches doing his impressions. Brad could tell that he was getting more than a little aggravated with Alison who had once more begun to treat him as if he were a performing seal.

'Do your Richie Benaud............Go on, do your John Cole.......... Mikey, Mikey - do that black people talking stuff, what's it called again? Parrot? Pattie? No that's it, Patois. Go on, do that Patois thing.'

Mikey managed to keep his patience and got everyone going with a few singalongs. Brad left Mikey to it, because he knew that the only part of the job that Mikey had been having problems with up until then had been microphone work on the coach. Mikey was really getting into his stride, with fifty or so drunk and happy holidaymakers all joining in. At last, he totally had them. After about fifteen minutes, Alison came stumbling up the aisle of the coach and plonked herself on Brad's lap.

"Ere Mikey. Gi'us mic'phone. Wanna do song,' she slurred, barely able to speak.

'Bloody hell Al. You're pissed.'

'Don' say ahm pissed.' She stopped to belch loudly. Her breath stank of onions. 'C'mon. Gi'us bloody mic'phone, I'll show you a song.'

Mikey handed her the microphone and sat down next to her.

'Right ev'one,' she screamed, then started singing, 'There's a bear that we all know, Yogi, Yogi, there's a bear that we all know Yogi Yogi bear. Yogi's got a little friend...' She stopped singing. 'Oh what's his fu'in frenz name again.'

She was barely legible and continued like this for more than five minutes. Although at first it was mildly amusing to see her so pissed, she soon became tiresome and clients at the back started yelling insults, which Alison responded to with a torrent of abuse that West Ham supporters would have thought twice about throwing at Millwall fans. Brad tried a couple of times to unsuccessfully prise the microphone from her, but she was having none of it. Just as he was about to give up he had a brainwave.

'Al, Mario wants to speak to you.'

'Does, he. Right. Where is he?'

Alison made her way towards the back of the coach. Mario

was sitting next to a blonde girl, with his rep's bag on his lap.

'Ah Mario, you...... you....mmmmm. C'mon, move y'bag so y'Resort Manager can sit on y'lap.' Mario didn't move and looked awkward. The girl next to him seemed to freeze. 'C'mon. Wassup? 'Ere. I'll move it.'

Alison grabbed the bag and almost ended up having a tug o' war with him. Eventually, she wrestled it from his grasp. When the bag was out of the way she looked at his lap and shrieked. The girl next to him still had her hand firmly grasped around Mario's massive cock, where she had been wanking him off. Mario closed his eyes and pushed his head back against the seat, in the vain hope that when he opened them again he would wake up to find that he was in the middle of a horrible dream. Alison blustered her way back to her seat, still reeling partly from the shock of what she had just seen and partly from shock at the size of what the blonde girl had in her hand. If she was in two minds about sleeping with Mario before she certainly wasn't any more. By the end of the season she wanted that thing inside her.

The bar crawl was probably the most subdued of the season, with most of the clients who had been to the hippy market and Monty's not making it. However, all of the reps had to turn out, but fortunately Alison did not join them until their last port of call at The Star Club, so for most of the evening they were able to take it easy.

Brad made a point of seeing Danny, the prop for Sgt. Pepper's, to get half a gram of coke, which he shared with Mikey to keep themselves going. He also got ten doves for Clare and Trudi. As the evening wore on he continued to wind them up about the threesome, but they didn't seem anywhere near as keen as they had earlier in the day in Es Cana.

Brad had been in The Star Club for half an hour when Romford Reg sauntered in. Brad walked straight over to him.

'Reg.' He stood in front of him and stopped him in his

tracks.

'Alright geezer. How's the car?' The way he said it was ambiguous enough for Brad to almost think that he was taking the piss. He was.

'The car?' said Brad trying to control his temper. 'Yeah, it's got four wheels and something that vaguely resembles an engine, so I guess broadly speaking you could call it a car.'

'Get me a San Mig luv,' said Reg to one of the girls in the group he had walked in with. 'Yeah. Got yourself a bargain there. Proper little motor that.'

Brad stared at Reg to see if there was any obvious sign that he was winding him up. He gave him the benefit of the doubt.

'Since I've had that 'car', it's been nothing but trouble. You know and I know that I paid over the odds for it.' Reg went to protest but Brad held up his hand to stop him, 'But I swallowed it on the understanding that you would look after any problems. First of all you didn't get over here when you said you would, and when you did eventually get here you're about as easy to find as a brass's hymen.'

'Not my fault I'm busy geeze.'

'And it's not my fault that lump of shit keeps breaking down either.' Brad put his hands in his pocket and gave him the key. 'This time you'll find it in the side road just up from the Hotel Pueblo.'

'Bollocks. I've already told you once........' protested Reg, refusing to take the keys.

'...And I've already told you,' snapped Brad, raising his voice and taking a step closer. 'It just so happens that I've spoken to a few people and they've told me how much you were trying to sell that car for the end of last season.'

'So what? You bought it for a fair price.'

'Don't take me for a mug you dopey fucker. The only reason I bought the poxy thing was because I had no choice and you knew it. Alright, you've had me over. But I tell you what, don't rub it in......or else.'

Reg looked at Brad. Although he was a couple of inches taller than Brad, Brad was at least two stone heavier. Reg could have a scrap, but there was something in Brad's eyes that made Reg feel a little uneasy. At that moment the blonde girl brought Reg his drink back. Reg had to show some bravado.

'Or else what?'

Brad glared at Reg. he held the keys out and dropped them on the floor in front of him without losing his gaze.

'Just get it fixed you soppy cunt, and stop trying to give yourself the big 'un in front of the girl.'

Brad walked away and went to the other side of the club. He was really wound up, and consequently didn't even acknowledge Mario or Lester and his friends as he barged passed them.

Lester in particular, had been goading Mario all night. There was nothing that Mario could say that would persuade him that he had actually shagged Lorraine. In truth, Lester, Ryan and Paul were also running out of money so the last thing they wanted to do was to give Mario a hundred pounds. Mario on the other hand, not only needed the money, but also did not want to lose face. He could not understand why someone as plain as Lorraine wanted nothing to do with him physically, but she had made it abundantly clear that this was the case. Mario was still drunk from earlier in the day, and he imagined that Lorraine was too. He knew that the only way he could win the bet and 'prove' to Lester and his friends that he had slept with Lorraine was for there to be some heavy physical contact with her displayed in front of them. This would mean having to force himself upon her. Clearly, Lorraine would hate him afterwards, but Mario figured that as she was none too keen on him as it was, it would not make that much difference. He could live with that.

Mario sat at the bar watching Lorraine, trying to plan the best way to get hold of her in front of Lester. He knew that he would have to be careful not to grab hold of Lorraine anywhere near Brad or Mikey, because they would obviously come over to see what was going on, and Lester or one of his friends would then realise during the commotion that Lorraine was an unwilling participant. After careful but drunken consideration, Mario got off of the bar stool, walked over to Lester and told him to stand about fifteen yards away from the ladies toilets. Mario waited for Lorraine to go to the loo. He knew it wasn't a foolproof plan, but he thought that the worst that could happen would be a slap around the face and for him to lose the bet.

Nearly half an hour after Lester and his friends had taken position, Lorraine at last walked over to the toilet. Mario almost missed her because he had his back to the loos, and it was Lester who had pointed out that she was answering the call of nature. Mario walked over to the entrance of the ladies toilets and waited for her to come out. Eventually she emerged.

'Lorraine.'

'Oh, hello Mario. Still pissed?'

'Yeah. You?' Mario leant one arm up against the wall blocking her path.

'Not as bad as I was.' A few seconds awkward silence followed. 'Anyway, suppose I'd better get back. If you'll 'scuse us....'

'I'm sorry about this Lorraine.'

With that Mario grabbed hold of her as tightly as he could and started kissing her. He held her arms so her wrists hurt, and then forced one of her arms round his back and then on to his bum, so it would seem to Lester and his friends that Lorraine was all over him. He did not see Alison come walking out of the toilet.

'Look, I've told you before Lorraine,' he said at the top of his voice for Lester's benefit, 'I'm not interested. Just leave me alone.' With that he swung on his heels and walked straight into Alison.

'Lorraine, Mario. What the hell is going on?'

'Ask him,' said Lorraine, almost in tears which were partly born of rage. 'I was minding my own business when he suddenly grabbed hold of me.'

'Mario?' said Alison turning to face him. Mario shrugged

219

his shoulders.

'It's like I said before. I don't want to get anyone in trouble.'

'So why did you grab me you bastard.'

'Oh come on Lorraine,' said Mario. 'Alison's not stupid. She probably knows.'

'Knows?' screamed Lorraine, 'Knows what? What have you been saying?'

'Calm down Lorraine,' said Alison. 'Look at the state of you. You're showing yourself up and you're showing up Young Free & Single. Go back to your hotel and come and see me after desk tomorrow morning. I'll deal with it then.'

Lorraine ran off sobbing.

'Sorry Alison,' said Mario. 'I did warn you. Thank God I did, otherwise you might have thought I was coming on to her.'

'You must be joking,' laughed Alison. 'What, you and her? I'd like to think you had better taste than that.'

'Too right I have.'

'Come on. I'll get you a drink,' said Alison. 'You and Lorraine. Ha, ha.' Alison walked away laughing.

As they went past Lester and his friends Mario dragged behind a little so he could whisper to Lester,

'Double or quits if I shag Alison. Whaddya reckon?'

'No free drinks. A straight two hundred quid bet, and then only if you can prove it beyond doubt,' said Lester.

'And how can I do that,' asked Mario.

'A picture. Or better still, a video,' replied Lester.

'You're on.'

It took Brad nearly an hour to calm down. Romford Reg left as soon as he finished his drink. Brad spent most of the time up at bar five chatting to some of the workers. Kelly The Vision was there briefly, but Brad only exchanged pleasantries with her. He also found out that Stella, the girl he had shared the coach transfer with a couple of weeks previously, had gone back to the UK.

Clare and Trudi kept coming up to Brad. He could tell by the size of their pupils that they were well and truly up. They had decided to conduct their own wobblability test on Brad's testicles, squeezing or slapping them at every opportunity. Brad contemplated dropping a pill himself, but thought better of it when he remembered how much he had drunk throughout the day, and how much Charlie he had put up his nose. Consequently, by two thirty he was more than ready to leave. As he made his way out of the club, Clare and Trudi were dancing near the exit.

'Right then ladies. Looks like you've missed your chance 'cos I'm off.'

'Oh you're not going are you?' said Clare. 'Stay a bit longer. We're having a brilliant time.'

'No honestly. Thanks all the same but I'm knackered.'

'Oh don't go,' joined in Trudi, 'We've got loads of energy left.'

'Yeah, well if you've got that much energy left you can walk me to the door.' The two girls went either side of Brad and put their arms through his. When he got to the door he kissed them both on the lips, and in a last ditch effort said,

'If you change your mind about the threesome I'm gonna have a quick cup of coffee in The Star Cafe.'

The two girls went back into the club and Brad sat down and ordered his drink. He was feeling outrageously horny, and although he had managed to avoid Melanie all day and all night she suddenly entered his thoughts. She was going home on a flight at five thirty, so if he hurried back he might have been able to just catch her for a quickie. He laughed to himself, at how only a few hours earlier he would have rather drank his own sick than have anything more to do with her. He tossed around the idea for a couple of minutes before abandoning it altogether, resigning himself to a night alone. Brad had another coffee before getting up to leave, his token effort to pay the bill waved aside by the owner, who's name he never could remember. As he waved goodnight to the doormen at The Star Club he noticed Clare and Trudi walking out arm in arm.

'Changed your mind then have we?' asked Brad as they came outside, not for one moment actually believing that they had. The girls said nothing, and grinning took hold of one of his arms each. 'Oh, I get it,' said Brad, 'You're gonna get your own back by winding up poor old Bradley. Is that it?' Still the girls said nothing, other than giggling to each other occasionally. 'Well, I'm getting a cab back, so if you want a lift you'd better be prepared to keep the wind up going a bit longer.'

Brad hailed a cab and all three of them got in the back. Brad felt his mouth begin to go dry as for the first time he began to imagine what could happen, before convincing himself once more that they were on a wind up. The last thing he wanted to do was to take them seriously, make a play for them and for them to start laughing and blow him out. He knew himself well enough to understand that once the blood started rushing to his groin, he would not have the same control over his actions as normal. The only thing he could do was to carry on, with tongue in cheek.

'So who's going to go first then. Have you decided yet or am I going to have to do you both at the same time? Oh, and there's one condition. I've got a fucking big spot on my bum, so if either of you start laughing then that's it.' They turned the road in which the hotel was situated and he tapped the driver on the shoulder. '*Aqui por favor* (Here please).'

They got to the bottom of the stairs. 'Right, my room or yours?' Brad tried to appear as indifferent as he could.

'Well, we're going to our room. I don't know about you,' said Clare.

Brad was not sure what she meant by that. Did she mean that they were going to their room and he wasn't invited and that was it, end of the game? Or was it an invitation for a night of hedonistic pleasure? He had to find out.

'Well, I'd rather go to my room, but part of my responsibility as a rep is to make sure you get home safely, so I'll walk you to your door.'

222

They all went up to the second floor. The girls room was the first door on the left. Once they were outside and the 'moment of truth' had arrived, Brad actually felt a little nervous, at both possible outcomes. He was sure that the two of them nudged each other, but again was unsure whether this was indicative of a continued wind up or of sexual intent.

'Well come on then,' Brad finally said, 'Invite me in. You know you're dying to.' Clare and Trudi looked at each other, but still Brad could read nothing from the look. 'Come on. If I'm gonna shag the pair of you I want to at least be sure you don't leave dirty underwear lying around your room.'

Clare opened the door and all three of them walked in. The room was tidy, with two single beds covered by the universal brown crocheted blanket that all of the rooms in the hotel had. On the bedside table was a make up bag with some birth control pills poking out of it, and a small hair dryer connected to a plug adapter. Brad sat down on the bed against the wall which divided the bathroom from the rest of the room. The two girls had said barely a word since leaving The Star Club. 'Fuck it' thought Brad, 'In for a penny, in for a pound.' Someone had to make the move and Brad figured that lightening the tone would be the way to do it.

'Right then. Tops off. We're going to have a proper wobblability test.' Brad winced a bit at his own naffness, but to his surprise, they both obediently removed their tops. 'Come on then, you first,' he said crooking his finger and getting Clare to come towards him.

He looked her in the eye and told her to bend towards him which she did, keeping her eyes locked on his. Their noses were a matter of inches apart, so he grabbed her round the back of her neck and pulled her towards him and started kissing her. As he did so she fell onto the bed and he rolled on top of her, his hands quickly exploring the rest of her underwear free body. He stopped and beckoned Trudi over. With one finger still inside Clare, he used his free hand and mouth to help Trudi remove the rest of her clothes. Once they were all naked, he got Trudi to grab hold of him and guide

223

him into Clare. He was hoping that the two girls would indulge each other, but it soon became clear that their intentions were totally heterosexual. Brad could find little to complain of though, as he looked down and saw the two giggling girls swapping his bursting cock from mouth to mouth, with one of them slowly rubbing him as the other took it as deep as she could. They even started having their own competition to see who could get most of it in, the winner getting Brad's cock to herself for five minutes (which the other timed to the second).

One of the girls had a bottle of a lubricant called Cyberglide, which they covered Brad in. They then sat astride one of Brad's legs each, rubbing themselves back and forth into an orgasmic frenzy. Brad was grateful for the lubricant, because as they were doing this they were both rubbing his cock and squeezing his balls with such ferocity that had it not been for the lubricant he would have had friction burns on his dick for the rest of the season. After the best forty five minutes of Brad's life he had to come. The two girls sat upright on the bed leaning against the wall. Brad stood on the bed astride them both and brought himself to a shuddering climax, which covered both girl's faces. Brad had a habit of laughing as he came, but his orgasm was so strong that his laughs were more of a moaning yelp. He felt his knees start to shake, which caused him to flop on the bed opposite, although all the time he still kept his eyes on the girls. Brad could not remember ever coming so much and even the girls were surprised at the quantity they were having to remove from their faces. 'Harry definitely is on the boat', Brad thought to himself. After a minute or so, when they had all got their breath back, Clare looked at her bedclothes,

'Oh bloody hell look,' she said pointing at a rather large dollop of freshly deposited semen, 'Why did he have to come over my bed?'

Brad sat there incredulous, as the two girls got into a heated argument over who was going to sleep in which bed.

'Ladies, ladies!', said Brad getting up and sitting between the two of them. He put his arms around both girls and they all started laughing. 'So when did the pair of you plan all this then?'

Trudi stood up, tugging her fingers through the ends of her recently matted hair, saying,

'Ah, well that's for us to know.'

Brad stood up and leant over to kiss Trudi on the forehead. It wasn't so much a sign of affection, more that her forehead was the only part of her face that wasn't covered in dried spunk. He did the same to Clare and started to get dressed. Once he had done so he gave them both a hug.

'Well I tell you what girls, you've made an old man very happy. If there's any chance of a repeat performance before you go home then, well, I'm available when needed.'

Brad walked out of the room with a spring in his step and a grin on his face. He was amazed at how light hearted the whole thing had actually been. He had waited most of his sexually active life for what he had just experienced, and he wanted to tell the world.

For now though, Greg and Mikey would have to do.

CHAPTER EIGHT

When she woke up her eyes were hurting. Crying. The soreness in her eyes only confirmed that she had not been dreaming. Maybe if she went to sleep again? That was the answer. The next time she woke up it would all have been a bad dream. God, she didn't want to lose her job. Why had Mario grabbed her? What did he mean by 'she probably knows anyway'? She was confused. Part of her wanted to rush to Alison to discover what it was all about. But she had a horrible fear of facing her - just in case. She really, really did not want to lose her job. The sad irony was that it had taken all of her courage to apply to be a rep. If her boyfriend had not left her; if there had been any job prospects. The thought of going back to that factory in Sutton Coldfield and folding boxes - Lorraine shivered. And now she was at last truly loving the job. She was growing in confidence daily. She adored being with people. Listening to them; helping them. It was as if her whole life had been leading to this. Another year in a different resort or maybe back to Ibiza. A year or two as a Resort Manager then a job in Head Office. Maybe on the road or in Training. Move down to London. Everything had seemed so simple before......Mario. Why? Nine a.m. Half an hour to go. No, Alison couldn't sack her. Once she'd explained......

The alarm started beeping. Nine a.m. She tried to ignore it. A nice lie in. But then she remembered. Just what she bloody needed. She knew she should have arranged it for mid-afternoon. It was all Mario's fault. The good looking bastard. She hadn't got home until nearly six. She was so close to inviting him in. So close.

She groaned. She had not had enough sleep to be able to make complicated decisions; to arbitrate; to absorb facts and based upon those facts to punish or reprimand or ignore. Screw being Resort Manager. Half an hour to get ready. How the fuck was she going to decide what to do? Brainwave. She reached onto the bedside cabinet and picked up a twenty five peseta coin. 'Heads she stays, tails she goes.' She spun the coin in the air.

Lorraine knocked on Alison's door.

'Come in.'

Lorraine walked in. It was only the second time that she had been in Alison's room. It was lovely and bright with a huge secluded balcony overlooking the beach. The balcony door was open and the crisp morning sun filled the room, reflecting off of the television with the satellite receiver on top of it. The room smelt very feminine, although the clothes scattered everywhere reminded Lorraine more of her old boyfriend's flat. Bastard. Alison was just making some coffee.

'If you want some coffee I've only got black.'

'No thanks Alison. I've already had some coffee downstairs.'

'Suit yourself.' Alison even had a kettle. She poured the hot water into a cup with 'Boss' written on it. 'Sit yourself down.'

Lorraine sat down. She had butterflies in her stomach.

'Right then,' said Alison drawing hard on her first cigarette of the day. It made her cough. 'So what's it all about then.'

'I haven't got a clue,' replied Lorraine. She was already close to crying. 'What did Mario say?'

'Never mind what Mario said. I've already heard his side of the story. I'm more interested in hearing what you've got to say for yourself.'

'I-I don't know really. I mean - I still don't really know what happened.'

'What do you mean 'what happened'? Do you mean that you

don't know what came over you? You just felt like grabbing hold of Mario in front of everybody. Is that it?

'No-no of course not. What do you mean? I didn't grab hold of Mario.'

'Well it certainly looked like it to me.'

Lorraine was confused. 'What, you think I grabbed hold of him?' It was beginning to sink in. She started laughing. 'You must be joking! I wouldn't touch him with a barge pole. He's - he's a creep.'

'A good looking 'creep'. Anyway, that's not his side of the story,' said Alison flatly.

'No way!' said Lorraine shaking her head. 'I came out of the toilets and he just grabbed hold of me. I haven't got a clue why.'

'Neither have I,' snapped Alison, looking her up and down disdainfully.

'Oh Jesus. I see what this is all about now. You think that I've been coming on to Mario. Is that it?'

'Basically - yes.'

'So why would you believe him rather than me?'

'I'd have thought that was obvious.'

'Not to me it isn't.'

Alison became slightly more matronly in tone. 'Look Lorraine. I can understand how you feel. Mario is good looking and worldly wise. It's understandable that someone like you would fall for him....'

'I don't believe I'm hearing this.'

'But do you really think that he'd see anything in you? Even if he wasn't constrained by the job? Come on Lorraine. Put yourself in my position. Mario even told -' Alison checked herself.

Lorraine pounced. 'Told? Told you what? What's Mario been saying? Come on, tell me. What's that fucking bastard been saying about me?'

'Alright Lorraine. Alright. I've tried being nice. Mario came and saw me before all of this happened and told me that you were coming on to him. And that 'fucking bastard' as you call

229

him; that 'creep' stuck up for you. That's right. Mario actually defended you.'

'Oh Alison. I can't believe that you've been taken in by all of this. I don't know what Mario is playing at, but please listen,' Lorraine said the next words one by one, 'I-do-not-fancy-Mario. Let's get him up here and find out what he's playing at.'

'I'm sorry Lorraine but that's not possible. Being Resort Manager is a tough job, and it involves making tough decisions. I've thought about this long and hard. I've carefully weighed up the facts,' she looked at the twenty five peseta coin that she had taken out of her bedside cabinet, '...and I'm afraid that on this occasion I believe Mario.'

'Oh, for Christ's sake,' sighed Lorraine. 'Well I hope you know what you're doing because it's not going to be the best working environment for the next few weeks...'

'I'm aware of that Lorraine.' She stood up and walked towards the balcony, 'That's why I'm sorry to say that we're going to have to let you go.'

'I beg your pardon?'

'I'm sorry Lorraine. As you implied, one of you has got to go and I'm afraid it's you.'

'WHAT!!!'

'I've got you on a flight this evening. I'll give you all of the details later. Of course, you can stay, but if you do then you will obviously be responsible for making your own way home.' Lorraine was walking up and down the room shaking her head in disbelief. 'Any Young Free & Single property will have to be returned to me by four o'clock otherwise I won't be able to issue you with a flight ticket.' Lorraine started crying. 'I'm sorry Lorraine but you really left me with no alternative. You know the rules about fraternising with other reps. As you said yourself - it would be impossible to work as a team. That's the very reason we have that rule.'

'But I didn't try and get off with him,' protested the sobbing Lorraine.

'Well-,' Alison just shrugged her shoulders.

'Please,' begged Lorraine, 'Please get him up here so we

can have this out face to face. Pleeeeaaase.' Lorraine crumpled into the chair.

'Come on Lorraine,' said Alison. 'This isn't doing either of us any good. Look, I've got things to do. You don't want to have to pay for your own flight do you?'

Lorraine looked up at her with red eyes. 'How can you do this to me? I've got nothing to go back to. Nothing. You can't just sack me on a whim..'

'It's not a whim,' contradicted Alison looking at the twenty five peseta coin again. 'I told you. I've thought about it long and hard...'

'Please Alison. Please give me another chance, I....'

'Oh for heaven's sake Lorraine. Pull yourself together and stop acting like such a baby. It's only a job. Unfortunately it's a job to which you're not suited. Now are you going to spend the rest of the day here or are you going to go and sort yourself out?'

Lorraine got up from the chair and ran for the door, still sobbing. Alison picked up the coin.

'Tails, she goes.'

It was a beautiful morning. Probably the most beautiful morning that Brad had ever witnessed. His whole body felt as though it had been on a battery charger all night. Full of energy; swimming a few lengths by nine o'clock. Funny though, he could have sworn that he saw Lorraine walking through reception as he got out of the deserted pool. She wasn't on desk that morning so there was no way she would have been up. Oh well.

It was all he could do to stop himself from standing on the edge of the pool and yelling out to all the balconies at the top of his voice, 'I slept with two women last night'. He dried himself off, had a croissant, and confused the early risers with his over enthusiastic 'Good mornings'. He couldn't wait until desk finished so that he could run over to The Bon or The

Delfin to tell Greg and Mikey.

Ten o'clock and apart from the psychotic Rafael behind the bar, he was alone. He was looking through the information book to see if anything needed adding or improving when Lorraine came running in from the street crying.

'Lorraine?'

She looked at him and started howling.

'Lorraine - what's up?' Brad stood up.

'Oh Brad,' she said, running over and burying her head in his shoulder.

'Come on darling, sit down and tell me what's wrong.'

Lorraine gasped for air in between sobs and tried to compose herself. Brad reached over to the next table and took some serviettes out of a glass and handed them to her to wipe her eyes. After a minute or so she stopped crying.

'Better?' asked Brad. Lorraine nodded. 'So come on then. What's happened?'

'I've-I've just been sacked.'

'WHAT!! Why? - I mean how?'

'Oh Brad, it's so unfair.' Brad looked at her, giving her a chance to tell him what had happened in her own time. 'I was in The Star last night, just minding my own business. I came out of the toilet and Mario started talking to me. Then all of a sudden he grabbed hold of me and started kissing me.'

'He what!?'

'I know - I couldn't believe it either. Anyway, Alison happens to be standing next to us and sees the whole thing, and says she wants to see me this morning.'

'Hang on a minute.' Brad sat back in his chair. 'I've missed something here. Why have you been sacked?'

'Exactly!' said Lorraine, looking as though she was about to start crying again.

'So I go and see the fucking bitch this morning to try and sort it out and she tells me that she thinks I've been coming on to Mario.'

'No way.'

'Yep. So I'm obviously denying it, but then it comes out that

Mario has actually told her that I've been coming on to him before any of this happened.'

'Whoa. Now I am confused. Why would Mario do that?'

'That's what I can't understand.'

'I mean, you definitely didn't - you know - I mean, even give him any indication-'

'NO WAY,' interrupted Lorraine. 'I can't stand him and he knows it. But surely even Mario wouldn't be that vindictive.'

'I wouldn't have thought so,' agreed Brad. 'But why would he do it?'

'Beats me. He's been acting a bit funny round me this last week but......' Lorraine's voice trailed off. They both sat there in silence for a few moments.

'Fuck it,' said Brad standing up. 'Stay here for a moment. I'm gonna go over and see Alison.'

'Do you think that's a good idea?'

'Well - too bad if it's not.'

'Who is it?'

'It's me - Brad.'

'What does he want,' Alison muttered under her breath. She opened the door and Brad marched in. She looked at her watch. 'Shouldn't you be on desk duty?'

Brad ignored the question. 'What's all of this nonsense with Lorraine?'

'I'm sorry?'

'I said, what's all of this nonsense with Lorraine?'

'That's what I thought you said,' Alison replied tersely. 'And what exactly has it got to do with you?'

Brad realised that he would have to soften his approach for the moment.

'Well I've just had a very distressed Brummie crying her eyes out on my shoulder and I wanted to find out what's upset her. She said something about being sacked, which I found a little hard to believe.'

'No, it's perfectly true - not that it should be any concern of yours.'

'Oh come on Alison,' protested Brad. 'You know how close you get to someone when you're working with them. I'm just worried about her. There must have been some kind of misunderstanding.'

'Well you needn't worry. There's been no misunderstanding.'

'So what's she done to warrant getting sacked?'

Alison sat down. 'Like I said, it really is none of your business, but......' She lit a cigarette. 'She's been hassling Mario, and last night I caught her forcing herself on him in front of clients. It left me with no choice.'

'Oh come off it. Can you really see Lorraine going after Mario?'

'A darn sight more than I could see Mario going after her.'

'You must be joking. How much time have you spent getting to know us all Alison?'

'What do you mean?'

'Exactly that. How much time have you spent getting to know us? It can't be a lot, because if you had you'd know that Lorraine can't stand Mario.' Brad sat down opposite Alison. 'In fact none of us can,' he added mumbling.

'Oh I get it,' said Alison. 'That's what it's all about isn't it?' She laughed. 'Mario told me that you and Mikey were always picking on him. If the pair of you were half as good at your job as him-'

Brad stood up. 'Do me a favour! Open your eyes Alison for fuck's sake. I don't give a monkeys about Mario. If you think he's Super Rep then that's your look out. All I know is that Lorraine wouldn't hurt a fly. All of the clients love her-'

'There you go again,' said Alison raising her voice. 'You think you know so much about repping don't you? How long have you been doing the job now? Four weeks? Four weeks and you think you know more about what makes a good rep than I do..'

'I don't need to know about repping. What I do know about

is people, and I'm telling you now that people like Lorraine. She takes time to talk to them and isn't wrapped up in herself like some I could mention, and if you get rid of her this team won't be the same.'

'I know it won't be the same - that's why I'm getting rid of her.' Alison smirked as if she'd just scored a winning point.

'Can't you give her another chance. How about if we get Mario up here and all sit down and discuss it?'

'You must think I was born yesterday,' said Alison shaking her head. 'All that will happen is that you and Mikey will go and threaten him and get him to say what you want him to say. Oh no. I've made my mind up and that's it.'

Brad sat back in the chair saying nothing. He looked at Alison directly in the eyes making her feel uncomfortable.

'What are you up to Alison?'

'What?'

'What are you up to?' Brad paused. 'There's something that just doesn't add up. I mean, you're obviously very able otherwise you wouldn't have got the job, would you? But, I don't know, I can't believe that you misjudge people so...so dramatically.' Brad thought he'd risk playing one of his aces. 'It just makes me wonder if running a happy resort is your main objective, or whether there's some kind of hidden agenda that I'm maybe, well.....missing.'

'What do you mean by that,' snapped Alison standing up.

'I dunno. You tell me.'

'How dare you! How dare you come in here you arrogant......If I were you I'd watch my step otherwise Lorraine won't be the only one on a flight home.' She walked to the door and opened it. 'Now get out of here while you've still got a job.'

It was seven thirty in the evening. It was the first extraordinary meeting of the season, and the first meeting to be held in Alison's room. By now all of the reps and most of the clients knew that Lorraine had gone. Alison knew that Lorraine had probably been telling the truth, but she didn't like her and Mario's actions had provided the perfect opportunity to be rid of her. Brad had seen Lorraine off in a cab only an hour before, and she was so upset that it had taken all of his self control not to crack up as well. No-one had seen hide nor hair of Mario all day, even though Brad had spent most of the day looking for him. The mood in the meeting was sombre. Brad had been so badly effected by Lorraine's dismissal that his morning euphoria had been totally forgotten - he'd not even bothered to tell Greg or Mikey about the eight points he'd scored the night before.

There was a knock on the door and Mario came in. Everybody looked at him, not smiling, and for the first time ever Mario actually appeared slightly sheepish. He sat down next to Heather and said nothing.

'Right, now we're all here,' said Alison. 'In case any of you don't already know, I've had to send Lorraine back to the UK today.' Alison paused but there was no reaction. 'It was not something that I enjoyed doing, and I had to do a lot of soul searching, but the end of the day the smooth running of this resort is the most important thing and in order for the resort to run smoothly rules have to be obeyed. Without going into too much detail, one of those rules forbids any fraternising between reps of the opposite sex, especially when it happens right under my nose. Unfortunately Lorraine chose to ignore this rule and let down both herself and the company, which left me with no choice other than to terminate her employment. The reason I've got you all together is to quash any rumours and to clarify exactly what the rules are, just in case any of you are in any doubt.'

'So what did she do exactly?' asked Heather.

'I caught her in a......a compromising position with another rep....'

'Mario,' offered Brad.

'Brad!' snapped Alison. 'I really don't see the necessity in naming names.'

'Why not?' continued Brad, 'It's not exactly the best kept secret.'

'Even so-'

'So go on then Mario. Tell us all what happened.' It was the first chance that Brad had to speak to him. Mario said nothing and looked at Alison feebly for help.

'I don't think this is the time or the place,' interjected Alison.

'Oh I don't know,' said Brad. 'I think that we'd all like to know what Lorraine did to Mario that was so bad that she's on her way to the airport.'

There was a general mumbling of agreement from the other three reps. As annoying as it was to her, Alison knew that because Brad had brought it out into the open forum, some kind of explanation would be needed.

'Ok. Seeing as you all seem so desperate to know. I caught Lorraine kissing Mario - against his will - in The Star Club last night in front of a load of clients.'

'How do you know it wasn't the other way round?' asked Mikey.

Mario started laughing. 'You must be mad if you think I'd fancy that... that....thing.' Heather looked at Mario with contempt, which Mario noticed. 'What? What's up with you? You don't think I fancied her do you? She was a pig.'

Heather looked away from him shaking her head. Alison decided to give him some help.

'The thing that Mario isn't telling you is that he came to see me yesterday morning to tell me that Lorraine was coming on to him.' Alison noticed the look of horror on Heather's face, 'And before any of you say anything I had to drag it out of him and even then he tried to stick up for her.'

'I bet,' mumbled Mikey.

'Anyway, next week we'll have a new rep on resort - I'll tell you more at the weekend. As far as the clients are concerned I don't want to hear any rumours. If anyone asks then just say she had to go back to the UK - nothing more, nothing less. If I hear anyone saying anything else then they'll be joining

Lorraine back in the UK. Do I make myself clear?' There was a general murmur of agreement. 'Good. Right then. We've got the Dickens excursion tonight. There's two coaches - Heather, you guide one, Greg, you do the other. Mario, I want you to stay in San Antonio to do a merchandise stock check, so if you wait here after the others have gone I'd like to have a word with you.'

Alison thought that this would be a good idea because it might then seem to the others that she was going to reprimand him, and if nothing else, would keep him out of the way of Brad's insistent questioning. But with or without Mario around, Brad had no intention of letting the matter drop.

Dickens was held in a large basement done out to resemble an old Workhouse. There were rows of tables, attended by buxom serving wenches (normally girls from the East End or Essex who wanted to work in Ibiza and do something marginally upmarket from persuading holidaymakers to go into bars). Proceedings were overseen by a Mr. Bumble type character who was resplendent in Town Cryer garb. He made all of the holidaymakers yell for their food and their 'tankards of ale' (jugs of San Miguel), and organised drinking games and competitions. The reps main function during this was to encourage everyone to join in the sing song (By the Light of a Silvery Moon etc.) and to prevent the inevitable food fights. After they were fed, the tables were cleared and music was played. None of the reps were in a particular buoyant mood, and with no Alison to watch over them they didn't get as involved as they normally would have done. In fact, they spent most of the latter part of the evening huddled around the bar talking about Lorraine.

After Dickens, all of the reps apart from Greg went home. Greg went down The Star, mainly because a young Scandinavian had put him on a promise the night before. He had been there for about half an hour when Lester came up to him.

'Greg. Fucking great club innit.' Lester had to yell over the music.

'Yeah, it's alright,' replied Greg looking around for the Scandinavian.

'I know that this probably isn't the best time to ask you, and I know that we're going home on Saturday, but how do I get some money sent over?'

'Oh, it's not that hard.' Greg saw the Scandinavian girl coming out of the toilets and waved at her to indicate that she should meet him by the door. 'So what, you've all ran out of money already then have you?' Greg laughed. 'You boys just don't know how to budget do you.' Greg picked up his yellow YF&S cardigan, ready to go.

'Oh I don't need it yet. It's just that I want to get some pressies before I leave. We'd be alright if we didn't have stupid bets with the reps.'

'Ha.' Greg gave a token disinterested laugh, not really taking in what Lester had said. 'Well that'll teach yer.' The Scandinavian was waiting by the door. 'If you look in the information book it gives details on how to get money sent over.'

'Yeah, alright. I'll pop in there to look tonight.' Lester was trying to prompt Greg to ask him what he meant by 'pop in', but Greg was pre-occupied with the Scandinavian, so Lester told him anyway. 'Yeah, we've pulled these three sorts. Want us to stay at their place around the bay. Definite shag.'

'Yeah,' said Greg. 'Nice one. Listen mate, I've gorra go. Any problems pop in and see me tomorrow. Alright?'

'Yeah sure,' said Lester. 'Probably see you Saturday.'

Lester went back to Ryan, Paul and the three girls who he had been with all day. None of them knew that Lorraine had been sacked.

Alison had told Mario where all of the T-shirts were and

instructed him to take them to his room at The Delfin to count them, saying that she would join him later to check that everything was ok. She spent most of the evening in The Cockney Pride, winding up Trev and getting pissed. At ten thirty she went to Mario's.

Mario had a gut feeling. He wasn't often wrong. It was the way she looked at him; some of the things she had said the night before when she was pissed; the way she touched him. He was sure that she was game on. And for some reason he thought that tonight could be the night. For the sake of pride and two hundred quid it had better be. He got the camera ready.

Lorraine still felt as though she was in a dream; the days events had not really caught up with her. She'd rang her mum and cried down the phone. Her mum had said not to worry. She had seen Mr Thomas earlier in the week and there was still a job in the factory for her. The flight was delayed by three hours. Estimated departure time was now just gone midnight.

She said she'd be there for between ten thirty and eleven. Mario wanted to make sure that he was wet and only had a towel on. He had prepared his eight foot by ten foot room as best he could. He only had a single bed, a bedside cabinet, a chest of drawers and a wardrobe, on top of which was hidden the video camera, all ready to go. The solitary light bulb provided only minimal illumination (Mario had bought himself a small table lamp to provide better quality videos). Even during the day the room was dark and dingy. It had grey floor tiles, brown curtains, green window shutters (with peeling paint) and dirty, off white walls. The room had not been decorated for at least ten years. The small bathroom had a shower curtain that was impossible to tell the original colour of, with fungus on the bottom where it rested against the bath. The shower was either scalding hot or freezing cold and normally did little more than dribble (even when it was switched off). Mario braved the shower at just gone ten thirty. He had only been out of the shower for a few minutes when there was a knock on the door. He opened it and pretended to be flustered.

'Oh, it's you. I didn't think that you were coming round until eleven. I was just having a quick shower. I've finished the stock check.'

Alison feasted her eyes over Mario's bronzed, hairless body. Although he didn't work out a great deal, he had a superb natural shape. Mario had played with himself a little in the shower, and his manhood was obvious to Alison through the towel. Because she was pissed she allowed herself to look at him longer than she normally would have done. Mario was not the only one who was wet.

'I feel really bad about what happened today Alison,' said Mario, rubbing his hair dry with a smaller towel. 'I feel like I put you in an awkward position, especially with Brad and that.' He walked over to the chest of drawers where there was an open wine bottle. 'Drink?'

'Yes please.'

Mario poured the wine into two glasses that he had got out of the bathroom. He gave one to Alison. 'Cheers.'

'Cheers,' she replied. 'Don't worry about Brad. It doesn't matter what he thinks. If he's not careful he'll be joining her.' Mario smiled at this comment. 'Anyway. You're enjoying the job, aren't you?'

'Oh yeah. It's great. You've really helped.'

'Well - that's what I'm here for.'

Alison felt an almost uncontrollable urge to jump on Mario. She knew that she would have to make the first move or at least make it obvious how she felt. She didn't think that Mario would risk his job by trying it on with her - not without a very clear green light. But suppose he didn't respond? God, the embarrassment. Of course, he would have to go if he rejected her. She thought this through. That wouldn't be so hard. The other reps didn't particularly like him. She could make something up relating to the incident with Lorraine; the other reps would probably even respect her for it. It would have to be a one off. Mario would be easy enough to manipulate. One word and she would sack him. The more accessible the idea seemed, the shorter her breathing became as she remembered the size of his cock and looked at his body. Any minute now she would have him. She was going to do it! But how? She didn't have to wait long for her opportunity. Mario brushed passed her and as he did so his towel 'accidentally' fell from his waist to the floor.

'Oh shit,' said Mario feigning embarrassment. He saw Alison's eyes head directly for his cock. She couldn't help herself. Slowly, she reached out and took it in her hand, pulling him towards her.

'This is a one off Mario.' She flicked the end of his fast growing cock with her tongue. 'If anyone finds out about this I'll deny it and sack you.' She took as much of him in her mouth as she could, and then rested it against the side of her cheek. 'And this is not going on the score sheet. Understood?'

'Loud and clear.'

'Good.' She put him back into her mouth and gave him a playful bite.

Within minutes they were both naked and Alison was on all flours. Mario was ramming her from behind. Alison reached onto the bedside cabinet where there was some baby oil that Mario had applied to his body just before Alison arrived to make himself glisten. She poured it between her buttocks.

'Fuck me in the other hole Mario. See if you can get that gorgeous cock of yours up there.'

'What, up your arse?'

Before Mario had a chance to even think about it she grabbed hold of him and guided him in. She screamed with a mixture of pleasure and pain.

'Push fuck you, PUSH! Come on, I want you to ram it into me.'

Mario tried half-heartedly, but it slipped up the small of her back. Alison swung around so that she was lying on her back and Mario started pumping her in a more conventional fashion.

The window was open, and outside the sound of cars and drunken holidaymakers was joined by the roar of a jet as it passed overhead. At that moment, Alison came. Whenever Alison came she started to cry, a whimper which sounded like a dog pleading for it's bone to be given back, appropriately enough. Mario pulled out and shot all over her stomach. As the jets roar disappeared into the distance she thought that it was a shame that she couldn't allow herself to screw him again. She looked at his travelling clock. Just gone midnight. She smiled at Mario - maybe she could sleep with him again. She wiped a tear from her cheek. It was still a long season.

The plane banked left and roared over the island. The Captain informed the passengers that San Antonio was to the right. Lorraine looked out of the window.

'Have you got the time please?' asked the middle aged man sitting next to her.

'Just gone midnight.'

She wiped a tear from her cheek. It had been a short season.

Brad was once again doing the last flight. He had not been able to sleep so he went over to The Bon to see Mikey. It was one o'clock in the morning. Mikey and Greg were sitting at a table both eating pie, chips and beans. Brad had already eaten in The Las Huertas, so he just ordered three beers. It was two days since Lorraine had left. Mario had been keeping out of everyone's way, but on the few occasions Brad had seen him he had seemed even more pleased with himself than normal. This had wound Brad up even more. Brad was still on a very short fuse.

When Greg finished eating he went through the up to date scores. Brad had been on a roll, and the threesome had helped to put him in joint first place with Greg on thirty four points. Mario was now on twenty eight, and Mikey had been through a relatively barren period, only increasing his tally to twenty six.

Brad had been there for about ten minutes when Lester came up to Greg.

'Alright Greg.'

'Alright mate.' Greg couldn't remember his name.

'We only got back from sorting those birds out today,' said Lester, trying to impress.

'Which birds were they then, like?' Greg didn't know what he was on about.

'Y'know - the ones who live round the bay. I pointed them out to you on Thursday night when we were down The Star.'

'Oh yeah.' Greg only vaguely remembered.

To the three reps slight annoyance, Lester pulled up a chair to join them. 'Do any of you want a drink?'

'No thanks lad,' said Greg, answering for all of them.

'Yeah mate,' continued Lester. 'Fucking gorgeous they were. Couldn't get enough.'

'Really?' Greg was not doing a very good impression of someone who was interested.

Lester changed the subject. 'I got that money sorted out.'

'Wha' money was that, then?' asked Greg on auto-rep.

'Remember, I told you I might need to get some money sent over.'

'Oh yeah, yeah - that's right.' Greg did have a distant recollection of the conversation.

'Yeah, popped into The Delfin. Got Mario to sort it out. Then again, I suppose it was in his interest.'

'Yeah, right.' Greg looked around the room.

Lester persisted. 'Where's Lorraine? I haven't seen her about lately. Mind you, I haven't been around much what with those birds round the bay and everything.'

'She got the sack,' said Brad, still with a hint of anger in his voice.

'Oh you're joking,' said Lester, 'I really liked her as well.'

'You're not the only one,' said Brad.

'So what did she get the sack for then?' asked Lester innocently.

'The boss saw her coming on to Mario down The Star Club,' said Mikey.

The colour drained from Lester's face. 'You're joking.'

'I wish he was,' said Brad.

'Oh shit.' Lester looked skyward. 'Oh fucking shit. Oh I don't believe it. That wasn't meant to happen......'

All three reps stared at Lester, suddenly interested in every word he had to say.

'What do you mean, "Wasn't meant to happen?" What wasn't meant to happen?' said Brad leaning forward.

'It-it was just a bit of harmless fun - a bet. I didn't think it would go that far. I mean, I thought Mario would say something. Oh fucking hell...'

'What bet?'

'We bet Mario a hundred quid that he couldn't shag Lorraine. We just wanted to shut him up 'cos he was giving it the superstud bit. I've got the money here,' Lester got out an envelope. 'If he'd been here I was going to give it to him, but seeing as he isn't, well.........'

Brad was almost speechless with rage, so Mikey continued the questions to make sure they had all the facts.

'So what you're saying,' said Mikey, 'Is that you had a bet with Mario, and the bet was whether or not he could shag Lorraine, is that right?'

'Basically, yeah, but-'

'And to prove it, he grabbed hold of Lorraine in front of you?'

'Yeah. He said he'd get a video or something first, but that was the next best thing. Course, when Alison caught him we just assumed....' Lester saw the look on Brad's faced and decided it would be prudent to say no more, especially about the double or quits bet.

'So Lorraine got the sack because Mario didn't speak up. Just for a poxy 'undred quid that 'e's not gonna get anyway,' said Greg, summarising the situation. This was too much for Brad.

'CUNT!!!' he screamed at the top of his voice turning the table over sending glasses flying everywhere. All of the ready to depart holidaymakers looked up. Brad was oblivious to them. 'FUCKING ITALIAN SHIT TOSS WANKING CUNT!!!' Brad had lost it. 'I'M GONNA FUCKING KILL HIM!' Brad went storming out of the apartments heading for The Delfin. Heather had been sitting outside and heard the commotion and came running in.

'Heather,' said Mikey. 'Look after this lot.' He turned to Greg. 'Come on mate. We've got to stop him before he does something stupid.'

They both ran after Brad. He was trotting, and was already half way to The Delfin. They both called after him but he heard nothing. Mikey sprinted and overtook him.

'Brad, stop.' He ignored him. 'Brad, for fuck's sake stop.'
'GET OUTTA MY FUCKING WAY.'

Greg hovered behind. This looked serious. Mikey was in a quandary. He could see in Brad's eyes and tell by the way he was breathing that Brad had totally lost his cool. Mikey was hard, seriously hard, but even he didn't fancy a set too with Brad the way he was at the moment. But he had to stop him. He ran at Brad from about ten yards and used an American football block to pin him against the wall. Before Brad had a chance to react he started talking.

'Brad, listen to me. Listen to me Brad. If you don't agree with what I have to say I'll let you go and I'll even come down there and we'll do the fucker together.'

Brad stopped struggling slightly and looked Mikey in the eye. Mikey could see that Brad was coming out of the blind rage, but he knew that if he didn't act quickly Brad could fly off again and then God knows what would have happened.

'Look. Whatever you do Lorraine isn't going to get her job back. If we do Mario over, especially after your performance in front of all of the clients, then we'll both get the sack. Where will that get us? Yeah alright, so we'll enjoy seeing the fucker bleed for a while but then what? We might even get nicked. You don't want to end up in Spanish jail do you? Come on Brad. That's one of the reasons I respect you - you think about things. Think about this. We won't let him get away with it but let's think our revenge through, let's be clever about this. We don't even have to let him know that we know. Let's just use the information to get back at him and that slag Alison as well if needs be. Yeah? Come on mate, calm down.'

Greg now felt it was safe to join in. 'He's right Brad. Filling Mario in won't achieve anything. Besides, I can't let you get the sack 'cos I'll 'ave no competition with the ol' score board.'

'Come on man,' pleaded Mikey, 'He's not worth it.'

Mikey could feel Brad relaxing so he let him go. Brad turned round and in a final vent of anger and frustration punched a solid wood door, sending a bang echoing around the empty streets and instantly cutting two of his knuckles. He leant against the wall and nodded at Mikey. Mikey just nodded back.

'You alright?' asked Greg.

'Yeah, sorry. Guess I was a bit of a knob.'

'I wouldn't say that,' said Greg, 'But Mikey's right. I know I don't really wanna ger' involved but...well, I understand.'

'Yeah, cheers.'

'You better go and get that hand cleaned up,' said Mikey.

'Yeah I will.'

They were only twenty yards from The Las Huertas, so Brad slipped in to clean himself up. Greg and Mikey continued to walk down the road towards The Bon.

'Fucking 'ell,' said Greg, 'I wouldn't like to ger' on the wrong side of 'im.'

'He really had lost the plot, hadn't he?' said Mikey. 'I've

seen people go like that before. They don't know what they're doing until it's all finished. Fuck me, if that's what the job does to you maybe Lorraine's the lucky one.'

'No lad,' said Greg, 'There's a lorra good bits to come yet.'

CHAPTER NINE

Jane Ward was stressed. It was always the same this time of the season. The middle of June and already five new reps had either left or been given the sack. Tom Ortega had just got back from Majorca where he had gone to investigate Jason Barnes, the Resort Manager. Unfortunately when he had got there Jason Barnes had already left, taking over twenty thousand pounds of excursion money with him. To top it all off, a tabloid journalist had somehow heard a rumour about what had happened and had been hassling Jane all week for the story. Jane had denied all knowledge of the incident, but now in front of her on page seven of the Daily Star was the headline 'MAJORCA'S MISSING MILLIONS - Young Free & Single Manager disappears with over 5 MILLION pesetas.'

'Is that not just bloody typical of the tabloids?'

'What's that, Jane?' said Tom.

'Well as if twenty five grand doesn't sound bad enough, they have to write five million pesetas.'

'Oh that, yeah, crock of shit isn't it?'

'I'd love to get my hands on the Judas who leaked this story. I don't suppose you've any idea which reps been blabbing?'

'To be honest Jane,' said Tom, getting up and going to the small vending machine in the corner of the room, 'I'm not even sure that it was one of our reps. You know what it's like out there. Everybody knows what everyone else is doing. Might have been a rep from another company or one of the props from the bars. Maybe even Kirstie......'

'Could've been Jason himself for that matter, the bastard,' interrupted Jane.

'Can we prosecute him?' asked Tom. 'Assuming he ever

turns up.'

'Not really. Well, we can but we'd have to do it through the Spanish courts which could take forever and cost a fortune. Then there's the problem of proving how much he took. You know as well as I do that we don't declare all of the money we get from excursions.'

'So basically he's got away with it then?'

'Basically.'

Tom whistled. 'Twenty five grand. I wonder where he'll go with that.'

'Well if he's got any sense he'll get out of Majorca,' said Jane. 'Where's my tea you selfish bastard?'

'Oh, sorry.' Tom stood up and returned to the vending machine. He changed the subject. 'How's Natalie getting on working for the lovely Alison Shand in Ibiza? She's been out there over a week now hasn't she?'

'Mmm, I think so. As far as I'm aware she seems to be doing fine.' Jane took the tea from Tom. 'Thanks. Anyway, what do you mean, 'the lovely' Alison Shand? Do I detect a note of sarcasm? What's she done to upset my wee laddie?'

'Oh nothing,' sighed Tom. 'It's just that every time I speak to her on the phone I get the impression that she doesn't like me.'

'You sound a bit paranoid - not been out clubbing again at the weekend have we? On a bit of a come down?'

'*Chupa me la polla*,' (Suck my dick) laughed Tom, reverting to his second language. Jane didn't speak Spanish but she knew what he meant, as he'd often playfully swear at her in his father's native tongue. She chuckled, and flicked a rubber band at him. 'It's not just me,' continued Tom, 'It seems as though she's none too keen on Brad either.'

'Really!?' Jane raised her eyebrows. 'Now that does surprise me. Mind you, I was disappointed with Lorraine. I thought she'd do really well - such a sweet girl. It just shows that you never can tell.'

'Yeah but come on Jane. Mario is a good looking bastard, and Lorraine was rather, well, plain.'

'Even so Tom. She seemed so level headed. I was sure that she'd complement the team perfectly, but - there you go.'

She was interrupted by the phone ringing. 'Overseas. Oh hello Adam.' It was Adam Hawthorne-Blythe, the Chairman. 'Yes, I've seen it - it's in front of me at the moment. I know. No idea - it could've been anyone right enough. Even him, yes. No-one seems to know. Not in Majorca he isn't. Pretty much common knowledge. Neither am I, Adam, neither am I. No, but I'll be going to see Sebastian in a few minutes. Yeah, sure. As soon as I hear anything. No, you can if you want. Well that's what I thought. That's it, but if it doesn't blow over then one of us will have to. There'll probably be something more newsworthy tomorrow, like a cat stuck in a tree. Ok Adam, thanks. Yeah, bye.'

'Adam?'

'Adam,' repeated Jane sighing. 'He's seen it.'

'And?'

'He's alright - just making sure that we're on top of things.'

'Had he heard about the death in Tenerife?'

'No, not yet,' said Jane sipping her tea. 'One thing at a time, eh Tom? Jesus, what is it with Tenerife? Two death's in as many weeks. Plus that one in Crete, and it's not even July until next week.'

'What was the full story in Tenerife?' asked Tom.

'Apparently the maid knocked on the door, then the client just turned round, ran for the balcony and jumped. Splattered himself about ten feet away from a load of our lot laying on their sunbeds.'

'Did know he was six floors up?'

'I think so.'

Tom shook his head laughing. 'Must've been a fucking ugly maid.'

Brad had made a point of staying out of Mario's way. It was all he could do to stop himself from letting Mario know that he was aware of the bet with Lester. But Mikey was right. Lorraine was gone and there was nothing he could do or say that would get her back. Besides, Natalie had already replaced her. Revenge on Mario was going to be best metered out surreptitiously.

Natalie was a nice girl. Sort of reminded Brad of a female Greg - wholly itinerant, not interested in resort politics and just there for a good time. Brad and her had hit it off straight away. There was no resentment from Brad for her taking over from Lorraine. From the day she arrived they spent nearly all of their time laughing, or taking the piss out of each other, which was made easier for Brad by Natalie's penchant for Spanish men. She had only been in Ibiza just under two weeks, but had already slept with one of the waiters at the Rodeo Grill, then the son of the owner of The Bon who worked in the supermarket, and finally (so far) a barman from Sgt. Peppers. She was a bubbly blonde Geordie, who had the endearing quality of being able to laugh at herself and send up her own shortcomings.

Brad took the key from behind the desk of The Delfin. Just as he did so, the night porter walked into reception from the bar. Brad thrust the key into his pocket.

'Hola.'

The night porter grunted a response. He really was a miserable old sod. Brad crept up the stairs towards Mario's room. When he got there he knocked on the door, just in case. No answer. He put the key in and opened it.

'Mario?' he whispered half heartedly.

Silence. Brad closed the door. Revenge time. He walked into the bathroom and picked up Mario's green bottle of Wash 'N Go. Carefully, he removed the top but as he did so he heard footsteps coming down the corridor. They were getting closer. Shit! They weren't stopping. Brad looked for a hiding place but there was nowhere. He waited for the key to go into the lock. Instead there was a knock on the door.

'Mario?'

It was a girls voice. Brad kept totally still.

'Mario, are you there? It's me, Kim.' She waited for a few seconds. 'Damn.'

Brad heard the footsteps disappear back down the corridor, and returned to his task. He took a bottle of Immac hair remover from out of his pocket, and poured the contents into the Wash 'N Go bottle. Smiling, he put the top back on and said out loud to himself,

'Vidal Sassoon - Wash 'N Gone.'

The invoice had been picked off of the floor, some weeks before, by a cleaner. She had placed it with a pile of other papers. A few minutes later she had picked up the Post-it note. 'Sebastian. Please see me about this, Felipe.' She hadn't a clue what it referred to, so she had thrown it into the bin.

Sebastian decided to clear his desk. Things had been piling up and it had begun to annoy him. Monday, the first Monday in July - the perfect day to have a sort out. By eleven thirty he had worked his way through the majority of documents, although admittedly, he had been there since seven o'clock. He loosened his tie and ran his fingers through his thick black hair, before picking up the sole remaining A4 sheet of paper left on his desk. An invoice. After four and a half hours he was dealing with invoices on auto pilot. However, when he saw the name of the company on top of the invoice, his routine indifference turned first to confusion and then to intrigue.

'Chamberlain Clinic,' he mumbled to himself. 'What on earth is this for?' In the 'Invoice to' box, there was no name, only a customer number. He took off his reading glasses and gently banged them against his teeth. After a few minutes deliberation, he pressed the on-hook button of his phone, and dialled their number. A well spoken female voice answered.

'Good afternoon - sorry good morning, Chamberlain Clinic. How can I help you?'

'Oh, hello. I'm just about to settle an invoice, number............six, two, one, seven, four, and I was won-'

The receptionist interrupted. 'Yes, please hold and I'll put you through to the right department. Thank you.'

There were two rings and another female voice answered. 'Accounts.'

'Hello yes, I was wondering if you could help me? I'm about to settle an invoice - would you like the number?'

'Yes please.'

'Ok. It's six, two, one, seven four.'

Sebastian could hear the number being tapped into a keyboard.

'Is that Mr. Gomez?'

Sebastian was slightly taken aback.

'Hello, Mr Gomez? Mr Gomez, are you there?'

'Uh, yes. Sorry about that - someone just came into my office.'

'That's ok Mr. Gomez. I can understand that you might want to keep this confidential.'

It crossed Sebastian's mind that Felipe might have had a penis extension. But why would he put it through the company? There had to be an explanation.

'So how can we help you Mr. Gomez?'

'Well,' said Sebastian, stretching the word out as long as he could to try and give himself time to think. 'For my company records I need a more detailed, um, a more detailed breakdown on the invoice of what the treatment was for. You know - tax deductible and all that.'

Just at that moment, Jane walked in. Sebastian beckoned her to ssshh and to sit down. Once again Sebastian heard a keyboard being tapped, whilst the woman said,

'That shouldn't be a problem Mr. Go- oh, hang on a minute.' The woman on the other end started laughing. 'Well I've heard of some creative accounting in my time, but I think the taxman might have something to say about this one.'

'Why? What do you mean?'

'Well you better get yourself an Accountant Mr. Gomez. Only make sure he's good.' She laughed again. 'He'll have to be if you want to claim tax back for a termination.'

'A WHAT?' Sebastian stood up.

'A termination.' The woman paused. 'A pregnancy termination.' Sebastian was speechless. 'Hold on a moment. That is Mr. Gomez isn't it?'

'What? Yes, yes. Look I'm sorry - must go. Someone's just come in. Bye.' Sebastian put the phone down and dropped into his chair.

'What on earth was all that about?' asked Jane.

Sebastian shook his head. 'Oh you'll not believe this.' He sat back in his chair and stared out of the window for a few moments whilst he collected his thoughts. 'I've just found this invoice on my desk. It's from a private clinic and do you know what it's for?' Jane shrugged her shoulders. 'An abortion.'

'Oh God no,' said Jane, suddenly looking as though she'd seen a ghost.

'It gets better. Guess who put it through?'

'It wasn't Felipe Leather Office Gomez by any chance?' asked Jane slowly.

Sebastian looked at Jane as though she had suddenly revealed a psychic talent. Jane looked at him sheepishly. 'Oh dear.'

'How did you -?'

'Oh Sebastian, I feel so stupid.'

Sebastian came over cold as the possibility struck him. 'Don't tell me it's you,' he said leaping to his feet and slamming his hands on the desk.

'No it bloody wasn't me!' said Jane indignantly. She glared across his desk at him.

Sebastian held up his hands. 'Sorry.'

Jane let him stew for a few seconds before replying. 'I got an anonymous call last week telling me to watch Felipe Gomez because he was having an affair with someone who works for Young Free & Single. She didn't say who though.'

'So the caller was female?'

'Aye - but there was nothing distinctive about the voice.'

They sat and looked at each other for a few moments.

'What I don't understand,' said Sebastian, breaking the

silence, 'Is why would he try and put it through the company?'

'And more to the point, who's it for - now we've established it wasn't me?' Jane added sarcastically.

'Alright, alright. I've said I was sorry.'

'Hmph.' said Jane. 'Well anyway, we know it's not his wife - she's about fifty.'

Sebastian picked up his phone and dialled seventeen, Felipe's extension. 'Let's find out a bit more then.'

'Felipe Gomez.'

'Felipe. It's Sebastian.' They never exchanged pleasantries, so Sebastian got straight to the point. 'Felipe, It's about this Chamberlain Clinic invoice.'

'Ah yes. I'm glad you've called, although to be honest I thought you would have called a couple of weeks ago.'

'Yes, well I've been very busy,' said a slightly confused Sebastian.

'Quite, quite, well never mind. So, is there a problem?' asked Felipe, spoiling for a fight. 'I thought there might be. That's why I put the Post-it note on asking you to call me so I could answer any queries.'

So that was it. Sebastian smiled to himself. The Post-it note had obviously become detached from the invoice. He would have to play this by ear - let Felipe do all of the talking.

'You see, the thing is Sebastian, my eyes have been deteriorating over the last year or so - I guess it's all those contracts I keep reading.' Felipe enjoyed slipping that one in. 'So during the winter I had laser corrective eye surgery, and I thought that because I had it done mainly for the purposes of reading, it would be appropriate for me to put it through the company. After all, were it not for all of the reading I have to do for my job I could have probably waited a few years.'

'So the invoice is for laser corrective eye surgery, is it?'

'Yes, that's right,' lied Felipe. 'Will there be a problem?'

'Um, no. Well at least there shouldn't be.' Sebastian was thinking as he spoke. 'I tell you what Felipe. If there are any problems I'll come back to you. Alright?'

'Fine. Speak to you later then Sebastian. Good-bye.' Felipe

put the phone down and smiled. He had not expected it to be that easy.

'What the hell is he up to?' said Sebastian, standing up and walking around the room.

'Did I get the gist of that? Is he saying the invoice is for eye surgery?'

'That's what he's claiming, yes.' Sebastian looked at Jane and smiled, handing her the phone. 'Do you fancy finding out who the 'lucky' woman was?'

'I don't know,' said Jane taking the phone, 'What shall I say?' Sebastian looked at her blankly. Jane's eyes lit up with inspiration. 'I know.' She dialled the number.

'Chamberlain Clinic.'

'I wonder if you can help me. I had an abortion there last summer, but the invoice has been sent to the father's address rather than mine.'

'Oh no!' said a concerned voice. 'I'm so sorry.'

'No, it's alright. Our fault - we should have said at the time. The only thing is I've moved since then and I wasn't sure whether or not you had my old address or my new one.'

'Hang on and I'll check for you. What's the invoice number?'

Jane looked at the invoice. 'It's six, two, one, seven, four.'

There was a pause. 'The address we've got is the one in Cambridge. Is that right?'

Jane was hoping that the woman would read out the whole address, but she didn't. Now what? She couldn't very well ask for her own address.

'No, I've moved.' Jane gave the address of an old university friend. 'Could you send it to forty five, Cheetham Rd, Hanwell, London W7. I'm sorry, I can never remember the post code.'

'That's alright. We'll get it off to you today.'

'Thanks.' Still no name. Jane looked at Sebastian and shrugged her shoulders. She'd failed. 'Thanks a lot. Good-bye.'

'Good-bye Miss Shand.'

'Wh'appen bal' 'ed?'

'What!?'

'Me say wh'appen bal' 'ed?'

Brad understood Mikey and started laughing. Mario didn't.

'Talk properly. We're not in Brixton or Jamaica. Now say it again slowly.' Mario could barely hear Mikey over the music pumping out of The Ku Club sound system.

Brad acted as translator. 'He said, "What's happening bald head." That's right isn't it Mikey?'

'Spot on dread.'

They both looked at Mario's confused face topped by his freshly shorn head and burst out laughing. Mario marched off sulking, which made them laugh even more.

'There you go Brad,' said Mikey in between giggles. 'I told you there were better ways of getting back at him, other than kicking his head in. Get him right where it hurts - his ego.'

'It's great isn't it. He was so proud of his hair as well. He's like Samson - totally lost his confidence. He hasn't pulled for nearly a week.' Brad picked up an unattended half full beer bottle. They didn't get free drinks in Ku, and a beer was nine hundred pesetas - nearly a fiver. He took a swig of it but immediately spluttered it out laughing. 'Fuck me.' he said and pointed up to the balcony, 'Look up there.'

Mikey looked up. Bent over the balcony of the luxurious aircraft hanger sized club was a girl with long blonde hair. She was totally out of it, which in part explained why she was allowing herself to be shagged from behind in full view of the whole club, by a grinning client of Brad's with cropped ginger hair called Rusty. Rusty was part of a group of five lad's who were all totally mad and complete 'E' monsters. They had been on the island a week, and were having a competition to see who could shag a girl in the most unusual place. Any claim had to be verified by another member of the party or a rep. As Brad and Mikey looked up at the balcony they saw Greg come and stand next to the fornicating couple. He gave a double thumbs up to the rest of the group who were on the dance floor standing about ten yards from Brad. There was a loud cheer from the group, and Rusty, still shagging, gave a victory salute, just prior to being hauled off of the girl and escorted from the premises by the uniformed security.

'I'll pop up there and check he doesn't get a kicking,' said Mikey. 'I think he's in the lead with that one though, don't you?'

Brad laughed and walked around the club. He was seriously thinking about popping a pill. The music was spot on and the atmosphere was great. Brad actually felt in quite a good mood. At one point he thought that maybe someone had laced his drink because he was sure that he saw Samuel Zakatek, the mad ex-Vietnam vet he'd met on the journey over. Brad shuddered, and made a point of not going to that part of the club again.

Even though he had got revenge on Mario by chemically scalping him with the Immac, he still had an inexplicable, primeval urge to let loose physically. Brad seldom got into fights and mostly went out of his way to avoid trouble. But after he had 'lost it' when he found out about Mario's bet with Lester, there was still an unresolved rage within him. Normally, with nothing else to provoke him, it would have probably worked it's way out of his system and that would have been the end of it. Normally.

Brad was standing near the entrance waiting for Mikey. He had the small white pill in between his thumb and forefinger, ready to pop it in his mouth as soon as he saw someone walk passed with a drink he could take a swig of. He looked up to the main doors. Romford Reg was coming in with three friends and four girls. The girls were all very attractive, and two of the friends were well over six foot. Reg had been avoiding Brad. Something had gone wrong with the car at least twice a week since the beginning of the season. The windscreen wipers had packed up totally, and a new motor for it was impossible to find. It was still overheating regularly and the exhaust had all but fallen off.

Over a week had passed since Brad had given Reg the keys

yet again and still the car had not been repaired. Brad had spent a small fortune on taxi's and not done half of the things that he had planned to do, without having the mobility that a car should have offered him. He was seriously pissed off at Reg. However, hitherto Reg had been quite smart. Although Brad sensed that he was taking the piss, Reg had always eventually backed down and had not been too much of a smart arse, at least not sufficiently enough for Brad to escalate the confrontation to a physical one. But tonight, Reg was feeling slightly more cocksure than normal, largely brought about by the fact that he had some friends with him from back home, and they had pulled some stunning girls. With Brad still on a shortish fuse, all of the ingredients were there for a more unpleasant exchange than normal.

'Ah, look who it isn't,' said Reg, as he saw Brad. Just seeing him wound Brad up, but he didn't feel in the mood to even converse with him. Possibly Reg took this as a sign of weakness. 'Would've thought this was a bit posh for you Brad.' The girls giggled. 'Yeah, thought The Star was more your cup of tea. Old Brad 'ere's a rep, girls - works for that Young Free & Single mob.' Two of the male members of Reg's party and one of the girls went to the bar. 'This is the geezer I was telling you about who bought that classic car of mine. Got 'imself a right bargain. Ha, ha, ha. See you later mate.'

Reg led the rest of his group to the bar to join the others. Brad stood there. At first he felt nothing. He put the pill back into his pocket and walked up to the balcony, where he looked down on Reg and his friends standing at the edge of the dance floor, all laughing. It started off as a calm rage; a calculated decision that tonight was going to be the night that Reg would wish that he had not followed the career path of Arthur Daley. He stared at Reg, remembering the catalogue of things that he had done, and then re-interpreting some of the things he had said so that there was no doubting in Brad's mind that Reg had been taking the piss all along. He began to feel his blood boiling. Mikey was walking towards him, but he had not seen Brad. Brad wanted to continue winding himself up in his own company, so he walked away.

As he started walking, the adrenaline once again began pumping around his body. Perhaps whatever Brad was going to do to Reg was in part misplaced and intended for Mario. It didn't matter. Because he had moved from his vantage point Brad lost sight of the black jacketed, blonde crew cut that distinguished Reg. The urgent need to find him and the quickening of pace put Brad's body into the final, fight or flight mode. He didn't realise that he was barging into people as he crossed the dance floor next to the swimming pool in Ku. Then he saw him. Walking down the stairs to the toilets. Brad almost broke into a trot. He knew exactly what he was going to do. He had seen it countless times in the film Scum, where Carling (played by Ray Winstone) chases the 'Daddy' Pongo into the toilets, bashes his head against the wall and then batters him to the floor, telling him exactly what he thinks of him. Brad felt surprisingly controlled. As he jumped down the last three stairs and skipped into the toilet though, he felt a sudden mad adrenaline rush. He was just about to grab Reg when he realised........it wasn't him! It was another clubber wearing a black jacket and sporting a blonde crew cut.

Brad panicked. His system was in overdrive and he had to do something. He ran up the stairs, frantically looking for Reg. Luckily (or unluckily for Reg) he saw him standing near the bar in the VIP lounge on the next level up. Brad bound up the stairs, totally focused on Reg but not now having such a clear idea as to what his course of action was going to be. He strode into the VIP section, and when he was about ten yards away he virtually ran at Reg.

SMACK! He whacked Reg with his right fist, side on so that he connected with his cheekbone directly under his left eye socket. Reg had no warning - Brad was not playing by Queensbury rules. It was a great shot. Reg's legs crumpled from under him. Brad had crossed the threshold. All he saw was a red mist; conscience, fear, pain and logic were at that moment totally alien emotions to him. Even though Reg was down and virtually out, a blind rage was surging through

Brad's veins. As Reg went down, Brad's right foot lashed out, just missing the falling Reg's head and instead connecting with his shoulder, causing him to scream with pain.

The biggest of Reg's friends went to grab Brad, but Brad pushed him away so hard that he fell over the table where the three girls were sitting, sending glasses and bottles flying everywhere. The smallest of Reg's friend came from behind Brad and managed to encircle him with his arms. Brad pushed backwards, causing the two of them to tumble so that the hapless friend had all of Brad's body weight fall on top of him. Somehow he managed to keep his arms around Brad and hold him on the floor. Reg was not completely out and was lying next to Brad's feet. Raging, and annoyed that Reg was still conscious, Brad kicked downwards with both feet, trying to connect Reg's face with the heels of his Timberlands and inflict as much damage as he could.

The next thing Brad remembered was being ran out of the club, prodded by four or five of Ku's security. He felt the hot flush begin to subside, as if someone had turned the gas down on a pan full of boiling liquid. Reason, shock and guilt immediately replaced the vacuum that the fast diminishing anger created.

The night's promoter, who knew Brad reasonably well and had been on the island for years, stopped the security and spoke to them in Spanish. From what Brad understood it seemed as though he was asking them what had happened and to leave it to him to deal with.

The promoter turned to Brad, and with his gentle Welsh accent said, 'So what's it all about Brad?'

'Sorry Gerry,' Brad was calming down fast. 'I guess I just lost it. That fucking wanker's been winding me up since the beginning of the season. I suppose I snapped.' His fast, shallow breathing was returning to normal. 'Fucking 'ell. Is he alright? What did I do to him?'

'I don't know. He's still in there. Look, I'm sorry Brad, but I'm gonna have to ban you for a couple of weeks.'

'Yeah sure. I understand.'

'Here,' he said giving him a bottle of San Miguel, 'Take this. Best thing you can do is stay out of the way of his mates and get a cab home. You know where the taxi rank is, don't you?'

'Yeah,' said Brad. 'Sorry Gerry.'

'Don't worry mate - shit happens.'

Brad made his way down to the taxi rank, where a constant flow of taxi's took the revellers back to their homes or hotels, or on to another club. There were about twenty people there. Brad sat himself down on a two foot high white wall, which sectioned off the road from a number of trees. Brad noticed that a group of people near the front of the queue were staring up at something. Brad glanced in the direction that they were looking but didn't pay much attention as he was still pre-occupied with the events of the previous half hour. His train of thought was interrupted when he became aware of someone calling his name. He looked round but could see no-one.

'Brad.' He looked to his left.

'Brad.' He looked further to his left.

'Brad.' He stood up.

'Brad you knob!' He looked to his right. Whoever was calling his name started laughing.

'BRAD!!' He looked all around but still could see nobody he knew.

'BRAD!!! - UP HERE!' Brad looked up towards where the rest of the crowd were pointing and either laughing or shaking their heads in disbelief. There, up a tree, with the same blonde girl that Rusty had been shagging on the balcony, was one of Rusty's mates, a stocky lad with short light brown hair.

'Whaddya reckon then Brad - does this count?'

It was fairly obvious what he was up to, but in case there was any doubt, his grinning bravado was interrupted by a cry of 'Oh shit.' He had gone a stroke too far. He pulled out of the girl, but as he did so a sticky white spurt landed on the head of a Spanish man in his early thirties who was standing in the queue. He was not amused. The crowd scattered, but quickly re-gathered to form a potential lynch mob. Brad had endured enough trouble for one night, so, as the crowd focused their attention on the branches above, Brad gave Rusty's friend a thumbs up to indicate that even if it turned out to be a posthumous award, the shag qualified. He jumped the queue into a waiting cab.

'Las Huertas, San Antonio por favor.'

Brad, now totally calm, sat back in the chair of the cab and smiled to himself. He didn't know Rusty's mate's name, but if he survived Brad decided that henceforth he would be called Squirrel........after all - he had just stored his nuts up a tree.

CHAPTER TEN

It had been nearly a year since Tom Ortega had last visited Ibiza. He had only been working for YF&S for three months when Jane Ward had sent him over to get a feel for what repping was like on resort. It seemed a lifetime ago now. Before putting on the YF&S badge he had heard how easy the reps had it with female hoidaymakers. The experienced reps had told him some of the stories during a party night that they had just before leaving for resort. At the time he found some of them hard to believe; the egotistically fertile imagination of vain young men trying to be the centre of attention for those few minutes more, by relaying stories of sexual prowess and perversion. Tom thought that some of the stories could have been built upon a grain of truth, but surely women could not be that easy? Tom had been in Ibiza less than four hours before he found out the answer for himself.

At the time, Jason Barnes was the senior rep, under Kirstie who was then Resort Manager. Tom had been standing in the reception of The Bon when he heard a girl ask Jason if he thought he could manage her and her mate. Unable to believe his ears, Tom had turned around. The girl noticed him and immediately spotted his badge.

'Are you a rep too?' she had asked.

'Uh, sort of,' Tom had replied nervously.

'You're not bad looking really, are you?' Tom remembered feeling embarrassed. 'Yeah, I think I'll have you by the end of the week.'

She fulfilled her threat that same night.

Since then Tom had made over a dozen resort visits and in that time, like many reps, had realised his potential with the opposite sex. He had inherited his Spanish fathers thick black hair, brown eyes, and six foot frame; his mothers Roman nose and refined English accent. The overall resulting effect combined with an easy going and amiable personality meant that every resort visit so far had brought him ample female attention.

Tom was aware that he had changed dramatically during the last year. His confidence had improved, and whereas when he first started the job he had been scared to say boo to a goose, he now had no qualms about using the authority that his position and closeness to Jane Ward gave him to throw his weight around to discipline reps where necessary. This meant that the reps were pretty much divided as to whether or not they liked him. Most of those who bothered to get to know him thought he was fine, whereas those who didn't thought he was a jumped up egomaniac from head office with ideas above his station. Brad fell into the former camp, Alison the latter.

About half a mile before coming into San Antonio, both sides of the road are lined by trees only a few feet apart. As well as giving motor cyclists and the odd reckless driver the perfect opportunity to become terminally at one with nature by crashing into them (virtually every tree has a story to tell), they also form a kind of natural tunnel. Even in the middle of summer only a flicker of sunlight penetrates their canopy. As Tom drove through this 'tunnel', he was in quite an introspective mood. Ahead of him he could see the bright, late afternoon sunlight, indicating the end of the row of trees and the beginning of San Antonio.

Tom wondered if having one of those 'near death' experiences would look anything like the view ahead; a flicker of light at the end of a long dark tunnel, growing ever closer and ever brighter. Would the light look the same, thought Tom, irrespective of whether you were bound for heaven or hell? Tom squinted as the trees gave way to the bright sunlight, and there it was; San Antonio - truly, some people's idea of heaven, but equally truly, some people's idea of absolute hell. It struck Tom that maybe heaven and hell are indeed the same place; all that is different is the individuals perception and expectations. If this was the case, then during his first visit Tom had slept with five women in as many days, and drank as much as he possibly could without spending a penny - now that was his idea of heaven.

Tom drove past the roundabout which had a giant white sculpted egg sitting in the middle of it. Apart from a night club called Extasis and a hotel called Piscis Park, this is the first thing the visitor sees as they come into San Antonio harbour. The harbour boasts a recently renovated promenade which overlooks the departure point for boats taking holidaymakers to local beaches (San Antonio has no real beach) or for outings in glass bottom boats. At the back of the promenade is a row of restaurants, where semi-interested diners can watch a fountain and lights display every evening, in between trying to find the English page of their menu, hoping that it's contents contain something other than 'bloody foreign muck'.

Tom remembered to be careful driving his hired Renault Clio along the promenade road. Even during the day, drunk or daydreaming, jaywalking Brits would forget that the Spanish were inconsiderate enough to be the same as the majority as the rest of the world, in that they drive on the right. Most locals were aware of the British lemming attitude to road safety, and drove to accommodate them. Any accidents were normally caused by British drivers not aware of their fellow countrymen's ignorance, or by Germans who were, but who had a vague memory of 1945 or 1966.

Tom successfully negotiated the promenade and drove a little faster as he came to the back of town. It was just coming up to seven thirty, so most of the people he saw frequenting the local bars were either families, or teenagers who had yet to come to terms with the fact that all of the bars did not ring last orders before eleven o'clock. He thought about making a slight detour to Cafe Del Mar to see what the quality of female worker was like this year and what type of pills were on offer. Instead, he sniffed his armpit and decided that a shower would probably be the course of action which would most improve his later social standing.

267

For once Brad had been given an early flight transfer. The flight was due to arrive at nine p.m. so Brad was in the coach and ready to go at seven thirty. He walked up and down the coach counting. Once satisfied that everybody was on board he made his way to the front and turned to the coach driver.

'Ok Jose - Vamos' (Let's go).

Jose started the engine and closed the door. As he did so, Brad saw a blue Renault Clio, and instantly recognised Tom Ortega removing his case from it's boot. Unluckily for Tom, Brad had the microphone switched on and in his hand.

'Right everyone. If you look out of the left window - that's the one nearest the apartments - you can see Tom Ortega who's our Overseas Controller, and he's come over to see us all from London. Well, when I say 'us', I don't mean you lot 'cos you're all about to go home. Ha! Ha!' All of the clients started jeering in a good natured way. 'But I'm sure you'll all be back next year - AM I RIGHT!?' There was a great big cheer. 'Brilliant. I can honestly say that you've been the best crowd that we've had all season...' Brad said this every week, '....So give yourselves a big round of applause.' More clapping and cheering. The coach started to pull away. 'Now the thing with our Overseas Controller is that he's come over here to try and persuade the hotels to put up the price of booze,' lied Brad, 'So instead of waving good-bye to the apartments, I want you all to give Tom the rudest gesture and to hurl the worst abuse that you can. And seeing as you're leaving you can say something really rude like 'flip' or 'bum'. Are you ready? One.....Two....Threeeeeee.'

There followed a sea of hand signals and a chorus of obscenities. Brad looked through the door and gave Tom a thumbs up. Tom responded with a hand gesture of his own.

Sitting at the front of the coach was a girl from Wolverhampton called Angela. Two nights before, she had come up to Brad full of Dutch courage and told him that he

268

had promised to sleep with her the previous week. Brad couldn't remember but, chivalrous as ever, obliged her that self same night. What Brad didn't know at the time was that Angela was the type of girl who religiously videoed Little House On The Prairie and always made sure that she listened to Simon Bates's Our Tune. A hopeless romantic, happiest with a wet handkerchief, she was now certain that Brad was her Anthony, and she his Cleopatra. However, the only 'infinite variety' Angela possessed was a huge repertoire of annoying habits that Brad had tired of after one night. She had been pestering him ever since and had told most of the holidaymakers that Brad was her boyfriend.

This had ruined Brad's chances with a gorgeous Irish girl the night before to say nothing of putting his job in jeopardy. He had sat Angela down to talk to her, but had given up when it was obvious that it was going in one ear and out the other. It was amazing how, in such a short space of time, she had positioned herself as probably being the singularly most irritating woman that Brad had ever met - certainly that he had ever slept with. But, he should not have been surprised - she was, after all, a single share.

Brad couldn't help it, but because she had caused him so much grief during the last two days he wanted to get her back. Not nastily - in fact he thought that she would probably enjoy what he had in store for her in her own perverse way - but she was the perfect candidate for Greg's new competition.

Brad finished his usual spiel about passports, the reunion and how to check in at the airport etc. Once he finished he switched off the microphone, turned to Jose and nodded.

'Ahora Jose' (Now Jose).

Jose looked at his watch and pressed a button which stared a stopwatch. Brad switched the microphone back on.

'So that's all of the information you should need at the airport. All that remains is for me to once again thank you all for being such a great crowd, and as we drive out of San Antonio I hope that you've all got some wonderful memories to take back with you.' Brad looked out of the window and the

269

harbour looked fantastic as the low sun and the bar lights reflected off of the water, with the final sun worshippers disembarking from the last boats of the day. Brad tried to sound as slushy as possible. 'As you look out of the window I'm sure you'll all agree that this island can be a magical place. Maybe some of you have met the boy or girl of your dreams and fallen in love, so if you have, I hope it all works out for you.'

He glanced at Angela. Almost. 'Like I said before, you've been the best crowd ever and I'm going to miss you all, and maybe I'll see some of you again one day.' He paused. Surely that would do it? Still not quite. 'Anyway, for once in my life I'm going to shut up and let the music do the talking.' He put in the cassette that he had been holding in his hand. 'When Will I See You Again' started playing. If that didn't work then he was sure that 'Leaving On A Jet Plane' would do the trick. He certainly hoped so - he'd spent a good couple of hours at The Anglers making up a tape of the slowest, slushiest songs with references to 'leaving' or 'lost love' that he could find. He needn't have worried. Within the first four bars of the tape he heard a sniffle, and sure enough it was Angela. He turned to Jose

'Jose amigo, cuanto tiempo?' (Jose my friend, how long?)

'Fifty three seconds,' replied Jose in his best English.

'Yes!'

Brad made a small punch in the air and sat back in his chair smiling to himself. Even Greg was going to have to go some to beat that. A blubber in less than a minute - it had to be a record.

Tom had a quick shower and got himself ready to meet Greg in the bar at midnight. Alison had allowed Greg the night off from airport duty so that he could escort Tom around town. She considered Tom's visit to be a minor irritation - she did not like him and had no intention of socialising with him nor spending any more time with him than absolutely necessary.

Tom was in the bar before Greg. Cases were piled in the hallway ready for the arrival of the coach to take their owners to the airport. Twenty or so subdued clients were sitting outside The Bon with the last drink of their holiday placed in front of them. Most of them were dressed in shorts and a T-shirt. Tom chuckled to himself. Before joining YF&S he worked at Gatwick airport and it never failed to amaze him how holidaymakers would often come off of their flight dressed in attire more suited to the climate of their place of departure. When Tom had left London it had been cold and raining - hardly T-shirt and shorts weather.

He chatted to Frank while he was waiting for Greg to turn up. Tom really wanted to converse in Spanish, but from the day he had joined YF&S Jane had told him to keep his linguistic skills secret from everyone but her. That way, she reckoned that he might be able to pick things up from hotel staff or Resort Managers, who assumed he could not speak the language. Tom knew that Alison spoke hardly any Spanish and that all of the other reps apart from Mikey only had the most basic grasp, but he kept to English nevertheless.

Just after midnight Greg walked in. When he saw Tom his face broke into a broad grin.

'Alright mate,' he said shaking Tom's hand.

'Not bad thanks. What you been up to?'

'Oh, plenty of caning. Over forty points now.'

Tom had been introduced to the points competition the year before by Jason Barnes. Greg had also been in Ibiza that year and Tom remembered how vigorously Greg had pursued first place. Tom and Greg had actually got on quite well. Greg wasn't interested in company politics, so his main criteria for judging whether or not Tom was 'alright' was by ascertaining Tom's capacity for alcohol and his appetite for women. As Tom had slept with five women in as many days, and had helped Greg in a two man attempt to keep San Miguel in business, they had successfully bonded.

'So, what have you got in store for us tonight?' Tom asked.

271

'Well, I thought we could go an' 'ave a look at a rather interesting church near San Augustine, then maybe go to a Flamenco recital, per'aps rounding off the evening with a cup of coffee an' a chat about airport procedure. On the other 'and, we could go into town, get pissed for nowt an' try to pull a couple o' slappers. What d'ya reckon?'

'Let's leave the cultural bit 'til tomorrow, eh?' Tom knocked back his drink. 'C'mon then - you lead.'

The West End of San Antonio is essentially one main road going up a hill which is adjacent to the harbour, with bars or clubs filling both sides. There are a few roads running parallel or which cut across this main hill which also have bars in them, albeit not huddled together so densely. The only other road which is more or less full of bars runs at a right angle to the main drag and starts just opposite Sgt. Peppers - Sgt. Peppers being where Tom and Greg chose to commence their crawl.

As Tom and Greg walked in, Ray the singer hadn't started playing. When he saw Tom he remembered him instantly, partly from the previous year, but mostly from the reunion. November had seen the YF&S reunion held at what used to be a Butlin's holiday camp, but was now a modernised 'holiday centre'. Ray had been one of the acts booked to play there. On the first night he had shagged a very pissed client in Greg's chalet, at the same time and along with Greg and Tom. After the initial renewal of acquaintances, the reunion was inevitably their first topic of conversation.

'So you gonna do the reunion again this year?' asked Tom, once they had all toasted each other and downed a Jaegermeister in one.

'Aye lad. Mind you, I'm trying to make sure me bird don't come after last year.'

'Of course,' said Tom, 'You're going out with that page three girl now aren't you? Cheryl Pitt isn't it? Or should that be Cheryl Fit?'

Ray laughed. 'Yeah she's certainly that. Definitely better than that monster we all shagged at the reunion.'

'I make yer right there,' said Greg. 'The thing that got me though was turning round and seeing old Barnesy in the corner wanking 'imself off. Remember? I asked 'im if 'e wanted a go and 'e just said -'

'Carry on, I'm 'appy 'ere,' interrupted Ray, finishing the story. They all laughed. 'How is old Jason? He's boss in Majorca this year in't he?'

Tom shuffled uncomfortably for a moment. 'He was. I had to go over there to sack him.'

'Wha'?' said Ray. 'Why?'

'Well as it turned out he beat me to it - already done a bunk. I thought you'd've heard about it,' Tom said to Ray. Ray shrugged his shoulders so Tom continued. 'Basically, Jason scarpered with about twenty five grand of company money.'

Ray whistled, 'Dodgy bastard.'

'You can say that again. Still it's done now.' He took a swig of beer and changed the subject. 'So what do you think of the new reps? Getting on alright with them?'

'Yeah, not bad. Mikey's safe. Brad's a nice bloke - I let 'im get on the ol' piano sometimes. That new bird - Natalie....?' Tom nodded, 'She's a fuckin' nutter. I think she's already 'ad one of the barmen.'

'What about Mario?' asked Tom innocently.

'I'm going for a quick slash. Fuck off when we get back?' said Greg.

'Yeah sure,' said Tom glancing at his half empty bottle. 'Yeah so what about Mario?' asked Tom again.

'Less said about 'im the better,' said Ray. Tom said nothing and Ray knew he would have to elaborate. 'Let's just say that we didn't ger'off to the best o' starts, an' if it weren't for Mikey I would've probably decked him.'

'Why, what happened?' persisted Tom.

'I'll leave it at that,' said Ray finishing off his drink. 'I've got to get up and do me bit. Good to see you again Tom. I'll catch up with y'later.' He saw Greg come out of the toilet and waved at him as he got on to stage, mouthing 'Later' as he did so.

As Tom and Greg left the bar Tom turned to Greg.

'What was all that nonsense between Mario and Ray at the start of the season?'

'Wha' did Ray tell you?' asked Greg.

'Not a lot really. Is everything alright now?

'Mario's not 'is bosom buddy if that's what yer mean. But Ray's too professional to let it affect the way 'e does 'is job so 'e tolerates 'im.'

'So what the fuck did Mario do?'

'What did 'e do?' Greg laughed. 'Let's just say that Mario isn't exactly the most popular rep on the island. Come on - let's go in to Rainbow.'

The Rainbow Bar is the first bar that you come to on the left when you walk down the road that runs at right angles towards the main hill. This season it hosted non-stop Karaoke, and as Tom and Greg walked in another tour company were in the middle of a bar crawl. It was nowhere near the size of a YF&S bar crawl - probably little more than twenty people - and the reps were certainly not used to entertaining. It amused Tom how reps from 'mainstream' companies (non-specialist companies which cater for families as well as young people) would try and copy YF&S, getting the younger members of the party out on crawls or certain excursions. He would often recognise the reps as ones who had failed to pass the YF&S interviews. This meant that not only was the 'raw material' not as good as a YF&S rep, but also they would not have undergone the intensive specialist training that all new YF&S recruits went through. The result was normally a shoddy, unprofessional imitation of a YF&S night out.

When the reps from the other company saw Tom and Greg they tried even harder to be lively and entertaining, which was actually quite embarrassing. Of course, it was great for business when YF&S were in the same bar or on the same excursion as another tour company. What would normally happen would be that the clients on holiday with the rival company would see how it should be done and how much fun everybody was having, and book with YF&S the following year. This was one of the reasons why YF&S reps always had to be the first up and dancing - so that people on holiday with a different company would be convinced that YF&S were the liveliest most fun loving tour operator on the planet.

Tom and Greg left Rainbow as soon as they had finished their first drink.

'I dunno about you mate, but I've had enough of drinking,' said Tom.

'Leave off. I've only just started,' said Greg.

'What about getting a couple of pills?'

'What, you mean E's?'

'Yeah, fancy it?'

For once, Greg looked almost bashful.

'Come on,' persisted Tom. 'You're a rep - you must know where to score some pills.' They stopped in the road outside a Scandinavian bar called Mermaid.

'Yeah, I do. It's just that, well, I've never - you know. Its not that...'

'Greg,' said Tom. 'Stop waffling. What's the problem?'

Greg shuffled uncomfortably. 'I've never taken ecstasy before.'

'You're joking!'

'No. I've never felt the need. I've always been 'appy with the ol' grog.'

'Oh mate - you don't know what you're missing. You've got to try one.'

'Nah - I'll stick to the beer.'

'Why Greg? What you scared of?'

Tom found it hard to believe that a supposedly streetwise scouser had never taken an E. Still, he had been working abroad for nearly four years, with free drink wherever he went. Maybe that was it - he wasn't scared, just tight.

'I'm not scared. I just don't fancy it. Come 'ed, let's 'ave a drink in 'ere.'

They went into Gorm's Garage, a long bar with a DJ which held about three hundred people when full. It was frequented by all of the different tour companies on their bar crawl nights. No single nationality had staked a claim on the bar, so it was a melting pot of Brits, Germans and Scandinavians. Despite this, there was seldom any trouble, mainly because it had a reputation as being a ravey dance bar rather than a 'drinkasmuchasyoucanandfallover' bar. Greg ordered two more beers before Tom had a chance to refuse. Because it was so busy they took their drinks outside, where Tom was the first to speak.

'I'm not trying to turn you into a junkie you know Greg.'

'I know you're not. It's just that no-one seems to know for sure what they do to you.'

'Maybe not, but I sure as hell know that booze fucks up your brain, liver and kidneys, as well as making you fat and anti-social. Give me E's any day.'

'What about if I 'ad an allergic reaction?' said Greg, for the first time beginning to actually contemplate the idea.

'There's more chance of having an allergic reaction to peanuts or tomatoes.'

'I still don't know......'

'Look. Just take a half to start with - I'll keep my eye on you.'

'I'm not sure,' said Greg. 'What was that bit about sex again?'

'It's fucking brilliant. Your whole body is like one big, fucking erogenous zone. It's almost impossible to come, and when you do......' Tom made an explosion type noise. Greg sat still for a moment or so. Suddenly he stood up and downed his drink in one.

'Fuck it. Let's go an' gerra couple.'

'Attaboy,' smiled Tom.

At the bottom of the main hill in San Antonio's West End is Night Life night club. A pretty girl with curly brown hair, kissed with orange streaks by two months of sunbathing, was herding the constant flow of people into the club.

'Come on lads, in you come......Free to get in..........Top

London DJ's........The best music in San An............Free schnapps with your first drink........Alright girls, all the talent's in here tonight...........You boys are too good looking to go anywhere else, get yourselves down there..'

Ninety percent of the drunk or drugged males who she vaguely addressed were convinced she fancied them. But she (Maddy) was immune to looks, chat up lines, phemerones or designer clothes while she was working. She was on auto pilot; looking through every face that appeared before her; hearing the same crap chat up lines and corny jokes twenty times a night. The only time she injected a mild dose of enthusiasm was when the bearded bespectacled manager came scurrying out to check that the other bars were not doing any better than Night Life. Even if Night Life was full he would be on her case;

'Maddy, those boys there........Come on, no drink so much......Plenty other girls want to work here.'

And of course, he was right. Even though it was seven hours a night for little more than the equivalent of fifteen pounds pay, at least four young people would come in every night asking for work. The main thing that Maddy had in her favour was that she had worked there the previous season, and she knew that Toni (the Manager) didn't want to let her go because she was good at her job and had showed a degree of resilience and loyalty. Most 'props' only lasted a few nights. It had therefore become Toni and Maddy's nightly ritual to wind each other up and to test each others boundaries to the full.

Greg had taken Tom back to Sgt. Peppers to score from Danny. Danny had some unusual E's called 'Mad Bastards'. The name alone almost put Greg off, but Danny re-assured him that they were 'really rushy' - which didn't particularly encourage Greg, and then that he would be really 'loved up' - which did.

Tom and Greg walked down the bottom road by the Tanit apartments. It was quieter and darker than all of the others which led to Night Life. Towards the bottom were two stalls on opposite sides of the road, both selling ready made rolls in cling film, ice creams, sweets and drinks. Tom bought a bottle of water.

'Right then mate,' he said. 'You sure you wanna do this?'

'You fuckin' muppet. You've spent the last 'alf hour talking me into it and now you ask me if I'm sure,' said Greg. 'Just give us 'alf the thing and let's gerrit over with.'

Tom broke the speckly pill along the line which bisected it. Tom knocked his back straight away and handed the bottle to Greg. Greg put it on his tongue, and swallowed.

'If I die you fucking twat, just make sure that Mario doesn't win The Competition.'

Tom laughed and put his hand around Greg's shoulder.

'Welcome to the slippery slope of druggy ruin,' Tom joked. Greg aimed a kick at his backside.

As they got to the bottom of the road Greg saw Maddy. There were a few people who Maddy came out of working zombie mode for - Greg was one of them. He'd shagged her when she was very pissed at the end of the previous season, and surprisingly, it had improved their friendship without there being the slightest intention on either of their parts for a repeat perfomance.

'Hello lover,' said Maddy, kissing him on the cheek. 'No airport tonight?'

'Nah - night off. I'm showing Tom around,' he said, nodding at Tom.

'Hi,' said Tom.

Maddy gave him a smile only slightly more genuine than the one she reserved for passing punters.

'So, you coming in tonight Greg?'

'Aye. I've just 'ad a fucking E.'

'You're joking!' exclaimed Maddy, knowing that countless people had tried to get Greg to take one without success. 'How come?'

'It's this fuckin' twat,' he said pointing at Tom. 'Caught me in a moment of weakness.'

'I told him he'd be shagging all night,' corrected Tom.

'That figures,' said Maddy. 'When did you take it?'

'Just now,' replied Greg. 'How long does it take?'

'Depends. Twenty, forty minutes. What did you take?'

'Dunno. Wha' was it again Tom?'

'A Mad Bastard,' said Tom. 'Any idea what they're like?'

'Oh they're mental,' said Maddy smiling. 'You get flickery eyes and they're rushy as anything. Good luck.' She saw Toni coming up the stairs. 'Gotta go. I might see you later.' She walked over to a group of four drunk teenage boys. 'Alright lads.......Where you off to tonight?........Come on, get yourselves downstairs......Free schnappps.....Hot babes.....Don't be shy.....'

Tom and Greg walked down the five tiled stairs. Each time the swing doors ahead of them opened they caught a snippet of the four/four beat emerging from the excited darkness. When they opened the doors for themselves a wall of sound and a blast of heat like a Savanna wind struck them, although once inside, the superb air conditioning system reduced the temperature to a tolerable level. The club was square and only about twenty metres by twenty metres. In the middle of the club was a square sunken dance floor surrounded by painted metal railings with steps leading to it in every corner.

The club's popularity was in no small part due to the cash incentives that Toni, the wiry, hustling Spanish manager, offered tour company Resort Managers. It was a good policy, because once clients had been in there they would normally go back. The club seemed to manage to strike the right balance between the 'Ere We Go brigade and the more ravey clientele, although it was mainly the younger provincial weekend ravers, rather than the seriously stylish clubbers who kept coming back.

Greg reluctantly accepted the bottle of water that Tom gave him, still finding it difficult to come to terms with being in a club without having a bottle of beer in his hand. Tom assured him that very soon he would not even fancy a beer. Once he had his drink, Greg went over to Irish Ben, the solitary bouncer in the club. At five foot nine, slightly overweight with a humorous Desperate Dan type face, he didn't exactly look like a typical bouncer. Moreover, he had a high, fast speaking voice which stuttered when excited, with an Eire accent so strong that most people only caught the gist of what he was saying.

Most workers new to the island would seriously underestimate him, normally dismissing him in a patronising way as a thick Paddy who only worked as a bouncer because no bouncer of any worth would work for such a paltry wage. However, anyone who had been on Ibiza for any length of time knew better. Irish Ben was in fact the highest paid bouncer on the island. A club the size of Night Life would normally employ two or three doormen, rather than just the one, which gave some indication of the respect in which he was held.

Irish Ben had a very sharp sense of humour, so much so that he would often take the piss out of people for his own amusement, when they thought that they were taking the piss out of him. He knew that people often had trouble understanding him, causing them to just nod or say 'Yeah' in what they thought to be the right places. Sometimes, Ben would say something totally nonsensical just to see if someone was actually paying attention. He set himself up as a figure of fun, and really did not care a jot what anybody thought of him, actually preferring it if they didn't know what he was capable of - and even at thirty eight, what he was capable of was awesome.

In his early twenty's he had been European karate champion three years running, and then one of his students had taken over the title for the following two years. He had subsequently got more involved in different martial arts disciplines. However he had suffered a number of personal tragedies which he kept totally to himself. Whatever these tragedies were, they had caused him to leave everything for a life in Ibiza when he was twenty nine.

He teamed up with an American and started off doing karate exhibitions in night clubs on the island; breaking bricks and slates, splitting melons on volunteers chests with a Samurai sword etc.. But his martial arts partner went off the

280

rails and as Ben had all but tired of doing exhibitions anyway, he started a local karate school. He stopped the school after two seasons and in latter years, Ben decided that he preferred the more social and what he thought to be less stressful option of door work.

Greg was about to start talking to him when a huge, muscle bound Swedish looking man pushed the swing doors open, closely followed by four mean looking bodybuilders. Those closest to the door froze, convinced that there was going to be trouble. However, when the five man mountains saw Ben their faces broke into a grin and there was lots of backslapping and little playful karate type pressure point holds exchanged. Once they were safely at the other side of the club, Greg went up to Ben.

'Thought it was going to go off then Ben,' said Greg. 'I was just about ready to jump in and sort it out for you.'

'T'anks a lot. Oi feel an awful lot safer now yis told me that,' replied Ben, raising his eyebrows and smiling.

'Big old lumps that lot - who were they then?'

'Danes. Just a bunch o' eejits. Yer man wi' the big arms is an awful gobshite, so he is. Says they're all bodyguards or something loike that. Oi had to educate them the other noight.'

'Whar' about?'

'Oh, nothing really y'know. They just got a wee bit boisterous, an' one of them t'ought he'd troy and get me in a strangle hold.'

'So what 'appened?'

'Oi just gave him a flip over me shoulder, and showed him a couple of little pressure points o' me own. Would y'loike t'see 'em?' asked Ben, grinning to himself and not giving Greg a chance to say no, as he gently dug the first joint of his finger into the small of Greg's back and then his collar bone.

'Ouch, ow!' yelped Greg.

Ben laughed. 'Will y'be wanting a drink?'

'No thanks mate, I've got one.'

'Water,' said Ben, noticing Greg's drink, 'That's not loike

you.'

Greg wasn't sure what Ben's attitude was towards drugs so he didn't say anything. 'I'll catch you later Ben - I've got me boss over.'

He had a real urge to go and dance. He looked around for Tom, and caught sight of him on the edge of the dance floor nodding his head, and moving his arms slightly. He went over to him.

'So what's meant to happen then?'

'You'll know,' said Tom.

'I can't feel a thing yet,' said Greg, his body unconsciously picking up on the beat.

'You will,' said Tom smiling knowingly.

Greg shrugged his shoulders and went to the toilet. He'd made his mind up that when he came back he'd get himself a beer and start drinking again. This E lark was obviously a lot of fuss about nothing.

Greg felt a little light headed as he made his way to the loos. The people around him seemed to be moving slower and looking at him more intently. He wasn't totally aware of it at first, and put it down to the fact that he'd had a few beers. By the time he got to the toilet however, he found himself in a cubicle, rather than standing by the urinal as originally planned. He stretched out his arm and rested it against the wall. His stomach had an empty hollow feeling, almost like he wanted to be sick, although it could have been that he wanted a dump. He took his trousers down and sat on the pan just in case. Behind his eyes, there was a warm sensation which travelled across the bridge of his nose. Not quite a throbbing, just an unusual rather pleasant heat. He couldn't focus properly, so he shut his eyes and rested his head on his hands, not realising that he was swinging his shoulders in time to the music that he could hear infiltrating into the cubicle from the club.

Slowly, it dawned on him - he was coming up on his first E. He panicked slightly, becoming aware of his shallow breathing and his heart thumping against his chest. Suppose this was it?

Suppose he was one of the unlucky ones? The more he thought about it the more scared he became. Where was Tom? He couldn't possibly go out to find him - everybody would be looking at him, knowing he was 'on one', or about to die. But equally, he needed someone around - now. The thoughts were racing through his head at such a speed that he couldn't absorb them all properly. He stretched his neck, pushing his head back and felt a tightening in his lower abdomen. Almost before he was aware, his bowels opened. It was a great feeling, one of the most wonderful shits he had ever had. His prostrate gland sent an unconscious message to his groin, and Greg noticed that he had started to get a hard on, although he was unable to focus because his eyes were all over the place. He stroked himself until he was almost hard, all thoughts of death or a fatal reaction long since passed. He laughed out loud at how he thought he must have looked - in the middle of a glorious shit, dripping with sweat, his head and eyes rolling whilst stroking a hard on. God, this was weird.

He wiped his backside and even that somehow felt sensual. His erection subsided, he pulled his trousers back up but straight away sat back down again, grinning to himself and becoming increasingly aware of the music even though he felt unable to do anything about returning to it's source. His thoughts were still racing - conscious, and controlled, but randomly intermingling with bizarre nano second daydreams and spurts of shape and colour. Out of one of these daydreams came a voice.

'Greg.....Greg....are you in there. Greg...open up.'

He jolted back to his newly discovered reality and opened the door. Standing in front of him grinning, was Tom. When Tom saw Greg he started laughing.

'Fuck me. You must've been in here at least ten minutes. What do you think of it then?'

Greg gave him a soppy smile and gurned, shaking his head.

'I tell you what Greg, these are fucking strong. Normally I have to take a whole pill to move even slightly, but these....'

Greg nodded his agreement and slowly rose to his feet.

'I'm not sure if I like this,' he said. 'Can we go outside for some fresh air?'

'Yeah sure. You'll be alright. Just get this first rush out of the way and you won't be able to stay off of the dance floor.'

'I'll believe that when I see it,' said Greg, looking at Tom quizzically to see if Tom's face gave any reaction to whether or not Greg was speaking legibly.

He felt a little paranoid about his appearance, and wasn't looking forward to walking through the club. He stuck very close to Tom, trying to look at the floor, but still finding it difficult to focus on one point.

When Maddy saw Greg emerge from the club with his chin sticking out and his huge eyes rolling, she burst out laughing. Greg was oblivious to her mocking - in truth, he was pretty much oblivious to everything. Tom ushered him away from the crowd and down to a bench by the harbour. Greg sat down and began to regain control of his breathing and was at last able to focus properly. The responsibility of looking after Greg had made Tom control the effects of his pill better than he would have otherwise been able. Even so, he had never known a pill like it for the way it made one's eyes flicker. He was glad that he had only taken a half. He looked at Greg who now seemed as though he was approaching a semblance of normality.

'You alright mate?'

Greg exhaled, shaking his head. 'I'm not sure if I like this, lad.'

'Don't worry,' said Tom, 'You'll be fine in a minute.'

'Fuckin' 'ope so.' Greg put his head between his own knees, rubbed his neck and then stood up. 'I tell you what la', I don't feel to steady on the ol' pins.' Tom just smiled at him re-assuringly. 'Fuckin' 'ell Tom. I'm really glad you're here. I don't think I'd've got through this without yer.' Tom smiled again and nodded. 'Seriously mate, you're a top bloke. It's a shame you're not 'ere for the season. You 'n me, we'd 'ave a right laugh - do some serious caning.' Greg was feeling good. 'So that's a rush then is it? I suppose it's not too bad, as long as there's someone like you around, y'know, someone that can be trusted. I suppose Maddy saw me like this, She's a great girl that Maddy. I should've treated 'er better. Maybe tomorrow I'll go and ask 'er out properly, y'know - make it up to 'er. It's a fucking great island this, innit? I mean, just look at the stars. It's weird, we're seeing those stars like a thousand or a million years after......y'know, like it's taken a thousand years or whatever to get......well......anyway........fucking amazing. Cor, look at that bird, she's fuckin' 'orny.

When should I take the other 'alf then?'

Chaos. It always was frantic but tonight was worse. Much worse. It started with the airport police. Nothing had been mentioned about the work permits since the beginning of the season, but now it had all come on top and typically, it was Brad and Mikey in the firing line. Brad's 'early' flight had been delayed by five hours. All of the other reps apart from Mikey had been and gone. Mikey was doing the perpetually late Manchester flight, so it was only him and Brad who were affected. At first the airport police wanted to arrest them, but thanks, once again, to Mikey's command of Spanish, they had agreed on a compromise. They would allow the YF&S reps to pick up their clients, just this week, but they were not allowed to actually set foot in the airport. If the permits were not ready by the following week then they would be thrown off of the island.

Mikey and Brad were sitting on the wall outside the airport, both seriously stressed.

'That fucking dozy cow,' said Brad, referring to Alison. 'I can't believe she hasn't got those permits sorted out. What the fuck does she do all day?'

'To be honest I'm beyond caring with her. Don't worry - what goes around comes around. Something'll happen to her one day.'

'I'll believe it when I see it. People like her get away with

285

murder. If there was any justice she wouldn't be Resort Manager in the first place. She really is fucking hopeless.'

'Don't let it worry you. I know what'll make you feel better,' said Mikey reaching into the breast pocket of his airport shirt and pulling out an already made spliff.

'Oh you diamond,' said Brad, 'But where can we smoke it?'

'We'll just take a walk down there,' said Mikey pointing to the end of the coach car park.

'Cool. I'll check that our flights haven't landed.'

Brad went to the doorway of the arrivals lounge to look through the door at the board. The flights weren't on the display. He caught Kelly's eye and beckoned her over. She knew of Brad and Mikey's plight, and had agreed to direct the YF&S clients out to them as best she could. Just her smile was enough to alleviate Brad's stress. As she approached the door it opened automatically, almost as if it too was in reverence of her beauty.

'Bit of a joke this, isn't it?' said Brad.

Kelly just smiled.

'Don't suppose there's any news on the flights yet is there?' asked Brad.

'There's a rumour that they'll both be arriving in about half an hour.'

'Oh good,' said Brad. He looked at Kelly, desperate for an opportunity to ask her out without making a prat of himself. For once, she actually started a conversation.

'So what will you do, if you don't get a work permit?'

'I dunno,' said Brad shrugging his shoulders, 'Go home I suppose.'

'Oh that would be a shame.'

Was that a green light? Or was she just being polite? Fuck it. Without giving it any more thought he blurted,

'Yeah it would be a shame. I was going to leave asking you out until August, you know, just to give me a chance to check that you weren't a woman of easy virtue. But I guess I'll just have to take a chance and ask you out now instead and if you are a woman of easy virtue, well...........I suppose I'll just have to deal with it. What about Wednesday?' Even as Brad was saying it he knew it was one of the naffest proposals for a date he had ever made. He just knew he'd fucked it.

'Ok.'

'Huh?'

'Yeah, Wednesdays fine.'

'What? Oh great. I mean - oh shit.' Brad remembered that he was working on Wednesday. 'Balls, I'm working Wednesday. Howzabout....' Brad quickly went through a mental diary, '.......Thursday. Eleven o'clock in The Charleston?'

'Eleven o'clock it is then.'

'Great.' they stared at each other for a few seconds. 'Right, I better go and see Mikey. Back soon.'

Brad skipped off back to Mikey, unable to believe his luck. He'd actually done it. He'd cracked 'The Vision'.

'Mikey - guess what?'

'Don't tell me. Both our planes have collided over The Bon, killing all passengers, holidaymakers and reps apart from Alison.'

Brad gave Mikey a confused look. 'You need fucking therapy mate. I've just asked out Kelly and she said yes.'

'I think I would've got more pleasure out of the plane crash. Here.' He passed Brad the spliff directly after lighting it.

Brad started laughing. 'Have you always had a warped sense of humour or did it take a lot of practice to develop it to it's current, sick level?'

'Oh I'm sure it's partly genetic. So when you taking her out?'

'Thursday, after the bar night. She's fucking gorgeous in't she?'

'I've seen you with worse.' Mikey re-lit the spliff which Brad had allowed to go out. 'Was Mario up here earlier?'

'Yeah - jammy bastard. His flight was actually ten minutes early. He can't have been at the airport for more than half an hour. He still winds me up y'know. Since Lorraine went he's been doing my head in. It's like he knows something we don't,

287

right smug. I wish I could put my finger on it.'

'Don't let it bug you,' said Mikey. 'We got our own back on him didn't we?'

Brad chuckled. 'When he had clumps coming out of his hair - before he shaved it all - I could not stop laughing. I'm surprised he didn't know it was us. He must have sussed it.'

'So what if he did. What's he going to do about it?'

'Yeah I s'pose you're right. Still, it's not like him to let things go - he's a vindictive bastard.'

'Fuck him.' Mikey flicked the remaining roach at the kerb. 'Looks like the first lot of people are coming through.'

Brad looked at the glass doors twenty metres away, and sure enough there were a flurry of people.

'This should be fun.'

Almost an hour later, the 'fun' was just about over. It had been hell. Kelly had been so busy herself that not all of the YF&S clients knew where to go. Some had initially got on to the wrong coach, others had been wandering aimlessly around the airport, which contributed to it looking as though it was hosting a football shirt manufacturer's convention. The ones that had found there way to the two respective coaches straight away had been sitting there for best part of an hour and were understandably getting restless. Mikey and Brad stood by the door and could see no sign of any further clients. They got another rep that they had spoken to briefly to check the airport for them. He came back and said that as far as he could see there were no more YF&S clients.

'How's it looking?' Mikey asked Brad.

'Still four missing. Fuck it. I'll have to leave them. What about you?'

'All aboard. Thing is there's forty nine blokes and three girls.'

'Oh you're joking,' said Brad.

'Wish I was. Some fucking week this is going to be.'

Brad got onto his coach. 'Morning every one.' Silence. Mikey was probably right - this was going to be 'some fucking week'.

CHAPTER ELEVEN

His arms were in the air. His jaw was hurting through chewing gum and smiling so much. He'd talked to numerous people - suddenly feeling as though he was part of a special society that he had previously only pretended to understand and belong to. It was the same club, with the same or the same type of people, but somehow The Star had changed. Greg normally spent his time cosily ensconced on a bar stool at bar five, either falling asleep or drunkenly trying to chat up any female within striking distance. But tonight was different. The normal rules and rituals of the blagging game no longer seemed to apply.

While he was dancing a pretty blonde girl kept smiling at him. She ended up dancing right next to him. When he caught her eye again she spoke.

'Hi. You're Greg aren't you?'

'Yeah.'

'I'm Jacqui. You work for Young Free & Single, don't you?'

'Yeah. How d'ya know?'

This was a particularly stupid question as Greg was wearing his badge. Jacqui didn't seem to notice.

'That's who I've come on holiday with.'

'Really? Where yer staying?'

'At The Bon.'

'How come I 'aven't seen you?' asked Greg. 'Not been on any of the excursions?'

'No. We only came over here for the clubbing and Young Free & Single was the cheapest package on offer.'

'So where you been going?'

'Space, Amnesia, Ku, Pacha - the clubs out here are amazing.'

'Yeah, they are aren't they?' Greg had only been to Ku.

They carried on dancing and smiling at each other for a few minutes. Occasionally Jacqui would brush against Greg. Each time she did he felt his whole body tingle. It wasn't long before they were dancing very close to each other and becoming quite tactile.

'What did you say your name was again?'

'Jacqui.'

'Right,' nodded Greg smiling. 'So what you taken then?'

'A dove. You?'

'A Mad Bastard.'

'A what?'

'A Mad Bastard. They're really rushy,' said Greg, now an authority on the subject. 'What's the dove like?'

'Usual sort of thing really.'

'Uh-huh.' Greg was none the wiser.

Yeah,' continued Jacqui. 'Quite Lovey.'

'Yeah - these too,' said Greg.

Jacqui turned her back on Greg. 'Do me a favour and massage my shoulders for me.'

Greg started massaging her shoulders. After a while he ran his fingers up the nape of her neck and then let his fingernails gently scratch her on the way back down. He couldn't believe how erotic it made him feel.

'Mmmm,' moaned Jacqui. 'That feels wonderful. I felt all stiff before.'

'Not as stiff as I'm feeling now,' said Greg, the words coming out before he had a chance to decide whether or not to verbalise his thoughts.

Jacqui playfully rubbed her backside against Greg's hard on. She giggled. 'So you are.'

She turned round, rested her arms on his shoulders and looked him directly in the eyes, still dancing in time to the music. They started kissing and it was all that Greg could do to stop himself from ripping her clothes off.

'Do you wanna leave?' asked Greg.

'I can't, I've got to find my friend.'

'She'll be alright.'

'No, honestly. Look, I might catch up with you later.'

Before Greg had a chance to argue she disappeared into the crowd. He carried on dancing for ten minutes then went to the bar where Tom was standing. The music didn't seem to be as captivating as before and the warm sensation had all but disappeared. Moreover, Greg felt that girls were no longer looking at him in the same way as they had been for the previous couple of hours.

'You alright?' asked Tom.

'Nah. I just pulled a blinding bird an' she's fucked off. Plus the music don't seem so good and I don't know - it's just not as good as it was a little while ago.'

'Sounds like you're coming down,' said Tom.

'Wha'?' said Greg.

'The pill - it's wearing off. Here..' he said, biting another pill in half. 'This'll sort you out.'

Greg popped it in his mouth and swigged it back without a second thought.

'Taken like a veteran,' said Tom.

Brad eventually got to sleep just before five in the morning. The transfer had been a disaster. Despite his attempts at winning them over, they had been the most miserable bunch of clients that he had ever brought back from the airport. Brad always sent himself up as soon as he got on the microphone, aware of the hostility that his bright yellow uniform, bronzed skin and seemed air of confidence could provoke. On this occasion it hadn't worked - there had even been a few mumbles of 'cockney bastard' (Brad had discovered that to northerners, anyone south of Luton was a cockney). They had also given him a hard time when he checked them into their hotels, so Brad wasn't holding out too much hope for a well attended welcome meeting.

He had been asleep for little more than an hour when he heard a loud bang and some screaming and shouting. It seemed to be coming from the floor below. Brad put on his shorts and ran downstairs to see what was going on.

As he walked onto the landing one of the doors was open. From it came a male voice yelling in Spanish. Brad walked into the room where he was confronted by Rafael, the hotel owner's son, about to punch a small blonde girl. Brad leapt between them and pushed him away. Rafael went into a karate stance. Brad looked in the corner where the blonde girl's friend was sitting. She had a black eye. Brad looked at Rafael, who went to move towards the blonde girl. Brad leapt between them.

'Yeah?' Rafael stopped in his tracks. 'Fancy your fucking chances do you?' He pushed Rafael. 'Well come on then. Try and give me a black eye dick head.' Brad thought Rafael was about to lash out so he stepped back slightly. 'Come on. What you waiting for? What's up you fucking wanker?' Brad wanted to provoke him. He remembered one of the phrases from a swear word session with Frank. 'Hijo de puta.' (Son of a whore)

Rafael glared at Brad. Brad smiled back to antagonise him further. Rafael looked at the two girls, glared again at Brad then barged passed him, spitting out Spanish that Brad had no chance of understanding. The two girls huddled together on the bed sobbing. A few other holidaymakers who had been woken up by the commotion put their heads around the door to see what was going on. Brad told them that everything was fine and to go back to bed. He closed the door and sat on the bed next to the girls.

'Right then, I think it might be a good idea to tell me what happened, don't you?'

The girls had stopped crying.

'Nothing, he's just mad,' said the blonde girl.

'What, so he just came in here for no reason and hit you?'

'Yeah, look at my eye,' said the girl with the black eye.

'I know it's bad. But I need to know why he hit you.'

'I told you - he's mad,' repeated the blonde girl.

Brad raised his eyebrows.

'Who's side are you on anyway?' asked the girl with the black eye, who looked as though she was about to start crying again.

'It's not a question of who's side I'm on,' said Brad, 'But if I'm going to help you I need to know exactly what happened.'

'These two blokes came back........' said black eye,

'Nothing in it though..' interrupted the blonde. 'They just came back to chill out for a little while.'

Black eye continued the story. 'Next thing there's a banging on the door. We opened it and that nutter came barging in. He started yelling in Spanish and attacked the two boys. They ran off and then he turned on us. God knows what he would've done if you hadn't stopped him.'

'Mmmm.' Brad digested the story. 'You're not meant to have anyone in your room who's not staying in the hotel, so that sounds like the reason he went mad. Having said that, there's no excuse for the way he reacted. It's not the first time he's done it and to be honest I can't believe that he's been allowed to get away with it as many times as he has.' He stood up. 'Look, there's not much I can do now. Will you be alright until later? I'll go and have a word with my boss before the welcome meeting.'

Brad left the two girls, but with the adrenaline still in his system he found it difficult to sleep. At about eight o'clock, totally exhausted, Brad crashed out.

The knocking confused Brad. Squinting at the clock he saw that it was five past nine. He could tell by the way that his head was hurting that he had not been sleeping for thirteen hours, which meant that he had only been in the land of nod for just over an hour. The knocking was very insistent. It crossed his mind that it could be Rafael, ready for round two. Brad was in no fit state for a physical confrontation.

'Who is it?'

'It's me - Alison. Open up.'

'Alright. Give me a minute.'

He put on his tracksuit bottoms and T-shirt, then opened the door. Alison stormed passed him and stood by the window with her hands on her hips. Alison was never one for small talk - shout first, ask questions later.

'You've annoyed me a few times during the season already Brad, but this time you've really done it.'

Brad went to speak, but he had learned through experience that it was almost impossible to interrupt Alison when she was ranting. The best way of dealing with her was to let her scream and shout before coming back at her.

'First of all the airport. What on earth do you think you were doing letting four clients get a taxi into San Antonio? They've just collared me in The Bon demanding the cab fare and threatening to sue us for more for the inconvenience. Next thing I'm confronted by the hotel owner downstairs who tells me that you've been letting clients bring non-residents into the hotel.' She shook her head. 'It makes me laugh. Everyone in head office was going on about how smart you're meant to be but I've yet to see any indication of it. You're lucky that you've still got a job. I know a lot of Resort Managers who would have had you off the island by now.'

'Yeah, and I know a lot of Resort Managers who would've got the work permits sorted out before the middle of July, so that the reps were actually allowed into the airport to do their job.'

'What?'

'Alison - I can't be bothered to talk to you about it now. I've had one hours sleep, there's a welcome meeting in just over an hour, then that meal with Felipe and the agency, then a bar crawl, then a cruise at eight in the morning. If you're just gonna come in here shouting and screaming, then don't expect me to listen to you when I could be getting some of that rare commodity called sleep.'

'What was that you said about the work permits? Mario didn't say anything about not being allowed in the airport and he was there after you.'

'Yeah, but as usual dear Mario got the best flight and was in and out of the airport within half an hour, whereas I was there for over six hours.'

'And what about this stuff with the hotel. I think we're going to have to move you somewhere else.'

'Alison, do what you fucking want,' said Brad beginning to lose his cool. 'But while you're at it go and have a look at that poor girl in room three two two who's nursing a black eye courtesy of that nutter Rafael.' Alison looked at him bemused. 'Yep, that's right. He's actually done it this time. Only rather than a bloke he's hit a five foot two girl. I warned you but you wouldn't listen.' Alison's brain went into survival mode, already thinking of a way out or a way of not shouldering the blame if it went any further. 'And as for the airport, we weren't even allowed to set foot in it. You're lucky that only four clients got a taxi back because it was hell up there. All the clients are totally pissed off so I wouldn't be counting on a very good week for sales if I were you.'

'Well I still can't claim to be very happy,' said Alison, stuck for anything else to say.

'Yeah? Well I can't claim to give a fuck. And if you want to put someone else in here then I don't care either because this time next week it'll be academic.'

'What do you mean?'

'The police said if we haven't got permits by next week we're all off the island.'

'I don't believe it.'

'Believe it or don't - it's true.' Brad sat on his bed and shook his head. 'Yeah, you've done a real good job Alison. You know what really confuses me though?' Alison looked at him with the hatred growing in her eyes. 'What confuses me is how you got the job in the first place.'

Alison was almost shaking with rage. She said nothing, flying past Brad and slamming the door behind her.

She was back in her room at The Bon within minutes. She lit a cigarette to calm herself down. She needed to think and act fast. She went downstairs and rang Jane Ward at home.

'Hello,' said a sleepy voice.

'Hi Jane. It's Alison Shand in Ibiza.'

'Alison? What on earth's the matter?'

'We've got something of a mini crisis here, and I really don't know what to do.'

'What's the problem? What crisis?'

'Well it's two things really. I sent through all of the reps details a good few weeks ago for the work permits but I've still received nothing....' Alison had in fact forgotten to send them.

'Hang on a minute,' said Jane, gradually waking up. 'What details? I remember asking you for them a few weeks ago but as I didn't receive them I naturally assumed you'd sorted out the permits on resort.'

'God no,' said Alison sounding surprised. 'I thought they were all going through your end. Don't tell me they've got lost in the post.'

'They must've done,' said Jane, unable to think of any other explanation. 'Look, give me a chance to get myself together and give me a call later with all of the reps details and I'll get it sorted out for you first thing in the morning.'

'Oh Jane, thanks ever so much.'

'That's fine. Now what was the other problem?'

'It's to do with Brad and The Las Huertas. He's not really been controlling his clients particularly well and they've been antagonising the hotel owner's son, y'know, parties, music at all hours. Anyway, a couple of times the owners son has lashed out.'

'What do you mean by lashed out?'

'Hit clients.'

'Jesus, why haven't I heard about it?'

'I managed to contain it to resort.'

'Didn't you get Brad to do a report?'

'Of course I did. I've asked him countless times but he hasn't or won't,' lied Alison.

'That's not good enough. If you tell him to do something he's got to do it. You're the Resort Manager after all.'

'That's half the problem Jane. He thinks he knows it all. I keep telling him but he won't listen. I think he's even turning Mikey against me.'

'Well there's only one answer to it.'

'What?'

'Sack him. It hurts me to say it because I must admit, even I thought that Brad would do really well. But I'm not there so............ Look, I tell you what. Tom's there, isn't he?'

'Yes,' said Alison.

'Have a chat to him about it and get him to call me and we'll get the whole thing resolved by tomorrow one way or another. Is that ok?'

'That's marvellous Jane. Thank you ever so much. You don't know how helpful you've been.'

'That's fine - I'm just doing my job. Now you talk to Tom, get those details and call me later.'

'Thanks again. Bye.'

Alison let out a sigh of relief. One way or another she had made the decision - Brad was going to go.

CHAPTER TWELVE

Just as Brad had thought, the welcome meeting was disastrous. For the first time he sensed some genuine animosity from some of his clients. A group of six lads from Burnley, who had arrived the previous Wednesday and were staying for ten days, had formed an unholy alliance with some of the other large groups that he and Mikey had brought in that morning. Sitting around the pool after the welcome meeting, there was not the normal friendly atmosphere. A hardcore of about thirty northern lads watched Brad's every move, making snide comments or jeering from the safety of the group. Brad went and sat with them for a while, trying to find a shared common interest, but nothing seemed to work.

He wanted to ascertain who the natural leader was so that he could give him some special attention, but half the problem was that no natural leader yet existed. It was an amalgam of three or four different sets of lads who were all still jostling to sort out their own hierarchy, and finding different ways of bonding. Unfortunately their common bond at that point seemed to be a shared hatred of YF&S, reps and in particular, Brad. Although he was exhausted, he was therefore glad when Mikey turned up in a taxi to take him down to Es Reguero, the restaurant where the company meal was to be held. Brad flopped into the back seat.

'Get much sleep?' asked Mikey, swivelling around from the front passenger seat.

'Don't ask,' replied Brad.

'That bad, huh?'

Brad sighed. 'I sometimes wonder if it's all worth it. Everyone thinks this job's all about getting a tan and shagging yourself senseless - if only they knew.'

'What, if only they knew it was about getting pissed for

nothing as well?' Brad was too knackered and had got to know Mikey too well to bite. Mikey realised this so continued. 'I know what you mean. I worked out that since I've been here I've averaged just over four hours sleep a night. Do you believe that?'

'Mate, I'd've been doing cartwheels if I'd got four hours last night. D'you know what happened when I got back here after the transfer?' Mikey shook his head. 'That fucking nutter beat up another client, only this time it was a girl.'

'No way!'

'Yep. Thought he was gonna have a pop at me as well. Stupid tosser started to give it all that karate stance shit. I called him an Hijo de puta -'

'Bet he loved that,' interrupted Mikey laughing.

'He wasn't over impressed. Still couldn't provoke him into hitting me though, which was the whole reason for me saying it.'

'Just as well,' said Mikey. 'Alison would've probably blamed you for it.'

'You haven't heard the best bit yet. I'd been asleep for about an hour when I heard someone banging on my door. I thought it was Rafael again, but it turned out to be our beloved leader.'

'What, Alison?'

'The very same. She started having a go at me 'cos those four clients we couldn't find at the airport got a cab to the hotel and wanted re-imbursing.'

'Sounds fair enough to me. Didn't you tell her about the permits?'

'You know what she's like - I didn't get a chance. When I did tell her she started having another go at me 'cos Rafael or his dad had just given her a load of bullshit about the girl he whacked.'

'Fucking hell - so what did you say?'

Brad winced. 'Basically I told her to fuck off.'

Mikey winced. 'Ouch. So what did Alison do?'

'Stormed out. She's gunning for me mate. I've sensed it since the day I arrived but now I'm sure.'

'I don't know what to say. Fuck me, I won't be so happy doing this job if you're not about. Do you think it could come to that, you know, the old heave-ho?'

'To be honest with you Mikey, after this week's arrivals I'm beginning not to give a fuck.'

'Yeah, I thought they'd be a handful. Most of my coach was for your hotel and they weren't the best bunch I've ever brought in. Mind you - two of those girls were quite fit.'

Brad burst out laughing. 'Did you speak to them?'

'No.'

'They came up to me this morning, moaning their bloody heads off. It's the first time they've been on a package holiday and they were expecting Holiday Inn type accommodation and a Riviera type resort.'

'Leave off.'

'Honest. Anyway, next thing - and I swear this is true, 'cos I couldn't make it up - they started to get hysterical. One of them says "You don't know how much this holiday means to us, it could be our last one".'

'What!? What did she mean?'

Brad shook his head laughing, still unable to believe what the girl had told him. 'She reckons they met each other last year at the Papworth Clinic - after they'd both had organ transplants.'

'Fuck off - you're winding me up.'

'No, as I live and breathe. They're still in the critical period where the organs could get rejected. I just hope Greg doesn't find out.'

'Why's that?'

''Cos he'll wanna shag 'em, of course.'

A long table was set out underneath one of the white canopies which protected Es Reguero's customers from either the sun or the rain - on this occasion it was most definitely the former. Although the restaurant was only a five minute walk from The

Star Club, very few tourists ever frequented it. However, because the food was so good, it was almost always busy with ex-pats and workers sampling the culinary delights, or just propping up the bar catching up on gossip. When Brad and Mikey arrived, everyone was there apart from Alison. Brad went and sat next to Tom and Greg, who were sitting at the end of the table with Felipe Gomez from head office and Luis from the agents, Viajes Diamante. Mikey went to the other end of the table with Natalie, Heather and Mario. A space at the end of the table was ready for Alison.

Alison arrived just after the wine was placed on the table. She kissed Felipe and Luis politely on the cheek and then turned to Tom.

'Tom, have you got a minute - I need to speak to you.'

'Yeah, sure,' said Tom leaning back to pull another chair over.

'In private.'

'Oh, right.' Tom stood up, 'Excuse me everyone.'

They walked inside to the cool, dark bar area, which was only ever normally used during the winter. Alison sat down first and Tom followed suit, after he had called out to the barman to order two beers.

'Don't you even know what beers are in Spanish?' asked Alison.

'I did, but I keep forgetting,' lied Tom.

'You'll have to learn Spanish if you want to make any progress you know.'

This puzzled Tom slightly, because his position was already senior to Alison's. Unfortunately, Alison was one of the 'old school' who had been with the company long enough to mistakenly believe that they were still higher up the company ladder than Tom.

'So what - you can speak Spanish, can you?' asked Tom, already knowing that she couldn't.

'Yeah, enough to get by.' As if to prove the point she said 'Gracias' as the drinks arrived.

'So, what's the problem?' asked Tom.

'I spoke to Jane this morning and she suggested that I spoke to you first,' replied Alison, to give what she had to say more credibility. 'There were two things really. The first problem was the airport. I don't know if you remember, but I sent all of the reps details through to you at the beginning of the season-'

'I don't remember receiving them,' said Tom.

'Well that's what Jane said, so they've obviously got lost in the post or something.' The lie didn't come as easily to Alison being face to face with someone as it had over the phone. 'Anyway, Jane said she would be able to sort that out so hopefully it won't be a problem - as long as it's done by the weekend. The other problem,' said Alison taking a sip of her drink, 'Is Brad.'

'Brad?'

'Yeah. It's a shame because like everyone else, I thought he was going to be really good when I first met him. But from the day he got here he's been trying to tell me how to do my job. Every time I tell him to do something he questions it. I wasn't going to say anything because to be honest, I could deal with it. The only reason that I'm saying something now is that it's got a little more serious.'

'In what way?'

'Well for starters, I think he's turning Mikey against me. As you know, Brad's got a really strong personality. Before we came out to resort even Kirstie told me he was a bit of a natural leader, so the last thing I want is for him to turn all of the other reps against me.' Alison paused for a moment. 'The other problem is The Las Huertas. He doesn't get on too well with the staff in there and he's more into having a good time than he is controlling the clients.'

'Yeah but come on Al, the whole job's about getting on and joining in with the clients.'

'You don't have to tell me - I have been doing this job for a few years you know. The thing with Brad is he doesn't know where to draw the line and that causes problems.'

'What sort of problems?'

'The clients get out of hand and someone else has to control them, and sometimes that person may not be the best person for doing that job.' Tom looked at Alison, not sure what point she was trying to make. 'For example, on a few occasions Brad's clients in The Las Huertas have got a bit lairy and Rafael, the owner's son, has taken the law into his own hands and hit them.'

'What!' said Tom. 'Why weren't we notified of this in head office?'

'Apart from the fact that it's probably not as bad as it sounds, I didn't want to get Brad into trouble.'

'What do you mean?'

'I thought Brad would make a good rep, so I didn't want anything to go on his record that might go against him. The thing is, I asked him time and time again to do a report, but..........' Alison shrugged her shoulders.

'So what did Jane say?'

'Jane said I should sack him, but to talk to you first.'

Tom sat back in his chair, taking it all in. Although everything Alison had said made sense, there was something that didn't seem quite right, but Tom wasn't sure whether that was just down to the fact that he liked Brad. After a minute or so's deliberation, he told Alison what he had decided.

'Alright Alison. I'll need to speak to Jane before I do anything. Obviously I'll also have to hear Brad's side of the story....'

'Of course. I mean clearly Brad's going to say that he did a report, but I swear he didn't give it to me.'

'Ok, just leave it with me and I'll sort it out. Let's go back and act as though nothing has happened.'

When they got back to the table Alison went to one end, where Heather was giggling and saying that she'd never slept with a man with a foreskin and wouldn't know what to do with one if ever she did. Tom went to the other end of the table and sat next to Felipe and Greg, where Greg had just finished telling Brad about his morning with Tom and the two girls. It reminded Tom that he still hadn't slept.

Tom needed to get the conversation with Alison out of his head so he could act normally towards Brad. He remembered that the husband of a girl who came away at the beginning of the season had rang up head office claiming that Greg had got his wife pregnant. Tom had forgotten to tell Greg this, so it was with great glee that he relayed the story in front of everybody, adding a bit of fabrication by telling Greg that the 'brick shit house' of a husband was arriving that Wednesday. He enjoyed watching the colour drain from Greg's face.

After the meal was finished everybody was pleasantly tipsy and in good spirits. Felipe, Luis and Tom were all smoking cigars and talking shop. Alison was quite drunk and had come down to the other end of the table, where she was sitting very close to Felipe. Tom watched them and noticed them exchange a couple of hand squeezes. He tried to imagine them in bed together. The mental picture he got made him glad that he'd finished eating, and he was relieved when Felipe's voice interrupted his thoughts.

'So Tomas, do you speak Spanish?'

'No, not really.'

'But I would have thought with a name like Ortega......'

'My great grandfather,' lied Tom. 'From Madrid.'

'Ah,' said Felipe. 'And what about the rest of the reps - do any of them speak Spanish?'

'Only me and Mikey,' interrupted Alison. Felipe almost laughed at this comment because Alison could barely speak a word. She was one of those people who rather than admit that they do not have command of a foreign language, say that they understand more than they speak.

'And Mikey,' continued Felipe. 'Which one is he again?'

'At the end, wearing the rimmed sunglasses,' said Brad.

'The black bloke,' said Alison.

'Good,' said Felipe realising that Mikey was out of earshot. 'Well if you'll all excuse me I need to speak to Luis and it will be easier for us to converse in our native tongue. Please do not think we are being rude.'

'No problem,' waved Alison, answering for everybody.

Tom thought that this was quite unusual because they both spoke impeccable English, so he kept one ear on the conversation, which at first was about general gossip, catching up on mutual friends etc. It made Tom laugh to himself how initially, Alison kept nodding as if she understood what they were saying. Once she felt that she had sufficiently impressed her juniors with her knowledge she slid off to the other end of the table to sit with Mario, Mikey and the girls. As soon as she left, Tom heard Felipe say, in Spanish,

'Fucking nuisance. I wish the whore would just leave me alone. I only fucked her twice and the stupid bitch got pregnant. I don't know how - I spent most of the time with my cock up her arse.'

Both men laughed at this point. They were speaking very quickly and in regional dialects, but Tom kept listening and understood more or less every word that they said.

The next five minutes of conversation left Tom totally gobsmacked. He was so engrossed in what they were saying that he wasn't able to join in any of the other conversations going on around him, and if anyone asked him a question he just grunted 'yes' or 'no'. It was almost too much to take in, in his present state. He thought that he might have been having some kind of verbal trip, but the conversation continued revealing more and more. When they finished Felipe smiled in his normal charming way and apologised,

'I'm sorry about that. We were just talking boring contracting stuff. Now, I think that seeing as this is on the company, we should order a bottle of champagne, what does everybody think?'

Tom was the only one who didn't reply. If what he had just heard was true, a bottle of champagne wasn't the only thing that Felipe had bought 'on the company'. He stood up and went to the bar.

'Is there a phone I can use to ring England?'

CHAPTER THIRTEEN

'Hello. Jane?'

'Yeah. Is that you Tom?'

Tom looked around to check that no-one could hear him.
'Yeah.'

'What's up? Have you spoken to Alison?'

'Yes, but-'

'What did she say?'

'She was going on about Brad and - but anyway, that's not-'

'So what did she say about Brad?'

'Just that he doesn't respect her. Look, I need-'

'Do you think we should get rid of him?'

'I don't know. Will you lis-'

'What do you mean, you don't know?'

'I mean I don't know. Now please-'

'Well what have you been doing-'

'Jane - SHUT UP!' There was a stunned silence on the end
of the phone. 'Thank you. Now if you'll kindly listen I've just
heard something that makes Brad, Alison and everything else
seem irrelevant by comparison.'

Tom had never spoken to Jane like that before, so she
guessed that it had to be pretty serious. 'Go on - I'm listening.'

'Right. You know how you've always gone on at me about
not letting anyone know I'm fluent in Spanish?'

'Uh-huh.'

'Well it's finally paid off.'

'How?'

'Felipe and Luis - you know, the guy from our agents, Viajes
Diamente - had a conversation in Spanish, but only after Felipe
checked that nobody else spoke the lingo. Oh, and you were
right about Alison and him. He did get her up the duff, but it's

not an ongoing romance.'

'But he is the father?'

'Definitely.'

'So do you think there's more to it? Is that why he was so keen for her to be given the Resort Manager's job?'

'Partly, but Jane, there's more to it than you could ever imagine.'

Tom looked around again to check that nobody was listening.

It took him nearly ten minutes to tell Jane the whole story. There were a few seconds silence before Jane said,

'Oh Christ Tom, this is really spooky.'

'Hardly the adjective I'd have chosen, still -'

'No, you don't understand,' continued Jane. 'Just before we found out about Alison's abortion I received an anonymous phone call from a woman to tell me that Felipe was having an affair. That same woman called me a couple of days ago to tell me that Felipe and Alison were on the fiddle.'

'Alison. Ah yes. I'll come on to her in a minute. Any idea who made the calls?' asked Tom.

'I haven't. It's obviously someone who's doesn't like Alison - or Felipe for that matter.'

'Well after seeing the way Alison is liked out here, that should narrow it down to half of Ibiza.'

'No I reckon it's someone over here. The calls didn't sound as if they were from abroad.'

'What about the voice?'

'It's so hard to tell Tom. It sounded a bit like someone from the west country trying to put on a posh voice, or a posh voice trying to sound regional. There's no way of knowing.' Jane paused to collect her thoughts. 'Jesus Tom. Do you realise how much he could have been making each season?'

'Um,' Tom did some quick mental arithmetic, 'Over quarter of a million pounds.'

'And the rest - more like half a million. Bugger.'

'It doesn't bear thinking about, does it?'

'So how does Luis from Viajes Diamente fit into all of this?'

asked Jane.

'Luis was the first person he started doing it with. Apparently they go way back - met at college or something. Luis put him onto a contact in each Diamante office and they got a cut. Let's face it - even a small cut of that kind of money's worth their while.'

'Let me just make sure that I've got this absolutely right. Felipe has been contracting a room for, let's say an average of one and a half mill.'

'Keep it in sterling - it'll make it easier.'

'Alright then. He contracts a room for seven pounds a night. He then gets the agency to invoice us for a tenner. We pay the agency, who pay the hotel and then cream off the difference. Right so far?'

'Yep.'

'So Felipe keeps more than half-'

'Nearer two thirds.'

'Whatever. Then what's left is kept by Luis or the agency on top of their normal commission.'

'That's about it.'

'So Felipe's making about two pounds a night on every room, in all of our accommodation. Phew! But how come the boss of the agency doesn't know what's going on?' Jane had lost the thread.

'Think about it. The agency invoice us for what they believe to be the correct amount. We pay them and they pay the hotel. Sometimes they pay the hotel in cash so when that happens it's easy - Felipe just takes the money and the hotel doesn't have to be any the wiser. But when they pay by cheque, the hotel has to know, so they give Felipe a kick back. That way the boss of the agency doesn't know.'

'But suppose a hotel or apartment isn't interested,' asked Jane, trying to cover all of the permutations.

'If they're not interested I guess they don't get contracted. Christ Jane, you know how competitive it is out here. Most of our accommodation is run by one man bands desperate for the business.'

'But what about some of the bigger contracts, the stuff the mainline companies use?' Jane was referring to other companies within the group that YF&S belonged to, which catered for families and therefore normally had to have accommodation of a higher standard.

'I don't know. Felipe didn't really say anything about that.'

'Do you not think that maybe some accommodation is being contracted legitimately.'

'Probably, yes. Don't forget that it's only happening in Spain and not in Greece.'

'ONLY!' repeated Jane ironically. 'And he's been doing it for at least two seasons?'

'Well I heard him talking about last season so he was definitely doing it then. I don't know if Kirstie was in on it and of course, it's always possible that he's been at it longer. And........' Tom had just thought of something else, 'Who are our agents in Andorra?'

'Diamente,' replied Jane slowly. 'Oh no, not the winter season as well.'

'It's possible, isn't it? And imagine if he's managed to pull a similar scam in France or Italy - there are affiliated Diamante agents there. He could be making even more than half a million a year.'

There was silence again as they both digested the implications.

'Oh, and there's something else. You know that house in Dulwich and all that fancy stuff in his office?'

'What, the house and stuff left by his relative?'

'Wrong,' sang Tom. 'He was bragging to Luis that the house is almost paid for by his 'little' scam. Did you know he'd also just bought a new Range Rover?'

'No. I thought he just had the company Audi.'

'I wouldn't mind betting he calls that his runaround.'

Jane didn't reply. She was too busy thinking what all of this meant. She started to think aloud down the phone.

'So if he contracts accommodation on the basis of whether or not they'll give him a backhander, then surely that means

310

that our clients aren't getting the most suitable places to stay? If quality or value for money isn't the main criteria...'

'Exactly,' agreed Tom.

'And if, as a company, we're paying more for our hotels and apartments than we could be,' said Jane, working out even more consequences, 'Then we pass that cost on to the holidaymakers, which means that-'

'Which means that the holidays cost more than they otherwise would,' said Tom, finishing Jane's sentence for her.

'It's fucking scandalous, right enough,' whistled Jane. 'Anything more I should know?'

'Yep. The lovely Alison Shand. He launders all of his money through Ibiza and she looks after all of his accounts while he's not here. For some reason they're all joint accounts with his wife but from what I can make out she knows hardly anything about them. Of course, the account only needs the one signature so he's probably just shoved the initial form under her nose to sign or forged her signature.'

'Why would he do that?'

'My guess is that he's got joint accounts simply to re-emphasise to Alison that he is married. I'm not sure whether the hotel and apartment owners know that she's in on it, but it wouldn't surprise me. Apparently some of our clients have been friends of Alison's. They get their holiday paid for in return for taking back some of the cash with them, so that's how most of it finds it's way to the UK. Felipe was laughing at the minuscule amount he's paying her. She's obviously not stupid and can see how much he's making, but he's told her that Diamente are taking a lot more than they actually are. From what I can gather, Alison really wanted to be Resort Manager in Ibiza, so Felipe's pulled some strings and partly used that as justification for not cutting her in. He told Luis that he's promised her ten grand at the end of the season, but he's even thinking about not giving her that. Mind you, he'd be silly if he didn't 'cos I'm sure his wife wouldn't be too happy to find out that her two sons almost had a step sibling.

'Unbelievable,' was all that Jane could say.

'So now what? Shall I sack Alison?'

'God no!' said Jane, who's sharp mind was well and truly in gear. 'No. If anything we've got to keep her there, even if she breaks every rule in the courier's manual.'

'Why's that?' asked Tom, who was now some way behind her.

'Because Alison is our whole key to catching Felipe. Don't you see that we can't possibly do anything on the basis of what you've heard? We need some proof.'

'Like what?'

'I don't know. A bank statement? Pictures? I really don't know. I'm going to have to give this some serious thought. I'll obviously have to speak to Sebastian and Adam. I think for now we'll just have to sit tight.'

'So what about this stuff with Brad?'

'Puts a bit of a different light on it, doesn't it? I don't know about you Tom, but I found it a little hard to believe that Brad had screwed up. Of all the new reps..'

'I know. That's what I thought too. And from what I've heard so far he seems to be doing great. The only one out here who I've heard anything bad about is Mario.'

'Mmmm. Well he was borderline. Still, Mario's the least of our problems. The question is what now?'

'I haven't spoken to Rafael or his father yet, and I haven't spoken to Brad. What should I do?'

Jane paused to think. 'Find out exactly what's going on. I was all for sacking Brad, but after this I'm sure there's more to it than meets the eye. In the unlikely event that Alison is telling the truth, do what you have to. The most important thing is that she doesn't suspect anything because we must keep her there. If that means that Brad has to go, then.......'

'Oh come on Jane - that's hardly fair.'

'So what do you suggest? We keep on a first year rep - albeit potentially a very good one - and let them get away with huge amounts of money? More expensive holidays next year, piss poor accommodation, more-'

'Alright, alright - you've made your point.'

'Tom, of course I want you to do everything you can to keep Brad on resort, but it's not the most important thing. Do you understand?' Jane emphasised the point. 'It is not the most important thing.'

'Alright Jane. I get the message. Cor, I thought this was gonna be a nice painless visit. Couldn't've been more wrong, could I?'

'All part of the job Tom.'

'I know. Alright then. I better get back to the meal before I'm missed. I'll speak to you later.'

'Ok. I'll call you as soon as there are any developments, assuming that you haven't called me first. Speak to you then.'

'Yeah. Adios.'

'Oh, and Tom.'

'Yeah, what?'

'Well done.'

CHAPTER FOURTEEN

'Women problems,' said Tom, to excuse his absence as he returned to the table.

The pills and the adrenaline quickly wore off leaving Tom with all the energy of a sixty a day septuagenarian crossing a triathlon finishing line.

Five hours blissful sleep later and he woke up to make his way over to the bar night at The Las Huertas, which was replacing the usual Sunday night bar crawl.

When he got there Brad had the bar rocking. Although some of the new arrivals had tried to disrupt the beginning of the evening, Brad had managed to get rid of them without causing any major problems. Alison had earlier instructed Brad to make the clients spend as much in the hotel bar as possible. The circle of seventy or so people had therefore been led through two hours of drinking games, causing them to pass their year's savings over the bar with unparalleled urgency. It was the first time that Brad had seen the hotel owner smile.

There was a group of three lads from Bradford who were drunk before the games had started. Brad had wanted to stop getting them drinks after only half an hour of games, but Alison had popped in and told Brad to keep persuading them to buy drinks and pour them down their necks. Two of them had already been sick, one of them all over the floor. But the one who was undoubtedly the most pissed (skinny, with a black denim shirt and Buddy Holly style glasses) had so far managed to keep down the contents of his stomach.

Brad finished off the games with 'Confessions.' This was where they would go around the circle and say something like, 'Take a sip, anyone who lost their virginity before they were sixteen.' The questions started out quite tame, but by the time everyone had taken a few sips the questions got nearer and nearer the mark. Brad was particularly interested in a girl in her late twenties who had so far taken a sip in response to:- losing her virginity before fifteen; having sex with more than one person at the same time; having a homosexual relationship; shagging on top of a fridge; having something bigger than a finger up her bottom; enjoying having Harry on the Boat (one of Brad's questions) and enjoying water sports (she was one of the few girls who understood that one, let alone admitting to enjoying it).

There was even a deaf Aussie playing the games, and although he didn't really understand everything that was going on, he was having a thoroughly good time being in the same proximity as other souls, who were consuming alcohol as fervently as he was.

After the games were finished, most of the clients went down The Star. Tom took Brad in the corner where they sat down for a chat. Tom told him what Alison had said about the hotel and him not filing a report. Brad pulled out a copy of the report he had written, and several more, none of which Tom had seen. This meant that they had not found their way back to head office. Luckily, the girl with the black eye was in the bar, and she also more or less validated Brad's story. It was all making sense to Tom.

Here was the classic case of an unsuitable hotel that was obviously being used because they were in on Felipe's scam. Tom realised that another consequence of contracting a hotel that was paying backhanders was that certain owners clearly thought that it gave them carte blanche to do as they pleased. But what was he to do? It was becoming apparent that Alison was lying and that Brad was in the right, but circumstances had twisted Brad's future. Brad also told him all about the airport, and although he didn't say so, Tom's opinion was that Alison had simply forgotten to get the permits sorted out - probably because she had been too busy looking after Felipe's accounts.

Brad was pissed, tired and depressed. He was not the type

of person to backstab someone even if they deserved it, but when the conversation got round to Lorraine he couldn't help himself from telling Tom about Mario's involvement.

Tom was left in a total quandary. Had things been different, he would most definitely have been on the phone to Jane Ward to get her on to resort to sack Alison. Instead, his orders were that if anybody had to go then it should be Brad. But he could not bring himself to sack Brad after all that he had just heard. Instead he settled on a compromise. He told Brad that he would put him and Natalie in The Bon, and bring Mario and Heather into The Las Huertas, effective from Wednesday. Brad was not doing cartwheels but he didn't moan either - he didn't have enough energy. Tom left to go down The Star at ten to one. Brad had not slept since Alison's intrusion that morning, so for once, all thoughts of music, dancing, drink, drugs or sex were overtaken by the need to rest his eyes, who's lids felt like they had opposing magnets attached to them. Brad was asleep by one o'clock.

Greg only just made the coach for the cruise and he looked like shit. After the bar night he had gone down The Star and taken another 'E' with Robbo. They had pulled a girl who was off her head and taken her round the back of The Star where, bending over, she had given Greg a blow job while Robbo shagged her from behind. The bit that Greg was happiest relating, was about when the pair of them decided to pick their noses and flick bogies over her back while they were keeping her busy at either end. Greg had a great time, but he could not remember when he had last slept.

The Competition was getting out of hand. Each rep was finding it difficult to keep tabs on their own score, let alone everyone else's. Brad knew that he'd already been to bed with over twenty girls, but how many of them had been a full on consumation......how many had just given him a blow job..........how many bonus points he'd scored.......he really

317

didn't have a clue.

The cruise set off from Ibiza Town, so Brad did the coach transfer from San Antonio. It occurred to him that he had finally mastered the art of sounding happy even when he was pissed off. Mario had met a gorgeous looking girl that he was keen to impress, so he took over the microphone from Brad after five minutes. He was actually mildly amusing, and when he finished he put on his Derek & Clive tape. Unfortunately, it was the racist sketch about 'darkies'. There were a black couple from Manchester on the coach who actually took it quite well, but Brad enjoyed watching Mario squirm, trying to decide whether to switch it off, thereby drawing attention to his 'error', or to leave it running and suffer everyone's embarrassed giggles.

On Espalmador, Greg almost immediately crashed out. Brad got a paper plate and ripped it into the shape of a phallus, which he placed on Greg's stomach with a small pebble on top of it so that it didn't get blown away. He was hoping to get half an hour or so without Greg moving, so that the sun darkening the rest of Greg's skin would slightly contrast against the lighter area where he'd placed the three inch high paper dick. Brad was therefore more than happy when Greg did not move from the one position for the whole day, leaving him with a well defined reminder of Brad's practical joke.

Brad was surprised that most of the people from the previous night's bar night had made the cruise. The three lads from Bradford hadn't turned up, but then again, they were absolutely legless by the end of the night. The dirty looking girl in her late twenties however, who was on holiday by herself, did turn up. Halfway through the afternoon Brad started talking to her. The conversation was loaded with innuendo. In the end, Brad could take no more.

'Look,' he said, 'I'm not very good at euphemism's. I really want to fuck you.'

They got a pedaloe over to Brad's favourite wall and had filthy, gekko free sex. She was quite petite, but listening to the noise she made, Brad wondered if she too had visited the

Papworth clinic, for her lungs surely belonged to a woman four times her size. Judging by the way Brad's dick barely touched the sides when he was inside her, he thought that there was a good chance that another part of her anatomy had been donated by a similarly sized woman.

On the coach back to San Antonio after the cruise had finished, Brad put on his Thunderbird's tape. Brad had a copy of a whole episode of the Gerry Anderson classic. Initially he had got it just for the countdown at the beginning, which he played at full volume from his balcony when he wanted to wake up his clients. But latterly, he had taken to playing the whole episode as a respite from the music tapes that he was growing increasingly bored with. He had also started playing Reader's Digest Spanish Language tapes, which he would put on during excursions, adding his own comments and getting the whole coach to repeat back the phrases like a group of infants. It had got to the stage where clients were actually asking him to put on the language tapes instead of music.

As the coach pulled up outside The Las Huertas, Alison and Tom were both waiting for Brad. They looked serious. Brad stepped off of the coach and Alison beckoned him over.

'Brad, can I have a word with you.'

She whispered something to Tom, who nodded and walked away. Alison led Brad through to the hotel bar and they both sat down.

'Brad, something quite serious has happened.'

'Here it comes,' thought Brad, looking at his arm and deciding that at least he'd have a decent tan to go home with.

'I've spoken to Tom. After what happened this morning you should be going home. However, after discussing it we've decided to move you to The Bon on Wednesday. I'm not happy with your performance, and if you step out of line again I think you know what the consequences will be.' Alison had to agree to this compromise that Tom had come up with, but she knew it would only be a matter of time before she got rid of Brad. 'Anyway, that's not why I want to talk to you.' Brad looked at her with a mixture of puzzlement, indifference and relief.

319

'Something happened last night, so I need you to have your wits about you.'

'Go on,' said Brad, leaning forward in his chair.

'One of your clients has died.'

'What! Which one?'

'Nick Harland. One of the lads from Bradford - the one with the Buddy Holly glasses.'

'Oh God, no. What happened?'

'His two friends got up for breakfast this morning and gave him a shout but he didn't move. They didn't think anything of it but when they got back he was still in the same position. When they looked closer they saw that he'd choked on his own vomit.'

'How?'

'Too much to drink.' Alison didn't look Brad in the eyes. 'Hopefully there won't be any repercussions. Apparently after they left the bar they were in town doing Tequila slammers, so.......'

'So we might be off the hook,' said Brad cynically.

'No, that's not what I meant. Obviously, it's not our policy as a company to get clients that pissed, just merry.'

'Like when I suggested they'd had enough to drink at nine o'clock last night and you told me to make them carry on drinking? Is that what you meant?'

'No that's not what I meant at all. If they hadn't drank in the hotel they'd have got drunk somewhere else.'

'Maybe. But it's not gonna look very good if the boys parents start asking questions and find out that the night their Nick died, we'd been doing drinking games and doing all we could to make him so drunk that he couldn't stand up.'

'No Brad,' corrected Alison. 'You did, not we. What each individual rep does in his or her hotel is down to them. If a rep oversteps the mark and goes outside of our stated company policy then we have only one course of action open to us.'

'Right, so what you're saying is if this goes any further then it's yours truly who's gonna carry the can, which means that to distance me from the company I'll be the sacrificial lamb and given the chop. Whereas if I'd done what I wanted to do last night and have been wanting to do since the beginning of the season, namely moderating these stupid fucking bar nights, then you'd've given me the chop anyway for going against you. Does that sound about right?'

Alison leaned forward and smiling, hissed at Brad, 'See, you're not as fucking smart as you thought you were. I told you to watch your step. Now we'll see-'

'I don't believe you,' snapped Brad. 'There's a poor guy just died and all you're worried about is using it to get one over on me. You're pathetic.' Brad stood up. 'I'm going upstairs 'cos if I have to listen to your drivel any longer I might do something I regret.'

As he went away Greg walked in. 'Wha's all that about?'

'Just giving Brad a few home truths,' said Alison. 'I suppose you've heard about the death?'

'Yeah, bad news.'

Tom walked over. 'Where's Brad?'

'Gone upstairs,' said Alison.

'Is he alright?' asked Tom. Alison shrugged her shoulders. 'I've rung head office,' continued Tom.

'What did they say?' asked Alison.

'Not a lot.'

'So how many deaths is that so far this season?' asked Alison, gathering her things together and standing up ready to leave.

'Um, two in Tenerife, one in Crete and one in Gran Canaria.'

'Well,' said Alison. 'We'd better get our finger out if we're gonna take the lead.'

Greg stayed in the hotel to cover Brad's desk duty. He'd been there for about ten minutes when Nick's two friends walked in. Greg beckoned them over.

'I'm really sorry to hear whar' 'appened to Nick. Are you alright?'

'Aye, still a bit shocked like, but......'

'I've just spoken to 'is mum,' said the other. 'That was fucking hard.'

Greg looked at them not really knowing what to say. He offered them a drink which they declined. The two boys stood there awkwardly, so Greg brought the 'conversation' to a close.

'Well if there's anything I can do for you.........'

'Actually,' said the boy who'd spoken first, 'There is summit you can do.'

'Just name it,' said Greg.

'I let Nick borrow two mill yesterday - any chance of getting it back for us?'

Greg looked at him, not sure at first if he was serious. He was.

'Uh, I'll see what I can do.'

The body had been upstairs all day, while the necessary arrangements were made. Alison came in just before eight and whispered to Greg that they were going to be bringing the body down within the next fifteen minutes, and to be sure that all of the clients were out of the way. A girl who was staying at The Las Huertas had been annoying Greg all week. She was a spiteful gossip, who had to know what everyone else was doing. Her father had been a pop star in the seventies - a guitarist in a band that Greg had heard of but couldn't remember the name of. Out of devilment he went up to her in the corner of the bar where she was sitting alone.

'How y'doing Jodie.'

'Hello Greg. What was all that whispering going on with your boss and Brad?'

'Well, y'know that lad Nick who died last night?'

'Yeah I heard. He choked on his own vomit, didn't he?'

'Yeah. Don't tell anyone but they're bringing the body down in a few minutes.'

Greg went and stood by the bottom of the stairs waiting for the body to come down. Sure enough, within five minutes a group of about ten clients had gathered, led by Jodie. Greg smiled to himself. Barely a minute or so after they arrived, the voices of two Spanish men could be heard echoing down the stair well. Nobody knew exactly what to expect, but it certainly was not the sight that greeted them. Both men had goatee beards, grey sawtooth trousers and dirty white tops. Cigarettes were dangling from each of their lips and they were laughing and joking. In between them, as if they were putting out some heavy rubbish, was a black bag, in which was obviously a body. However, either the bag wasn't zipped up properly or there was a hole in it, because one by one, Greg and the clients noticed a steady drip coming out of the bag and onto the stairs.

'What's that?' asked Jodie.

'Must be his fluids,' answered Greg.

'His what?' asked Jodie.

'His bodily fluids. When you die all the fluids in your body - y'know, piss, shit an' all that - they pour out.'

He looked at Jodie who swung to her left and threw up all over the wall. Grinning, Greg walked away.

Brad didn't wake up until just before midnight. He really felt like getting 'on one'. Natalie was doing desk in the morning so he could have a late night if he wanted.

It was without doubt, the most down he'd been since he'd arrived in Ibiza. Unless something dramatic happened he felt that it was only a matter of time before Alison sacked him. He was always tired, knew he was drinking too much, hated this weeks clients - he was even getting bored with sex. Greg had said this would happen earlier in the season. He remembered what Greg had said about forming relationships and he was right. True, it was easy to shag yourself senseless, a different girl every night if you really put your mind to it. It was also true that girls fell in love with you. But Brad had learned that it was always a classic holiday romance. The phone calls and letters would stop; the old boyfriend would re-appear - 'Patricia Syndrome' time and time again. As for relationships with other reps or workers - well that was fine for normal rep's. But YF&S rep's had such a bad reputation for womanising that to forge such a relationship was a mammoth task, especially with such a small amount of free time. Still, Brad was looking forward to his date on Thursday with Kelly 'The Vision'.

Mikey was due round at twelve thirty. At just gone quarter past, Brad heard a commotion on the stairs. He went down a couple of floors and a scruffy looking bloke ran past him and down the corridor into a room. Two girls voices started shouting and screaming, so Brad quickened his pace. He was about ten yards away when the bloke came running out of the room, with what looked like a wallet in one hand and a knife in the other. Instinctively Brad tripped him up and sent him flying. As he did so, the jolt on his leg made him brush against the wall, where a protruding nail ripped Brad's shirt and scratched his skin. The intruder went flying, and the wallet and knife skidded along the corridor. Brad skipped over and picked them up. The intruder looked at Brad, who was now in possession of the knife. He obviously didn't fancy his chances and ran off down the stairs. The two girls came hurtling out of the room. They were both cockneys.

'Where'd 'e fuckin' go?'

''E's nicked our passports.'

'What, these?' said Brad, showing them what he thought previously to be a wallet.

'Fuckin' 'ell,' said one of the girls, with wavy bleached hair and a pretty, freckly tanned face. ''Ow d'ya get that. 'E 'ad a bleedin' knife, did'n'e?'

'What, this?' said Brad, showing them the knife.

'Look, 'e's striped ya,' said her friend, who had dark hair and the battered features of a girl who would not have looked out of place in a gritty Channel 4 documentary.

Brad looked down at the graze that the nail had caused.

324

'Are you alright?' asked the prettier girl, bending down to look at Brad's 'wound'.

'Yeah, it's nothing.'

'Bastard reckoned we owed 'im some wonga. Came up 'ere and took our passports when we told 'im we 'ad nuffink,' said the dark haired girl. 'You must be a bit tasty to get that knife off 'im.'

Brad liked the thought of being 'tasty'.

'It wasn't too hard. It's what I'm here for.'

'Yeah, but could've bin nasty,' said the pretty one. 'If 'e'd slashed yer face or sumfink....'

'No chance. I've done a bit of, uh, a bit of karate.' Brad made a chopping motion to emphasise the fact.

'Let me 'ave a butchers.'

'No, it's fine, honest,' said Brad moving away from the dark haired girl in case she noticed that the slash mark wasn't as bad as it obviously looked from a distance.

'We're trying to find work,' she said. 'Anyfink abaht?'

'Not that I know of. Sorry.' Brad began to realise that they were probably a couple of scallies. 'Anyway - gotta go. I'm glad you're both alright.'

'Yeah, cheers mate,' they said almost at the same time.

Brad had just changed his shirt when Mikey, Tom and Greg all turned up, dressed to the nines and filling Brad's room with the scent of different after shaves and deodorants. Greg produced a small bag of pills. Tonight they were all going for it.

Brad was rushing his tits off. Robbo had got hold of some E's called Apples which Greg had bought and they were brilliant. All four of the boys had dropped one in Brad's room, although Tom and Mikey had only done half each. Greg had taken a pill on each of the last three nights.

Brad loved Es Paradis. The spacious white club was beautifully designed around a central circular dance floor which was surrounded by sculpted columns. It was quite a bright club and as such attracted more of a posey, cosmopolitan crowd. Looking round at the smiling faces and feeling the great atmosphere, Brad guessed that Robbo had had a profitable night. Rusty, Squirrel and all of their mob were there and apparently on the same buzz. None of them had yet surpassed Squirrel's effort up the tree, although they had all shagged the same girl. Rusty told Brad that to his knowledge she had slept with twenty blokes in her first week. The night before, she had taken on three of Rusty's group and four other lad's one after the other. No sooner had they finished talking about her than she walked down the stairs leading into the club. Brad had an idea. He waved her over.

'Donna, over here.'

She came over smiling. She looked really sweet and was actually a very attractive girl.

'How's young Donna tonight then?'

'Great. I've had a couple of those Apples. Wicked. What about you?'

'The same,' replied Brad. 'I've got to be a bit careful though. I've got my boss over from London.'

'Oh, which one's he then?'

Brad pointed to the bar that was halfway up towards the balcony, where Tom was standing and laughing with Greg.

'He doesn't look old enough to be your boss,' said Donna. 'He's good looking though isn't he?'

'Yes,' thought Brad, silently punching the air.

'Funny you should say that Donna, 'cos he noticed you yesterday and was asking questions about you.'

'Really?' Donna's face lit up.

'Really,' repeated Brad. 'I'm gonna go and have a word with him in a minute, so you go and have a dance and I'll see what I can do.'

Brad walked up behind Tom and winked at Greg. They both threw their arms around him - Brad realised that they'd consumed more drugs. After general 'E' talk, Brad pointed out Donna to Tom, making a ssshhhing gesture to Greg as he did so.

'See that girl over there Tom?'

'Which one?'

'That really fit blonde in the middle of the dance floor. The one in the short yellow dress with the gorgeous tits.' Brad thought he might as well lay it on.

'Yeah,' said Tom, finally spotting her.

'I don't know why I'm telling you this - 'cos I doubt if you'd do the same for me - but a little birdie tells me she's got the hots for you, which is a real fucker 'cos everyone on resort has been trying to crack her all week without any luck.'

Greg almost gave the game away by choking on his water at the last comment.

'Really?' said Tom in Apple induced innocence and gullibility.

'In't that right Greg?'

'Oh aye,' said Greg recomposing himself. 'When you've finished Tom, all we ask is for you to let us sniff yer fingers.'

Tom put his drink down and went to make his way over to her.

'But before you go,' said Greg, 'I've gorra new competition.'

'Oh not another one,' groaned Brad. 'What is it this time?'

'Right, we've all got cassette recorders 'aven't we.'

Brad nodded. Mikey had just joined the group and nodded as well.

'I've got a Sony Walkman,' said Tom.

'Does it record?' asked Greg.

'Yeah, I think so.'

'Perfect,' said Greg. 'Right, what we do is 'ave a phrase of the week that we 'ave to get whoever we pull to say while we're shagging 'em.'

'What sort of phrase?' asked Mikey.

'Well, I thought for the first week the phrase should be 'Fluffyflops'.'

'WHAT!?' screamed the other three laughing.

'Yeah, Fluffyflops,' repeated Greg. 'So while you're at it you've gorra get 'er to say 'Fluffyflops'. Doesn't matter 'ow yer

327

do it, as long as yer don't tell 'er it's part of a competition.'

The other three all shook their heads in disbelief, whilst secretly already trying to think of a devious way to get their next victim to say 'Fluffyflops'.

Tom headed off towards Donna and within ten minutes was leaving with her, much to the other's amusement.

The pretty girl who had the knife wielder in her room earlier that night turned up without her friend, and within an hour Brad left with her.

Mikey left Greg alone for a while. When he came back, Greg was in a terrible state and all over the place, barely able to stay conscious.

'What's up mate?'

Mikey couldn't understand Greg's reply, and seconds later Greg passed out. Nearby was Vince, who ran The Madhouse.

'Any idea what's up with him?' asked Mikey.

'Dunno. 'E's 'ad a lorra drink.'

'Well that's why then,' said Duffy from The Charleston leaning over. 'He had a load of that GHB stuff earlier on. Mixed with alcohol it's fucking lethal. I'd get him down the medical centre if I were you.'

Mikey tried to wake him up but he barely stirred. There was a medical centre less than a hundred yards from Es Paradis, so Mikey got Duffy to give him a hand to carry Greg up there. Mikey told the doctor what he thought Greg had taken and the doctor gave him an injection.

Fortunately Greg had not had as much GHB or alcohol as everyone thought. However, when he came round just under two hours later he panicked, having no recollection of passing out or the events leading up to it. For a few moments he thought he was dying. One of his first conscious thoughts was a strong desire not to expire at that particular moment. It was not for the love of his family or because he had unfulfilled ambitions that he needed to achieve. It was because the last girl he had shagged had been a monster, and he could not stand the posthumous embarrassment of having her face next to his, plastered all over The Sun, detailing her 'Last Night

With Dead Young Free & Single Rep', especially as he had made an absolute hash of shafting her. Fortunately, by dawn he felt fine, and with such tabloid infamy spared him, was able to leave under the protective wing of Mikey.

Brad took the pretty girl to his room because her room mate had 'pulled'. The pretty girl's name was Amanda. Amanda had made it clear to Brad that they were not going to have sex, but ten minutes later, with her hand firmly placed around his weapon, he figured that she'd probably changed her mind. She had. Brad had only taken the one 'E', which had more or less totally worn off - at least sufficiently enough for him to have to concentrate on not coming. He was enjoying keeping himself as close to orgasm as possible.

Greg had been right. Sex was so abundant that the other participant had almost become irrelevant. Trying to master a certain technique or doing something different or outrageous to tell the others the next day had become the most important thing - next to scoring points, of course. Although a can of deodorant had found a new temporary home during the liaison with Amanda, he could not for the life of him think of a way of getting her to say 'Fluffyflops'. He was considering this and trying not to come when he was aware of someone or something behind him. What Brad had not seen was the hotel mongrel, Brad's 'confidante', push the door of Brad's room open with it's nose, and inquisitively start to sniff around. Dogs seem to have a natural affinity with smelly body parts, so it was not long before he was attracted to the two bodies grunting and sweating on the bed.

The dog's timing could not have been better. Just as Brad was slowing down to stop himself from coming, the dog nudged it's cold nose up Brad's arse and licked his balls (out of canine curiosity rather than desire). It finished Brad off. He pulled out and whipped the condom off, aiming for Harry on the Boat but ending up with Harry somewhere on Amanda's mid-stomach. Brad turned round and glared at the dog, who slinked out of the room wagging it's tail. Had Brad been in possession of a Hitch Hiker's Guide type Babel Fish all purpose translator, the little yelp that the dog gave as he left the room would have undoubtedly sounded like Muttley laughing.

The pool was buzzing with two topics of conversation. The night before there had been what appeared to be a massive fight down Night Life. The Scandinavian bodybuilders had gone in drunk, and started on Irish Ben. Ben had tried to avoid trouble but was eventually left with no option. Everybody had scattered, scared to look back to see how badly Ben had been injured. Nobody had wanted to get involved because the Scandies were all so massive and were all bouncers or bodyguards in their own right. However, the next minute was destined to pass into Ibiza legend and folklore, for at the end of it, each Scandinavian was laying spark out on the floor. Ben had then calmly ordered himself a drink from the bar, and the police carried the bodybuilders out (they were so heavy that each one needed four policemen).

The other topic of conversation was Tom getting off with Donna. All of the reps, Rusty, Squirrel Mikey and about ten other clients had either a sheet of paper or cardboard with the number '21' written on it. When a very self satisfied Tom walked into the pool area at just gone midday, they held up their placards and started chanting 'twenty one'. Tom took a long while to accept that he was the twenty first of Donna's vacational victim's and when he did, the way that the colour drained from his face suggested that he had probably not worn a condom.

CHAPTER FIFTEEN

The slap hurt. Rick's instinctive reaction was to give her a Glasgow kiss; a knee jerk reaction to the stinging pain, but the impulse passed in seconds.

'What did you do that for?' he pleaded, hoping that she hadn't found out about his periodic visits to Viv in Lochaber, or to Lena in Park Head.

'I can't trust you to do anything,' said Carmen.

'What are you on about?'

'Sandy,' she said referring to her Yorkshire Terrier.

'What about her?'

'Don't give me the innocent. Alistair told me all about what happened.'

'Oh,' said Rick sheepishly.

'And what was it that almost killed my poor wee dog? The same thing that causes us not to see each other every weekend; the same thing that made you lose your job; the same reason you're incapable of anything before Wednesday - bloody drugs.'

'Och, that's hardly fair hen. It was'nae pills that she swallowed.'

'So an eighth of puff is alright, but?'

'I didn't mean to leave it lying around. The wee bugger'll eat anything. It didn't do any harm though, did it?'

'God knows. And what about when you almost garrotted her with her lead?'

'That was an accident. Anyway you can't blame that on drugs.'

'Can't I? When did it happen?'

'Sunday morning.'

'And where had you just got back from?'

'Um, The Arches.'

'And I suppose you were straight.'

'Well, I'd taken a couple, but -'

'But nothing. You were off your head.'

Rick remembered what happened only too well. He'd got back home from The Arches in Glasgow, totally nutted. Thinking it would be a good idea to take the dog out for a walk, he had attached the extending lead to Sandy's collar and set off. It was a beautiful sunny morning and he started running. Sandy, her little legs a blur, struggled to keep up, so Rick let more of the lead out. All of a sudden, he felt a sharp yank on the lead. When he looked behind, the dog was airborne, swinging around a tree for the second time. Rick had ran passed the tree on one side and the dog on the other.

Carmen had entrusted him with her beloved Sandy for a week while she went to visit her sister, in London. The dog was like a Tasmanian Devil, zooming around his small flat and yapping incessantly. On the third day of the dog's residence, Sandy was unusually quiet and immobile. Rick remembered the pleasure he'd felt at the respite from the stress the dog had been causing him. He decided to reward himself with a spliff. Ten minutes later, still unable to find the eighth he'd bought the day before, he put two and two together made the correlation between the dog's inactivity and the sudden loss of his hash. His stomach knotted as he raced to the extremely stoned dog. Sandy didn't move for six hours and for once, Rick was thankful when the dog resumed its previous level of boisterousness.

Like a fool, he'd told his friend Alistiar McBride about what happened because he thought that it actually made quite a good story. He should have known better. Alistair never could keep a secret.

For Carmen, the dog was the final straw. She'd tired of Rick some months before. He was twenty nine, divorced and had just discovered clubbing and ecstasy. For the last six months he had been out on his own or with his friends almost every Saturday. He was still at the stage where the whole scene for him was not about the music, more an excuse for reliving his youth and giving him the opportunity to pull girls barely out of their teens. This was particularly naive of him, as Carmen was beautiful and intelligent and was really way out of his league. She looked a little like the actress, Nicole Kidman, but with softer rounder features, brighter red hair and captivating translucent blue eyes. She was quick witted, with an appetite for life that during her time with Rick had been reduced to that of a super model on amphetamines. She had met Rick just after finishing a short, passionate affair and had most definitely been on the rebound. Plus, she had known him for a number of years because he had been in the same class as her sister, who always spoke very highly of him. Even if he had not got into the club scene she would have probably finished with him. But on the rare occasions they had been to a rave together, he had embarrassed her with the unsophisticated way he conducted himself when 'on one'. Carmen had been clubbing for at least six years, since she was seventeen. She was able to more or less control her buzz and was quite contemptuous of 'lost it's' in clubs - guys walking around with gormless, grinning faces, dancing to anything and homing in on any girl that gave them the briefest of eye contact. Rick most definitely fell into this category. She was sure that he was sleeping around, but cared so little for him that she wasn't too bothered, especially as they hadn't had full sex for over a month.

The incident with the dog presented her with the perfect excuse to finish things.

Afterwards, it left Rick confused as to how she could get upset enough to chuck him over something as trivial as the episode with the dog. Over the next few weeks he would realise the mistake he had made, beat up Alistair, take load more drugs and constantly ring Carmen to try and get her back. Carmen knew that she would never go back with him. She also knew that she dearly wanted to get out of Scotland and make a fresh start - a new challenge. Maybe something abroad?

Mario had just got off of the scales outside the main chemist in San Antonio, down the road from Night Life. It was seven o'clock and the restaurants along the front were springing into action; coloured lights on, music playing and waiters scurrying. Natalie was with him buying some tampons, so Mario was loitering outside waiting for her to complete the purchase. A Spanish youth approached him, just as Natalie emerged.

'Hey, you want a cheese?' asked the Spanish boy.

'Do what?' asked Mario.

'You want a cheese?'

'A cheese?'

'Si, a cheese.'

Natalie tugged Mario's arm. 'Mario-'

'Hang on a sec Nat - I'm trying to understand this Spanish kid. Now then mate, you say I want a cheese, yes?'

'Si,' replied the Spanish boy nodding enthusiastically.

'Ok. A cheese what? Fromage?' he said reverting to basic French, before he remembered Spanish for cheese. 'Queso?'

'No,' said the Spanish boy. 'You want a cheese.'

'Si,' said Mario. 'A cheese - queso.'

'No queso,' said the boy, a little more impatiently.

'Mario,' said Natalie, tugging his arm again.

'Look, leave me a minute will you. Can't you see I'm trying to speak Spanish? Everyone keeps having a go at me for not bothering to learn any, and when I try you keep attempting to stop me.'

'Yes, but Mario, he's not-'

'Just shut up a sec, will you. Right then. Queso. Boacadillo de queso,' said Mario, smiling that he'd remembered what cheese in French bread was.

'No, no queso de bocadillo conjo. I say do you want A CHEESE!' The boy was now getting quite irritated.

'Yes, I know you say a cheese. But a cheese what?'

'Mario, I-'

'Natalie, for the last time - will you shut up?'

'Hijo de puta. You want a cheese. Yes or no,' said the Spanish boy finally.

'Sorry - I don't know what you mean.' Mario gave up. The boy turned on his heels in disgust.

'Mario.'

'Oh for God's sake Nat - WHAT!?'

'He was asking you if you wanted hashish - not a cheese.'

'Oh.'

The mood in the boardroom was sombre. Adam Hawthorne-Blythe sat at the head of the table, looking as calm as ever. Jane Ward was sitting opposite Tom, who's main desire was for the day to end as quickly as possible so he could catch up on some much needed sleep. He had caught a flight in the early hours of Tuesday morning and had gone straight to work from the airport. He had tried to sleep by the pool all day on Monday, but the constant piss taking of Brad, Greg, Mikey and most of the clients once they had found out that he had slept with Donna, had made it all but impossible.

Sebastian was pacing up and down the room, his tie loosened and the sleeves of his blue striped shirt rolled up to just below his elbows. A pen was placed behind his ear and a calculator was in his hand.

'You're right you know,' he said, finishing off some calculations. 'It could run into hundreds of thousands - maybe even a million if he's been at it for longer. No wonder we've been struggling to compete with our rivals.'

'What's done is done,' said Adam Hawthorne-Blythe. 'Our main focus of attention should now be to ensure that we gather sufficient evidence to bring the perpetrator to justice, so that future accommodation is contracted for our customers benefit rather than the fiscal gain of a rogue director.'

'Easier said than done,' said Jane, wondering if anything ever ruffled Hawthorne-Blythe.

'Why can't we just tell him we know what he's up to, give him the boot and make him pay the money back?' asked Tom.

'Were it only so easy,' replied Hawthorne-Blythe.

'The problem is Tom,' offered Sebastian, 'That we have to be careful what accusations we throw at him without evidence. He's a devious little sod, and I would imagine with the money he's now got behind him, he could hire himself a good lawyer....'

'Unfair dismissal, slander - shoot ourselves in the foot, sure we could,' said Jane.

'Precisely,' agreed Hawthorne-Blythe. 'What we need is some evidence. But the question is, how?'

'We could always ask Alison,' suggested Jane sarcastically. 'God, if you hadn't found that invoice Sebastian........'

'No wonder Felipe was so keen for her to get the job,' said Tom. 'What about if we sacked her? Don't you think that might ruffle his feathers enough for him to slip up?'

'Possibly,' said Jane, 'But I think that our best bet is to keep her out there. If she's looking after his accounts I reckon we've got much more chance of getting something on him - certainly more than we have back here.'

'Most definitely,' agreed Hawthorne-Blythe. 'He would be very foolish indeed to leave any evidence back in the UK. I could probably find out a little about his affairs over here, but frankly it would prove nothing. He would almost certainly use this fictitious relation of his as an excuse and most of his money is no doubt laundered in Spain.'

'Mmmm,' said Sebastian thoughtfully. 'As much as I hate to agree, getting rid of Alison is the worst thing we could do at the moment. No, if anything she must stay there at all costs.'

'But you should see how she's screwing up the resort, Sebastian. The reps are all demotivated, no one has a good word to say about her,' said Tom.

'It's unfortunate, but this is so big that even if we have to write off the season out there and change all of the reps, we must get some evidence,' said Sebastian, sitting down. 'Alison must stay.'

'But how are we going to get some evidence?' asked Tom.

'We need someone out there,' said Jane.

'What about Brad?' asked Tom.

Jane raised her eyebrows, to indicate that she took the suggestion seriously. 'He's certainly bright enough,' she said thinking aloud. 'And from what you've said he dislikes her sufficiently enough to have the right motivation.'

'She's almost certainly gonna sack him,' said Tom, 'And he knows it. Can't think of any better motivation.'

'Sorry, about whom are we talking?' asked Hawthorne-Blythe, peering over the top of his glasses.

'Bradley Streeter,' said Jane.

'Who is he, exactly?' asked Hawthorne-Blythe.

'He's a first year rep,' said Jane, hesitating as the words came out of her mouth, realising how it must have sounded.

'Absolutely not. Preposterous idea,' said Hawthorne-Blythe. 'If you think we can entrust what is tantamount to the future of this company to someone who has been with us for little more than three months, and with whom we've had no previous dealings, well........' Hawthorne-Blythe didn't need to expand any further.

'Apart from anything else,' added Sebastian, 'If there's already animosity between him and Alison it would make it even more difficult for him to get anything worthwhile.'

'I guess you're right,' said Tom, watching Brad's lifeline disappear.

'No, what we need is someone who either has Alison's trust or who isn't known to her. It also needs to be someone we can count on for loyalty one hundred and ten percent - somebody with the same blood running through their veins as we have,' said Hawthorne-Blythe.

They all looked at each other blankly. 'Maybe Brad'll turn something up,' said Tom lamely.

The bookings for Aguamar, the water park next to the airport, were abysmal. In fact the excursion bookings for the whole week were. Brad had been having a terrible time. There were now five large groups of lads who were all gunning for him. They had vandalised his information book, defaced his posters and tried to disrupt his bar nights while he was in The Las Huertas. He had been in The Bon for one night, sharing a two bedroom apartment with Natalie. Three of the groups of lads were staying in The Las Huertas, but they had turned two other groups of northern lads in The Bon against him. Brad really had done nothing wrong other than be the rep on a particularly bad week for weather and women.

He had seen Alison laughing and joking with the lads on different occasions. Judging by the way the group looked over at him from time to time, Brad correctly suspected that Alison had not exactly been helping him. He couldn't wait until the weekend when all five groups were going home. He only hoped he didn't get their coach to take to the airport because it had almost gotten nasty on a few occasions and he was fairly certain that they would be out to do him before they left.

Brad got on the coach that Greg was guiding to Aguamar. Greg cracked a few funnies, and got everyone in the right mood. He told everyone that it was his birthday the next day. He did this every two weeks to get presents and as another angle for scoring points. Sitting at the front of the coach was a chubby, mousey haired girl called Felicity that Greg had slept with the previous night and had successfully got to say Fluffyflops, proved by the tape he had played to the other reps that morning.

When it seemed he had finished his spiel, Greg furrowed around in his bag. Brad was sitting a few seats back, and guessed he was looking for the Thunderbirds tape, because the episode had finished only half way through on the coach journey back from Hoe Down the night before, and most of the clients wanted to hear it's conclusion. However, Brad didn't recognise the tape that Greg got out. He placed it in the cassette player but before pushing it in, switched the microphone back on.

'Right then everyone. Whoever guesses who this is, gets a free bottle of champagne.' He pushed the cassette in.

'Oh Greg. I'm not sure I want to.'

'Look, I'm not gonna force yer. If yer don't wanna do it like, just say so I can get some shut eye.'

Felicity sank in her chair turning beetroot.

'I bet you get loads of girls. Why me?'

''Cos loadsa girls ain't 'ere and you are.'

Noise of clothes rustling, springs creaking and slurping.

'Oh Greg. That feels wonderful. Oh yes. Don't stop. Why are you stopping? No, not up there. Greg, stop it. Ow!!! Get it away and put it back in where it was.'

Greg heard muttering 'fuck it' on tape. Coach howling. Felicity sinking further into chair. Friend next to her wins champagne.

'C'mon, um, oh shit - I've forgotten your name.'

'Felicity.'

'C'mon Felicity - talk dirty to me.'

'I can't. I'm too shy.'

'Course you're not. No one else can hear.'

'I don't know.'

'Oh please. It'll really turn me on.'

'What do you want me to say exactly?'

'Just say "Fuck me Fluffyflops",'

'WHAT!?'

'Oh come on. 'You've gorra say it. I won't be able to come if yer don't.'

Pause.

'Alright then. Fuck me Fuffyflops.'

Brad got back from his date with Kelly just before four o'clock in the morning. Natalie was in the apartment sitting by the table taking off her make up when he walked in. Brad thought she looked a little down.

'You alright darling?'

339

'Oh, nothing I won't get over. What about you? How did you go with the lovely Kelly?'

Brad scratched his head and sat down opposite her.

'To be honest I don't know. It was a bit of a weird night. I mean we got on alright but there was no, no.............I dunno - I can't put me finger on it.'

'Oh dear,' said Natalie reaching behind her to the breakfast bar and getting a bottle of Southern Comfort and two glasses. 'Sounds like we'd better have a drink 'cos I've had a shit night too.' She poured the golden liquid into the tall glasses which had little red tulips running down their sides. 'You go first.'

'It wasn't really a shit night. I suppose I was looking forward to it so much that it all seemed a bit of an anti climax.'

'In what way?'

'There wasn't any rapport. I mean all she did was smile sweetly and look lovely. We didn't talk about anything of any consequence but we didn't argue; she laughed at my jokes but she didn't guffaw; she didn't give me a knock back but it didn't seem right to make a lunge. I don't know. Like I said, it was weird.'

'So what did you talk about?' asked Natalie.

'I asked her about what she did before she came away, what her ambitions were, a bit about relationships.....'

'Did she ask you anything?'

Brad thought for a moment. 'Actually, I can't remember if she did.'

Natalie chuckled. 'Well there you go. It sounds to me like she's totally wrapped up in herself. To be honest I've spoken to a few people about her.....'

'Why?'

'When a woman looks like she does Brad, just believe me that other women want to know as much about her as blokes do - probably more so.' Brad shrugged his shoulders and accepted Natalie's insight. 'Most people I've spoken to say that she's pleasant but with not a lot to say for herself.'

'Pleasant,' repeated Brad slowly. 'Yeah, that's a good word for her.'

'You often find that with good looking people. They're so used to using their looks to get what they want that they don't develop their personalities as much.'

'Is that why you've got such a good personality?' asked Brad. 'Were you an ugly child?'

'Was that a complement or an insult?'

Brad smiled. 'Anyway. Enough of my wailing. Suffice to say that I don't think I'll be bothering with her again. I wish there was someone here who was a bit of a challenge, y'know, someone who really flicked my switch.'

'Tell me about it,' said Natalie. 'All I end up with are Spaniards or bastards. I met this bloke at the beginning of the week - a punter as well - he's lovely. We've had a couple of really nice nights out and now he's started fucking me about. I just don't seem to be able to stay in a relationship.'

'I don't know,' sighed Brad, 'Maybe we're just waiting for cupid to shoot us up the arse with his arrow. Don't you think it would be nice to be with someone who you were so into that any time an epic love story comes on you could totally empathise with it? So that when old Burt Lancaster and whatever her name is are rolling around lovestruck in the waves you could totally relate to it, rather than arguing with someone in Tesco's over whether to get skimmed or non-skimmed milk.'

'But that's the real world Brad.'

'Yeah - that's probably why we're all here.'

The five men were squeezed into a corner of The Village Inn. The owner, a sarcastic seventeen stone cockney called Big Al hated reps and wouldn't give them free drinks, which was why the tour companies never normally bothered frequenting his bar. It was for this very reason that Mario thought it would be the ideal place to meet his brothers friends.

Two of them had been in Ibiza for the season, based in Ibiza Town rather than San Antonio. They were mugging,

341

robbing, ducking and diving - anything to avoid working and to sustain a reasonable lifestyle. The other three had just arrived on an indefinite holiday. None of them really had much time for Mario but one of them was his cousin and they were all friends of his small time gangster elder brother, so it was more out of respect to him than any desire to assist Mario that they indulged the white sheep of the family.

Big Al looked at the group suspiciously. He had been around enough criminals to recognise 'wrong 'un's' when he saw them. He tried to eavesdrop on what they were saying but they were whispering and he was unable to make out a single word. All of the group apart from Mario looked like bruisers; a mixture of broken noses, scars and steroid filled muscles. Mario's hair had grown to a respectable length so he no longer had the appearance of one who had just escaped from the foreign legion. However, his face had the bitterest scowl. Mario had not forgotten the humiliation that the Immac in his hair shampoo had caused him. If Big Al's attempts at eavesdropping Mario's conversation had been successful, the word most frequently heard would have been 'revenge'. Mario was giving them all the information that they needed to give a hiding to the perpetrator. Where he stayed, what time he walked passed the waste land (the best place to jump him), what sort of state he was likely to be in, what kind of fight he'd be liable to put up. Mario had all of the information that they needed and it was all correct - all correct apart from one crucial element.

The name being mentioned was Mikey, and not Brad.

CHAPTER SIXTEEN

Brad was still pissed when he woke up. He couldn't remember who the girl was laying next to him. She had her back to him, so he lifted her leg up and shagged her anyway. He emptied out within five minutes. The girl turned round but he still couldn't remember who she was. He didn't much respond to her idle chat, and a few minutes later she left suitably unimpressed. Brad wasn't sure if it was the girl's fault, but there seemed to be flies everywhere. They had been annoying him all season, but as he tried to get back to sleep they were more persistent than normal. He'd feel them tickle his skin, hear them buzzing his ear and one in particular was trying to enter every available orifice. That was it - Brad was declaring war on flies.

Half an hour later he was in the supermarket under The Bon. He bought a fly swat, some spray and a device that you put into a plug. Feeling dehydrated, he went to the drinks fridge to get himself some peach juice which he liked because it was also silky smooth on the throat. As he did so, he noticed a suave looking Clark Gable lookalike - a sort of debonair squaddie - buying some fruit. Until then, Brad had completely forgotten that he had given him a severe talking to the night before because he was the guy that had been messing Natalie around. Brad was trying to remember what he had said to him, when a very sunburnt Brummie boy of about eighteen approached.

'Alright Brad - you got a minute?'

'Yeah, sure,' said Brad, wincing at the red outline of a vest, blistering the Brummie's naked torso. 'What's up?'

'Well you know during the welcome meeting you said that if we got sunburnt, then yoghurt was a good cure?'

'Not a cure, but it'll offer some relief, yes.'

The Brummie picked up a black cherry yoghurt from the fridge.

'Does it matter what flavour you get?' he asked.

'Shouldn't,' said Brad. 'Natural's normally the best.'

'Really?' said the Brummie, putting down the black cherry and picking up a carton of natural. 'Oh, that's a shame.'

'Why?' asked Brad.

'I don't really like natural yoghurt.'

Brad laughed politely, but then looked at him and realised he wasn't joking.

'Um, actually you're not meant to drink it.'

'What are you supposed to do with it then?'

Brad couldn't resist. 'Rub it round your balls and in your hair. See you later.'

When he got back upstairs, Natalie was making a cup of tea.

'Two sugars please.'

'You were wrecked last night,' she said, as she looked in the cupboards trying to find where Brad had put the tea bags. 'Do you remember the picture?'

'The group one outside The Cockney Pride? Yeah course I do. Those bloody National Police.......'

'That's not what I meant, but they were bastards weren't they?'

'I felt such a pillock,' said Brad. 'That girl came running in saying the police were hitting all the clients. So I went out there giving it the big 'I'm a rep, I'll sort it out bit' - I couldn't fucking believe it. I pointed at my badge and said 'Soy Guia' (I'm a rep), and the bastard whacked me around the leg with his truncheon.'

'I've never seen you move so fast,' laughed Natalie.

'Too right - don't wanna mess with those guys. I was surprised that Alison made us do it when they'd gone. Probably didn't want to lose her commission.'

'So do you remember the picture then?' repeated Natalie.

'What do you mean?'

'Do you remember seeing it?'

344

'I don't actually, no. Why?'

Natalie giggled and went and got one of the pictures. Brad looked at it but it took nearly thirty seconds for his face to change.

'Oh no,' he groaned. Natalie started laughing more loudly. 'I don't believe it.'

Brad looked closer. 'My left bollock's hanging out.'

'That'll teach you to go out not wearing any pants.'

'Oh fuck. How many have we sold so far?'

'Last count, one hundred and eighty three I think.'

'Oh fucking great,' said Brad. 'So we're going have all these clients going back saying 'look mum, that's our rep's left testicle.' Bloody marvellous.'

They both went onto the balcony and sat down to drink their tea in the morning sun.

'I'm getting a bit worried about Greg, you know,' said Brad.

'Why?' asked Natalie.

'I think he's taken a pill every night since he had that first one when Tom came over. He told me the other day that morning desk duties were a bind - he's missed two in the last week.'

'I'm not surprised,' said Natalie. 'He's not normally getting in 'til seven. And then he's usually got some girl with him so God knows what time he's getting to sleep.'

'Probably five past,' said Brad sarcastically. 'I think I might have a word with him later.'

They sat quietly for a couple of minutes. They were by now relaxed enough in each others company for silences not to feel uncomfortable.

'What transfer are you on tonight,' asked Natalie, placing her empty cup on the floor.

'Dunno. As long as it's not those bastards who've been making my life hell all week I don't give a fuck. You? It's your night off tonight, isn't it?'

'Was. I swapped it with Mikey 'cos I was gonna see that bloke but he's stopped messing me about and come clean. He's got a wife back home.'

The talking to obviously worked, thought Brad.

'So, I've swapped it back. Mikey's off tonight.'

Just then, the door burst open, and there was Greg, still in the same clothes as the night before. It was clear that he hadn't slept and he still seemed slightly charged.

'Fuckin' 'ell lad. I've gorra tell yer wha's just 'appened to me.' He flopped onto the settee. 'I've just shagged that girl who's on 'oneymoon.'

'What?' said Natalie. 'Where was her old man?'

'He'd gone 'ome early pissed. I did 'er in that spare room on the first floor.'

'Hang on a minute,' said Brad, remembering the couple because he thought it particularly sad that someone should come on honeymoon with YF&S. 'Correct me if I'm wrong Greg, but doesn't she look like Olive from that old sitcom On the Buses, and.........' Brad suddenly remembered the worst bit, 'Isn't she eight months pregnant?'

'Yeah,' said Greg enthusiastically. 'Fuckin' great what E's do, innit?

'You and me are gonna have to talk.'

Alison had made a decision. She was going to get rid of Brad by the end of the following week and at last she had worked out how. From the conversation she had with Tom, she guessed that it would have to be something pretty drastic to get rid of the blue eyed boy. God she hated him. Still, he might have been the blue eyed boy, but he obviously wasn't as smart as her, she thought. If he was, then the fourteen thousand pounds would have been sitting in front of him instead of her. Of course, there was still the money to come from Felipe for her part in helping him with his 'pension'. All this money and it was only just August. Alison looked at the transfer sheets. She smiled as she put Brad's name next to the Birmingham flight which had fifty two other male names on it.

Mikey gave the joint to Brad and a bit of spliff to Raoul, the caretakers son who had let them up onto the roof of The Bon. Whenever they wanted to get away from it all this is where they would come, in between the washing but overlooking The Med.

'So what you gonna do?' asked Mikey.

'Well, for starters,' said Brad reaching into his shirt pocket, 'I've been saving this for a special occasion,' he pulled out a gram of coke, 'And it's either going up my nose or in that spliff.'

'Do you think that's a good idea?'

'Got a better one?'

'I could always come with you.'

'Mmm.' Brad thought about it. He liked that idea - he could certainly do with the back up. 'Yeah, alright then. Cool. Still gonna do the charlie though.'

Mikey laughed and nodded.

'I just can't believe after the week I've had that she'd be stupid enough to give me that transfer. They'll fucking lynch me.'

'If the ICF don't first.'

'Yeah, do you believe that? I've got to meet the coach down at Parking rather than the hotels,' said Brad, referring to a pick up point on the front at San Antonio harbour. 'And who are the ICF over here beating up? Reps. And where did that last bloke get done? Parking. Alison might as well go and get me a Millwall scarf and put some fucking posters up. If the ICF don't get me, the punters will.' Brad laughed ironically. 'Well she can go fuck herself, 'cos I'm gonna do the pick ups at the hotels.'

'Fair enough,' agreed Mikey, nodding.

'And I tell you what else. I'm getting on that coach tooled up. Old wotisface from The Star is gonna get me some gas. I've had enough of all this bollocks.'

By the time the coach arrived, the coke had worn off and Brad was feeling mellow. He was so stoned that he didn't give a toss about anything other than winning the bet with Pedro, the mad coach driver. For the last four weeks the reps had been having a bet with him to see how quickly he could get back from the airport after doing the first transfer. Even in a car, the airport would take about half an hour to get to. Realistically, with a coach full of clients to drop off and pick up, the journey should have taken at least an hour and a half, or more likely over two hours. The early Gatwick flight was hardly ever late and the only proviso was that if it was, then all bets were off. It had been Mikey's idea. Mikey got on well with Pedro, but the bet had arisen largely because Mario nearly always got the desirable early Gatwick transfer. It was Mikey's way of making Mario's journey more 'interesting', and the stiff drink and look of abject horror on Mario's face every time he saw that Pedro was driving was a fair indication that Mikey's plan worked.

The time limit on Pedro was an hour and fifteen minutes. Brad was sitting on his balcony in his airport uniform when he heard a coach come screeching around the corner and skid to a halt outside the apartments. Brad looked over the balcony and saw that week's holidaymakers disembarking, looking as though they had just been on the Nemesis roller coaster. He sat back smiling and then heard Mikey and Pedro arguing in Spanish as to who had won the bet.

When he got on the coach the hostility towards him was obvious. Brad hadn't bothered to get the CS gas - he'd got too pissed and stoned. As the coach pulled away there was silence. Brad switched on the microphone. Mikey was sitting next to him looking out of the window. Brad looked at all of the miserable faces. 'Fuck it,' he thought.

'Right then everyone,' he said in his happiest Hi-De-Hi voice. 'Have we all got our passports?'

Silence.

'Have we all had a good time?'

348

Oh shit, thought Mikey. He's going to start taking the piss.

'Have any of you little treasures fallen in love this week?'

Silence.

'Not even one of you?'

Shout of 'Fuck off' from somewhere near the back of the coach.

'No? Oh that's a shame. Well I'm sure you've all had a wonderful time, nevertheless.'

Cry of 'Sit down you cockney bastard,' from halfway down the coach.

'Yes, well I'll sit down in a moment.' Mikey caught Brad's eye with a look that said please don't. Brad ignored it. 'Before I do, I'd just like to say that I hope that if any of you have somehow managed to score during this last week or two, you wore a condom. Now please, don't for one moment think that I give a toss about any of you catching AIDS, it's just that I can't stand the thought of any of you fuckers breeding and populating the planet with any of your sorry offspring.' Mikey sank into his seat and pulled his baseball cap over his eyes. 'Ok. As we drive past San An harbour, I'd like to take the opportunity to point out some of the sights for the last time. If you look to the right you can see the boats in the harbour. Take one long last look at them all lads, moored and ready to go to your favourite beaches tomorrow. Now spare a thought for your poor rep Brad, laying on a beach and going even browner while you're stuck indoors looking at the situations vacant column of your local paper - that's for those of you who can read.' The coach drove passed a group of girls all wearing short skirts. 'Take one last look at all of those lovely girls, and think about your poor rep Brad, shagging who he wants - maybe even your girlfriends.' The coach drove past the road that led to The Star. 'Take one long last look at The Star and think about your poor rep Brad getting into all of the clubs for nothing, when you're getting turned away from clubs back home because you can't afford any decent clothes and are too fucking scruffy to get in..................' Brad continued the barrage of insults for almost five minutes before finally saying,

'.......And I hope you all have a safe flight home, but if you don't then I hope it crashes near Burnley (where most of the clients were from) 'cos by the look of you lot they must be used to having shit all over their streets. Hope to see you with Young Free & Single again. Bing bong.'

The coach fell into a stunned silence.

'You shouldn't've said that, man,' said Mikey.

'Fuck 'em,' said Brad.

However as it sank in what he'd done he began to feel a bit twitchy. Even Pedro sensed that something was wrong.

'Brad - *que pasa?*' (What's happening?)

Brad shrugged his shoulders.

'*Problemas?*' he asked. Brad shook his head. 'Hey Brad, *no pasa nada,*' (Don't worry,) he said, showing Brad a baseball bat by his seat. He said something else which Brad didn't understand.

'What did he say?' Brad asked Mikey.

'He said any big problems and he'll just call the police.'

'Fuck that,' said Brad, beginning to relax again. 'Let's just get them off the island.'

Miraculously, the coach was almost totally silent for the whole journey. At the airport, Brad sent them all to the wrong gate, just for good measure and instead of checking them all in, made his way straight to the arrivals lounge. An hour later, he had his clipboard in his hand and the first client came through.

'Young Free & Single?'

Looking around the group gathered in the bar of The Las Huertas, it struck Mikey that YF&S clients had a certain blandness about them. Apart, that was, from three cockney slappers from Leyton, who had a certain brainlessness about them. The group was probably the most rowdy that Mikey had to control all season. Even before the crawl started a Mancunian lad had to go to the medical centre because he had been having a bundle with his two friends and one of them had bit his dick and made it bleed.

Mikey was dividing his duties between The Las Huertas where Mario was now staying, and The Bon. Mikey had started winding Mario up again, which was proving to be particularly easy as Mario had just tried to impress one of the girls from Leyton by placing a food order in Spanish. The self satisfied smile turned to a scowl when Mikey informed him that the waiter's hysteria was brought about by Mario requesting a dog on heat instead of a hot dog.

Earlier in the day, the company photographer had been over to take some pictures for the following year's brochure. They had gone up to the Rodeo Grill where the photographer had got Mario to pose on one of the mechanical bulls. Mario had been getting on everyone's nerves all day with his 'when I was on an assignment' talk, so Mikey had started the bull on full speed sending Mario flying off and only just landing on the inflatable, designed to break the riders fall.

During the day, Mikey had a long chat with the photographer. He was told how a few years before, a picture had been taken of a group of holidaymakers in a swimming pool. Amongst the bathers was a black youth. At the time, it was not felt to be in keeping with the YF&S image to have blacks in the brochure, so during processing the youths head was changed to a multi-coloured beach ball. Thankfully, the photographer said, times had changed.

The bar crawl was the biggest of the season, and as the massive line of singing and shouting YF&S holidaymakers wound it's way through the streets of San Antonio, Mikey could feel the disgust with which other holidaymakers viewed them. Mario was at the front of the group leading the singing and obviously enjoying the power trip of having more than two hundred people doing more or less exactly what he wanted.

Two girls, both called Mary, were giving Mikey the come on. He wasn't sure at first which one to make a play for. The choice was narrowed somewhat when the darker haired of the pair was found in the toilets of The Cockney Pride giving one

351

of the clients a blow job. This must have set some kind of precedent, because later Mario and Greg emerged triumphant from the same toilet, having received a wank and a blow job respectively from a girl called Geraldine. They spent the next hour bragging about it to anyone who would listen. Later when all of the group were in Sgt. Peppers, Mikey found Geraldine sitting outside crying. She'd been off her face when she had indulged Greg and Mario and was regretting it, more so because by now, almost everyone knew about it. Mikey spoke to her for nearly ten minutes trying to console her, but she would not stop sobbing and the incident seemed to have stirred up a hornet's nest of repressed guilt and self loathing. Brad came out but to see what was wrong. As Mikey was telling him what had happened, she suddenly stopped crying. Instead, she stared directly ahead, with an emotionless watery gaze.

Without warning, she jumped up and ran into the road, into the path of an oncoming van. Luckily the van was only doing about thirty miles an hour and Mikey was quick enough to push her out of the way. The van swerved and screeched to a halt, stopping just so that it gently touched a moped which was parked next to five others outside Sgt. Peppers. As if in slow motion, the bike eventually toppled over, causing each of the other bikes in turn to fall like dominoes. Heather came out to see what was going on. Mikey brought Geraldine back across the road and took her into a restaurant next to Sgt. Peppers and ordered her a coffee. He waved Heather in to look after her and marched up to Brad. They looked at each other, both thinking exactly the same thing.

'Well?' said Mikey accusingly.

'Yeah, I know - it's all getting a bit out of hand. Let's go and have a word.'

They walked into the bar to find Greg and Mario. Greg was in the middle of the dance floor, contemplating taking his second pill of the night. Mario was next to him surrounded by three girls. Brad escorted Greg from the floor and Mikey guided away a protesting Mario. They stood in a darkened corner at the back of the bar.

'It's got to stop,' said Brad.

'Wha'samarrer?' said Greg gurning and putting his hand around Brad's shoulder.

'This points thing's getting out of hand,' said Mikey.

'You don't like it 'cos you're in last place,' said Mario mockingly.

'I don't give a toss which place I'm in. Did you see what just happened to Geraldine?'

'Who?'

'GERALDINE!' yelled Mikey impatiently.'

'The girl in the bogs,' laughed Greg, slapping hands with Mario.

'I'm glad you find it funny,' said Brad. 'She's just almost tried to kill herself 'cos of you two.'

'What?'

'This whole points thing's gotta stop,' said Mikey.

'It was just a bit of fun at first,' said Brad, 'But it's turned into a fucking obsession.'

'All you seem to want to do is humiliate anyone unfortunate enough to end up in bed with you,' said Mikey.

'Oh, you've changed your tune, soft lad,' said Greg, more towards Brad than Mikey.

'Yeah, maybe I have. I'm as guilty as anyone else,' admitted Brad, 'But lately half the girls I've shagged I might as well just have wanked off in for all it meant.'

'Listen to yerself,' said Greg, '"All it meant". Pah! I've told yer before that shaggin's all they're good for.'

'You've gotta draw the fucking line somewhere,' said Brad. 'I know a lot of them are idiots or know the score, but it's got to the stage where we don't even treat them like people. To be honest, hard though it may be to believe, I'm actually getting bored with it.'

'Well I'm not,' said Mario belligerently.

'It's just a phase,' said Greg. 'You'll ger' over it.'

'No. I've had enough. I'm all for a laugh but-'

'There's a laugh, and there's a laugh,' completed Mikey.

'You two were bang out of order-'

'Oh shut up you wanker,' said Mario.

Almost before Mario had finished the sentence Mikey had him pinned up against the wall.

'No more warnings. No more messing. Cross me again and you'll be the sorriest Italian on this island.'

Mikey stared at him for a few seconds. Mario could tell he was serious, and for all his bravado there was no way that he wanted to fight Mikey - not on his own at any rate. Mikey let him go and stormed out. Mario straightened his shirt and sneered after him. Brad took Greg to one side.

'Listen mate. These pills you're doing - slow down a bit, eh? There's nothing wrong with them but it's like anything - moderation.'

'But they're fuckin' great. Ten times better than being pissed. And sex.....!!!'

'Just be careful, I know it's hard. Fuck me, if I'd started taking pills out here, getting them for nothing, partying every night then I'd probably be the same. Just make sure you control them rather than the other way round.'

Brad walked away not entirely convinced that Greg had heeded his advice. He brushed past Mario who looked surprisingly unruffled following his confrontation with Mikey. Mario looked at his watch. Another couple of hours and Mikey would know all about 'no warnings'.

It was less than a week since Brad had taken out Kelly. Although he had decided not to pursue her further, he was less than happy when he got down The Star and discovered that she had just started seeing someone called Digger. Digger worked at the Go Kart track and was classically tall dark and handsome. Partly because of his job, people would often associate him as looking like Eddie Kidd when describing him. The only unusual thing about his appearance was a pair of sideburns that he had cultivated into points aimed towards the corners of his mouth. He drove around a bright yellow Karmann Ghia which always drew admiring looks, more so when he was sitting at the wheel. He had a vain arrogance about him that annoyed most other males, and as he had started seeing Kelly, Brad felt particularly antagonistic towards him. Brad was at bar five in The Star surrounded by Thomson's reps, none of whom particularly liked Digger. They therefore thought it quite funny when Brad started calling Digger Noddy Holder and singing Slade songs. However as Brad got more and more pissed, the laughter become politer and politer, until eventually a very drunk Brad was by himself at the bar, having exhausted his repertoire of the Wolverhampton quartet's hits.

Mikey came up to him. 'Brad, I'm off.'

'Mikey me old chum. See that twat over there. Noddy fucking Holder. Remember? That geezer from Slade. "Cum on feel the noise...." Brad started singing.'

Mikey laughed. 'See you later mate.'

Mikey walked back towards the apartments the same way that he always did. As he went passed the waste land he was aware of some people lurking in the shadows. He got closer and was able to make out five large male silhouette's, speaking what at first he thought to be Spanish, but then figured to be Portuguese or, more likely, Italian. Something didn't feel right, so he crossed the road. The group sprang into life, and within seconds were surrounding him. Mikey relaxed onto the balls of his feet, with his fists loosely clenched by his side, and tried to position himself so that none of the group were behind him.

'What do you want?'

'What do we want?' repeated the closest of the group.

'We're here to teach you a lesson,' said another.

'Yeah, you black cunt,' said the biggest.

Mikey knew that there was no point in trying to reason and all escape routes were cut off. Mikey lashed out with his right foot and his instep connected with the groin of the one who made the last comment. Six foot four and eighteen stone of bully doubled up, and as he was heading for the ground,

Mikey swivelled on his left foot so that he was side on, and without his right foot being placed back on the floor, aimed a sideways karate kick at his head. There was a loud crack as a jaw broke, and the bully was unconscious before he hit the floor. Mikey threw a vicious right fist out behind him. It glanced the cheek of the smallest of the group, stunning him temporarily.

Then Mikey felt a blow to the back of his head that almost made him sick. Despite his efforts he couldn't stay on his feet, falling face down towards the dusty floor. Before he hit it, a foot volleyed him in the face jolting his whole body. It was a miracle that he stayed conscious. He tried to huddle up in a ball. Fists and boots pummelled into him. Occasionally one would break through his defences and connect with his groin or head. He thought it would never stop. Despite the pain caused by every blow, he tried to stay as still as possible so it would seem that he was finished and they would leave him alone. Eventually it stopped and they ran off. Mikey lay there, drifting in and out of consciousness and unable to move. As the bodies natural pain killers wore off, his body ached. He groaned and tried to look up through his swollen eyes. The fight had taken him away from the road and passers by. Mikey knew he was in trouble.

Brad eventually stumbled out of The Star and into the cafe next door. He sat in a corner, drinking coffee and throwing food down his neck like a caveman. Half an hour later he weaved his way to the taxi rank but there was a massive queue. Cursing under his breath he started the walk back, still singing Slade songs. Halfway through 'Good-Bye To Jane,' his bladder guided him towards The Anglers. By the time he got there he'd sobered up a bit, but when he went to push the door open it was locked and the bar was closed. 'Wankers,' he said, booting the door. Fortunately the wasteland was only yard away, but in case he couldn't make it he started pissing as he was walking. The initial relief was wonderful and whilst in full flow he aimed for a thorn bush about ten feet away, but as the velocity of his torrent reduced he settled for writing 'Noddy' in the dirt. He ran out of pee by the first 'd'. Brad shook himself dry and stared up at the stars. A low groan and rustling from about twenty yards away brought him back to earth. At first he thought it was a stray dog or cat, so he made a point of giving it a reasonable berth. As he got closer he realised it was a person.

'Are you alright mate?'

Brad approached cautiously. It could have been someone luring him into a trap. But as he got closer, there was something familiar about the figure on the floor.

'Mikey!' Brad ran over. He lifted Mikey's bloodied head and cradled it in his arms. 'Shit. What happened? Are you alright?' Brad was sobering up fast. Mikey just groaned. 'Fuck, you need help. Stay there.'

'I'm hardly going anywhere you moron,' said Mikey through broken teeth.

'Oi, any more of your lip and I'll do you myself,' said Brad trying to make light of the situation.

Brad took off his shirt and cardigan. He placed the shirt under Mikey's head and draped the cardigan over him.

'I won't be long.'

Mikey nodded. 'Hurry up Brad. I think I'm in a bad way.'

'It's a fucking miracle,' said Brad, as Mikey eased himself into an upright position in bed. 'I thought that was your lot for the season.'

'I thought it was my lot full stop,' said Mikey, wincing as he rested his bruised kidneys against the wall at the top of his bed.

'So what was the final tally then?' asked Brad.

'Two teeth, broken nose, concussion, a couple of black eyes and loads and loads of bruises. Not even a cracked rib. I must admit, I thought it was a lot worse.'

'So did I. I've never sobered up so fast. I can't believe that of all people it was me who found you. Wish I hadn't now. You've ruined my shirt and cardigan, bleeding all over them. It's me who should be getting treatment, coming into contact with your blood without wearing surgical gloves.'

'If you don't watch it you'll be coming into contact with your own blood,' joked Mikey. 'If you think about it though, not many people come along that road and only someone who works here would normally venture on to the waste land. I guess I was lucky that you needed a piss so bad.'

Brad went over to the fridge and poured out a couple of orange juices. When he brought them back and sat down, a wad of money fell out of his tracksuit bottoms.

'What's that?' asked Mikey.

'Er, just some money I had sent over to get the car sorted out. The gearbox has gone and I can't be arsed with Reg anymore. Plus I just picked up some money from The Charleston and The Madhouse for the condoms.' Brad quickly changed the subject. 'So, do you still reckon that your little bashing was down to our friend?'

'Who else could it have been? They didn't try and rob me, they were Italian and they said that they were going to teach me a lesson. No, it was down to Mario alright.'

'So now what?'

'I dunno. Something will happen before the end of the season, I know it will. The doctor reckons the bruising will go down in a few days, so we'll see then.'

'Yeah, well taking the advice you gave me when I wanted to do him, I'm gonna get him back in another way.'

'Oh yeah - and how's that?'

Brad pulled out a bottle of laxative.

It was a hundred and twenty degrees. There were going to be a few burnt bodies after the beach party. Greg did the microphone on the boat to the beach where it was held. Brad went round with the pouron - he still got a cheap thrill out of seeing the wine dribble down a decent looking girl"s chin when her mouth was full.

The official Ibiza Beach Party was one of the most popular excursions, so there were six boats transporting almost three hundred expectant revellers to the private beach where it was held. It was very well organised, with the groups being split into two teams for the beach games and competitions. The reps normally took turns to captain the teams, and on this occasion the honours fell upon Brad and Mario's shoulders. When the games were finished, a meal of chops, salad and spuds was laid on, during which there were a few drinking games. At the end of the competitions, the two teams were neck and neck. It presented Brad with the perfect opportunity.

Brad went to the bar and got a couple of La Mumba's. He'd decided that this would be the best drink to disguise the taste and colour. Into one he poured almost half a bottle of the powerful laxative, then he went to the table that Mario was sitting at, stood on an empty chair and blew his whistle. Everyone looked up.

'If I could have your attention please,' yelled Brad. As he did so, a girl who was sitting next to Mario came back to her seat. Brad didn't see her move the two La Mumba's on the table to make room for her bag. 'Me and Mario are going to settle the competition by seeing who can down a La Mumba first.'

There was lots of cheering which meant that Mario could not back out. Mario stood on his chair. Brad bent down to pick up the two drinks. He was horrified to see that they had been moved - he no longer knew which one had the laxative in it. For a moment he froze, but by now three hundred clients were clapping and egging him on. First he went to pick up one, then the other, but whilst he was dithering Mario grabbed the glass which Brad was now absolutely certain was the unspiked one. But Brad could do nothing, for fear of alerting his intended victim. Instead he brought the glass in his hand up to his lips -

he was going to have to drink it and hope for the best.

The next half an hour was one of the longest in Brad's life. It was small consolation that he won the drinking race. To try and take his mind off of the expected gurgling from his bowels, he picked up a pretty brunette he had noticed earlier in the week and ran into the sea with her, throwing her in when they were knee deep. Unfortunately, she landed on some jagged rocks and gashed her leg open. Brad suddenly felt about as popular as a hurricane at a wig makers convention. The toilets were round the back of the bar, so he made his way over there and sat down, waiting for the inevitable. A couple of times he felt his stomach rumble. 'Here it comes', he thought. He strolled over to the one functioning toilet and sat down to prepare himself. At first, nothing abnormal happened but he felt it would be safer to sit there a bit longer. Suddenly there was a desperate banging on the door.

'Open up, open up. Quick!'

'I recognise that voice,' thought Brad.

The door didn't have a lock on it and it flew open to reveal Mario standing there clutching his stomach, with two girls standing next to him who had been patiently waiting to use the toilet.

'Let me in for fuck's sake,' gasped Mario.

Brad pulled his shorts up. Mario barged passed him and slammed the door.

Once inside, Mario lent forward to hold the door shut, and crouched over the toilet. His bowels exploded with such force, that hardly any of their contents made it in to the pan. But the relief was so great that Mario could do nothing to alter the trajectory, or to stop the expulsion. It was almost two minutes before he was able to turn around and see the damage that he had done. When he saw the mess he was flabbergasted. Throwing water from the sink over the back of the toilet only made it worse. He pulled the door open slightly and looked out. There were now more than half a dozen girls waiting to use the loo. Brad was in the throes of trying to round up some more.

'Go away,' said Mario, 'You can't come in here.'

'Why not,' said one of the girls. 'We've been waiting here for ages.'

'Just fuck off,' hissed Mario, 'I'm not well.'

'There's no need to talk like that,' said the same girl.

'Piss off,' said Mario.

The girl turned to her friend. 'I'm not going to let him speak to me like that.'

She yanked the door open. As she did so, seven mouths dropped open at what they were confronted with. She let go of the door and it gently swung shut. She turned away and puked up. From the toilet came the most ferocious sound of flatulence imaginable. Mario was off again.

The weeks seemed to be getting shorter and shorter - Saturday transfer day had arrived yet again. Kevin Roundtree, the Training Manager from head office was on resort. So was Kirstie Davies, the Resort Manager from the previous year. Kirstie had received a windfall and she wasted no time in telling Alison what a fabulous lifestyle she now enjoyed. Anyone who knew how much they really hated each other would have been surprised at what great friends they gave the appearance of being.

Kevin Roundtree was in his mid-forties but his thick grey moustache and grey, thinning hair contributed to his appearing at least ten years older. He was flying back on Sunday so that he could get on a Saturday incoming and outgoing airport transfer to assess a couple of reps microphone work on the coach. Everybody was dreading that it was going to be them, apart from Mikey. Although Mikey was now more or less back to normal, his face still looked somewhat battered. It was therefore felt that he would not be the ideal choice to meet the new arrivals, so he had been given the night off. Mario, who had only just recovered from a two day intimate relationships with Spanish toilets, was chosen to have Kevin accompany him for the outgoing journey, Natalie the inbound.

It was just gone seven o'clock in the evening and the bar of The Bon was packed. Kevin was having a drink and chatting to Brad and Natalie when Alison burst in.

'Everyone - reception quick,' she said addressing the three of them.

Brad looked at Natalie and raised his eyebrows, then along with Kevin the two followed Alison out to reception. Alison was standing by an open locker.

'See - all gone,' she said.

'What's all gone?' asked Kevin.

'The money.' Still nobody knew what she was on about. 'The excursion money. I reckon it must be at least fifteen grand.'

'WHAT!?' said Kevin.

'Fifteen grand's worth of unliquidated excursion money,' replied Alison. 'I was just about to take it and check it so Jaime could collect it for banking.'

'Who's Jaime?' asked Kevin.

'He's from Viajes Diamente. He collects the money on Saturdays or Sundays.'

'Did anyone else have a key?' asked Natalie.

'No, only me. The master key doesn't even fit my locker.'

'When did you last check it?' asked Brad

'This morning.'

'Where was the key between then and now,' asked Natalie.

'In my room, on the table.'

'So it's possible that someone could have got into your room and taken the key for a while,' said Kevin.

'Yes, but - I don't know. Who would do that? It'd have to be someone........'

Alison's voice trailed off.

'Well, I don't think any of us even knew that you kept the excursion money there,' said Brad, realising what Alison was thinking.

'Oh I'm sure that Alison wasn't implying anything,' said Kevin. 'Anyway, leave this to Alison and I - I'm sure you've both got to get things ready for the airport.'

Once they had left the room, Kevin turned to Alison. 'Any ideas?'

'Not really. I can't see how it happened.'

'Was the key where you left it?'

'To be honest I can't remember. It's possible.'

'Someone must have been into your room and it must have been someone who knew about the excursion money.'

Kevin paused to let Alison work it out for herself.

'Oh no,' said Alison, realising what Kevin meant, 'Not one of my reps, surely.'

'Can you think of anyone else?'

Alison shook her head. 'I guess not.'

'I'll ring head office. Put your thinking cap on and see if you can come up with anything.'

'Here we go again,' said Sebastian, walking into Jane's office and slamming the door shut. 'It's already started. Just had Kevin on the phone. Allegedly fifteen thousand pounds of excursion money's been stolen from Alison's locker in Ibiza.'

'Oh no,' said Jane. 'How?'

'Your guess is as good as mine. I'm waiting for more info, but Kevin reckons that it's probably one of the reps.'

'Which one?'

'Don't know.'

'Kevin's not in on what's happening out there with Alison and Felipe, is he?' asked Tom.

'Christ no,' said Sebastian. 'He gets on too well with the pair of them. The only people who know about what's going on, apart from Hawthorne-Blythe, are in this room.

'So now what?' asked Jane.

'We sit tight and see what transpires,' said Sebastian.

'Is there any way of putting a tap on Felipe's phone?' asked

Tom.

All of the reps apart from Mikey had gone to the airport. Mario and Natalie were glad that the locker had been broken in to - it meant that Kevin wasn't going to the airport with them to check on their microphone work. Alison had suggested that while the reps were at the airport, each of their rooms were checked for any sign of involvement in the theft. Alison was going to check Mario and Greg's rooms with Jaime from Viajes Diamente. Mikey was to accompany Kevin, after his room had been given the once over by Kevin and Alison.

Heather's room was clean. Mikey noticed that Kevin spent a long time going through the drawers next to her bed. When Mikey glanced into them he noticed that they were full of panties.

When they went into Brad and Natalie's apartment, Mikey looked in Natalie's room, and Kevin in Brad's. Mikey was just thinking what a messy bitch Natalie was, when Kevin called him.

'Mikey, in here.'

Mikey walked into Brad's room. The mattress was on the floor, the bed base leant up against the wall and three boxes of condoms were stacked up in the corner. Kevin was standing there holding up the bedclothes.

'Look.'

Poorly hidden underneath a sheet were several empty brown envelopes. 'Excursion money' was printed on them and Alison's signature was across the seal. Mikey remembered the wad of money that had fallen out of Brad's pocket.

'Oh no.'

The airport was the busiest that Brad had ever seen it. Greg had excelled himself and pulled a girl and taken her into the

364

toilets for a shag as soon as he had ticked her name off of the clipboard. Brad had agreed to check in the rest of the flight. Everybody had come through except for one male single share who's surname was Fisher. Greg was in and out of the loos within ten minutes. The girl looked a mess.

'Harry on the Boat?' asked Brad.

Greg grinned. 'Thought y'wouldn't approve - y'know, me not respecting women........'

'My attitude might have changed a bit, but not that much mate. Good effort!'

Greg waited another five minutes to see whether the stray client turned up. In the end Brad agreed to look out for him so that Greg could get on his coach. No sooner had Greg gone than Brad was interrupted from checking down his list by a voice.

'Are you the rep for Young Free & Single?'

Brad looked up and turned around but could see nobody. He heard the voice again.

'Young Free & Single?'

Brad looked down at a man who was less than three feet tall.

'Mr. Fisher?'

Dennis Fisher sat down with Brad for the half hour it took for Brad's flight to arrive, then next to him for the coach transfer back to San Antonio. It pleased Brad that rather like 'Pacemaker Peggy' earlier in the season, the dwarf had a similarly alliterative Christian name. Fortunately, Dennis had a wicked sense of humour, having Brad in stitches for most of the journey. By the time that they got to the apartments, Brad had persuaded Dennis to star in a dwarf throwing contest on the cruise the next day. If he didn't feel tired, Brad decided to do a poster to advertise it when he got back to his room.

'I'm shocked,' said Alison.

'Brown envelopes with your signature on them - just like

you described putting in the locker. You can even ask Mikey. Good idea that was, having two of us there. Just as well seeing as best part of fifteen grand is missing and having two of us finding it means that no-one else can be suspected,' said Kevin.

'But what was Brad thinking of? How stupid of him. I had such high hopes for him, you know.'

'Well you can forget those,' said Kevin, 'Because I'm sure that once I've got in touch with someone else from head office, he'll be in a cab to the airport and home.'

Just then a coach pulled up outside. 'Right,' said Kevin. 'That'll be Greg's coach, so Brad will be here soon and I've got to make some calls. I'll be in my room or on the phone if you need me, but try and make sure that I'm not interrupted - unless someone find's the rest of the money.'

Brad was surprised to see Kevin in reception.

'When you've checked them all in, can you come up to my room?' asked Kevin.

'Yeah sure,' said Brad. 'Five one two, isn't it?'

'That's the one.'

Brad checked the clients in without a hitch. He got himself a coffee, went up to Kevin's room and knocked on the door.

'Come in.' Kevin was sitting at a square table made of a light coloured wood. He had the chairs positioned opposite each other, as if prepared for an interview. 'Sit down,' he beckoned to the empty chair.

Brad made himself comfortable, and smiling, waited to see what Kevin wanted.

'Brad, I'm afraid we're going to have to let you go.'

It didn't sink in at first. 'I'm sorry,' said Brad, looking at him blankly.

'We're letting you go. As of now you are no longer employed by Young Free & Single. All uniforms, merchandise and other property that belong to the company should be returned within the next hour. I've managed to get you on the

eight twenty flight this morning which leaves in.....' Kevin
looked at his watch, '.....four and a bit hours. Obviously if you
miss that you will have to make your own way back to
England.'

Brad was reeling. Although none of what Kevin had just
said really sank in, he understood that he was sacked. But he
was racking his brain to think why. Had someone found out
about the money that he'd taken from Duffy at the beginning
of the season? Was it the free meals he'd had in The Angler's?

'I should warn you also, that it would not be in your
interests to stay on the island. If needs be, we will sometimes
get the police involved in this kind of incident when we
consider it to be relevant. We certainly don't want you having
any further contact with any of the reps.'

'Hang on a sec - what's this all about? Why are you sacking
me? What am I supposed to have done?'

'I'm sorry, I'm not allowed to say.'

'What do you mean you're not allowed to say? This is my
future you're talking about.'

'Sorry Brad. I'm just here to do the dirty work. If you've any
questions they should be addressed to head office.'

'Too right I will,' said Brad, 'In fact I'll ring them now.'

'Don't be silly. It's only every other Saturday that they're in
the office and even then they leave at eight. By all means give
them a call first thing Monday.'

It sunk in that he really meant it. 'You can't sack me without
telling me what I've done. I haven't done anything wrong.
What's that useless slag Alison been saying about me, eh?'

'It's got nothing to do with Alison. As I've said, when you're
back in the UK....'

'But what's the point in sending me back?' asked Brad,
raising his voice. 'I'm gonna have to pack all my things up only
to get home, unpack them and pack them again when this is
all sorted out and I come back here on the next flight.'

'Whether you come back or not is clearly something that
you will have to discuss with head office. In the meantime I'd
get your things together otherwise you'll be paying for your

own flight.'

Although Brad knew that he could afford his own flight, all he could think of was getting back as soon as possible to see what the hell was going on. Then suddenly it dawned on him.

'This is about that money, isn't it?'

'As I've already stated Brad, I cannot divulge the reason for your dismissal.'

'This is fucking pathetic,' said Brad getting angry and standing up. 'I'm going to see Mikey and Alison.'

Kevin stood up. 'I should warn you Brad if that you make any attempt to approach any of the other reps, then I will call the police. I've sent Natalie to The Manolo, so you can get your things from your room.'

Brad looked at Kevin. He could tell that he was serious.

For Brad, the season was over.

CHAPTER SEVENTEEN

Carmen had put the mattress back on to the bed. The three condom boxes were still in the corner, which made her chuckle. She found some group pictures. 'So that's Brad,' she thought. She'd heard a lot about him and he seemed interesting. Seeing the pictures, she thought he looked interesting too.

It had all happened rather quickly for Carmen. One minute she was in Glasgow, in a relationship and in a rut and after a phone call, a meeting and some basic training she was in Ibiza, sharing Brad's old apartment with Greg. Natalie had been moved to The Las Hurdes, where she was working with Heather and Mario. Mikey was by himself at the phoneless Adelino, and as such, had still not spoken to Brad.

It was the Thursday after Brad's sudden departure. The only person who had spoken to him was Natalie. She had told everybody that as suspected, Brad had been sacked for stealing fifteen thousand pounds worth of excursion money. Although none of them wanted to believe it, Greg and Natalie both knew that Brad was quite sharp and not adverse to the idea of the odd scam. He's told them both of dealings he'd had back home which were not exactly on the right side of the law. Even Mikey had his doubts. He had told Greg, in confidence, about the money he had seen Brad with. Greg had, in confidence, told Heather. Heather had, in confidence, told Natalie. Natalie had, in confidence, told Mario and Mario had, in confidence, told Alison. Alison had smiled.

Felipe saw Tom's reflection in the window opposite his slightly open door, so he started to speak louder.

'Yes, I've heard all about it Alison. He stole fifteen thousand, didn't he? You say he what? My my. So even Mikey thinks he did it? My my. It just goes to show. Well thank you ever so much for calling. You take care now. Bye.'

Tom hurried into Sebastian's office, unusually, without knocking. Jane was there and had been having one of her rare snogs with Sebastian at work.

'Haven't you heard of knocking,' said Sebastian.

'I was just standing outside Felipe's office,' said Tom, ignoring the comment. 'I heard him on the phone to Alison. Looks like I was wrong after all. From what he was saying Brad did do it.'

'What did he say exactly?' asked Jane.

'Just that Mikey thinks Brad did it as well, and you know how close they were. Other than that, he didn't seem to know much about it or be too interested.'

'Well I'll be....' said Jane. 'I'd've put money on it being something to do with Alison.'

'Looks like your famous gut feelings were wrong for once,' said Sebastian, almost too smugly. He caught Jane's admonishing look and hurried on. 'Well it doesn't matter now anyway - Brad's history.'

Just then the phone rang.

'Hunter,' said Sebastian before handing the phone to Jane.

Jane nodded and said 'yes ok' a couple of times before putting the phone down. She looked at Tom.

'It's Brad again,' she said. 'He wants to see me.'

'That's the fourth day running, isn't it?' said Sebastian.

Although Brad had explained everything and although Jane actually believed most of what he said, she could do nothing.

'Look I'm sorry Brad. There really is nothing more to say on the matter. You can deny all knowledge of the money but the fact is the empty envelopes were found in your room. You can tell me that Alison's on the take, but without any proof there's not much I can do. Anyway, your replacement arrived on resort yesterday.'

Brad felt a sick feeling in the pit of his stomach, as he finally realised that no matter what happened, he wouldn't be going back as a rep for YF&S.

'I don't believe it,' was all he could say. 'I was so sure that I'd be going back out there that I even left my car behind. Admittedly, it wouldn't have been worth bringing it back, but..........I honestly thought that of all people you'd believe me Jane.'

'I'm sorry Brad, but even if I did believe you - which I'm not saying I do - then I would still be able to do nothing.'

'My replacement - what's he like?' asked Brad, winding the conversation up, knowing that this really was it.

'It's a she actually. Her name's Carmen.'

'Oh.' Brad had run out of the desire to converse any further. 'Well I guess there's not much more left to say, is there?'

Jane shrugged her shoulders. 'I'm sorry it had to end like this Brad.'

'So am I Jane, so am I.'

'What are your plans?' she asked, standing up to open her office door for him.

'Dunno. Get my head together and sort out what I'm going to do.'

Looking at Brad she felt quite sorry for him and she stretched up and kissed him on the cheek.

As he left she had another one of her gut feelings.

Alison opened the giant box of Persil under the sink in her apartment. She reached through the first inch or so of powder and pulled out a plastic bag. The bank statements and documents that it contained were quickly spread out over the table, along with the money she had made in the last few days. It gave her considerable pleasure to see it all there. Alison chuckled to herself. Seeing Brad go had been the highlight of her season - even better than screwing Mario.

Although he couldn't hear the other person talking, Tom was able to hear Felipe's part of the conversation. A friend of Tom's had got him a plug adapter that contained a hidden microphone. Tom had swapped this with the normal adapter in Felipe's office and spent as much time as he could with his Walkman headset tuned in. Two days had passed without anything untoward being said. In fact, hardly anything had been said because Felipe was seldom in his office. It was just a hunch Tom had. He knew that it was too late to help Brad, but for his own piece of mind he wanted to know what had happened.

It was Friday afternoon at work and Tom was bored. He tuned in his Walkman, not for one moment expecting Felipe to be in his office, so when he heard Felipe talking Tom was pleasantly surprised. It soon became clear it was Alison on the other end of the phone. Tom pressed the record button

'Yes, I'm sorry about that. Of course I knew what you were on about. It's just that I'd noticed Tom standing outside my office. Of course he did - hook line and sinker. Now don't worry - everything will be fine. Yes, I'll be there in a week or so. I just hope you're happy that - what was his name again? Brad, that's it. Well, I hope you're happy now he's gone. Well whether he did or whether he didn't doesn't matter now, does it? Look, I must dash. I'll see you soon. You too. Good-bye.'

'Told you so,' said Tom throwing the cassette on Sebastians desk after walking into his room for the second time without knocking. As was becoming increasingly frequent, Jane was in there too.

'Told you so, what?' asked Sebastian.

'Told you Brad was innocent.'

'How so?' asked Jane.

372

Tom played them the tape. When it was finished, Tom turned to Jane.

'Shall I call Brad and offer him his job back?'

'You know we can't Tom - Carmen's already there. Anyway, he didn't categorically say that Brad didn't do it. All it really tells us is that Felipe made up the conversation you heard the other day because he saw your reflection and knew you were standing outside his office.'

'But why would he do that unless he was hiding the fact that Alison set him up?' asked Tom. 'It seems so unfair.'

'Life's unfair,' said Sebastian. 'It's too late. There's always the risk that Alison might smell a rat - albeit a small risk, but a risk that I'm not prepared to take.'

Tom looked at Jane.

'He's right, Tom,' she said. 'It's a terrible shame I know, but we all understand what's at stake here.'

'Oh well - that's the end of Brad then.'

CHAPTER EIGHTEEN

A little over two weeks had passed since Brad had arrived back in Ibiza and already he was making Alison's life hell.

He wasn't sure what was going to happen when he first returned to San Antonio. A lot of bar owners made out that they liked reps all of the time that they were bringing in clients, but as soon as the clients were no longer around the majority of reps got given the cold shoulder. Brad was grateful that he had gone out of his way to get on with everyone, and most of the bar owners and workers actually liked him, rather than his badge. This had been reflected in the number of jobs Brad had been offered. Brad had deliberately chosen jobs to plague Alison. Ray had got him a job DJ'ing in Sgt. Peppers; Giles, who ran the beach party, had offered him a job taking the group photographs and videoing the day; Irish Ben had pulled a few strings and got him a job as a bouncer in The Star a couple of nights a week, and Woodsy had persuaded Manny to let him work as a bouncer on the excursions. This meant that virtually everywhere Young Free & Single went, Brad would be working, and if ever Alison turned up, Brad would make his hatred of her more than evident.

Brad was loving not having the pressures of repping. It meant that he was able to go out clubbing a lot more and the only days he needed to get up early were when he was due to work on the beach party - which wasn't normally until eleven. Not having to get up for desk was marvellous, as were little things such as being able to go to what bars or clubs he wanted to go to and then being able to stay as long as he liked. Brad actually felt sorry for Mikey and the gang when he saw them having to herd around all of the piss heads on bar crawls. Brad still even got free drinks in most places. Before coming back to Ibiza, Brad thought that he might miss all of the female attention that being a rep brought. He discovered that holidaymakers weren't as interested, but he had more success with other reps and workers. One of these was Zena, a Dickens wench, who had told him that she always thought he looked 'dirty'. When Brad established that she was not referring to his personal hygiene he did his best not to ruin her expectations by shagging her on the roof of The Bon and tying her up with the washing line. He contemplated leaving her in her bondaged state for a few hours but thought better of it.

He had found an apartment round the back of town not far from The Delfin. He was sharing with a girl called Sally, who was propping for Koppas Bar, a bloke called Roly (short for Roland as opposed to being a description relating to his girth), who sometimes worked with Brad as a bouncer on the excursions, and another bloke called Hicksy, who wasn't really working and had an annoying hissing laugh, like a leaky pressure valve. He got on alright with Sally and Roly, but he was none too keen on Hicksy, who Brad had decided was definitely a scally.

Some things had gone missing out of the apartment and Brad had heard that one of Hicksy's dodgy friends had gone into The Madhouse to try and sell an Olympus Trip camera, which coincidentally was the same type of camera as Sally had stolen the day before from her room. Nothing was proved but the finger of suspicion was most definitely pointing at Hicksy. It made the whole atmosphere in the crowded apartment uncomfortable, and every night there seemed to be more of Hicksy's scummy friends scattered in varying degrees of senselessness around the living room floor..

The previous few days Brad had been staying back at The Bon with Mikey. He had to be careful that Alison or the owners didn't find out, but Raoul, the night porter's son was cool and always kept a lookout. Mikey had been moved back to The Bon to work with Greg and the new rep, Carmen. This meant that Natalie had replaced Mikey at The Delfin. Mikey was pleased when Brad finally convinced him that he hadn't stolen the excursion money. They both agreed that it must have been Alison because only a Resort Manager was given a skeleton key and knew where the money was put prior to liquidation.

Before going to the Bronco Bar-B-Q Brad went to The Bon to help Mikey with his paperwork, which was still causing him problems. He had been nearly a hundred pounds short the week before when he went to liquidate his excursion money and Alison had made him pay it out of his own pocket.

Mikey continued to fill Brad in on what had been going on for the three weeks that Brad had been away. He told him about the massive row Natalie had with the owner of The Las Huertas and his son, over yet another client getting beaten up after he refused to pay an extortianate amount for a pair of curtains that they claimed he had torn. When Natalie got back from a beach party, all of her belongings had been dumped in reception. To her credit Alison had actually backed her up, but to avoid further trouble had moved her to The Delfin, which was why there had been another change round.

As the night wore on the two friends chatted about a whole host of things. Brad realised that he had formed a strong relationship with Mikey and that during the course of the few months on resort they had learned a lot from each other. Although Mikey rarely got on his soap box about his colour, he was very good at subtly pointing things out and making Brad look at things in a different perspective. Brad would never have considered himself racist, but he began to realise how he accepted things around him that were discriminatory. Through no longer repping, Brad had more time to think and it pleased him that he had gained a good friend and something unexpected from his stay in Ibiza.

Brad told Mikey about the frustration caused by his attempts to clear his name back in the UK. All of the new reps had known that Brad had been Jane's blue eyed boy and most had got to like and respect him during the week's training course in the UK that they all attended prior to going out to resort. News of his dismissal had apparently spread around the other resorts like wildfire. Brad was still unable to understand why Jane had not backed him up, as he had shown her the reports that he had written that Alison had not sent on, told her how Alison was on the fiddle and had even offered to show Jane where Alison was making her money.

Eventually, impulsively, Brad had bought a flight to Ibiza and left on the same day before he had a chance to change his mind. When he arrived, the airport seemed like an old friend. He came in on a Thomson's flight and managed to get a lift into San Antonio on Kelly's coach. Digger had stopped seeing her and thankfully for Brad, she had fallen off of her pedestal. It was frightening to him to see how boring she actually was, looking at her through a pair of dodgy Ray Bann's rather than rose coloured spectacles.

The Triumph Herald, which as a rep he had little use for, was proving invaluable. Whereas previously he had bolted and unbolted the detachable roof, he now left it off all of the time. Although the car still played up on occasions, he had it overhauled and the only remaining problem was the ignition light staying on. This was rectified by disconnecting the battery whenever he stopped the car. He had got so used to doing this that it was no longer the inconvenience that it originally was.

It was YF&S's night up at the Hoe Down. Brad normally drove to work, but whenever it was a YF&S night he got a lift up in the coach - just to annoy Alison. Alison had complained to Manolo, but as Brad was working for him and it was also his coach company, Alison had to lump it.

Brad watched the reps running back and forth to get more drink for all of the clients, pretending that they were having the time of their lives. Brad knew the truth; that after more than four months of doing the same thing, the smiles plastered across most of the reps faces were as false as the two replacement teeth that Mikey had on order.

The most beautiful smile in Brad's eyes, false or otherwise, was the one belonging to Carmen. Mikey had told Brad that there was something about her that didn't seem right. She spent a lot of time with Alison and Mikey didn't trust her. Despite this, Brad had warmed to her instantly when they first met. She was obviously intelligent and quick witted. She didn't suffer fools gladly, which meant that she gave Mario almost as much stick as Mikey did. There was something deeper than that though that Brad couldn't quite put his finger on. She was slightly confrontational; never maliciously or spitefully - just a rational, fiery spirit that tore from her pale blue eyes, seductively challenging anyone to take up the gauntlet of a conversation. Since they had met, Brad and Carmen had teased and wound each other up. But the pleasure that they both got out of it was from the intellectual fencing - the uncertainty that ambiguous or loaded comments would cause. Neither was sure if there was genuine interest or potential for a relationship.

Had it not been for her sister's persuasion, Carmen would almost certainly not have bothered to become a rep. She had decided to take the job in a slightly superior way, feeling that it would provide an experience rather than an education. Before meeting them, she had assumed that all other reps would be simple, fun loving souls with little depth to them. That was not to say that she considered them to be her sub-ordinates, but she certainly didn't expect any of them to be smarter than her or to make her have to think too hard.

She first met Brad on a bar crawl at The Star, where he was working as a bouncer. Although Carmen had seen photograph's of Brad she didn't recognise him in the flesh, partly because during his return to the UK he had shorn his hair, and partly because he had facetiously introduced himself to her as 'Billy Bouncer'. They had a brief chat and Carmen found him pleasant enough. He made her laugh a few times and she thought he was reasonably attractive - in a bouncer sort of way. Following that, Carmen would not normally have done much more than exchange pleasantries with him. When she had been there for a week, and had seen Brad working at three other different jobs, she asked Natalie who he was. When she realised it was the same Brad that she had replaced, he began to intrigue her. The first time that they conversed at any length was the next time she was down The Star. They spent almost two hours taking the piss out of each other and anyone else unfortunate enough to attempt to join in.

The second conversation was when they were sitting at a table in The Star Cafe. It was a lot more deep and Brad really got into her head. When Brad walked away from the table he knew that he had really left her thinking, He smiled to himself as he got into his car and drove off, seeing her still sitting at the table trying to digest the conversation. He was pulling out all of the stops for this one.

Luigi Canelli reached under the desk in his office at the back of his Basildon restaurant and pulled out a mirror tile. He placed it on the desk top and sprinkled some of the creamy coloured powder on to it. A gold credit card was used to chop it into a line and a stripey straw, which had been cut down to a length of about two inches, transferred the powder from the mirror to Luigi's nose. He tilted his head back, sniffing vigorously.

'Mmmm. Good gear. It's not a re-press, is it?'

'Nah mate. Pucker charlie that is. Best I've 'ad for ages.'

'Alright then. How much for a key?'

'A kilo? Thirty two grand.'

Luigi sucked in through his teeth. 'Bit steep. Sharpen your pencil a little?'

'Nah. Can't be done. You can see the quality. I'm barely getting a drink out of it meself.'

Luigi paused for a few seconds to see if the silence reduced the price any. When it was apparent this ploy wasn't going to work he spoke,

'Ok. I'll get one of my boys to come and pick it up tomorrow. Usual place?'

'Yeah.'

'And,' said Luigi standing up, 'Don't forget that last lot of pills were eighteen short. What do you wanna do - knock it off the bill or make it up with the next lot?'

'I'll make it up.'

They shook hands and the dealer left. Luigi chopped out another line and snorted it. He checked in the mirror to see if any of it had fallen into his black goatee beard. Out of the inside pocket of his dark blue Armani suit he took a comb, which he ran through his jet black receding hair. It irritated him that at thirty two, male pattern baldness had already taken a hold. The excessive amount of forehead on display was annoying enough, but in the last year he had noticed more skin showing through his crown. Vanity was a family trait, but fortunately so were good looks. Luigi's sharp features and healthy bank balance provided him with ample opportunity to cheat on his wife of four years.

In recent years, drugs had provided Luigi with an income and status which he had previously only dreamt of. He was by no means a major player, but had befriended Adam Wilson, head of the local 'family', who had provided Luigi with the muscle to enable him to deal in largish quantities of cocaine and ecstasy without being ripped off. However, during the winter Wilson had been shot and killed which meant that although Luigi now had his own little firm, he had scaled down his operation and was only dealing with people he was fairly sure that he could trust. Deep down he knew that it was only a matter of time before he was caught by the police, or maybe worse. For this reason he had tried to legitimise his source of income by opening an Italian restaurant and by investing in his cousin's clothes shop.

The door of his office opened and one of the waiters popped his head around it.

'Luigi, your brother's on the phone - reverse charge. Shall I take the call and put it through?'

'Of course.' A minute later the phone rang. 'Mario? How's sunny Ibiza?'

'Yeah, wicked,' replied the voice on the phone.

'So what, you ran out of money again?'

381

'No - just didn't have any change. How's things?'

'Can't complain. Could do with a break though.'

'Yeah. Good. Might be able to kill two birds with one stone then.'

'Whaddya mean?'

'I've got a bit of a problem out here.'

Luigi stood up. He was fiercely protective of anything to do with his brother.

'What kind of problem?'

'There's a couple of reps who are giving me a lot of stick. I've dealt with one of them already-'

'I'll speak to Don at Young Free & Single,' interrupted Luigi. 'I'm still sorting him out the you-know-what so I can pull a few strings....'

'It's gone passed that stage. They've got a little gang together, some of the other workers,' lied Mario.

'What about Sergio and the other boys? Can't they deal with it?'

'They dealt with one of 'em a few weeks ago, but Sergio got a bust jaw.'

'What!?'

'Serious man. All eighteen stone of him spark out. One of the other rep's is a fucking great nigger who's a black belt or something. The other reps about fifteen stone. I mean, I can look after myself but, now they've got these other workers involved I need some help.'

There was silence on the other end of the phone. Mario pressed home the point, knowing his brother's Achilles heels.

'They've been insulting momma too. A flight's only eighty quid, I could find somewhere cheap for you to stay....'

'Hey, hey, hey! What's all this 'cheap' talk. This is family. Give me a week or so to tie up things here and I'll be there, ok?'

Mario hung up the phone and smiled to himself. It was payback time.

The Bronco Bar-B-Q was rocking. Woodsy was on top form, but seemed determined to get Brad and himself as pissed as possible. When Brad worked at the Bar-B-Q, one of his jobs was to help clear away the amps and keyboards from the ampitheatre. A couple of musicians would play in the amphitheatre some afternoons, performing to Scandinavian clients who visited the former zoo on a jeep safari. Every time that Brad tried to leave Woodsy to put the equipment away, Woodsy would grab him and give him another drink.

By the time everybody was due to go up to the amphitheatre, Woodsy was unconscious. However, it wasn't until nearly all three hundred clients were seated that anybody noticed his absence. It was Heather who discovered him unconscious by the pool with his dick in his hand, and when word got round all of the reps that Woodsy was incapable of anything other than snoring, there was a blind panic. They could have gone on stage and sang without music, but it would have definitely lacked atmosphere. Moreover, the pre-show singalong that Woodsy did was vital to warm things up. The reps were standing around the edge of the amphitheatre not knowing what to do. Brad was leaning against the railings trying to sober up, realising that the situation unfolding in front of him could not have been planned better. If all else failed, he thought, he would just have to volunteer, but he dearly hoped that Manolo or one of the reps would ask him.

Alison was screaming at Manolo, who was trying to be helpful but was fast losing patience with her unreasonable intolerance .

'We've got three hundred fucking people here Manolo, and that useless bastard's unconscious.'

Manolo shrugged his shoulders. 'It is bad but it is only one part of the evening. You can still sing without music.'

'No we can't. The clients expect a show, not just a few reps getting on stage by themselves and singing out of tune.'

Alison continued yelling at Manolo, which made him even less inclined to help her even if he'd been able to. As Alison yelled, Carmen walked over to Brad.

'Bit of a disaster this, isn't it?'

'Guess so,' replied Brad.

'Shame none of us can play guitar. Don't suppose you can, can you? Any more hidden talents?'

'Oh joy,' thought Brad. 'What do you mean?'

'Well, so far I've seen you working as a DJ, a bouncer and a photographer. I thought you might be able to play guitar as well.'

'No,' said Brad, 'I can't play guitar.'

Carmen smiled. 'Oh well, never mind.'

'But,' he continued, 'I play a bit of piano.'

Carmen laughed, thinking at first that he was joking. 'You are joking aren't you?'

'Nope.' Brad tried not to be too smug. He couldn't have planned it better. 'It's what I used to do. I've been playing in bands for years.'

'Well what are you waiting for?' asked Carmen. By now the clients had started a slow handclap and were singing 'why are we waiting.' Carmen rushed over to Alison and Manolo who were still arguing. 'Alison, I've found someone who can play and compere.'

'Who?' asked Manolo.

'Brad,' replied Carmen.

'What!?' said Alison. 'Don't be stupid.'

By now Brad had walked over.

'Brad, is this true?' asked Manolo. 'Can you play guitar?'

'No, but I play keyboards.'

'Yes, we have keyboards there,' said Manolo, pointing at the stage.

'No way!' screamed Alison.

Brad looked at Manolo. 'I'll give it a go if you want. Don't expect me to be as good as Woodsy though.'

Brad's back was hurting where so many people had slapped

him on it to congratulate him. When he had got on stage he'd not been able to believe his luck when he saw that there was a drum machine on top of the keyboard which was exactly the same as the one he had at home. It had helped to compensate for his not particularly good voice, and to cover up some of the wrong chords that he had played when each of the reps had come on to sing their song. The compering had been no problem because he had seen Woodsy do it on countless occasion's and had copied him as best he could. When she saw how well he was doing, Alison had stormed off.

He was sitting at the bar of the Bar-B-Q, having just been offered a job compering and playing the following season by Manolo. As he sat there watching all of the clients leaving he felt on top of the world. Carmen popped in to the bar just before making her way down to her coach.

'Is there anything else about you that I should know?'

Brad turned round. 'Oh hi. Not too painful on your ears then?'

'Och, you were fine, so don't go fishing for any complements. You're a bastard sure you are for taking the piss out of my nipples like that after you'd thrown me in.'

'Well, what do you expect if you don't wear anything underneath your T-shirt? Great thing, water.......'

'I noticed that you didn't put a sock over your willy like Woodsy does.'

'Couldn't find a sock small enough,' said Brad.

'Aye, they don't have a branch of Mothercare in Ibiza, do they?'

'Do you know what I like about you Carmen?'

'What?'

'Nothing.'

Carmen giggled. 'See you down The Star later?'

'It's not beyond the realms of probability.'

'Good.' Carmen kissed Brad softly on the lips. 'See you there then.'

Brad felt butterflies in his stomach. Any doubts as to whether or not he fancied Carmen as more than a friend, in that moment disappeared. The only remaining doubt was did she fancy him?

The smell of burning filled Brad's nostrils, and awoke him from his drunken slumber. He didn't react immediately, because apart from his head hurting he needed a few moments to get his bearings. He was in his room. It came back to him that after his session with the group of lads he had staggered home to his apartment to find yet more of Hicksy's friends strewn across the floor, with one of them even having the audacity to be in Brad's bed. It was unfortunate for this particular individual, because any somnambulistic activity he had been enjoying had been rudely interrupted by Brad booting him in the kidneys and telling him to 'get the fuck out of my bed'.

Brad stumbled out of his room towards the smell of the burning. On the stove was a saucepan with flames coming out of it. One of the uninvited guests had obviously got up to boil some water and had then fallen asleep again. Brad grabbed a tea towel, put it under the tap to soak it and then placed it over the flaming saucepan. Even in such a short space of time, acrid smoke had filled the kitchen. Brad went into the living room where three bodies lay comatose. He started kicking them.

'Wake up. Come on you dozy fucks, wake up.' They gradually stirred. 'Which one of you wankers left a saucepan on, eh? Come on, fuck off the lot of you.' Brad picked up any clothes he didn't recognise as being his and threw them out of the front door. 'Come on - move.' His kicking became harder.

'Ow! Alright man,' said the one who had been in Brad's bed the night before. 'Chill out. We're mates of Hicksy.'

'I don't give a toss who you're mates of - just fuck off. Come on, hurry up.'

Brad kicked another one of the three really hard up the backside. He yelped and peered out from his blanket to see if it was worth retaliating. He decided it wasn't.

Once they had all gone, Brad banged on Hicksy's door.

'Hicksy. Wake up. Hicksy......'

'Fuck off - I'm sleeping.'

'I'll give you sleeping you mug. If you don't come out here now you'll be sleeping for good.'

'Piss off and leave me alone.'

Brad booted the door. In the passageway was Hicksy's suitcase. Sally's room was locked and she obviously hadn't been back all night. Roly's room was open but Roly was nowhere to be seen. Brad remembered that he had said he was going to go to Space that morning. In frustration, Brad opened Hicksy's suitcase. Inside it was a Nick Coleman shirt which Hicksy wore all of the time and never stopped telling people, cost ninety pounds. Brad took the shirt and walked through the kitchen to the garden. On the way, he picked up a white lighter with 'Ibiza' written down the side of it. When he got into the small back garden he held the shirt out at arms length and set fire to it. Once he was sure it was properly alight, he placed it on the concrete and returned to his room where he packed up all of his things. Before leaving he wrote a note:-

Roly, Sally.

Can't stand living here any more. I think we're all square on the rent, but if there's anything outstanding let me know.

Hicksy - you're a fucking lowlife. Your Nick Coleman shirt's in the garden. One of your stupid mates almost set fire to the apartment so I guess somehow your shirt caught alight. I tried to wake you up to tell you but you told me to piss off. Shame.

Brad.

387

CHAPTER NINETEEN

The beach looked glorious as Brad stopped his car and looked down on the sheltered bay - it could have graced any postcard. Today he was doing the group photographs instead of the video and Young Free & Single were the clients. The boats had just moored and once they had been divided into their two teams Brad gathered them together for the group photographs.

He spent just under an hour collecting orders. Normally he would have left straight away to get the pictures developed so that they would be ready for handing out when the boats brought all of the Beach Party attendees back to San Antonio, five hours later. But on this occasion Carmen was there and he wanted to spend some time with her. He was fairly sure, judging by the way that she had seemed so genuinely disappointed that he hadn't turned up at The Star after the Bar-B-Q, that she wanted to be more than just friends. It was as if something had happened that night, something that made it seem as if they were already an item without anything actually being said even remotely to that effect.

They spent some time together messing around in the sea, both urging the other to say something that was not obfuscated by double entendre or cerebral sparring. When they came out of the sea Brad went and sat with Mikey.

'She's definitely game on, Brad.'

'You reckon?'

'Brad, you're so into each other that you can't see passed your noses.'

Brad felt a warm glow. 'I dunno mate. Maybe she's just a friend.'

'Bollocks. Tell me something. How many girls have you got out here who are just friends?'

'Three or four probably.'

'And why don't you sleep with them? Don't you fancy them? Wouldn't you shag them?'

'All apart from Jessica, I probably would.'

'So why don't you?'

'I dunno. I suppose half the fun is the chase. I mean, if I was into hunting deer then I would imagine that the fun would come out of stalking it; pitting your wits against it; lining it up in your sights. If it suddenly appeared in your telescopic lens with a grin on it's face saying 'Go on then - shoot me,' it would all be pretty pointless. It's the same with some women. On top of that, because they all work here it would be all the hassle afterwards. I mean, I already know that I wouldn't want a long term relationship with any of them so what's the point? I'd spend a night or a week trying to get into them; ten or fifteen minutes actually in them, so to speak, then the rest of the season trying to get out of them. It's not like scoring points with clients. I actually enjoy the relationship I've got with them now. If that sexual tension disappeared then the relationship probably wouldn't be the same.' Brad reflected on what he'd just said for a moment. 'Having said that, if we were off our heads and it was just a laugh with neither party expecting anything then I guess I'd bonk 'em.'

'So how's Carmen different?' asked Mikey.

'I didn't say she was,' said Brad.

'I'll tell you what the difference is then, shall I? You actually think you could have a long relationship with Carmen. You wouldn't be spending the rest of the season trying to wriggle out of things after you'd slept with her. She stimulates this,' said Mikey pointing to his head, 'As well as this.' He pointed to his groin.

Brad looked pensive. 'So what do you reckon then?'

'What do I reckon of her, or what do I reckon you should do?'

'Both,' replied Brad.

'She's gorgeous looking, sexy, intelligent and witty. But, there's something about her that personally I'm not sure about. It's as if she's acting or hiding something.'

'Like what?'

'Dunno. It's irrelevant. What's relevant is that you fancy her and you should go over there right now and ask her out.'

Brad sat there for a few seconds. 'Fuck it - you're right.'

He walked across the beach to where she was standing, near the steps which led up to the bar.

'Bikini line needs doing,' said Brad, nodding at her crotch.

'Willy needs extending,' said Carmen, nodding at his.

'It'll need thickening as well if it's gonna make any impression on that gaping chasm,' he said, 'When you get in the water the sea level of the Med drops as all the water disappears.' Brad made a sucking noise to indicate the disappearance of vast quantities of sea water up the aforementioned orifice.

'You disgusting bastard,' laughed Carmen, screwing her face up.

'Anyway, enough of these complements,' said Brad. 'After we've finished showing the video in Night Life I'm taking you out for a meal.'

'You are, are you?'

'Yeah, I'll book a table at The Copper Pot for twelve thirty.'

'Is this your bashful way of asking me out, taking me to dinner?' teased Carmen.

'No, but if we go for a meal then your mouth might be full just long enough to stop you from coming out with the normal crap you're prone to spouting. Is that a yes then?'

'Well seeing as you put it so charmingly, yes.'

'This room brings back memories,' said Brad, as he walked into his old bedroom which was now occupied by Carmen. 'Where's Greg?'

'He's gone to Amnesia. He's got heavily into pills and charlie you know,' said Carmen.

'I didn't know about the charlie,' said Brad. 'I'll have to talk to him.'

'I wish someone would. He hardly ever sleeps and for such a good looking boy he's looking rough.'

Carmen made some coffee and they sat on her bed, which now had the mattress placed back on the bedstead which Brad had placed vertically against the wall during his occupation of the room. It took a superhuman effort for Brad to keep his hands off of her. He was waiting for an obvious signal, but none came. He could feel his heart sinking. After a while, the conversation was no longer as light as it had been, nor was it deep and meaningful. It was the verbal equivalent of piped muzak. In the end Brad could take it no more.

'Carmen. I'm mad about you.'

It was as if someone else had said it. But there it was. Out. All of the innuendo and guessing was over. The possibility of mammoth rejection stared Brad in the face and for one moment, he wished he'd kept his mouth shut; wished that he could scurry back to the comfort zone of the games that they hitherto had been playing with each other.

Carmen looked at him and smiled. She lent forward and kissed him gently on the lips.

'I was hoping you would say something like that.'

Brad's heart started pounding and he felt a natural rush that made the hairs on the back of his neck stand on end. All of the possible scenarios he had played out in his mind could not prepare him for the excited reality that he was now experiencing. They kissed more passionately, but Carmen was quite reserved. After more than ten minutes of kissing, Brad wanted her desperately. He tried every trick he could think of. He got her to sit between his legs with her back to him while he massaged her shoulders. He let his hands settle at the top of her chest, then made her boobs rise and ride against her T-shirt by gently pulling up the skin at the top of each breast.

Carmen's nipples went hard as they brushed against her T-shirt. Brad let his fingers slowly glide passed her nipples outside the T-shirt, not quite or only just touching them. He kissed her shoulder, then bit it slightly harder. She moaned.

392

As Carmen got more excited Brad laid her on her back and got on top of her, then began to grind his hip bone or his hard on between her legs. He began to explore more of her body with his hands and his mouth. It had almost got to the point where Brad was sure that it was going to go all of the way when Carmen suddenly switched off,

'No Brad - not tonight.'

Brad said nothing, hoping that continued physical perseverance might wear down what he hoped to be token resistance.

'Please Brad - stop.'

Brad got off of her and retracted his hands with fumbling obedience. He put his arm around her and she snuggled up to his chest. Once his erection had subsided he was happy to be just as they were.

Carmen was special.

'Why do men always do that?' giggled Carmen.

'Do what?' asked a naked Brad as he walked back into the bedroom with a towel to clean up the mess he had just made. It had taken three nights together before they had fully consummated their relationship, but for the following two days they had been at it, at every available opportunity.

'As soon as a bloke comes he either falls asleep or loses interest. All us girls want is a cuddle.'

Brad laughed. 'Actually I've got a theory about that.'

'And what theory is that then?'

Brad sat on the bed and handed her the towel.

'Well, most basic things are somehow related back to our prehistoric ancestors, aren't they?' Carmen nodded. 'I read an article the other day that said that not all sperm are produced to fertilise eggs, and that some are actually there to fight off other sperm. If you look at apes or other mammals, the female often gets shagged by several males on the trot.'

'A bit like Young Free & Single holidaymakers then,' said

393

Carmen.

'More like the female reps,' said Brad. Carmen tweaked his nipple. 'Ouch! Anyway, as I was saying. Basically, given that we still produce these little spermies designed for combat, it seems a fair assumption that somewhere deep down, us men must still have this primeval need to make sure that it's our sperm that does the fertilising.'

'What on earth's this got to do with falling asleep or jumping off after you've come?'

'Well I reckon that after we've come one of two things happen. If you think about it, if a bloke falls asleep as soon as he's come - which taken to it's logical conclusion would actually mean falling asleep while he was still inside his partner - then no other male can get in. On the other hand, if we jump off straight away it's probably so we're ready to fight off any other males who are waiting to try and do the business. Now obviously, we no longer need to do this, so I reckon that it's somehow mutated into the male of the species going and making a bacon sandwich or sitting in an armchair and watching Match of the Day.'

Carmen shook her head. 'You need help.'

Brad smiled. He had fallen for Carmen in a big way, more than any other girl in his life. In the short time they had been together he had opened up to her about things he never had to anybody else. Yet it had not left him feeling in any way vulnerable. Their growing together seemed the most natural thing in the world. She occupied his every thought, and even though there were some gorgeous girls on holiday with YF&S, Brad could not be bothered to give them a second glance. The only subject which caused any tension was Alison. Carmen flatly refused to talk about her and Brad could not understand why she was so friendly towards Alison despite everything that Brad had told Carmen about her.

The eleven men barely fitted into the hotel room. The Jet

Bossa was a hotel near the airport where Luigi and his five travelling companions were staying. Luigi had promised himself a break, so Mario's request for assistance had given him the perfect opportunity for a holiday. With him was Alberto, his main debt collector. The other four were friends or waiters, all part of his little 'firm'. Luigi figured that taking care of Mario's tormentors would be a simple enough task. Even though Mario had told him that Mikey was a black belt and that Brad was on the large side, he wasn't expecting any serious problems. Part of the reason for assembling so many for such a small task was to make it more of a social occasion. On the other hand it also helped to bolster Luigi's own ego.

When Mario came into the room he felt quite intimidated. He was still very much looked on by Luigi's friends as the 'kid brother'. This of course made Mario try to act as tough and as in the know as he could, inventing at least four people he'd beaten up during the season and claiming to know the main dealers on the island.

It was arranged for Brad and Mikey to be jumped in the car park of Ku the following night. Mario knew that they were going to be going up there in Brad's car at eleven o'clock, because one of Mikey's friends from back home was the first DJ playing. Sergio was going to lead the attack; his jaw a reminder of the previous encounter with Mikey. This time he was determined the outcome would be different.

Taking the photographs and collecting the orders on the beach party had been done on autopilot. Brad was in a daze. He had not been able to get the previous night's conversation with Mikey out of his mind. They hadn't come to blows, but Brad had snapped more than he ever had with Mikey before. The thing was, Brad knew that Mikey's comments were not born out of any petty vying for Brad's friendship but a genuine concern for his happiness. That was what made it all the more worrying. The more he thought about it, the more it made sense. But how could he have been so completely suckered? Brad was experienced with women and perceptive to most of their wiles, but Carmen had hooked him and reeled him in. As he drove back to San Antonio he tried to convince himself that it wasn't so.

Mikey had told Brad that he was almost certain that Carmen was in cahoots with Alison. As if this wasn't bad enough, during the course of the morning, two different people had told Brad that they had seen her go into Mario's room after leaving The Star Club. The only reason that Brad had spent the night in Mikey's apartment rather than Carmen's was because Carmen had said that Alison was going to be visiting her first thing in the morning and didn't want her to think that Brad had been staying with her. The thought of Carmen with Mario made Brad feel physically sick. He thought he had found a soul mate, and the betrayal of that soul mate going with someone as shallow as Mario was almost too much to bear. The niggling thought of Mario's nine inch dick didn't help.

Mikey had said that Carmen had spent a lot of time with Alison, sometimes even being in Alison's room when Alison wasn't there, which no other rep ever did. A large portion of the money that was stolen when Brad got the sack, had never been recovered. Mikey had a theory that Carmen was Alison's friend and was trying to find a way of planting more evidence on Brad to deflect any suspicion away from Alison and to maybe make it serious enough to get Brad prosecuted. As their imaginations had run wild, fuelled by Spanish wine and Dutch skunk, they even contemplated the possibility that Alison and Carmen were trying to set Brad up to get arrested by planting drugs on him. As far fetched as this was, in Brad's current state of mind even this seemed plausible.

Brad pulled up at the photo lab, walked in and put the camera on the table.

'What's this?' laughed Mason, the American owner of the photo lab, opening the back of the camera.

'What?' said Brad, still miles away.

396

'There's no film in here.'

'Huh?'

Brad looked in the camera and sure enough, he had forgotten to load up the film.

'Oh for fuck's sake,' Brad groaned.

'Heavy night?' asked Mason.

Brad ignored him, grabbed the camera then jumped into the Triumph and sped back to the beach, perversely grateful that there was something other than Carmen to occupy his thoughts.

Once at the beach he managed to assemble the groups again and take another couple of pictures. He got back to San Antonio and managed to get the photos developed just as the boats from the beach party were pulling back into the harbour. Thankfully Giles, the beach party owner, had kept the beach party going a little longer than normal so they arrived at six thirty rather than six o'clock. Giles gave Brad a look that meant one more time and you're sacked.

When he got back to The Bon Brad went to Mikey's room. Mikey looked serious.

'You better sit down Brad.'

'What's up.'

Mikey hesitated. 'Someone has definitely been snooping through your things, and Carmen definitely went back to Mario's last night.'

Brad went cold. He just looked at Mikey helplessly. 'Oh bollocks.'

'I'm sorry mate. After you left I got a couple of brown envelopes and put money and different bits of paperwork in them. I didn't seal them, but I tucked one flap in and left the other one out. When I looked at them they were both tucked in.'

'Yeah, but it could have been Alison,' said Brad desperately.

Mikey shook his head. 'I asked Raoul to try and keep one eye on my room and he saw Carmen hovering around, plus Alison was in Ibiza Town all day.' Brad shook his head in disbelief. Mikey continued. 'I spoke to Antonio, the new night porter at The Las Huertas. Carmen went into Mario's room at two in the morning. He didn't see what time she came out because he fell asleep, but.........'

Mikey didn't have to say anymore. Brad stared into space, breathing shallowly, then flopped back on the settee.

'Now what do I do?' said Brad, thinking aloud.

'I'm really sorry it had to be me who told you Brad.'

Brad stood up. 'Well you're my best mate over here, so if anyone was gonna tell me, I suppose I'm glad it's you.'

For no particular reason Brad shook his hand and they hugged each other.

'Right then,' said Brad, beginning to compose himself. 'Guess I better go and sort this out.'

He walked to Carmen's room as slowly as he could. When he got there, he stood outside for a few moments before knocking. Carmen came to the door dressed in a YF&S white T-shirt and bikini bottoms. She looked surprised when she saw it was Brad.

'Where's your key? Why did you knock?'

'I wasn't sure if you'd have anyone in there with you.'

Carmen searched Brad's face for an explanation as he walked passed her and into the room.

'What do you mean?'

'I thought maybe Mario might be in here with you - you know, continuing where you left off last night.'

Carmen looked at him guiltily.

Brad gasped out loud. 'God. You're not even going to deny it, are you?' Carmen sat down and put her head in her hands. 'And,' continued Brad, 'I know that you've been going through my things.' Carmen looked up in horror. 'Fucking hell Carmen. If you think nothing else of me, the one thing I would've hoped you wouldn't think I was, was stupid. You must've known I'd find out.'

'Oh Brad, if only-'

'If only what? If only I hadn't found out that you and Alison were trying to stitch me up even more-'

'No Brad, that's not-'

'As if getting me branded a thief and losing my job wasn't enough. What else did you have in store for me, eh? Fucking hell, I can't believe that someone can hate me enough to want to do this.' A tear rolled down Carmen's cheek. 'Why did I have to go and fall for you? God, I really am not as smart as I thought I was, am I? The first time I let someone in, in God knows how long and it turns out to be a conniving, two faced bitch.' By now Carmen was crying. 'Save the fucking water works. You've wrapped me around your fingers enough for one lifetime.' Brad started to gather up his things.

'Brad, please listen. It's not like what you think.'

'Alright then.' Brad dropped the things that he had just picked up and stood facing her with his hands on his hips. 'Supposing you tell me what it is 'like'.'

'I'm not trying to stitch you up.'

'Did you or did you not go through my things?'

'Yes, but-'

'And did you or did you not go into Mario's room after The Star last night?'

'I did, but.........' Her voice trailed off.

'Go on then, I'm listening.'

'Oh I can't explain. You'll just have to trust me.'

'Trust! You!? There's more chance of me trusting Greg to stay drug free and celibate in a brothel with a jar full of E's than there is of me ever trusting you again. Crawl back to that slag Alison and tell her whatever it was you were plotting against me ain't gonna work. And if you're thinking about grassing me up for staying in Mikey's don't bother, 'cos I'm out of here.'

'Where are you going. You're not leaving the island, are you?'

'No I'm not - not that it should be any concern of yours. Do you know what the ironic thing about all this is? Initially I was obsessed with wanting to get revenge on that stupid bitch Alison. But you know, I'd more or less decided she wasn't worth it, 'cos I'm actually really enjoying doing my own thing and not repping. It's not until you step back from it and see

399

how wrapped up in themselves that reps are that you realise how a couple of years doing the job could turn you into a total egomaniac, not caring about anyone other than yourself.' Brad opened the door and looked at Carmen. 'Well, at least you've got a head start there. Have a nice life.'

Mario looked everywhere for his three video tapes. He wanted to show them to his brother and all of his friends, so they could see how many girls he had shagged. Three tapes containing twenty two of the fifty three girls he had slept with in the four and a half months he had been away, but he couldn't find them anywhere. Over a week had gone since he had video'd one of his conquests. Although he was sure they would turn up he was really pissed off that they were not there ready to show his brother.

He sat in the bar of The Las Huertas doing his desk duty. He had been there for five minutes or so when Antonio came in to tell him that he was wanted on the phone. It was Luigi.

'Hello.'

'Mario. It's me. Are they still going up to Ku tonight?'

'Yep.'

'You do know that we're gonna give 'em a fucking good hidin', don't you?'

'Yeah, course I do.'

'We won't tell 'em, but they'll probably guess it's from you.'

'Just make sure that you do 'em good.'

'Alright. Consider it done.'

Alison couldn't find some of Felipe's bank statements. She had got very pissed with Trevor a couple of nights before - so pissed that she'd actually wanked him off. When she'd returned to her apartment she had drunkenly gone through her finances to see how much money she had made, so she merely assumed that she had simply misplaced various bits and pieces.

She had already made nearly twenty five thousand pounds. A huge amount of money had gone into Felipe's account, so she had quite easily been able to filter off a couple of thousand pounds to add to her own growing nest egg, without it even being noticed. A lot of Felipe's money had been received in cash, although there had been some cheques paid in directly by different hotels. Her parents and her boyfriend Jonathan were coming over at the weekend and they were going to take back some of the money for her. The way things were going, Alison was beginning to consider doing another season - Jonathan would just have to lump it. All in all she was pleased with the way things had gone. Brad was out of the picture, and although he was still a minor irritation he couldn't do her any damage. Mikey was a lot easier to control without his influence, and Lorraine had been effortlessly disposed of early on. The money had been rolling in, and she had shagged all of the people that she wanted to apart from Spanish Jimmy at The Star. As far as she was concerned, Jane Ward thought that she was doing a good job, so with Felipe's continued string pulling another season as Resort Manager should be a formality. She smiled to herself and out of sheer devilment, took out a thousand peseta note and with it, lit a cigarette.

There were less than a dozen other cars in the car park. Ku didn't really get going until midnight, and it was only a quarter to eleven. Brad got out of the Triumph and as normal, lifted the bonnet to disconnect the battery. As he had his head under the bonnet he heard Mikey say something.

'What did you say Mikey?'

When Brad closed the bonnet he saw a group of about a dozen large males getting out of three cars and walking towards them.

'I said 'shit',' repeated Mikey.

'Who are they?' asked Brad, fearing that he had already guessed the answer.

'It's the fuckers who did me over - plus a few.'

Brad felt as though his legs were starting to shake. He remembered the state of Mikey after getting battered by only five of them. Now there were more than twice as many, and a couple were carrying what looked suspiciously like pick axe handles.

'Remember me?' said Sergio when they were a few metres away.

Mikey looked at him without speaking. Brad reached into the back of the Triumph Herald and grabbed a wheel spanner that was laying on the back seat.

'We're going to teach you two a lesson,' said Luigi.

'Look, I don't know what this is all about,' said Brad, 'But we don't want any trouble.'

'It's too late boy. You've already got it,' said Luigi, pulling out a flick-knife.

Brad went cold. 'Oh for fuck's sake.' He dropped the wheel spanner to his side, trying not to look aggressive.

'I'm gonna break more than your jaw, you stinking nigger,' said Sergio.

Mikey said nothing. Brad looked at him and wondered if he was shitting himself anywhere near as much as he was.

'What's this all about?' asked Brad.

'What's it all about?' laughed Luigi, 'It's all about you two getting the biggest kicking of your lives - however short they might be.'

Brad looked at him closely. The family resemblance suddenly struck him.

'Hang on a minute - you look like Mario. Is that what this is all about? Are you two related?'

'Yeah,' swaggered Luigi, 'He's my kid brother.'

Brad could feel himself getting wound up. He couldn't take anyone seriously who was related to someone he held in such contempt - not even someone with a flick knife.

'So young Mario's your brother.' Brad shook his head

402

laughing. Mikey looked at him - he'd seen that look before. Brad didn't speak for almost fifteen seconds before looking up, his eyes wide and glaring. 'Well I tell you what - HE'S A FUCKING WANKER!' Brad raised the wheel spanner back up to chest level. 'And if your his brother then so are you.'

This time Mikey was glad that Brad had lost it because it was obvious that they were going to have to fight their way out of their predicament. That being so, Mikey would most definitely have wanted a Brad who was completely wild by his side, rather than the normal 'ever friendly, ever smiling' rep.

'You're gonna regret saying that,' said Luigi.

'And Mario's gonna regret this, 'cos whatever you do to us, we're going to do to him twice as bad,' said Mikey.

'Big talk, black man,' said Sergio.

Alberto came and stood at the front of the group. When they saw him, both Brad and Mikey began to lose a little of their bravado. He was just over six foot, almost as wide and had a face of pure evil, with a voice to match.

'I don't think so. I don't think you're going to be doing anything.'

The tranquil, violent detachment in his voice sent a shiver up both Brad and Mikey's spines. For a moment there was silence; an unnatural calm before an inevitable violent tornado that would leave a trail of destruction over the bodies of the two reps. The mute tension was broken by a car entering the car park. Weapons were dropped to the side, out of sight, as the car headed towards the group. As it got closer there was something familiar about the blowing exhaust. When it was twenty metres away Brad could make out that it was a jeep.

'Oh fuck me, no,' he said.

The jeep pulled up next to the group, with it's headlights shining on them. Out of the drivers side got a man with a large, bandanna'd head.

'Brad!'

It was Samuel T Zakatek.

'Sammy?'

'Shit. I don't believe it. Brad man - how y'doing?' He came

over and hugged him. 'So what you bin up to? Jeez. I bet you never thought you'd see me again.' Sammy seemed oblivious to the situation that he'd walked into. 'So what y'doing up here?'

'Who is this clown?' said Luigi.

'Sammy. We've got a bit of a problem. You'd better go.'

'An' what koind o' problem would yis all be havin', exactly?' said the passenger as he got out of the jeep. It was Irish Ben.

'It's gonna be your problem as well if you don't fuck off, you stupid Paddy,' said Sergio.

'Now tha's no way t'be talkin' t'someone yeh've never met. Did yeh ma never teach y'any manners?'

'Go away my Irish friend, or it will be you who'll be getting a lesson in manners,' said Alberto.

'Bejaysus, yeh's an ugly lookin' bloighter, so y'are. I bet y'can eat a few o' them there Shredded Wheat t'ings.'

'I only eat people,' he growled.

'Well yis wan' t'be careful there big feller, 'cos us Paddy's have an awful habit o' causin' indigestion, so we have.'

Alberto made a lunge at Irish Ben with a knuckle dustered hand. Ben stepped to one side and as Alberto's momentum carried him past, the outside of Ben's fist came crashing down on his temple, knocking him out instantly.

Luigi was too busy incredulously watching what was happening to Alberto to see Brad's wheel spanner come crashing down to break his collar bone. The knife fell out of his hand and Brad knee'd him in the face as Luigi dropped to the floor.

Sammy leapt in the air and, with a Kung Fu kick that Bruce Lee would have been proud of, sent the pick axe handle flying out of Sergio's hand. When he saw this, Mikey span around and with an airborne reverse kick, gave Sergio a broken nose to go with his previously broken jaw. He sunk to his knees and the now raging Brad ran up and connected with the side of his face, booting him into unconsciousness. One of the other Italian's who was almost as big as Sergio punched Brad just under his eye, then picked up Luigi's flick-knife that was by

404

Brad's feet. From nowhere, Sammy came flying through the air and connected with his chest. He fell against the hired Renault 19 and doubled up, dropping the knife. As he did so, Brad caught him with a glorious uppercut, and Mikey swept his legs away for good measure. Brad picked up the knife. Mikey looked at him with horror,

'NO BRAD! DON'T!'

Mikey didn't see Luigi's head waiter come up behind and club him on the back of the head with both fists. Mikey stumbled towards Brad and the knife. Brad threw the knife away and caught him, before pushing him out of the way as the head waiter came for them. He aimed a punch at Brad's head but Brad ducked and swung his elbow into his face with a satisfying crunch. By the Triumph Herald, Sammy and Irish Ben were surrounded by the other six members of the gang. Before Brad or Mikey could even attempt to help them, Irish Ben's hands were a blur of movement and within no more than a couple of seconds, four of the group were either on, or heading for the floor. Sammy was making whooping noises as he kicked one, then punched the other to join their colleagues. With the adrenaline pumping, Brad was frustrated that there was no-one left to hit, so he went round kicking some of the remaining semi-conscious assailants, who were crawling or dragging themselves or the others to the three hired cars.

The four of them sat in the VIP bar of a still relatively empty Ku.

'So let me get this straight, 'cos I still can't fucking believe it,' said Brad, his eye swelling up as he spoke. 'You both arrived in Ibiza at more or less the same time and it was Sammy that you used to do the Karate exhibitions with ten years ago?'

'Have yis ever t'ought about apploying fer tha' University Challenge?'

'Alright, you piss taking bastard,' laughed Brad. 'I just can't believe it.'

'Tell him Sammy,' said Irish Ben.

'It's true Brad. I studied martial arts in 'Nam, so when I got here me an' Ben met up an' decided t'make a few bucks doin' exhibitions. That was before I went to the beach. Did I tell y'about when the King of Spain visited -'

'Um, yeah,' interrupted Brad hurriedly.

'What I don't understand is why you were both up here,' said Mikey.

'Well oi was goin' t'get y'man Sam's car fixed in the mornin'. Tha' meant givin' him a lif' t'work so oi had the car, y'see.'

'So you really do work in Ku, then?' said Brad, still half expecting to wake up.

'Yeah man. Dontcha remember me tellin' y'in France.'

'Yeah, yeah of course,' said Brad.

'So what're yis gonna be doin' about this Mario feller?' asked Irish Ben.

Mikey looked at Brad. 'I think we'll pay him a visit down The Star, don't you?'

Brad nodded in agreement. 'Definitely. But let's make a little detour - I've something I want to pick up first.'

Brad pulled up on the main road outside The Star and Es Paradis. He felt quite light headed.

'Don't forget to disconnect the battery,' said Mikey.

'Oh yeah,' said Brad.

Mikey watched as Brad lifted the bonnet and pulled off the positive terminal. As he did so all of the street lights went out.

'Shit,' said Brad, immediately replacing the battery lead on the terminal.

They both realised at about the same time that it was just a coincidence that there had been a power cut at the exact moment that Brad had disconnected his battery. When it dawned on them they burst out laughing. The power cut only lasted a few moments and the lights came back on to a big

406

cheer from everyone waiting to get back into the club.

Walking into The Star one of the first people they saw was Carmen.

'Oh my God,' she said when she saw Brad's almost totally closed eye. 'What's happened?'

'Mario thought he'd get his brother and a few of his friends to show us what he really thinks of us,' said Mikey.

Carmen went to touch Brad's eye. 'Are you alright?'

Brad wanted to say that his injuries were nothing compared to what she had done to him. But he decided it would sound too pathetic, and settled for a more ambiguous,

'All wounds heal with time, Carmen.'

They marched through the club towards bar five. Because of their dishevelled appearance a lot of the people in the club stared at them or moved out of their way. Gus, the head bouncer, was standing next to the DJ stand so Brad went up and asked him to turn a blind eye to what they were about to do.

They saw Mario just before Mario saw them. He had a couple of girls around him by bar five and was laughing and joking with them. When he saw Brad and Mikey his face froze. Roughly, they grabbed hold of him and frog-marched him through to the gents toilets.

'Out,' said Mikey to the two holidaymakers using the urinals.

Roly, who was working as a bouncer down The Star, stood guard at the entrance to the loos to stop anyone from going in. Mikey threw Mario up against the wall. He booted him in the groin and although he pulled the kick, Mario still doubled up in excruciating pain.

'Right Mario. I'm going to give you three punches head start and then I'm going to beat the living shit out of you.'

'No, I don't wanna fight you,' he wheezed.

'We know that Mario,' said Brad. 'You'd rather get your brother and his mates to do it for you, wouldn't you?'

Mario looked at them both, realising that their mere presence meant that they had somehow got the better of Luigi.

'C'mon then Mario,' said Mikey sticking his chin out, 'What are you waiting for?'

'I've already told you,' he said pathetically, 'I don't wanna fight.'

'No?' said Mikey. 'Do you wanna hear an alternative?'

'Yeah,' whispered Mario.

'Can't hear you,' said Mikey.

'I said yes,' repeated Mario, more loudly.

'Right then. You get your sorry racist ass off of this island first thing tomorrow morning-'

'But there aren't any flights home tomorrow,' protested Mario.

'Tough. Get a flight to Majorca. Just get the fuck off of Ibiza, and,' continued Mikey, 'You don't tell Alison or anyone else that you're going. Understood?'

Mario nodded, totally defeated.

'Finally,' said Mikey, 'You tell that cardboard gangster brother of yours, that if this goes any further, not only will it be you who suffers most, but you'll also have a whole load of angry niggers to deal with back home, and they'll break every racist bone in your motherfucking bodies. Clear?'

Mario nodded again, glad that he had got off so lightly. He hadn't.

'The only other thing Mario,' said Brad, 'Is that I've got this real bad problem. You see, if someone hurts me I've just got to do something back to them.' Brad looked at his swollen eye in the mirror. 'Now I reckon that this eye is gonna be with me for a week or so. Therefore, it's only fair that we give you something a little more permanent to remember us by. What d'you reckon Mikey?'

'For sure.'

Mikey noticed that a trickle was running down Mario's shaking leg.

'Oh dear,' said Mikey, 'Young Mario appears to have pee'd his pants.'

Mario was almost in tears, worrying about how he was going to be scarred. Mikey grabbed him and bundled him into a cubicle, pushed his head down the pan and flushed the cistern. He yanked him back up and pinned him against the wall.

'If I were you Mario,' he said, 'I'd keep pretty still.'

Mario looked at Brad with wide eyed fear as Brad reached for his back pocket. From it he pulled out a flick-knife, one of the two things he'd stopped for on the way to the club.

'Now don't move Mario.'

Mario screamed so loudly that even Roly put his head around the door to see what was going on. He screwed his face up in fearful anticipation and lost control of all of his bodily functions.

Brad looked at Mikey and they grinned at each other. He handed him the flick-knife and took out of his pocket the other thing he had picked up from his apartment - a Bic razor.

Five minutes later, an eyebrowless, wet-legged and crying Mario went running out of The Star, heading for The Las Huertas, his suitcase, and the first available flight to Majorca.

CHAPTER TWENTY

A shapely pair of sun-tanned legs came into the viewfinder as Brad scanned the YF&S beach party for an interesting subject. He zoomed in and noticed faint writing on her legs. It read, 'In case you're wondering, I didn't shag you.'

'What's all that, then,' Brad asked the girl as he carried on filming.

'Go away,' she shrieked, holding her hand out to shield her face from the camera and closing her legs. 'Go and ask that bastard Greg, if you really want to know.'

Brad switched off the camera and went over to Greg, who he knew was hiding at the top of the beach on a sundbed, catching up on some much needed sleep. Brad wiped his finger round his own backside and put it under the dormant Greg's nostrils. Greg's nose started twitching like an inquisitive dog, until his olfactory glands sent a message to his subconscious that something interesting was nearby. Greg's eyes opened. When he realised that the source of the smell was nothing to do with female genitalia, he sat bolt upright, yelling 'Fuck off.'

'So what went down with you and the girl with the writing on her legs?' asked Brad.

'You dirty bastard,' said Greg, still more concerned with Brad's digital assault. Once he had got his head together he started chuckling. 'You must be talking about Kimberley. Yeah, I nearly 'ad a threesome with 'er an' 'er mate last night.'

'You jammy fuck. What happened?'

'I gorrem both t'come back to me apartment t'play strip spoof. They were both pissed, like, but ol' Kimberley went an' fuckin' passed out on us. Up 'til then the threesome was definitely on, but after that 'er mate - can't remember 'er name - she went a bit cold. I tried t'grab 'old of 'er, but she jus' told

411

me to stick summit up Kimberley.'

'She what!?' said Brad.

'Serious, mate. She wanted me to stick one of them big Elnette 'air spray bottles up 'er.'

'Fuck off!'

'Honest. In the end I gorra beer bottle. That didn't wake 'er up so I shagged 'er. That didn't wake 'er up either.' Brad started laughing. 'Yeah, I know - sad innit? After that I gorr'er mate to wank me off over Kimberley's back. When I'd emptied me sac, I wrote that stuff on 'er leg with one o' them there magic markers. Made sure it was indelible ink.'

'You bastard,' said Brad.

'Cheers.'

Brad shook his head. Only Greg would consider that a complement.

'Best bit was in the morning,' continued Greg. 'Ol' Kimberley wakes up an' feels all me dried 'Arry over 'er back an' goes, 'Oh no, my back's peeling'. I almos' wet meself lad, I'm tellin' yer.'

'So why is it still written all over her leg?' asked Brad.

'Apparently she spent ages scrubbing it, but because it's indelible ink it wouldn't come off.'

Brad left Greg and walked over to Kimberley for another look. Even though he saw it with his own eyes he still had trouble believing it.

Alison had brought her parents and her boyfriend, Jonathan along to the beach party. Her parents spent most of the time at the bar. Jonathan knew nothing about the animosity between Brad and Alison, so made an effort to talk to Brad when he saw him going around with the video camera. He even told Brad that he was a bit pissed off because Alison was talking about coming back the next year. Brad found him a thoroughly nice bloke, which made him wonder what on earth he was doing with Alison.

Brad spent the whole day on the beach doing the video. Carmen continually tried to speak to Brad, but each time she approached him he walked away. When they got on to the boats back to San Antonio, she made a point of getting on the same boat as Brad which meant that try as he might, he was unable to avoid her. Eventually she cornered him.

'Brad, I really need to speak to you.'

'There's nothing left to say.'

'But things need to be explained.'

'No they don't Carmen.'

She looked up at him and all he wanted to do was to take her in his arms. The weeks she had spent in the sun had made her eyes even more striking and had brought out cute freckles across the bridge of her button nose. She was desperate to communicate with Brad and her normally challenging eyes now had a vulnerable warmth that Brad had to call upon all of his reserves of will power to resist.

She stretched up and kissed him on the cheek, then took his hand and squeezed it.

'Things are going to change Brad - sooner than you think.' She kissed him again and whispered into his ear, 'I love you.'

This made Brad feel as confused as a Dutch Lemming. His basic feelings for Carmen hadn't really changed, and as wonderful as it was to hear her say what she just had, that there was no way he could trust or respect her after what she had done. He walked away.

When everyone got back to The Bon, they were surprised to see Jane Ward and Tom Ortega. Alison was particularly surprised because she had no prior warning of their visit and as Resort Manager she expected that she would have been informed - particularly as they were both there at the same time which was quite unusual. Alison rationaled that they were probably over to see what was going on following Mario's recent sudden departure. Alison had heard rumours that Brad and Mikey were involved and she was looking forward to sharing those rumours with both Jane and Tom.

Once all of the reps had said their hello's Tom noticed that

Brad was leaving. Brad had moved back in with Sally and Roly as he had already paid the rent and Hicksy had fled the island after being done with a stolen credit card. Tom caught Brad just as he was getting into the Triumph Herald.

'Brad.'

'Alright Tom. Thought I'd leave you all to it.'

'Yeah thanks, but actually I was wondering if you wouldn't mind hanging around in the bar for half an hour or so.'

Brad looked puzzled. 'Well, I've got to go and edit the beach party video for tonight......'

'How long will that take?'

'Dunno. Hour or two I guess......'

'Please Brad. I'd be really grateful if you could hang around for a little while. It's quite important.'

Brad shrugged his shoulders. 'Ok.' He could easily spare the time and he was growing curious.

In the bar Alison was proudly going through her achievements to Jane Ward, Jonathan and her parents.

'Oh yes, you've only got to ask people like Trevor. They say that this has been one of the best seasons out here. I'm even thinking about coming back next year, aren't I Jonathan?' Jonathan grunted and Alison continued. 'Obviously I can't take all of the credit. Some of the reps have been a great help. It's such a shame about Mario. Actually Jane, I wanted to talk to you about that-'

'Yes, well Alison. Perhaps we could go up to your room and talk about it there.' Jane turned to Alison's parents and Jonathan. 'If you'll excuse us.'

Carmen went to go upstairs with them.

'Where are you going?' asked Alison, before sarcastically adding, 'Have you suddenly been promoted?'

'Actually Alison, I'd like Carmen to come upstairs with us, if it's all the same with you,' said Jane.

'Oh, alright,' said Alison.

As the four of them got into the lift, Alison wondered what Carmen had been up to. She was surprised that she hadn't been consulted but guessed it probably wasn't anything too serious.

When they got into the room, Alison and Jane sat down, Tom and Carmen remained standing. Alison sensed a certain tension in the air. Once again she wondered exactly what Carmen had done that was so serious.

Jane looked at Tom who nodded. Jane broke the silence.

'Right Alison. The game's up.'

'What?'

'We know exactly what's been going on.'

Jane paused deliberately, to see how Alison would initially react. Alison wasn't sure to which particular misdemeanour Jane was referring.

'Sorry Jane. What are you on about?'

'For the whole of the season you have been banking money for Felipe, who has been undertaking a massive fraud involving contracting accommodation for an amount different to that which we have been invoiced for. You have been lying about how much the bars have been paying and how many people have been visiting them. We also strongly suspect that it was you and not Brad who was responsible for the theft of the unliquidated excursion money.' Jane lent forward. 'You have ran this resort with an unimaginable degree of incompetence. Frankly, you should never have been given the job and had it not been for your liaison with Felipe - and yes, we know about the Chamberlain Clinic - then I am sure that you would never have been appointed. However, they say that if you give someone enough rope then they'll hang themself and that's exactly what you've done. It's just a tragedy that you have ruined what should have been a great season for so many people. Your selfishness is almost incomprehensible.'

Alison sat there stunned. 'I don't know what you're talking about. I swear that I didn't take the excursion money.'

Tom thought that she actually sounded genuine, but he took up the mantle nevertheless. 'We've been around to all of the bars threatening to withdraw our custom next year if they failed to co-operate. Russell from The Anglers, Jimmy from The Star, Noel from Sgt. Peppers - even darling Trevor. All of them have told us what you've been up to.'

'I don't believe you. You can't prove a thing.'

Alison turned to Carmen. 'Carmen.'

Carmen went over to the two giant boxes of washing up powder and reached inside them.

'Carmen - what are you doing?' asked a horrified Alison.

Carmen pulled a plastic bin bag out of each box. She emptied the contents over the table; millions of pesetas and sheet upon sheet of incriminating documentation.

'Alison,' said Jane almost smiling. 'I'd like to introduce you to Carmen Ward.' She allowed Alison a few seconds to let the surname to sink in.

'What!?' said Alison slowly, looking skyward. 'Oh please tell me you're joking.'

''Fraid not,' said Carmen. 'I've been her sister for......well, must be at least all of my life. I've been over here all this time gathering evidence on you. It took me a while to find your hiding place - shame you took laundering money so literally. It beats me how you lie so easily - I've hated having to do it.'

'Anyway, all that aside,' said Jane. 'Clearly we want every penny of the money back. We'll take this for starters.' She scooped the money on the table towards her. 'We know that your parents and boyfriend are about to take some to the UK for you, so unless you'd rather I did it, I'd suggest that you get it off of them.'

'I suppose we could arrange for them to be stopped at customs,' said Tom.

'Alright, alright,' said Alison throwing her arms out. 'But I'm telling you - whatever else I have or haven't done, I definitely did not touch that excursion money.'

'Well that will obviously have to be investigated. We couldn't get you on a flight tonight,' said Tom, 'But you're on a flight tomorrow morning at eleven o'clock. We'll decide whether or not to prosecute you based upon how much money we retrieve. The only other thing that will save your bacon is agreeing to testify against Felipe.'

Alison looked horrified.

'Right then,' continued Jane, 'That's about it. I thought you might be interested to know that we're going to ask Heather to take over running the resort. We've also got someone who I suppose will effectively be your replacement. Remember Lorraine?'

Alison nodded expressionlessly.

'Poetic justice, don't you think?' said Tom. 'She was so excited when I told her, but I bet she'll be even more pleased when she knows that you won't be her manager.'

Jane stood up. 'Right then Alison. If I were you I'd go down and speak to your parents. Tom, get the reps assembled in the empty room down the corridor.' She looked at Carmen. 'And Tom - you'd better bring a certain young man up here who I think deserves an explanation.'

Felipe had been trying to get through to Luis at Viajes Diamente in Ibiza all day. When he had not been able to, he had tried his contacts at all of the other Diamente offices with an equal lack of success. He knew something was wrong. Jane and Tom were abroad, Sebastian and Adam Hawthorne-Blythe were in meetings all day. At first he had panicked, but as the day progressed he knew that there would be nowhere to run to. With the calmness of a condemned man who had accepted his fate, Felipe left his company flat and sat waiting in the front room of his Dulwich home to prepare himself for the inevitable - he could at least keep his dignity.

At seven twenty in the evening an unmarked Vauxhall Cavalier swept up the gravel drive. Three men with short hair got out and walked up to the front door and rang the bell.

'Are you expecting anybody Felipe?' yelled his wife from the kitchen.

'Yes,' said Felipe, smoothing his clothes down as he stood up. 'I am.'

Brad walked into Alison's room behind Tom, totally confused as to what was going on, especially when he saw Jane and Carmen in the room.

'Sit down Brad,' said Jane, gesturing to the seat that Alison had just vacated.

'What for?' asked Brad, slightly arrogantly.

They weren't his bosses anymore, so why should he do what they told him?

'Please,' said Jane, 'We've something to tell you and when you hear it, I think you'll want to sit down.'

Jane and Carmen smiled at each other. Brad sat down.

'Ok - I'm listening.'

'Well,' said Jane, 'Where to start?' She paused. 'Felipe Gomez has been defrauding the company of hundreds of thousands of pounds. You will appreciate the gravity of such an accusation, so clearly we have had to gather some proof to substantiate it. The majority of his illegal gains were being laundered.......' Jane, Tom and Carmen all smiled again at this word, '........through Ibiza by one Alison Shand.'

'You what?' said Brad.

'At the time of the incident with the excursion money,' continued Jane, 'We knew what was going on and we more or less knew everything that she was up to and what a dreadful manager she was. But we could do nothing about your predicament for fear of blowing our investigation into what you must now understand to be a major travel industry scandal.'

'We felt dreadful at the time,' said Tom, 'But there really was nothing we could do.'

'Thank God you're so bloody minded,' said Jane. 'When we found out that you were back over here you don't know how happy it made us.'

Brad sat there taking it all in, but was beginning to wonder what Carmen was doing in the room. Jane sensed what he was thinking.

'Of course,' said Jane, 'We needed to gather together some evidence to prove what they were up to. We needed someone that we could trust; someone intelligent who would blend in and could get Alison's confidence. The only person we could think of as being suitable was my younger sister. Carmen.'

Carmen looked at Brad, searching his face for a reaction. For the first few seconds all she got was a blank stare. Then, Brad flopped forward on the table.

'No, no no,' he started laughing, lightly banging the table with his forehead each time he said the word. 'Aaaaaaggggghhhhh.' He sat back in his chair, his face flushed. 'Why didn't you - couldn't you - what was...........fucking hell.' Brad was speechless.

Jane nodded at Tom to join her in leaving the room.

'I daresay that you two have a lot to discuss. We'll talk again later Brad. I just want to say that if you want it, then you've a bright future with Young Free & Single.'

Jane and Tom left Carmen and Brad alone. As soon as the door closed, Carmen started speaking.

'All the time you thought I was going through your things I was just trying to see if there was anything that I could use against Alison, not you. I went through all of the reps things. I even got this.....' she said, throwing Brad a bag with three video tapes in it. 'I think they're tapes of Mario's conquests. That's what I was doing in his room that night, looking for anything that would help to incriminate Alison or Felipe. I'll admit that I flirted with him a bit to see if he'd any useful information, but I left after an hour, I promise you. I went back into his room the next day when he was out and took the video's and an envelope. I only took the video's because I saw the name Alison written on one of them. But when I got it home there were a load of other girls names on them as well, so Alison's obviously just some client he shagged rather than a film of our beloved Alison counting her money or whatever. Even the envelope had nothing interesting in it. I hated Mario. When I heard about what he almost did to you and Mikey I wanted to kill him myself.'

Carmen looked at Brad, not sure what to do. There was a moment of uncertainty, before Brad held his arms out, beckoning her to come and sit on his lap. As soon as he did so she sprang over and excitedly kissed him.

'Oh Brad, I'm so sorry. I've missed being with you so much. I'm so glad that it's all over.' She placed a hand on either side of his face and gave him a lingering kiss. 'How can I make it up to you?'

Brad made out he was thinking. 'Uuuummm......... how about earning three points?'

She slapped him playfully.

'Actually,' he said picking her up and carrying her into Alison's bedroom, 'Make that four.'

CHAPTER TWENTY ONE

Kirstie was excited and feeling on top of the world. She hadn't seen her boyfriend for more than a week and he was due any minute. Her travel agency was looking marvellous, especially since the Reggio low voltage lighting had been installed. Business had been brisk and she had bought a cottage near Brecon in Talybont-On-Usk which was ready for moving into that weekend.

She sat by the window and looked at her watch. It was six thirty - he was normally punctual. Sure enough, almost on the dot his light blue TVR pulled up outside. Kirstie opened the door and let him in.

'Jason!' she squealed, throwing her arms around Jason Barnes' neck. 'Have you missed me?'

'Course I have, you old slapper,' he teased, kissing her fondly. 'This place is looking good.'

'Thanks to Young Free & Single,' laughed Kirstie.

'Nice of them to pay for it,' said Jason, laughing too. 'And still a bit left over for a few of life's little extravagances,' he said, nodding at the car.

'We could have had a few more, if I hadn't screwed up in Ibiza,' said Kirstie, pushing him onto a chair so that she could sit on his lap.

'You didn't screw up - someone just beat you to it. Anyway, let's just be happy with the twenty seven grand we knicked from Majorca.'

'You must admit - another fifteen would have been nice. What I can't work out is how Brad knew where the money was kept.'

'Well he did and that's that. Good luck to him is what I say.'

He picked up the two champagne glasses that Kirstie had poured just before he arrived and handed one to her.

'To Brad,' he said.

'To Brad - the thieving bastard,' said Kirstie.

When Alison walked in to Night Life, Jane Ward could not believe her audacity. All of the YF&S clients were there to watch the beach party video that Brad was late in bringing to show them on the big screen. The reps all now knew the full story, so they just stared at her, amazed that she had turned up. She sat in the corner with her parents and Jonathan.

'Fuck 'em all,' she thought. She had told her parents and Jonathan what had happened. However, she played it down by saying that all managers were 'at it' and that she was just unlucky to have been caught. Taking them to where YF&S were that night, would, she thought, help to emphasise that what she had done was not particularly serious. Jonathan was actually quite pleased that she had been caught because it meant that she would not be going back the next year. Alison had decided to testify against Felipe if necessary, and consoled herself in the knowledge that with Jonathan's earning power, she would still be able to live in the manner to which she thought she should become accustomed.

The place was packed with over three hundred YF&S holidaymakers and a hundred or so others. The manager of Night Life was scurrying around even more frantically than normal because Brad was nearly an hour late with the video. Eventually a lively Brad came running through the door hand in hand with a giggling Carmen. Mikey was standing by the entrance.

'What kept you? he asked.

'Oh mate,' replied Brad. 'Wait until you see what we've found. Can't stop - gotta go and play the video.'

Brad put the video in and came back and stood with Mikey, who had been joined by Greg.

After about ten minutes, the video was showing the egg throwing contest, and through the powerful system, the screams and sounds of the days entertainment could be heard perfectly. Suddenly, the screen flickered and the picture changed. Brad and Carmen nudged each other like a pair of excited school children about to see Father Christmas for the first time.

On to the screen came the back of a naked male. After a few seconds the face turned around to the camera and winked. It was Mario. As he moved to the side viewers could make out a girl on all fours, pouring oil between her own buttocks. Some dialogue came out of the sound system, and spread over the almost hushed room and its agog inhabitants.

'Fuck me in the other hole Mario. See if you can get that gorgeous cock of yours up there.'

'What, up your arse?'

When Alison heard the voices she spluttered out the drink she was sipping. She jumped up and looked at the screen then as soon as she saw what it was, sank into her chair, wishing it would stop. It didn't.

'Push fuck you. PUSH! Come on, I want you to ram it into me.'

Everyone in Night Life was falling about and pointing at Alison. Jonathan glared at her, took off the engagement ring Alison had given him the previous October and threw it at her before storming out of the club. Her parents, just sat there with their mouths open. Alison went running out, chasing after what was now her former boyfriend. She had to squeeze passed people to get out of the club. As she barged passed the reps, a hysterical Greg called out after her, 'Well done Al - bonus points for that one.'

*　　*　　*　　*　　*　　*

Luis from Viajes Diamente sat alone in the yacht club in Ibiza drinking a carjillo. The October sky was mottled with orange coloured clouds which were blowing across the island quicker than in previous months, heralding the onset of the coming winter. Most holidaymakers had gone home, and all of the holiday reps had left or were about to leave. Everybody in the bar was either Spanish or a resident of Ibiza. He looked at the last of the days pleasure craft mooring on the jetty, many of them doing so for the last time that season. The Sunseeker he had just bought was nestled between a speedboat and a small cabin cruiser, the low sun reflecting off of her white gleaming hull. He had named her Rosa.

The perfume filled his nostrils before he saw her. Her smell was as distinctive as her appearance was distinguished. Even at fifty she was beautiful. Striking features, a well maintained body with clothes and make up that oozed class and style.

He stood up and kissed her, then clicked his fingers to the barman to bring over the champagne he had already ordered. The waiter brought it over and popped it open. They toasted each other.

'What to?' said Luis.

'To us?'

'No.' Luis coughed, then smiling and deepening his voice, raised his glass. 'To a woman who's masterly plan has brought us together. To a woman who has had to suffer the infidelites of a cheating husband for as long as I can remember. To a woman who has made phone calls, left clues, broken her rivals and finally - I hope - cleared her husband's accounts because he was stupid enpugh to underestimate her and will now pay the consequence.' Luis changed from his grandiose speech makers voice to his normal one to add, 'You did clear the accounts alright didn't you?'

She nodded at a huge suitcase. 'Of course. Nobody else could touch the accounts and Felipe wasn't about to tell anyone about them, was he?'

'Excellent.' He resumed his speech. 'To a woman who I hope I can spend the rest of my life with, be it here or in that Sceptered Isle.........'

'Oh Luis,' she giggled, 'You sound almost English.'

424

'To the woman who I have loved from the first day I met; to the woman who married the wrong man; to the woman who shall soon marry the right man, please, raise your glass to..................the former, Mrs Gomez.'

Rosemary Gomez gave an embarrased smile and took a sip from her glass.

'Not quite the former,' she said. She took Luis's hand. 'Oh Luis. This has worked out better than I could have ever imagined. I'm not sure if I would have gone through with it if I hadn't found that invoice. Knowing that Felipe was sleeping with all of those reps and managers was one thing, but getting that dreadful Alison pregnant and then making her have an abortion - well it really was the last straw. I have done the right thing haven't I Luis? I just couldn't stand it anymore. I've always known that you and I should be together, but out of loyalty, and for the sake of the children, even when I knew about his...........'

'I know, I know,' said Felipe, squeezing her hand.

'But now everything seems so clear. Oh Luis, I'm so happy.'

They hugged each other.

'So your conscience is clean then?' asked Luis.

'Of course it is,' she replied. She sat up for a moment. 'You know the only thing I feel a little bad about is that rep getting the sack.'

'What, Brad?'

'Yes - that's the one. Why did you put the empty envelopes in his room?'

'I had to put them somewhere to leave a false trail. That bitch Alison was planning to get rid of him anyway.'

'It seems such a shame.'

'I know. But don't worry about Brad - he's in for a nice surprise.'

'I don't fucking believe it,' said Brad, kicking the hissing Triumph Herald. 'That noise isn't steam you know - the fucking thing's laughing at me.'

'What's wrong?' asked Carmen.

'The bloody fan belt again.'

They were just outside Paris on their way back to the UK and it was close to midnight. The last few weeks of the season had passed with Brad and Carmen becoming inseperable, so much so that a leisurely drive through France with Brad had appealed to Carmen much more than a rushed two hour flight into Gatwick.

'Come here and give us a kiss,' said Brad.

Carmen walked around to Brad and they cuddled each other.

'D'you know what?'

'What?' replied Carmen.

'Getting the sack was the best thing that ever happened to me.'

'Course it was,' said Carmen squeezing him tightly and tucking her smiling face into his chest. 'Otherwise you wouldn't have met me.'

'Exactly.' Brad kissed her and walked to the front of the car. 'You might as well get inside.'

'Ok.'

'All I need now is for a sodding jeep to come trundling up the road,' mumbled Brad.

'What was that?' said Carmen.

'Nothing. I was just thinking about an old friend. I'll check my case to see how much money I've got and we'll have to find a B&B to stay in until the morning.'

Brad went to the back of the car and fumbled around in his case to find his wallet. In one of the corners he felt an envelope that he didn't remember packing. Curious, he pulled it out. Carmen was sitting in the car so couldn't see what Brad was doing. He opened the envelope and was startled to see a wad of pesetas. With it was a note.

Brad
I can't explain what this is all about. You should not have

been sacked but it was partly my fault that you were. From what I can gather, Alison would have sacked you anyway. Although Alison got her just desserts, she was not in fact responsible for stealing the money and planting the envelopes.

This million pesetas (about £5000 I believe) may seem a lot, but after what you have been through it is probably no more than you deserve. All I ask is that you tell no-one about this. Clearly, I cannot reveal my identity.

Gracias.

A shocked Brad stood in silence for a few moments. Once he had composed himself he took the cases out of the car and opened the passenger door.

'Come on, out you get - there's been a change of plan.'

'What do you mean?'

'Sod staying in a B&B, I feel like splashing out. Let's get a taxi into Paris and spend a romantic weekend in a top hotel. I'll get the car sorted out tomorrow.'

'Are you feeling alright?'

'Yeah - never better.'

'What are you up to Bradley Streeter?' asked Carmen suspiciously. 'What kind of sexually perverted act are you trying to bribe me into doing now? 'Cos I'm telling you this for nothing - anything that involves one of those horrible French Poodles and we're history.'

Brad laughed. 'I'll have to give Greg a call and see if there's any bonus points for that. Anyway, we've already done virtually every perverted act possible and you've come up with half of those.'

Carmen playfully slapped him. 'So what's the catch?'

'No catch. Let's say I've only just realised that I've got more out of this season than I previously thought.'

He locked the door and they made their way back to the main road.

'You know what Brad?' said Carmen linking her arm through his.

'What?'

427

'It's actually been quite a short season.'
'Funny. Everyone says that.'

THE END

About the Author

Colin Butts is a direct descendant of the former Russian royal family. His childhood was spent between Iceland, Kenya and Bermondsey. After Cambridge he joined the RAF where he was selected by NASA in 1984 to join their space program. Six months into his training it was discovered that he suffered from horizontal vertigo, a rare complaint which effects the inner ear and balance. This curtailed his career and on his return to the UK he resumed his studies. After gaining a degree in Marine Biology he spent a number of years working with dolphins at the now closed Windsor Safari Park. He specialised in monitoring the emotional stress and psychological traumas that these mammals undergo, brought about by their tendency to mate for life. Since the closure of Windsor Safari Park, Colin has divided his time between Formula Two race driving and lollipop man duties near a school in Peckham.